THE UNTAMED WEST

**Center Point
Large Print**

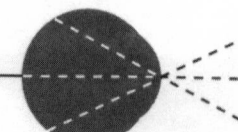

**This Large Print Book carries the
Seal of Approval of N.A.V.H.**

THE UNTAMED WEST

Three Classic Westerns by
Louis L'Amour, Zane Grey, and Max Brand

edited by
JON TUSKA

CENTER POINT PUBLISHING
THORNDIKE, MAINE

This Center Point Large Print edition
is published in the year 2008 by arrangement with
Golden West Literary Agency.

The text of this Large Print edition is unabridged. In other
aspects, this book may vary from the original edition.
Printed in the United States of America.
Set in 16-point Times New Roman type.

ISBN: 978-1-60285-115-3

Library of Congress Cataloging-in-Publication Data

Stories of the golden West. bk. 5.
   The Untamed west : three classic westerns by Louis L'Amour, Zane Grey and Max Brand /
Jon Tuska, editor. -- Center Point large print ed.
      p. cm.
   Originally published: Stories of the golden West: book five, a western trio. Waterville, Me. :
Five Star, c2004.
   ISBN 978-1-60285-115-3 (lib. bdg. : alk. paper)
      1. Western stories. 2. Large type books. I. Tuska, Jon. II. Grey, Zane, 1872-1939.
Canon walls. III. Brand, Max, 1892-1944. Black sheep. IV. L'Amour, Louis, 1908-1988.
Showdown on the hogback. V. Title.

PS648.W4S75 2007
813'.087408052--dc22

2007034524

TABLE OF CONTENTS

Foreword   7

Cañon Walls by Zane Grey   13

Black Sheep by Max Brand   85

Showdown on the Hogback by Louis L'Amour   175

Foreword

A short novel is a story too short to be a novel—40,000 words or less—and too long to be a short story. It was a literary form that once was encouraged and flourished when there were numerous fiction magazines published weekly, monthly, or quarterly in the United States, and it is a form at which numerous American writers excelled. Although a great many authors have written excellent Western fiction, beginning with Mark Twain and Bret Harte, only three managed as a result of their Western stories to attract a sufficient readership to become wealthy. Zane Grey, Max Brand, and Louis L'Amour were the three, and their work has endured with generations of readers throughout the world. For this collection I have selected a short novel by each of these authors, consisting of stories I regard as among their best work.

The greatest lesson the pioneers learned from the Indians is with us still: that it is each man's and each woman's *inalienable* right to find his own path in life, to follow his own vision, to achieve his own destiny—even should one fail in the process. There is no principle so singularly revolutionary as this one in human intellectual history before the American frontier experience, and it grew from the very soil of this land and the peoples who came to live on it. It is this principle that has always been the very cornerstone of the Western story. Perhaps for this reason critics have

7

been wont to dismiss it as subversive and inconsequential because this principle reduces their voices to only a few among many. Surely it is why the Western story has been consistently banned by totalitarian governments and is sneered at by the purveyors of political correctness. Such a principle undermines the very foundations of totalitarianism and collectivism because it cannot be accommodated by the political correctness of those who would seek to exert power over others and replace all options with a single, all-encompassing, monolithic pattern for living.

There is no other kind of American literary endeavor that has so repeatedly posed the eternal questions—how do I wish to live?, in what do I believe?, what do I want from life?, what have I to give to life?—as has the Western story. There is no other kind of literary enterprise since Greek drama that has so invariably posed ethical and moral questions about life as a fundamental of its narrative structure, that has taken a stand and said: this is wrong; this is right. Individual authors, as individual film-makers, may present us with notions with which we do not agree, but in so doing they have made us think again about things that the herd has always been only too anxious to view as settled and outside the realm of questioning.

The West of the Western story is a region where generations of people from every continent on earth and for ages immeasurable have sought a second chance for a better life. The people forged by the clash of cultures in the American West produced a kind of human being very different from any the world had ever known before. How else could it be for a nation emerging from so many nations? And so stories set in the American West have never lost that sense of hope. It wasn't the graves at Shiloh, the white crosses at Verdun, the vacant beaches at Normandy, or the lines on the faces of their great men and women that made the Americans a great people. It was something more intangible than that. It was their great willingness of the heart.

What alone brings you back to a piece of music, a song, a painting, a poem, or a story is the mood that it creates in you when you have experienced it. The mood you experience in reading a Western story is that a better life *is* possible if we have the grit to endure the ordeal of attaining it, that it requires courage to hope, the very greatest courage any human being can ever have. And it is hope that distinguishes the Western story from every other kind of fiction. Only when courage and hope are gone will these stories cease to be relevant to all of us.

Jon Tuska
Portland, Oregon

THE UNTAMED WEST

Cañon Walls
Zane Grey

Zane Grey (1872-1939) was born Pearl Zane Gray in Zanesville, Ohio. He was graduated from the University of Pennsylvania in 1896 with a degree in dentistry. He conducted a practice in New York City from 1898 to 1904, meanwhile striving to make a living by writing. He met Lina Elise Roth in 1900 and always called her Dolly. In 1905 they were married. With Dolly's help, Grey published his first novel himself, *Betty Zane* (Charles Francis Press, 1903), a story based on certain of his frontier ancestors. Eventually closing his dental office, Grey moved with Dolly into a cottage on the Delaware River, near Lackawaxen, Pennsylvania. It is now a national landmark.

Although it took most of her savings, it was Dolly Grey who insisted that her husband take his first trip to Arizona in 1907 with C.J. "Buffalo" Jones, a retired buffalo hunter who had come up with a scheme for crossing the remaining bison population with cattle. Actually Grey could not have been more fortunate in his choice of a mate. Dolly Grey assisted him in every way he desired and yet left him alone when he demanded solitude; trained in English at Hunter College, she proofread every manuscript he wrote and polished his prose; she managed all financial affairs and permitted Grey, once he began earning a good income, to indulge himself at will in his favorite occupations, hunting, fishing, sailing, and exploring the Western regions.

After his return from that first trip to the West, Grey wrote a memoir of his experiences titled *The Last of the Plainsmen* (Outing, 1908) and followed it with his first Western romance, *The Heritage of the Desert* (Harper, 1910). It remains one of his finest novels. The profound effect that the desert had had on him was vibrantly captured so that, after all of these years, it still comes alive for a reader. In a way, too, it established the basic pattern Grey would use in much of his subsequent Western fiction. The hero, Jack Hare, is an Easterner who comes West because he is suffering from tuberculosis. He is rejuvenated by the arid land. The heroine is Mescal, desired by all men but pledged by the Mormon church to a man unworthy of her. Mescal and Jack fall in love, and this causes her to flee from Snap Naab, for whom she would be a second wife. Snap turns to drink, as will many another man rejected by heroines in other Grey romances, and finally kidnaps Mescal. The most memorable characters in this novel, however, are August Naab, the Mormon patriarch who takes Hare in at his ranch, and Eschtah, Mescal's grandfather, a Navajo chieftain of great dignity and no less admirable than Naab. The principal villain—a type not too frequently encountered in Grey's Western stories—is Holderness, a Gentile and the embodiment of the Yankee business spirit that will stop at nothing to exploit the land and its inhabitants for his own profit.

Almost a century later, he is still a familiar figure in the American West, with numerous bureaucratic counterparts in various federal agencies. In the end Holderness is killed by Hare, but then Hare is also capable of pardoning a man who has done wrong if there is a chance for his reclamation, a theme Grey shared with Max Brand.

Grey had trouble finding a publisher for his early work, and it came as a considerable shock to him when his next novel, *Riders of the Purple Sage,* arguably the greatest Western story ever published, was rejected by the same editor who had bought *The Heritage of the Desert.* Grey asked the vice president at Harper & Bros. to read the new novel. Once he did, and his wife did, it was accepted for publication. However, the version that ultimately appeared was extensively bowdlerized. Finally, after more than ninety years, this novel as *Riders of the Purple Sage: The Restored Version* (Five Star, 2005) will be published as Zane Grey wrote it.

The same censorship process that had plagued *Riders of the Purple Sage* was also much in evidence when Grey wrote his sequel to it, *The Desert Crucible* (Five Star, 2003). Significant parts of this story were suppressed at the time the book, titled *The Rainbow Trail,* was published by Harper & Bros. in 1915. Among the most significant of these parts of the story is that Fay Larkin, the heroine, is forced into a marriage with one of her Mormon captors, a man with five wives and fifty-five children, forced for two years to live as a sealed wife, during which time she gives birth to a child. A confession concerning all of this is brought into evidence at her trial before a Supreme Court judge following her arrest by the Department of Justice on a charge of polygamy. Actually, due to editorial interventions at the time Zane Grey wrote his finest fiction, what he really wrote in his best books has not been published until now in the Five Star Westerns, making worthless much of the literary criticism of Grey as an author since it has been based on bogus editions. These restorations follow other equally notable Zane Grey titles published for the first time in book form, based on his holographic manuscripts: *Last of the Duanes* (Five Star, 1996), *Rangers of the Lone Star* (Five Star, 1997), *Woman of the Frontier* (Five Star, 1998), *The Great Trek* (Five Star, 1999), *Open Range* (Five Star, 2002), and *Tonto Basin* (Five Star, 2004). Similarly it was necessary to go back to Zane Grey's handwritten manuscripts to publish his short stories, contained so far in two collections: *The Westerners* (Five Star, 2000) and *Rangle River* (Five Star, 2001). In *Stories of the Golden West: Book Three* (Five Star, 2002) "*Tappan's Burro*" appears for the first time as Zane Grey intended.

Yet, despite the difficulties Grey encountered in getting his stories published as he wrote them, what did appear led to a degree of success that exceeded even his wildest dreams. The magazine serials, the books, the motion picture versions—and Grey at 108 films still holds the world's record for cinematic derivations based on the works of a single author—brought in a fortune. He had homes on Catalina Island, in Altadena, California, a hunting lodge in Arizona, a fishing lodge in the Rogue River area in Oregon.

Whatever his material prosperity, Grey continued to believe in the strenuous life. His greatest personal fear was that of growing old and dying. It was while fishing the North Umpqua River in Oregon in the summer of 1937 that Grey collapsed from an apparent stroke. It took him a long time to recover use of his faculties and his speech. Cardiovascular disease was congenital on Grey's side of the family. Despite medical advice to the contrary, Grey refused to live a sedentary life. He was convinced that the heart was a muscle and the only way to keep it strong was to exercise it vigorously. Early in the morning on October 23, 1939, Dolly was awakened by a call from her husband. Rushing to his room, she found Grey clutching his chest. "Don't ever leave me, Dolly!" he pleaded. He lived until the next morning when, after rising and dressing, he sat down on his bed, cried out suddenly, and fell over dead.

Even more than with Bret Harte, there has always been a tendency among literary critics to dismiss Zane Grey, although, unlike Harte, Grey at no point enjoyed any great favor with them. Part of this attitude may have come about because he was never considered a realistic writer—and yet that is in so many ways precisely what he was! "There was so much unexpressed feeling that could not be entirely portrayed," Loren Grey once commented about his father, "that, in later years, he would weep when re-reading one of his own books." The ultimate reason for the tears, I suppose, was the author's keen awareness that his editors had effectively prevented him from telling his Western stories as he wanted to tell them and felt they must be told. Readers of the present generation now have the opportunity to do precisely that, something Zane Grey surely never imagined possible.

I

"Wal, heah's another forkin' of the trail," ejaculated Monty, as he sat cross-legged on his saddle and surveyed the prospect. "Thet Mormon shepherd back a ways gave me a good steer. But dog-gone it, I hate to impose on anyone, even Mormons."

The scene was Utah, north of the great cañon, with the wild ruggedness and magnificence of that region exemplified on all sides. Monty could see clear to the Pink Cliffs that walled the ranches and villages northward from this country of breaks. He had come up out of the abyss, across the desert between Mount Trumbull and Hurricane Ledge, and he did not look back. Kanab must be thirty or forty miles, as a crow flies, across this dotted valley of sage. But Monty did not know Utah, or anything of this north-rim country.

He rolled his last cigarette. He was hungry and

worn out, and his horse was the same. Should he ride on to Kanab and throw in with one of the big cattle companies north of there or should he take to one of the lonely cañons and hunt for a homesteader in need of a rider? The choice seemed hard, because Monty was tired of gunfights, of two-bit rustling, of gambling, and other dubious means by which he had managed to live in Arizona. Not that Monty entertained any idea he had been really dishonest! He had the free-range cowboy's elasticity of judgment. He could find excuses even for his last escapade. But one or two more stunts like this last one at Longhill would make him an outlaw. He reflected that, if he were blamed for the Green Valley affair, also, which was not improbable, he might find himself an outlaw already, whether he agreed or not.

If he rode on to the ranches north, sooner or later someone from Arizona would come along; if he went down into the breaks of the cañon, he might find a job and a hiding place where he would be safe until the thing blew over and was forgotten. Then he would take good care not to fall into another. Bad company and a bottle had brought Monty to this pass, which he really believed was undeserved.

Monty dropped his leg back and slipped his boot into the stirrup. He took the trail to the left and felt relief. It meant that he was avoiding towns and ranches, outfits of curious cowboys, and others who might have undue interest in wandering riders.

In about an hour, as the shepherd had directed, the

trail approached and ran along the rim of a cañon. Monty gazed down with approving eyes. The walls were steep and very deep, so deep that he could scarcely see the green squares of alfalfa, the orchards and pastures, the groves of cottonwoods, and a gray log cabin. He espied cattle and horses toward the upper end. At length the trail started down, and for a while then Monty lost his perspective, and, dismounting, he walked down the zigzag path, leading his horse.

He saw, at length, that the cañon boxed here in a wild notch of cliff and thicket and jumbled wall, from under which a fine stream of water flowed. There were many acres that might have been under cultivation. Monty followed the trail along the babbling brook, crossed it above where the floor of the cañon widened and the alfalfa fields shone so richly green, and so on down a couple of miles to the cottonwoods. When he emerged from these, he was close to the cabin, and he could see where the cañon opened wide, with sheer red-gold walls, right out upon the desert. Indeed, it was a lonely retreat, far off the road, out of the grass country, a niche in colored cañon walls.

The cottonwoods were shedding their fuzzy seeds, that like snow covered the ground. An irrigation ditch ran musically through the yard. Chickens, turkeys, calves had the run of the place. The dry odor of the cañon here appeared to take in the fragrance of wood smoke and baking bread.

Monty limped on, up to the cabin porch, which was spacious and comfortable, where no doubt the people who lived there spent many hours during fine weather. He espied a girl in the open door. She wore gray linsey, ragged and patched. His second glance made note of her superb build, her bare feet, her brown arms, and eyes that did not need half their piercing quality to see through Monty.

"Howdy, miss," hazarded Monty, although this was Mormon country.

"Howdy, stranger," she replied very pleasantly, so that Monty ceased looking for a dog.

"Could a thirsty rider get a drink around heah?"

"There's the brook. Best water in Utah."

"An' how about a bite to eat?"

"Tie up your horse and go 'round to the back porch."

Monty did as he was bidden, not without a couple more glances at this girl who, he observed, made no movement. But as he turned the corner of the house, he heard her call: "Ma, there's a tramp Gentile cowboy coming back for a bite to eat!"

When Monty reached the rear porch, another huge place under the cottonwoods, he was quite prepared to encounter the large woman, of commanding presence, but of more genial and kindly face.

"Good afternoon, ma'am," began Monty, lifting his sombrero. "Shore you're the mother to that girl out in front . . . you look alike an' you're both arfel handsome . . . but I won't be took for no tramp Gentile cowpuncher."

21

The woman greeted him with a pleasant laugh. "So, young man, you're a Mormon?"

"No, I ain't no Mormon, either. But particular, I ain't no tramp cowboy," replied Monty with spirit, and just then the young person who had roused it appeared in the back door with slow, curious smile. "I'm just lost an' tuckered out, an' hungry."

For reply she motioned to a pan and bucket of water on a nearby bench, and Monty was quick to take the hint, but performed his ablutions very slowly. When he came out of them, shivering and refreshed, the woman was setting a table for him and bade him take a seat.

"Ma'am, I only asked for a bite," he said.

"It's no matter. We've plenty."

Presently Monty sat down to a meal that surpassed any feast he ever attended. It was his first experience at a Mormon table, the fame of which was known on every range. He had to admit that distance and exaggeration had not lent enchantment here. Without shame he ate until he could hold no more, and, when he arose, he made the woman of the house a gallant bow.

"Lady, I never had such a good dinner in all my life," he said fervently. "An' I reckon it won't make no difference if I never get another. Just rememberin' this one will be enough."

"Blarney. You Gentiles shore have the gift of gab. Set down and rest a little."

Monty was glad to comply, and leisurely disposed

his long, lithe, dusty self in a comfortable chair. He laid his sombrero on the floor, and hitched his gun around, and looked up, genially aware that he was being taken in by two pairs of eyes.

"I met a shepherd lad up on top an' he directed me to Andrew Boller's ranch. Is this heah the place?"

"No. Boller's is a few miles farther on. It's the first big ranch over the Arizona line."

"Shore I missed it. Wal, it was lucky for me. Are you near the Arizona line heah?"

"We're just over it."

"Oh, I see. Not in Utah a-tall," said Monty thoughtfully. "Any men about?"

"No. I'm the Widow Keitch, and this is my daughter Rebecca."

Monty guardedly acknowledged the introduction, without mentioning his name, an omission the shrewd, kindly woman noted. Monty was quick to feel that she must have had vast experience with men. The girl, however, wore an indifferent, rather scornful air.

"This heah is a good-sized ranch . . . must be a hundred acres just in alfalfa," went on Monty. "You don't mean to tell me you two women run this ranch alone?"

"We do mostly. We hire the plowing, and we have to have firewood hauled. And we always have a boy around. But year in and out we do most of the work."

"Wal, I'll be darned!" ejaculated Monty. "Excuse me . . . but it shore is somethin' to heah. The ranch ain't so bad run-down at that. If you'll allow me to say so, Missus Keitch, it could be made a first-rate ranch. There's acres of uncleared land."

"My husband used to think so," replied the widow, sighing. "But since he's gone we have just managed to live."

"Wal, wal! Now I wonder what made me ride down the wrong trail . . . ? Missus Keitch, I reckon you could use a fine, young, sober, honest, hard-workin' cowboy who knows all there is about ranchin'."

Monty addressed the woman in cool, easy speech, quite deferential, and then he shifted his gaze to the dubious face of the daughter. He was discovering that it had a compelling charm. She laughed outright, as if to say what a liar he was. That not only discomfited Monty, but roused his ire. The Mormon baggage!

"I guess I could use such a young man," returned Mrs. Keitch shortly, with penetrating eyes on him.

"Wal, you're lookin' at him right now," said Monty fervently. "An' he's seein' nothin' less than the hand of Providence heah."

The woman stood up decisively. "Fetch your horse around," she said, and walked off the porch to wait for him. Monty made haste, his mind in a whirl. What was going to happen here? That girl! He ought to ride right on out of this cañon, and he was making up his mind to do that when he came back around the house to see that the girl had come to the porch rail. Her great eyes burned at his horse. Monty did not need to be told that she had a passion for horses. It would help some. But she did not appear to see Monty at all.

"You've a wonderful horse," said Mrs. Keitch. "Poor fellow! He's lame and tuckered out. We'll turn him loose in the pasture."

Monty followed her down a shady lane of cotton-woods, where the water ran noisily on each side, and he sort of trembled inwardly at the content of the woman's last words. He had heard of the Good Samaritan ways of Mormons. And in that short walk Monty did a deal of thinking. They reached an old barn beyond which lay a green pasture with an orchard running down one side. Peach trees were in bloom, lending a delicate and beautiful pink to the fresh spring foliage.

"What wages would you work for?" queried the woman earnestly.

"Wal, come to think of thet, for my board an' keep. Anyhow till we got the ranch payin'," replied Monty.

"Very well, stranger, that's a fair deal. Unsaddle your horse and stay," said the woman.

"Wait a minnit, lady," drawled Monty. "I got to sub-stitute somethin' for that recommend I gave you. Shore I know cattle an' ranchin' backwards. But I reckon I should have said I'm a no-good, gun-throwin' cowpuncher who got run out of Arizona."

"What for?" demanded Mrs. Keitch.

"Wal, a lot of it was bad company an' bad licker. But at that I wasn't so drunk I didn't know I was rustlin' cattle."

"Why do you tell me?" she demanded.

"Wal, it is kinda funny. But I just couldn't fool a kind woman like you. Thet's all."

"You don't look like a hard-drinking man."

"Aw, I'm not. I never said so, ma'am. Fact is, I ain't much of a drinkin' cowboy a-tall."

"You came across the cañon?" she asked.

"Shore, an' by golly thet was the orfellest ride, an' slide, an' swim, an' climb I ever had. I really deserve heaven, lady."

"Any danger of a sheriff trailing you?"

"Wal, I've thought about that. I reckon one chance in a thousand."

"He'd be the first one I ever heard of . . . from across the cañon at any rate. This is a lonesome, out-of-the-way place . . . and, if you stayed away from the Mormon ranches and towns. . . ."

"See heah, lady," interrupted Monty sharply, "you shore ain't goin' to take me on?"

"I am. You might be a welcome change. Lord knows, I've hired every kind of a man. But not one of them ever lasted. You might."

"What was wrong with them?"

"I don't know. I never saw much wrong, but Rebecca could not get along with them, and she drove them away."

"Aw, I see!" exclaimed Monty, who did not see at all. "But I'm not one of the moonin' kind, lady, an' I'll stick."

"All right. It's only fair, though, to tell you there's a risk. The young fellow doesn't live who could let

Rebecca alone. It'd be a godsend to a distracted old woman."

Monty wagged his bare head, pondering, and slid the rim of his sombrero through his fingers. "Wal, I reckon I've been most everythin' but a godsend, an' I'd shore like to try thet."

"What's your name?" she asked with those searching gray eyes on him.

"Monty Bellew . . . Smoke for short . . . an' it's shore shameful well known in some parts of Arizona."

"Any folks living?"

"Yes, back in Iowa. Father an' Mother gettin' along in years now. An' a kid sister growed up."

"You send them money every month, of course?"

Monty hung his head. "Wal, fact is, not so regular as I used to. Late years times have been hard for me."

"Hard, nothing! You've drifted into hard ways. Shiftless, drinking, gambling, shooting cowhand . . . now haven't you been just that?"

"I'm sorry, lady . . . I . . . I reckon I have."

"You ought to be ashamed. I know boys. I raised nine. It's time you were turning over a new leaf. Suppose we begin by burying that name Monty Bellew?"

"I'm shore willin' an' grateful, ma'am."

"Then it's settled. Tend to your horse. You can have the little cabin there under the big cottonwood. We've kept that for our hired help, but it hasn't been occupied much lately."

She left Monty then, and he stood a moment, irresolute. What a balance was struck there! Presently he slipped saddle and bridle off the horse, and turned him into the pasture. "Baldy, look at that alfalfa," he said. Weary as Baldy was, he lay down and rolled and rolled.

Monty carried his equipment to the tiny porch of the cabin under the huge cottonwood. He removed his saddle-bags, which contained the meager sum of his possessions. Then he flopped down on the bench.

"Dog-gone it," he muttered. His senses seemed playing with him. The leaves rustled above and the white cottonseeds floated down; the bees were murmuring; water tinkled swiftly by the porch; somewhere a bell on a sheep or calf broke the stillness. Monty had never felt such peace and tranquility, and his soul took on a burden of gratitude.

Suddenly a clear, resonant voice pealed out from the house. "Ma, what's the name of our new hand?"

"Ask him, Rebecca. I forgot to," replied the mother.

"If that isn't like you!"

Monty was on his way to the house and soon hove in sight to the young woman on the porch. He thrilled as he spied her, and he made himself some deep wild promises. "Hey, cowboy. What's your name?" she called.

"Sam," he called back.

"Sam what?"

"Sam Hill."

"For the land's sake! That's not your name."

"Call me Land's Sake, if you like it better."

"*I* like it?" She nodded her curly head sagely, and she regarded Monty with a certainty that made him vow to upset her calculations or die in the attempt. She handed him a bucket. "Can you milk a cow?"

"I never saw my equal as a milker," asserted Monty.

"In that case I won't have to help," she replied. "But I'll go with you to drive in the cows."

II

From that hour dated Monty's apparent subjection. He accepted himself at Rebecca's valuation—that of a very small hired boy. Monty believed he had a way with girls, and at any rate that way had never been tried upon this imperious young Mormon miss. Monty made good his boast about being a master hand at the milking of cows. He surprised Rebecca, although she did not guess he saw it. For the rest Monty never looked at her—when she was looking—never addressed her, never gave her the slightest hint that her sex was manifest to him.

Now he knew perfectly well that his appearance did not tally with this kind of a cowboy. She realized it and was puzzled, but evidently he was a novelty. At first Monty sensed a slight antagonism of the Mormon against the Gentile, but in the case of Mrs. Keitch he never noticed this at all, and less and less from the girl.

The feeling of being in some sort of a trance persisted with Monty, and he could not account for it, unless it was the charm of this lonely Cañon Walls Ranch, combined with the singular attraction of its young mistress. Monty had not been there three days when he realized that sooner or later he would fall, and great would be the fall thereof. But his sincere and ever-growing admiration for Widow Keitch held him true to his inherent sincerity. It would not hurt him to have a terrible case over Rebecca, and he resigned himself. Nothing could come of it, except perhaps to chasten him. Ordinarily he would never let her dream of such a thing. She just gradually and imperceptibly grew on Monty. There was nothing strange in this. Wherever Monty had ridden, there had always been some girl before which he had bowed down. She might be a fright—a lanky, slab-sided, red-headed country girl, but that made no difference. His comrades had called him Smoke Bellew, because of his propensity for raising so much smoke where there was not any fire.

Sunday brought a change at the Keitch household. Rebecca appeared in a white dress, and Monty caught his breath. He worshipped from a safe distance through the leaves. Presently a two-seated buckboard drove up to the ranch house, and Rebecca lost no time climbing in with the young people. They drove off, of course, to church at the village of White Sage, some half dozen miles across the line. Monty thought it odd that Mrs. Keitch did not go.

There had been many a time in Monty's life when the loneliness and solitude of these dreaming cañon walls would have been maddening. But Monty found strange ease and solace here. He had entered upon a new era of thinking. He hated to think that it might not last. But it would last if the shadow of the past did not fall on Cañon Walls.

At one o'clock Rebecca returned with her friends in the buckboard, and presently Monty was summoned to dinner, by no less than Mrs. Keitch's trenchant call. Monty had not anticipated this, but he brushed and brightened himself up a bit, and proceeded to the house. Mrs. Keitch met him as he mounted the porch steps. "Folks," she announced, "this is our new man, Sam Hill. Sam, meet Lucy Card and her brother Joe, and Hal Stacey."

Monty bowed, and took the seat assigned to him by Mrs. Keitch. She was beaming, and the dinner table fairly groaned with the load of good things to eat. Monty defeated an overwhelming desire to look at Rebecca. In a moment he saw that the embarrassment under which he labored was silly. These Mormon young people were quiet, friendly, and far from curious. His presence at Widow Keitch's table was more natural to them than it seemed to Monty. Soon he was at ease and dared to glance across the table. Rebecca was radiant. How had it come that he had not seen her beauty? She appeared like a gorgeous, opening rose. Monty did not risk a second glance and he soliloquized to himself that he ought to go far up the cañon and crawl into a hole. Nevertheless, he enjoyed the dinner and did ample justice to it.

After dinner more company arrived, mostly on horseback. Sunday was evidently the Keitches' day at home. Monty made several unobtrusive attempts to escape, once being stopped in his tracks by a single glance from Rebecca, and the other times failing through the widow's watchfulness. He felt that he was very dense not to have seen sooner how they wished him to be at home. At length, toward evening, Monty left Rebecca to several of her admirers, who outstayed the other visitors, and went off for a sunset stroll under the cañon walls.

Monty did not consider himself exactly a dunce, but he could not see clearly through the afternoon's experience. There were, however, some points he could be sure of. The Widow Keitch had evidently seen better days. She did not cross the Arizona line into Utah. Rebecca was waited upon by a host of Mormons, to whom she appeared imperiously indifferent one moment and alluringly coy the next. She was a spoiled girl, Monty argued. Monty had not been able to discover the slightest curiosity or antagonism in those visitors, and, as they were all Mormons and he was a Gentile, it changed some preconceived ideas of his.

Next morning Monty plunged into the endless work needful to be done about the ranch. He doubled the water in the irrigation ditches, to Widow Keitch's delight. That day passed as if by magic. It did not end, however, without Rebecca's crossing Monty's trail, and earned for him a very good compliment from her, anent the fact that he might develop into a milkman.

The days flew by then, and another Sunday came, very like the first one, and that brought June around. Thereafter the weeks were as short as days. Monty was amazed to see what a diversity of tasks he could put an efficient hand to. But then he had seen quite a good deal of ranch service, aside from driving cattle. And it so happened that here was an ideal farm awaiting development, and Monty put his heart into the task. The summer was hot, especially in the afternoon under the reflected heat from the walls. He had cut alfalfa several times. And the harvest of fruit and grain was at hand. There were pumpkins so large that Monty could scarcely roll one over, bunches of grapes longer than his arm, great, luscious peaches that shone gold in the sunlight, and other farm products in proportion.

The womenfolk spent days putting up preserves, pickles, fruit. Monty used to go out of his way to smell the fragrant wood fire in the backyard under the cottonwoods, where the big, brass kettle steamed with peach butter. "I'll shore eat myself to death when winter comes," he said.

Among the young men who paid court to Rebecca were two brothers, Wade and Eben Tyler, lean-faced, still-eyed young Mormons who were wild-horse hunters. The whole southern end of Utah was run over by droves of wild horses, and according to some of the pioneers they would become a nuisance to the range. The Tylers took such a liking to Monty that they asked Mrs. Keitch to let him go with them on a hunt in October, over in what they called the Siwash. The widow was prevailed upon to consent, stipulating that Monty should fetch back a supply of venison. Rebecca said she would allow him to go if he brought her one of the wild mustangs with long mane and tail that touched the ground.

So when October rolled around, Monty rode off with the brothers, and three days brought them to the edge of a black forest called Buckskin. It took a whole day to ride through the magnificent spruces and pines to the rim of the cañon. Here, Monty found the wildest and most wonderful country he had ever seen. The Siwash was a rough section where the breaks in the rim afforded retreat for the thousands of deer and wild horses, and the cougars that preyed upon them. Monty had the hunt of his life, and, when those fleeting weeks were over, he and the Tylers were fast friends.

Monty returned to Cañon Walls Ranch, pleased to find that he had been sorely needed and missed, and keen to go at his work again. Gradually he thought less and less of that retreating Arizona escapade that had made him a fugitive; a little time in that wild country had a tendency to make past things seem dim and far away. He ceased to start whenever he saw strange riders coming up the cañon gateway. Mormon sheepmen and cattlemen, when in the vicinity of Cañon Walls, always paid the Keitches a visit. Still Monty never ceased to pack a gun, a fact that Mrs. Keitch often mentioned. Monty said it was a habit.

He went to clearing the upper end of the cañon. The cottonwood, oak, and brush were as thick as a jungle. But it appeared to be mowed down under the sweep of Monty's axe. In his boyhood on the Iowa farm he had been a railsplitter. How many useful things came back to him! Every day Rebecca or Mrs. Keitch or the boy Randy, who helped at chores, drove up in the big sled and hauled firewood. When the winter's wood, with plenty to spare, had been stored away, Mrs. Keitch pointed with satisfaction to a considerable saving of money.

The leaves did not fall until late in November, and then they changed color slowly and dropped reluctantly, as if not sure that winter could actually come to Cañon Walls. Monty doubted that it would. But frosty mornings did come, and soon thin skins of ice formed on the still pools. Sometimes, when Monty rode out of the cañon gateway upon the desert, he could see the white line reaching down from Buckskin, and Mount Trumbull had its crown of snow. But no real winter came to the cañon. The gleaming walls seemed to have absorbed enough of the summer sun to carry over. Every hour of daylight found Monty outdoors at one of the tasks that multiplied under his eye. After supper he would sit before the little stone fireplace he had built in his cabin, and watch the flames, and wonder about himself, and how long this could last. He did not see why it could not last always, and he went so far in calculation as to say that a debt paid cancelled even the acquiring of a few cattle not his own, in that past which got further back all the time. He had been just a wild cowboy, urged by drink and a need of money. He had asked only that it be forgotten and buried, but now he began to think he wanted to square that debt.

The winter passed, and Monty's labors had opened up as many new acres as had been cleared originally. Cañon Walls Ranch took the eye of Andrew Boller who made Widow Keitch a substantial offer for it. Mrs. Keitch laughed her refusal, and the remark she made to Boller mystified Monty for many a day. Something like Cañon Walls someday being as great a ranch as that one of which the Church had deprived her!

Monty asked Wade Tyler what she'd meant, and Wade replied that he had heard how John Keitch had owed the bishop money, and the great ranch, after Keitch's death, had been taken. But that was one of the few questions Monty ever asked. The complexity and mystery of the Mormon Church did not interest him. It had been a shock, however, to find that two of Mrs. Keitch's Sunday callers, openly courting Rebecca's hand, already had wives. *By golly, I ought to marry her myself,* declared Monty with heat, as he soliloquized to himself beside his fire, and then he laughed at his dreaming conceit. He was only the hired help to Rebecca.

How good to see the green burst out upon the cottonwoods, and then the pink on the peach trees! Monty had been at Cañon Walls a year. It seemed incredible. He could see a vast change in the ranch. And what transformation had that labor wrought in him!

"Sam, we're going to need help this spring," said Mrs. Keitch. "We'll want a couple of men and a teamster . . . a new wagon."

"Wal, we shore need aplenty," drawled Monty, "an' I reckon we'd better think hard."

"This ranch is overflowing with milk and honey. Sam, you've made it bloom. We must make a deal. I've spoken to you before, but you always put me off. We ought to be partners."

"There ain't any hurry, lady," replied Monty. "I'm happy heah, an' powerful set on makin' the ranch go big. Funny no farmer hereabouts ever saw its possibilities. Wal, thet's our good luck."

"Boller wants my whole alfalfa cut this year," went on Mrs. Keitch. "Saunders, a big cattleman . . . no Mormon, by the way . . . is ranging south. And Boller wants to gobble all the feed. How much alfalfa can we cut this year?"

"Countin' the new acreage upward of two hundred tons."

"Sam Hill!" she cried incredulously.

"Wal, you needn't Sam Hill me. I get enough of that from Rebecca. But you can gamble on the ranch from now on. We have the soil an' the sunshine . . . twice as much an twice as hot as these farmers out in the open. An' we have water. Lady, we're goin' to grow things."

"It's a dispensation of the Lord!" she exclaimed fervently.

"Wal, I don't know aboot that, but I can guarantee results. We start new angles this spring. There's a side cañon up heah that I cleared. Just the place for hogs. You know what a waste of fruit there was last fall. We'll not waste anythin' from now on. We can raise food enough to pack this cañon solid with turkeys, chickens, hogs."

"Sam, you're a wizard, and the Lord merely guided me that day I took you in," replied Mrs. Keitch. "We're independent now and I see prosperity ahead. When Andrew Boller offered to buy this ranch, I saw the handwriting on the wall."

"You bet. An' the ranch is worth twice what he offered."

"Sam, I've been an outcast, in a way, but this will sweeten my cup."

"Wal, lady, you never made me no confidences, but I always took you for the happiest woman I ever seen," declared Monty stoutly.

At this juncture the thoughtful Rebecca Keitch, who had listened as was her habit, spoke feelingly: "Ma, I want a lot of new dresses. I haven't a decent rag to my back. And look there!" She stuck out a shapely foot, bursting from an old shoe. "I want to go to Salt Lake City and buy things. And if we're not so poor any more. . . ."

"My dearest, *I* cannot go to Salt Lake," interrupted the mother in amaze and sorrow.

"But I can. Sue Tyler is going with her mother," burst out Rebecca, passionately glowing.

"Of course, Daughter, you must have clothes to wear. And I have long thought of that. But to go to Salt Lake? I don't know. It worries me. Sam, what do you think of Rebecca's idea?"

"Which one?" asked Monty.

"About going to Salt Lake to buy clothes."

"Perfectly ridiculous," replied Monty blandly.

"Why?" flashed Rebecca, turning upon him with great eyes aflame.

"Wal, you don't need no clothes in the first place. . . ."

"Don't I?" demanded Rebecca hotly. "You bet I don't need any clothes for *you*. You never look at me. I could go around here positively stark naked and you'd never even see me."

"An' in the second place," went on Monty with a wholly assumed imperturbability, "you're too young an' too crazy aboot boys to go on such a long journey alone."

"Daughter, I . . . I think Sam is right," rejoined the mother.

"I'm eighteen years old!" screamed Rebecca. "And I wouldn't be going alone."

"Sam means you should have a man with you."

Rebecca stood a moment in speechless rage, then she broke down. "Why doesn't the damn' fool . . . offer to take me . . . then?"

"Rebecca!" cried Mrs. Keitch in horror.

Monty, meanwhile, had been undergoing a remarkable transformation. "Lady, if I was her dad. . . ."

"But you're not," sobbed Rebecca.

"Shore it's lucky for you I'm not. For I'd spank some sense into you. But I was goin' to say I'd drive you back from Kanab. You could go so far with the Tylers."

"There, Daughter . . . and maybe next year you *could* go to Salt Lake," added Mrs. Keitch consolingly.

Rebecca made a miserable compromise, an acceptance rendered vastly significant to Monty by the deep, dark look she gave him as she flounced away.

"Oh, dear," sighed Mrs. Keitch. "Rebecca is a good girl. Now she often flares up like that and lately she has been queer. If she'd only set her heart on some man!"

III

Monty had his doubts about the venture to which he had committed himself. But he undertook it willingly enough, because Mrs. Keitch was tremendously pleased and relieved. She evidently feared this high-spirited girl. As it happened, Rebecca rode to Kanab with the Tylers, with the understanding that she would return on Monty's wagon.

The drive took Monty all day and there was a good deal of upgrade. He did not believe he could make the thirty miles back in daylight hours, unless he got a very early start, and he just about knew he never could get Rebecca Keitch to leave Kanab before dawn. Still the whole prospect was one of adventure, and much of Monty's old devil-may-care spirit seemed to rouse to meet it.

He camped on the edge of town, and next morning drove in and left the old wagon at a blacksmith shop for repairs. The four horses were turned into pasture. Then Monty went about executing Mrs. Keitch's instructions, which had to do with engaging helpers, and numerous purchases. That evening saw a big, new, shiny wagon at the blacksmith shop, packed full of flour, grain, hardware, supplies, harness, and what not. The genial storekeeper who waited upon Monty averred that this Keitch must have had her inheritance returned to her. All the Mormons were kindly inter-ested in Monty and his work at Cañon Walls, which had become talk all over the range. They were likable men, except the gray-whiskered old patriarchs who belonged to another day. Monty did not miss seeing several very pretty Mormon girls, and their notice of him pleased Monty immensely when Rebecca hap-pened to be around to see.

Monty ran into her every time he entered a store. She spent all the money she had saved up, and all her mother had given her, and she borrowed the last few dollars he had.

"Shore, you're welcome," said Monty in reply to her thanks. "But ain't you losin' your haid a little?"

41

"Well, so long's I don't lose it over *you,* what do you care?" she retorted gaily, with a return of that dark glance which had mystified him.

Monty replied that her mother had expressly forbidden her to go into debt for anything.

"Don't you try to boss me, Sam Hill," she warned, but she was still too happy to be angry.

"Rebecca, I don't care two bits what you do," said Monty shortly.

"Oh, don't you? Thanks. You always flattered me," she returned mockingly. It struck Monty then that she knew something about him or about herself which he did not share.

"We'll be leavin' before sunup," he added briefly. "You'd better let me have all your bundles so I can take them out to the wagon an' pack them tonight."

Rebecca demurred, but would not give a reason, which must have meant that she wanted to gloat over her purchases. Monty finally prevailed upon her, and it took two trips for him, and a boy he had hired, to carry the stuff out to the blacksmith's.

"Lord, if it should rain!" ejaculated Monty, happening to think that he had no extra tarpaulin. So he went back to the store and got one, and hid it, with the purpose of having fun with Rebecca in case a storm threatened.

After supper Rebecca drove out to Monty's camp with some friends.

"I don't like this. You should have gone to the rim," she said loftily.

"Wal, I'm used to campin'," he drawled.

"Sam, they're giving a dance for me tonight," announced Rebecca.

"Fine. Then you needn't go to bed a-tall, an' we can get an early start."

The young people with Rebecca shouted with laughter, and she looked dubious.

"Can't we stay over another day?"

"I should smile we cain't," retorted Monty with unusual force. "An' if we don't get an early start, we'll never reach home tomorrow. So you just come along heah, young lady, aboot four o'clock."

"In the morning?"

"In the mawnin'. I'll have some breakfast for you."

It was noticeable that Rebecca made no rash promises. Monty rather wanted to give in to her—she was so happy and gay—but he remembered his obligations to Mrs. Keitch, and remained firm.

As they drove off, Monty's sharp ears caught Rebecca complaining—". . . and I can't do a solitary darn' thing with that Arizona cowpuncher."

This rather pleased Monty, as it gave him distinction, and was proof that he had not yet betrayed himself to Rebecca. He would proceed on these lines.

That night he did a remarkable thing, for him. He found out where the dance was being held, and peeped through a window to see Rebecca in her glory. He did not miss, however, the fact that she did not outshine several other young women there. Monty stifled a yearning that had not bothered him for a long

43

time. "Dog-gone it! I ain't no old guffer. I could dance the socks off some of them Mormons." He became aware presently that between dances the young Mormon men came outside and indulged in fist fights. He could not see any reason for these encounters, and it amused him. "Gosh, I wonder if thet's just a habit with these *hombres*. Fact is, though, there's shore not enough girls to go 'round. Holy Mackerel, how I'd like to have my old dancin' pards heah! Wouldn't we wade through thet corral? I wonder what's become of Slim an' Cuppy, an' if they ever think of me. Dog-gone."

Monty sighed and returned to camp. He was up before daylight, but not in any rush. He had a premonition what to expect. Day broke and the sun tipped the low desert in the east, while Monty leisurely got breakfast. He kept an eye on the lookout for Rebecca. The new boy, Jake, arrived with shiny face, and later one of the men engaged by Mrs. Keitch came. Monty had the two teams fetched in from pasture, and hitched up. It was just as well that he had to wait for Rebecca, because the new harness did not fit and required skilled adjustment, but he was not going to tell her that. The longer she made him wait, the longer would be the scolding she would get.

About nine o'clock she arrived in a very much overloaded buckboard, gay of attire and face, and so happy that Monty, had he been sincere, could never have reproved her. But he did it, very sharply, and made her look like a chidden child before her friends.

This reacted upon Monty so pleasurably that he began afresh. But this was a mistake.

"Yah! Yah! Yah! Yah!" she screamed at him. And her friends let out a roar of merriment.

"Becky, you shore have a tip-top chaperon," remarked one frank-faced Mormon boy. And other remarks were not wanting to hint that one young rider in the world had not succumbed to Rebecca.

"Where am I going to ride?" she asked curtly.

Monty indicated the high driver's seat: "Unless you'd rather ride with them two new hands on the other wagon."

Rebecca scorned to give reasons, but climbed to the lofty perch.

"Girls, it's nearer heaven than I've ever been yet!" she called gaily.

"What you mean, Becky?" replied a pretty girl with roguish eyes. "So high up . . . or because . . . ?"

"Go along with you," interrupted Rebecca with a blush. "You think of nothing but men. I wish you had . . . but good bye . . . good bye. I've had a lovely time."

Monty clambered to the driver's seat, and followed the other wagon out of town, down into the desert. Rebecca appeared moved to talk.

"Oh, it was a change. I had a grand time. But I'm glad you wouldn't let me go to Salt Lake. It'd have ruined me, Sam."

Monty felt subtly flattered, but he chose to remain aloof, and disapproving.

"Nope. Hardly thet. You was ruined long ago, Miss Rebecca," he drawled.

"Don't call me Miss," she flashed. "And see here, Sam Hill . . . do you hate us Mormons?"

"I shore don't. I like all the Mormons I've met. They're just fine. An' your ma is the best woman I ever knew."

"Then I'm the only Mormon you've no use for," she retorted with bitterness. "Don't deny it. I'd rather you didn't add falsehood to your . . . your other faults. It's a pity, though, that we can't get along. Mother depends on you now. You've certainly pulled us out of a hole. And I . . . I'd like you . . . if you'd let me. But you always make me out a wicked, spoiled girl. Which I'm not. Why couldn't you come to the dance last night? They wanted you. Those girls were eager to meet you."

"I wasn't asked . . . not that I'd've come anyhow," stammered Monty.

"You know perfectly well that in a Mormon town or house you are welcome," she said. "What did you want? Would you have had me stick my finger in the top hole of your vest and look up at you like a dying duck and say . . . 'Sam, please come?' "

"My Gawd, no. I never dreamed of wantin' you to do anythin'," replied Monty hurriedly. He was getting over his depth here, and began to doubt his ability to say the right things.

"Why not? Am I hideous? Aren't I a human being? A *girl?*" she queried with resentful fire.

Monty deliberated a moment, as much to recover his scattered wits as to make adequate reply. "Wal, you shore are a live human creature. An' as handsome as any girl I ever seen. But you're spoiled somethin' turrible. You're the most awful flirt I ever watched, an' the way you treat these fine Mormon boys is shore scandalous. You don't know what you want more'n one minnit straight runnin'. An' when you get what you want, you're sick of it right then."

"Oh, is that *all?*" she burst out, and then followed with a peal of riotous laughter. But she did not look at him or speak to him again for hours.

Monty liked that better. He had the thrill of her presence, without her disturbing chatter. The nucleus of a thought tried to wedge into his consciousness— that this girl was not indifferent to him. But he squelched it.

At noon they halted in a rocky depression, where water filled the holes, and Rebecca got down to sit in the shade of a cedar.

"I want something to eat," she declared imperiously.

"Sorry, but there ain't nothin'," replied Monty imperturbably, as he mounted to the seat again. The other wagon rolled on, cracking the rocks under its wheels.

"Are you going to starve me into submission?"

Monty laughed at her. "Wal, I reckon if someone took a willow switch to your bare legs an' . . . wal, he might get a little submission out of you."

"You're worse than a Mormon," she cried in disgust, as if that was the end of iniquity.

"Come on, child," said Monty with pretended weariness. "If we don't keep steppin' along lively, we'll never get home tonight."

"Good! I'll delay you as much as I can. Sam, I'm scared to death to face Mother." And she giggled.

"What about?"

"I went terribly in debt. But I didn't lose my 'haid' as you say. I thought it all out. I won't be going again for ages. And I'll work. Then the change in our fortunes tempted me."

"Wal, I reckon we can get around tellin' your mother," said Monty lamely.

"You wouldn't give me away, Sam?" she asked in surprise with strange, intent eyes. She got up to come to the wagon.

"No, I wouldn't. 'Course not. What's more, I can lend you the money . . . presently."

"Thanks, Sam. But I'll tell Mother."

She got up and rode beside him for miles without speaking. It seemed nothing to Monty, to ride in that country and keep silent. The desert was not conducive to conversation. It was so sublime as to be oppressive. League after league of rock and sage, of black ridge and red swale, and always the great landmarks looming as if unattainable. Behind them the Pink Cliffs rose higher the farther they got, to their left the long, black fringe of the Buckskin gradually climbed into obscurity, to the fore rolled away the colored desert, an ever-widening bowl that led the gaze to the purple chaos in the distance—that wild region of the rent earth called the cañon country.

Monty did not tell Rebecca that they could not get even halfway home, and that they would have to camp. But mentally, as a snow squall formed on the Buckskin, he told her it likely would catch up with them and turn to rain.

"Oh, Sam!" she wailed, aghast. "If my things got wet!"

He did not give her any assurance or comfort, and about mid-afternoon, when the road climbed toward a divide, he saw that they would not miss the storm. But he would go in camp at the pines and could weather it.

Before sunset they reached the highest point along the road, from which the spectacle down toward the west made Monty acknowledge that he was gazing at the grandest panorama ever presented to his enraptured eyes. He was a nature-loving cowboy of long years on the open range.

Rebecca watched with him, and he could feel her absorption. Finally she sighed and said, as if to herself: "One reason I'll marry a Mormon . . . if I have to . . . is that I never want to leave Utah."

They halted in the pines, low down on the far side of the divide, where a brook brawled merrily, and here the storm, half rain and half snow, caught them. Rebecca was frantic. She did not even know where her treasures were packed.

"Oh, Sam, I'll never forgive you!"

"*Me?* What have I got to do with it?" he queried in pretended amazement.

"Oh, you *knew* it would rain," she said. "And if you'd been half a man . . . if you didn't *hate* me, you . . . you could have saved my things."

"Wal, if thet's how you feel aboot it, I'll see what I can do," he drawled.

In a twinkling he jerked out the tarpaulin and spread it over the new wagon where he had carefully packed her cherished belongings, and in the same twinkling her woebegone face changed to astonished beatitude. Monty thought she might kiss him and he was scared stiff.

"Ma was right, Sam. You are the wonderfullest fellow," she said. "But . . . why didn't you *tell* me?"

"I forgot, I reckon. Now this rain ain't goin' to amount to much. After dark it'll turn off cold. I put some hay in the bottom of the wagon heah, an' a blanket. So you can sleep comfortable."

"*Sleep!* Sam, you're not going to stop here?"

"Shore am. This new wagon is stiff, an' the other one heavy loaded. We're darned lucky to reach this good campin' spot."

"But Sam, we can't stay here. We must drive on. It doesn't make any difference how *long* we are, so that we keep moving."

"An' kill our horses, an' then not get in? Sorry, Rebecca. If you hadn't delayed us five hours, we might have done it, allowin' for faster travel in the cool of mawnin'."

"Sam, do you want to ruin me?" she asked with great, childish, accusing eyes on him.

"Wal! Rebecca Keitch, if you don't beat me! I'll tell you what, miss. Where I come from, a man can entertain honest desire to spank a crazy girl without havin' evil intentions."

"You can spank me to your heart's content . . . but . . . Sam . . . take me home."

"Nope. I can fix it with your ma, an' I cain't see thet it amounts to a darn otherwise."

"Any Mormon girl who laid out on the desert . . . all night with a Gentile . . . would be ruined!" she declared.

"But we're not alone!" yelled Monty, red in the face. "We've got a man an' boy with us."

"No Mormon would ever . . . believe it," sobbed Rebecca.

"Wal, then, to hell with the Mormons who won't!" exclaimed Monty, exasperated beyond endurance.

"Mother will make you marry me," ended Rebecca with such tragedy of eye and voice that Monty could not but believe such a fate would be horrible.

"Aw, don't distress yourself, Miss Keitch," responded Monty with profound dignity. "I couldn't be druv to marry you . . . not to save your precious Mormon Church . . . nor the whole damn' world of Gentiles from . . . from conflagration!"

IV

Next day Monty drove through White Sage at noon, and reached Cañon Walls about mid-afternoon, completing a journey he would not want to undertake again under like circumstances. He made haste to unburden himself to his beaming employer.

"Wal, Missus Keitch, I done aboot everythin' as you wanted," he said. "But I couldn't get an early start yestiddy mawnin', an' so we had to camp at the pines."

"Why couldn't you?" she demanded, as if seriously concerned.

"Wal, for several reasons, particular thet the new harness wouldn't fit."

"You shouldn't have kept Rebecca out all night," said the widow severely.

"I don't see how it could have been avoided," replied Monty mildly. "You wouldn't have had me kill four horses?"

"Did you stop at White Sage?"

"Only to water, an' we didn't see no one."

"Maybe we can keep the Mormons from finding out," returned Mrs. Keitch with relief. "I'll talk to those new hands. Mormons are close-mouthed when it's to their interest."

"Wal, lady, heah's the receipts, an' my notes on expenditures," added Monty, handing them over. "My pore haid shore rang over all them figgers. But I got the prices you wanted. I found out you gotta stick to a Mormon. But he won't let you buy from another storekeeper, if he can help it."

"Indeed, he won't. Well, Daughter, what have you to say for yourself? I expected to see you with the happiest of faces. But you look like you used to, when you stole jam. I hope it wasn't your fault Sam had to keep you all night on the desert."

"Yes, Ma, it was," admitted Rebecca, and, although she spoke frankly, she plainly feared her mother.

"So. And Sam wouldn't tell on you, eh?"

"No, it seems he wouldn't, *wonderful* to see. Come in, Ma, and let me confess the rest . . . while I've the courage."

The mother looked grave. Monty saw that her anger would be a terrible thing.

"Lady, don't be hard on the girl," he said with his easy drawl and smile. "Just think. She hadn't been to Kanab for two years. Two years! An' she a growin' girl. Kanab is some shucks of a town. I was surprised. An' she was just a kid let loose."

"Sam Hill! So you have fallen into the ranks, at last," ejaculated Mrs. Keitch, while Rebecca telegraphed him a passionately grateful glance.

"Lady, I don't just savvy that aboot the ranks," replied Monty stiffly. "But I've fallen from grace all my life. Thet's why I'm. . . ."

"No matter," interrupted the widow hostilely, and it struck Monty that she did not care to have him confess such facts before Rebecca. "Unpack the wagons

53

and put the things on the porch, except what should go to the barn."

Monty helped the two new employees to unpack the old wagon first, and then directed them to the barn. Then he removed Rebecca's many purchases and piled them on the porch, all the while his ears burned at the heated argument going on within. Rebecca grew less and less vociferous while the mother gained, until she harangued her daughter terribly. It ended presently with the girl's uncontrolled sobbing. Monty drove out to the barn, disturbed in mind.

"Dog-gone! She's hell when she's riled," he soliloquized. "Now I wonder which it was. Rebecca spendin' all her money an' mine, an' then runnin' up bills . . . or because she made us stay a night out . . . or mebbe it's somethin' I don't know aboot. Whew, but she laid it on thet pore kid. Dog-gone the old Mormon! She'd better not pitch into me."

Supper was late that night and the table was set in the dusk. Mrs. Keitch had regained her composure, but Rebecca had a woebegone face, pallid from weeping. Monty's embarrassment seemed augmented by the fact that she squeezed his hand. But it was a silent meal, soon finished; and, while Rebecca reset the table for the new employees, Mrs. Keitch drew Monty aside on the porch. It suited him just as well that dusk was deepening into night.

"I am pleased with the way you carried out my instructions," said Mrs. Keitch. "I could not have done so well. My husband John was never any good in business. You are shrewd, clever, and reliable. If this year's harvest shows anything near what you claim, I can do no less than make you my partner. There is nothing to prevent us from developing another cañon ranch. John had a lien on one west of here. It's bigger than this and uncleared. We could acquire that, if you thought it wise. In fact, we could go far. Not that I am money-mad, like many Mormons, but I would like to show them. What do you think about it, Sam?"

"Wal, I agree, 'cept makin' me full pardner seems more'n I deserve. But if the crops turn out big this fall . . . an' you can gamble on it . . . I'll make a deal with you for five years or ten or life."

"Thank you. That is well. It insures comfort in my old age as well as something substantial for my daughter. Sam, do you understand Rebecca?"

"Good Lord, no!" exploded Monty.

"I reckoned you didn't. Do you realize that where she is concerned you are wholly unreliable?"

"What you mean, lady?" he queried, thunderstruck.

"She can wind you 'round her little finger."

"Huh! She just cain't do anythin' of the sort," declared Monty, trying to get angry. She might ask a question presently that would be exceedingly hard to answer.

"Perhaps you do not know it. That'd be natural. At first I thought you a deep, clever cowboy, one of the devil-with-the-girls kind, and that you would give Rebecca the lesson she deserves. But now I think you a soft-hearted, easy-going, *good* young man, actually stupid about a girl."

"Aw, thanks, lady," replied Monty, most uncomfortable, and then his natural spirit rebelled. "I never was accounted all that stupid aboot Gentile girls."

"Rebecca is no different from any girl. I should think you'd have seen that the Mormon style of courtship makes her sick. It is too simple, too courteous, too respectful, and too importantly religious to stir her heart. No Mormon will ever get Rebecca, unless I force her to marry him. Which I have been pressed to do and which I should never want to do."

"Wal, I respect you for thet, lady," replied Monty feelingly. "But why all this talk about Rebecca? I'm shore sympathetic, but how does it concern me?"

"Sam, I have not a friend in all this land, unless it's you."

"Wal, you can shore gamble on me. If you want I . . . I'll marry you an' be a dad to this girl who worries you so."

"Bless your heart! No, I'm too old for that, and I would not see you sacrifice yourself. But, oh, wouldn't that be fun . . . and revenge?"

"Wal, it'd be heaps of fun." Monty laughed. "But I don't reckon where the revenge would come in."

"Sam, you're given me an idea," spoke up the widow in a thrilling whisper. "I'll threaten Rebecca with this. That I could marry you and make you her father. If that doesn't chasten her . . . then the Lord have mercy upon me."

"She'd laugh at you."

"Yes. But she'll be scared to death. I'll never forget her face one day when she confessed you said she should be switched . . . well, it was quite shocking, if you said it."

"I shore did, lady," he admitted.

"Well, we begin all over again from today," concluded the widow thoughtfully. "To build anew! Go back to your work and plans. I have utmost confidence in you. My troubles are easing. But I have not one more word of advice about Rebecca."

"I can't say as you gave me any advice a-tall. But mebbe thet's because I'm stupid. Thanks, Missus Keitch, an' good night."

The painful, pondering hour Monty put in that night, walking in the moonlit shadow under the gleaming walls, only augmented his quandary. He ended it by admitting he was in love with Rebecca, ten thousand times worse than he had ever loved any girl before, and that she could wind him around her little finger. If she knew! But he swore he would never, never let her find it out.

Next day seemed the inauguration of a new regime at Cañon Walls. The ranch had received an impetus, like that given by water run over rich, dry ground. Monty's hours were doubly full. Always there was Rebecca, singing on the porch at dusk—"In the gloaming, oh, my darling"—a song that rushed Monty back to home in Iowa, and the zigzag rail fences, or she was at this elbow during the milking hour, an ever-growing task, or in the fields. She could work, that girl, and he told her mother it would not take long for her to earn the money she had squandered.

Sunday after Sunday passed, with the host of merry callers, and no word was ever spoken of Rebecca having passed a night on the desert with a Gentile. So that specter died, except in an occasional mocking look she gave him that, he interpreted, meant she could still betray herself and him.

In June came the first cutting of alfalfa—fifty acres with an enormous yield. The rich, green, fragrant hay stood knee-high. Monty tried to contain himself. But it did seem marvelous that the few simple changes he had made could produce such a harvest.

Monty worked late, and a second bell did not deter him. He wanted to finish this last great stack of alfalfa. Then he espied Rebecca, running along the trail, calling. Monty let her call. It somehow tickled him, pretending not to hear. So she came out in the field and up to him.

"Sam, are you deaf? Mother rang twice. And then she sent me."

"Wal, I reckon I been feelin' awful good aboot this alfalfa," he replied.

"Oh, it is lovely. So dark and green. So sweet to smell! Sam, I'll just have to slide down that haystack."

"Don't you dare!" called Monty in alarm.

But she ran around to the lower side and presently

appeared on top, flushed, full of fun and desire to torment him.

"Please, Rebecca, don't slide down. You'll topple it over, an' I'll have all the work to do again."

"Sam, I'll just have to, like I used to when I was a kid."

"You're a kid right now," he retorted. "Go back an' get down careful."

She shrieked and let herself go and came sliding down, rather at the expense of modesty. Monty knew he was angry, but he feared he was some other things.

"There! You see how slick I did it? I could always beat the girls . . . and boys, too."

"Wal, let thet do," growled Monty.

"Just one more, Sam."

He dropped his pitchfork and made a lunge for her, catching only the air. How quick she was! He controlled an impulse to run after her. Soon she appeared on top again, with something added to her glee.

"Rebecca, if you slide down heah again, you'll be sorry," he said warningly.

"What'll *you* do?"

"I'll spank you."

"Sam Hill! You wouldn't dare."

"So help me heaven, I will."

She did not in the least believe him, but it was evident that his threat made her project only the more thrilling. There was at least a possibility of events.

"Look out. I'm coming!" she cried with a wild, sweet trill of laughter.

As she slid down, Monty leaped to intercept her. A scream escaped Rebecca, but it was because of her treacherous skirts. That did not deter Monty. He caught her and held her high off the ground, and there he pinioned her.

Whatever Monty's intent had been, it escaped him. A winged flame flicked at every fiber of his being. He had her arms spread, and it took all his strength and weight to hold her there, feet off the ground. She was not in the least frightened at this close contact, although a wonderful speculation sparkled in her big gray eyes.

"You caught me. Now what?" she said challengingly.

Monty kissed her squarely on the mouth.

"Oh!" she cried, divinely startled. Then a rush of scarlet waved up from the rich, gold swell of her neck. She struggled. "Let me down . . . you Gentile cowpuncher!"

Monty kissed her again, longer, harder than before. Then, when she tried to scream, he stopped her lips again.

"You . . . little Mormon . . . devil!" he panted. "This heah . . . was shore . . . comin' to you."

"I'll kill you!"

"Wal, it'll be worth . . . dyin' for." Then Monty kissed her until she gasped for breath, and, when she sagged, limp and unresisting, in his arms, he kissed her cheeks, her eyes, her hair, and like a madness whose hunger had been augmented by what it fed on he went back to her red, parted lips.

Suddenly all appeared to grow dark. A weight carried him down with the girl. The top of the alfalfa stack had slid down upon them. Monty floundered out and dragged Rebecca from under the fragrant mass. She did not move. Her eyes were closed. With trembling hand he brushed the leaves and seeds of alfalfa off her white face. But her hair was full of them.

"My Gawd, I've played hob now," he whispered, as the enormity of his offence dawned upon him. Nevertheless he felt a tremendous drag at him as he looked down on her. Only her lips had a vestige of color. Suddenly her eyes opened wide. From the marvel of them Monty fled.

V

Monty's first wild impulse, as he ran, was to get out of the cañon, away from the incomprehensible forces that had worked such havoc with him. His second was to rush to Mrs. Keitch and confess to her, before Rebecca could damn him forever in the good woman's estimation. Then by the time he reached his cabin and fell on the porch, those impulses had given place to others. But it was not Monty's nature to be long helpless. Presently he sat up, wringing wet with sweat, and still shaking.

"Aw, what come over me?" he breathed hoarsely. And suddenly he realized that nothing so terrible had happened. He had been furious when he held her, close and tight, with those challenging eyes and lips right at his. All else except the sweetness of momentary possession had gone into eclipse. He loved the girl and had not had any realization of the magnitude of his love. He believed he could explain to Mrs. Keitch, so that she would not drive him away. But, of course, he would be dirt under Rebecca's feet from that hour on. Yet, even in his mournful acceptance of this fate, his spirit rose resentfully to wonder and inquire about this Mormon girl.

Darkness had almost set in. Down the land Monty saw a figure approaching, quite some distance, and he thought he heard a low voice singing. But Rebecca would be weeping.

"Re-becca!" called Mrs. Keitch from the porch, in her mellow, far-reaching voice.

"Coming, Ma," replied the girl.

Monty sank into the shadow of his little cabin. He felt small enough to be unseen, but dared not risk it. And he watched in fear and trepidation. Suddenly Rebecca's low contralto voice rang on the quiet, sultry air.

> In the gleaming,
> Oh, my darling
> When the lights are
> dim and low
> And the flickering shadows falling
> Softly come and softly go.

Monty's heart swelled to bursting. Did she realize the truth and was she mocking him? He was simply flabbergasted. But how the sweet voice filled the cañon and came back in echo from the walls.

Rebecca, entering the square between the orchards and the cottonwoods, gave Monty's cabin a wide berth.

"Isn't Sam with you?" called Mrs. Keitch from the porch.

"Sam? No, he isn't."

"Where is he? Didn't you call him? Supper's getting cold."

"I haven't any idea where Sam is. Last I saw of him, he was running like mad," rejoined Rebecca with a giggle.

That giggle saved Monty a stroke of apoplexy.

"Running? What for?" queried the mother as Rebecca mounted the porch.

"Mother, it was the funniest thing. I called Sam, but he didn't hear. I went out to tell him supper was ready. He had a great, high stack of alfalfa up. Of course, I wanted to climb it and slide down. Well, Sam got mad and ordered me not to do any such thing. Then I *had* to do it. Such fun! Sam growled like a bear. Well, I couldn't resist climbing up for another slide. Do you know, Mother, Sam got perfectly furious. He has a terrible temper. He commanded me not to slide off that stack. And when I asked him what he'd do if I did . . . he declared he'd spank me. Imagine! I only meant to tease him. I wasn't going to

slide at all. Then you could see I *had* to. So I did. I
. . . oh, dear! . . . I fetched the whole top of the stack
down on us . . . and, when I got out from under the
smothering hay . . . and could see . . . there was Sam,
running for dear life."

"Well, for the land's sake!" ejaculated Mrs. Keitch
dubiously, and then she laughed. "You drive the poor
fellow wild with your pranks. Rebecca, will you
never grow up?" Whereupon she came out to the
porch rail and called: "Sam!"

Monty started up, opened his door to let it slam, and
replied, in what he thought the funniest voice:
"Hello?"

"Hurry to supper."

Monty washed his face and hands, brushed his
hair, while his mind whirled. Then he sat down
bewildered. *Dog-gone me! Can you beat that girl?
She didn't give me away. She didn't lie, yet she never
told. . . . She's not goin' to tell. Must have been funny
to her. But shore it's a daid safe bet she never got
kissed thet way before. I just cain't figger her out.*

Presently he went to supper and was grateful for the
dim light. Still he felt the girl's eyes on him. No doubt
she was now appreciating him as a real Arizona Gentile rowdy cowboy. He pretended weariness, and soon
hurried away to his cabin, where he spent a night of
inexplicable dreams and waking emotions. Remorse,
however, had died a natural death after Rebecca's
story to her mother.

With dawn came the blessed work into which

Monty plunged, finding all relief except oblivion. Rebecca did not speak a single word to him for two weeks. Mrs. Keitch finally remarked it and reproved her daughter.

"Speak to *him?*" asked Rebecca in haughty amazement. "Maybe . . . when he crawls on his knees!"

"But, Daughter, he only threatened to spank you. And I'm sure you gave him provocation. You must always forgive. We cannot live at enmity here," said the good mother persuasively.

Then she turned to Monty.

"Sam, you know Rebecca has passed eighteen and she feels an exaggerated sense of maturity. Perhaps if you'd tell her you were sorry. . . ."

"What aboot?" asked Monty, when she hesitated.

"Why, about what offended Rebecca."

"Aw, shore. I'm awful sorry," drawled Monty, his keen eyes on the girl. "Turrible sorry . . . but it's aboot not sayin' an' doin' *more* . . . an' then spankin' her to boot."

Mrs. Keitch looked aghast, and, when Rebecca ran away hysterical with mirth, she seemed positively nonplussed.

"That girl! Why, Sam, I thought she was furious with you. But she's not. It's sham."

"Wal, I reckon she's riled all right, but it doesn't matter. An' see heah, lady," he went on, lowering his voice, "I'm confidin' in you an' if you give me away . . . wal, I'll leave the ranch. I reckon you've forgot how you told me I'd lose my haid over Rebecca. Wal,

I've lost it, clean an' plumb an' otherwise. An' some-times I do queer things. Just remember thet's why. This won't make no difference. I'm happy heah. Only I want you to understand me."

"Sam Hill," she whispered in ecstatic amaze. "So that's what ails you? Now all will be well."

"Wal, I'm glad you think so," replied Monty shortly. "An' I reckon it will be . . . when I get over these growin' pains."

She leaned toward him. "My son, I understand now. Rebecca has been in love with you for a long time. Just let her alone. All will be well."

Monty gave her one mute, incredulous stare, and then he fled. In the darkness of his cabin he persuaded himself of the absurdity of the sentimental Mrs. Keitch's claim. Then he could sleep. But when day came again, he found the harm had been wrought. He lived in a kind of dream and he was always watching for Rebecca.

Straightway he began to make discoveries. Gradu-ally she came out of her icy shell. She worked as usual, and apparently with less discontent, especially in the mornings when she had time to sew on the porch. She would fetch lunch to the men out in the fields. Often Monty saw her on top of a haystack, but he always quickly looked away. She climbed the wall trail; she gathered armloads of wildflowers. She helped where her help was not needed.

On Sundays, she went to church at White Sage and in the afternoon entertained callers. But it was noticeable that her Mormon courtiers grew fewer as the summer advanced. Monty missed in her the gay allure, the open coquetry, the challenge that had once been marked.

All this was thought-provoking for Monty, but nothing to the discovery that Rebecca watched him from afar and when near at hand. Monty could not credit it. Only another instance of his addled brain! It happened, morever, that the eyes that had made Monty Smoke Bellew a great shot and tracker, wonderful out on the range, could not be deceived. The hour he lent himself, in stifling curiosity, to spying upon Rebecca he learned the staggering truth.

In the mornings and evenings, while he was at work near the barn or resting on his porch, she watched him, thinking herself unseen. She peeped from behind her window curtain, through the leaves, above her sewing, from the open doors—from everywhere the great, gray, hungry eyes sought him. It began to get on Monty's nerves. Did she hate him so that she planned some dire revenge? But the eyes that watched him in secret seldom or never met his own any more. Sometimes his consciousness took hold of Mrs. Keitch's strangely tranquil words, and then he had to battle fiercely to recover his equilibrium. The last asinine thing Smoke Bellew could ever do would be to give in to vain obsession. But the situation invoked and haunted him.

One noonday Monty returned to his cabin to find a magical change in his single room. He could not recognize it. Clean and tidy and colorful it flashed at him. There were Indian rugs on the clay floor, Indian ornaments on the log walls, curtains at his windows, a scarf on his table, and a gorgeous bedspread on his bed. In a little Indian vase on the table stood some stalks of golden daisies and purple asters.

"What happened around heah this mawnin'?" he drawled at meal hour. "My cabin is spruced up so fine."

"Yes, it does look nice," replied Mrs. Keitch complacently. "Rebecca has had that in mind for some time."

"Wal, it was turrible good of her," said Monty.

"Oh, nonsense," returned Rebecca with a swift blush. "Ma wanted you to be more comfortable."

"Ma did? How you trifle with the precious truth, Daughter! Sam, I never thought of it, I'm ashamed to say."

Monty escaped somehow, as he always managed to escape when catastrophe impended. But one August night when the harvest moon rose, white and grand, above the black cañon rim, he felt such a strange, impelling presentiment he could not leave his porch and go in to bed. It had been a hard day—one in which the accumulated cut of alfalfa had mounted to unbelievable figures. Cañon Walls Ranch, with its soil and water and Sam, was simply a gold mine. All over southern Utah the ranchers were clambering for that alfalfa.

The hour was late. The light in Rebecca's room had long been out. Frogs and owls and night hawks had ceased their lonely calls. Only the insects hummed in the melancholy stillness.

A rustle startled Monty. Was it a leaf falling from a cottonwood? A dark form crossed the barred patches of moonlight. Rebecca! She passed close to him as he lounged on the porch steps. Her face flashed white. She ran down the lane and stopped to look back.

"Dog-gone! Am I drunk or crazy or just moon-struck?" ejaculated Monty, rising. "What is that girl up to? Shore she seen me heah. Shore she did!"

He started down the lane, and, when he came out of the shadow of the cottonwoods into the moonlight, she ran fleetly as a deer. But again she halted and looked back. Monty stalked after her. He was roused now. He would see this thing through. If it were another of her hoydenish tricks! But there seemed to be an appalling something in this night flight out into the cañon under the full moon.

Monty lost sight of her at the end of the lane. But when he reached it and turned into the field, he espied her far out, lingering, looking back. He could see her moon-blanched face. She ran on, and he followed.

That side of the cañon lay clear in the silver light. On the other the looming cañon wall stood up black, with its last rim moon-fired against the sky. The alfalfa shone brightly, yet kept its deep dark, rich, velvety hue.

Rebecca was making for the upper end where that

day the alfalfa had been cut. She let Monty gain on her, but at last with a wild trill she ran to the huge, silver-shining haystack and began to climb it.

Monty did not run; he slowed down. He did not know what was happening to him, but his state seemed to verge upon lunacy. One of his nightmares! He would awaken presently. But then the white form edged up the steep haystack. He had finished this mound of alfalfa with the satisfaction of an artist.

When he reached it, Rebecca had not only gained the top, but was lying flat, propped on her elbows. Monty went closer—right up to the stack. He could see her distinctly now, scarcely fifteen feet above his head. The moonlight lent her an exceeding witchery. But it was the mystery of her eyes that seemed to end all for Monty. Why had he followed her? He could do nothing. His threat was but an idle memory. His anger would not rise. She would make him betray his secret and then, alas! Cañon Walls could no longer be a home for him.

"Howdy, Sam," she said in a tone that he could not comprehend,

"Rebecca, what does this mean?" he asked.

"Isn't it a glorious night?"

"Yes. But the hour is late. An' you could have watched from your window."

"Oh, no. I had to be out in it. Besides, I wanted to make you follow me,"

"Wal, you shore have. I was plumb scared, I reckon.

An' . . . an' I'm glad it was only fun. But why did you want me to follow you?"

"For one thing I wanted you to see me climb your new haystack."

"Yes? Wal, I've seen you. So come down now. If your mother should ketch us out heah. . . ."

"And I wanted you to see me slide down *this* one."

The silvery medium that surrounded this dark-eyed witch was surely charged with intense and troubled potentialities for Monty. He was lost and he could only look the query she expected.

"And I wanted to see terribly . . . what you'd do," she went on, with a seriousness that must have been mockery.

"Rebecca, child, I will do . . . nothin'," replied Monty, almost mournfully.

She got to her knees, and leaned as if to see him closer. Then she turned around to sit down and slid to the very edge. Her hands were clutched, deep in the alfalfa.

"You won't spank me, Sam?" she asked in impish glee.

"No. Much as I'd like to . . . an' as you shore need it . . . I cain't."

"Bluffer. Gentile cowpuncher . . . showing yellow . . . marble-hearted fiend!"

"Not thet last, Rebecca. For all my many faults, not thet," he said sadly.

She seemed fighting to let go of something that the mound of alfalfa represented only in symbol. Surely the physical effort for Rebecca to hold her balance there could not account for the strain of body and face. All the mystery of Cañon Walls and the beauty of the night hovered over her.

"Sam, dare me to slide," she taunted.

"No," he retorted grimly.

"Coward."

"Shore. You hit me on the haid there."

Then ensued a short silence. He could see the quivering. She was moving, almost imperceptibly. Her eyes, magnified by the shadow and light, transfixed Monty.

"Gentile, dare me to slide . . . into your arms!" she cried a little huskily.

"Mormon witch! Would you . . . ?"

"Dare me!"

"Wal, I dare . . . you, Rebecca . . . but, so help me Gawd, I won't answer for consequences."

Her laugh, like that other sweet, wild trill, pealed up, but now full of joy, of certainty, of surrender. And she let go her hold, to spread wide her arms, and come sliding on an avalanche of silver hay down upon him.

VI

Next morning, Monty found work in the fields impossible. He roamed about like a man possessed, and at last went back to the cabin. It was just before the noonday meal. Rebecca hummed a tune while she set the table. Mrs. Keitch sat on her rocker, busy with work on her lap. There was no charged atmosphere. All seemed serene.

Monty responded to the girl's sly glance by taking her hand and leading her up to her mother.

"Lady," he began hoarsely, "you've knowed long my feelin's for Rebecca. But it seems . . . she . . . she loves me, too. How thet come aboot I cain't say. It's shore the wonderfullest thing. Now, I ask you, for Rebecca's sake most . . . what can be done about this heah trouble?"

"Daughter, is it true?" asked Mrs. Keitch, looking up with serene and smiling face.

"Yes, Mother," replied Rebecca simply.

"You love Sam?"

"Oh, I do."

"Since when?"

"Always, I guess. But I never knew till this June."

"I am very glad, Rebecca," replied the mother, rising to embrace her. "As you could not or would not love one of your own creed, it is well that you love this man who came a stranger to our gates. He is strong, he is true, and what his religion is matters little."

Then she smiled upon Monty. "My son, no man can say what guided your steps to Cañon Walls. But I have always felt God's intent in it. You and Rebecca shall marry."

"Oh, Mother," murmured the girl rapturously, and she hid her face.

"Wal . . . I'm willin' . . . an' happy," stammered Monty. "But I ain't worthy of her, lady, an' you know that old. . . ."

She silenced him. "You must go to White Sage and be married at once."

"At once! When?" faltered Rebecca.

"Aw, Missus Keitch, I . . . I wouldn't hurry the girl. Let her have her own time."

"No, why wait? She has been a strange, starved creature. Tomorrow you must take her, Sam."

"Wal an' good, if Rebecca says so," said Monty with wistful eagerness.

"Yes," she whispered. "Will you go with me, Mother?"

"Yes," suddenly rang out Mrs. Keitch, as if inspired. "I will go. I will cross the Utah line once more before I am carried over. But not White Sage. We will go to Kanab. You shall be married by the bishop."

In the excitement and agitation that possessed the mother and daughter then Monty sensed a significance more than just the tremendous importance of an impending marriage. Some deep, strong motive urged Mrs. Keitch to go to Kanab, there to have her bishop marry Rebecca to a Gentile. One way or another it did not matter to Monty. He rode in the clouds. He could not believe in his good luck. Never in his life had he touched real happiness until then.

The womenfolk were an hour late in serving lunch, and during that the air of vast excitement permeated their every word and action.

"Wal, this heah seems like a Sunday," said Monty, after the hasty meal. "I've loafed a lot this mawnin'. But I reckon I'll go back to work now."

"Oh, Sam, don't . . . when . . . when we're leaving so soon," remonstrated Rebecca shyly.

"When are we leavin'?"

"Tomorrow . . . early."

"Wal, I'll get that alfalfa up anyhow. It might rain, you know. Rebecca, do you reckon you could get up at daylight for this heah ride?"

"I could stay up all night, Sam."

Mrs. Keitch laughed at them. "There's no rush. We'll start after breakfast. And get to Kanab early enough to make arrangements for the wedding next day. It will give Sam time to buy a respectable suit of clothes to be married in."

"Dog-gone I hadn't thought of thet," replied Monty ruefully.

"Sam Hill, you won't marry *me* in a ten-gallon hat, a red shirt, blue overalls, and boots," declared Rebecca.

"How about wearin' my gun?" drawled Monty.

"Your gun!" exclaimed Rebecca.

"Shore. You've forgot how I used to pack it. I might need it over there among them Mormons who're crazy about you."

"Heavens! You leave that gun home."

Monty went his way, marveling at the change in his habits and in his life. Next morning, when he brought the buckboard around, Mrs. Keitch and Rebecca appeared radiant of face, gorgeous of apparel. But for the difference in age anyone might have mistaken the mother for the intended bride.

The drive to Kanab with fresh horses and light load took six hours. The news spread over Kanab like wildfire in dry prairie grass. For all Monty's keen eyes, he never caught a jealous look, nor did he hear a nasty word. That settled with him the status of the Keitches' Mormon friends. The Tyler brothers came into town and made much of the fact that Monty would soon be one of them, and they planned another fall hunt for wild mustangs and deer. Waking hours sped by and sleeping hours were few. Almost before Monty knew what was happening he was in the presence of the august bishop.

"Will you come into the Mormon Church?" asked the bishop.

"Wal, sir, I cain't be a Mormon," replied Monty in perplexity. "But I shore have respect for you people an' your church. I reckon I never had no religion. I can say I'll never stand in Rebecca's way, in anythin' pertainin' to hers."

"In the event she bears you children, you will not seek to raise them Gentiles?"

"I'd leave that to Rebecca," replied Monty sagely.

"And the name Sam Hill, by which you are known, is a middle name?"

"Shore, just a cowboy middle name."

So they were married. Monty feared they would never escape from the many friends and the curious crowd. But at last they were safely in the buckboard, speeding homeward. Monty sat in the front seat alone. Mrs. Keitch and Rebecca occupied the rear seat. The girl's expression of pure happiness touched Monty and made him swear deeply in his throat that he would try to deserve her. Mrs. Keitch had evidently lived through one of the few great events of her life. What dominated her feelings, Monty could not divine, but she had the look of a woman who asked no more. Somewhere a monstrous injustice or wrong had been done the Widow Keitch. Recalling the bishop's strange look at Rebecca—a look of hunger—Monty pondered deeply. The ride home, being downhill with a pleasant breeze off the desert and that wondrous panorama coloring and smoking as the sun set, seemed all too short for Monty. He drawled to Rebecca, when they reached the portal of Cañon Walls and halted under the gold-leaved cottonwoods: "Wal, wife, heah we are home. But we shore ought to have made thet honeymoon drive a longer one."

That supper time was the only one in which Monty ever saw Widow Keitch bow her head for the salvation of these young people so strongly brought together, for the home overflowing with milk and honey, for the hopeful future.

They had their fifth cutting of alfalfa in September, and it was in the nature of an event. The Tyler boys rode over to help, fetching Sue to visit Rebecca. And there was merry-making. Rebecca would climb over mounds of alfalfa and slide down, screaming her delight. And once she said to Monty: "Young man, you should pray under every haystack you build."

"A-huh. An' what for should I pray, Rebecca?" he drawled.

"To give thanks for all this sweet-smelling alfalfa has brought you."

The harvest goods smiled on Cañon Walls that autumn. Three wagons plied between Kanab and the ranch for weeks, hauling the produce that could not be used. While Monty went off with the Tyler boys for their hunt on the Buckskin, the womenfolk and their guests, and the hired hands, applied themselves industriously to the happiest work of the year—preserving all they could of the luscious yield of the season.

Monty came back to a home such as had never been his even in dreams. Rebecca was incalculably changed, and so happy that Monty trembled as he listened to her sing, as he watched her work. The mystery never ended for him, not even when she whispered that they might expect a little visit from the angels next spring. But Monty's last doubt faded, and he gave himself over to work, to his loving young wife, to waltz in the dusk under the gleaming walls, to a lonely pipe beside his little fireside.

The winter passed, and spring came, doubling former activities. They had taken over the cañon three miles to the westward, which, once cleared of brush and cactus and rock, promised well. The problem had been water and Monty solved it. Good fortune had attended his every venture.

Around the middle of May, when the cottonwoods were green and the peach trees pink, Monty began to grow restless about the coming event. It uplifted him one moment, appalled him the next. In that past which seemed so remote now he had snuffed out life. Young, fiery, grim Smoke Bellew! And by some incomprehensible working out of life he was about to become a father.

On the 17th of June, some hours after breakfast, he was hurriedly summoned from the fields. His heart appeared to choke him.

Mrs. Keitch met him at the porch. He scarcely knew her.

"My son, do you remember this date?"

"No," replied Monty wonderingly.

"Two years ago today you came to us. And Rebecca has just borne you a son."

"Aw . . . my Gawd! Have . . . how is she, lady?" he gasped.

"Both well. We could work no more. It has all been a visitation of God. Come."

Some days later the important matter of christening the youngster came up.

"Ma wants one of those jaw-breaking Biblical names," said Rebecca, pouting. "But I like just plain Sam."

"Wal, it ain't much of a handle for such a wonderful boy."

"It's your name. I love it."

"Rebecca, you kinda forget Sam Hill was just a . . . a sort of a middle name. It ain't my real name."

"Oh, yes, I remember now," replied Rebecca, her great eyes lighting. "At Kanab . . . the bishop asked about Sam Hill. Mother had told him this was your nickname."

"Darlin', I had another nickname once," he said sadly.

"So, my man of mysterious past, and what was that?"

"They called me Smoke."

"How funny! Well, I may be Missus Monty Smoke Bellew, according to the law and the church, but *you,* my husband, will still always be Sam Hill."

"An' the boy?" asked Monty, enraptured.

"Is Sam Hill, too."

An anxious week passed, and then all seemed surely well with the new mother and the baby. Monty ceased to tiptoe around. He no longer awoke with a start in the dead of night.

Then one Saturday as he came out on the wide front porch, at a hallo from someone, he saw four riders. A bolt shot back from a closed door of his memory. Arizona riders! How well he knew the lean faces, the lithe shapes, the gun belts, the mettlesome horses!

"Nix, fellers!" called the foremost rider, as Monty came slowly out.

An instinct and a muscular contraction passed over Monty. Then he realized he packed no gun and was glad. Old habit might have been too strong. His hawk eye saw lean hands drop from hips. A sickening, terrible despair followed his first reaction.

"Howdy, Smoke," drawled the foremost rider.

"Wal, dog-gone! If it ain't Jim Sneed," returned Monty, as he recognized the sheriff, and he descended the steps to walk out and offer his hand, quick to see the swift, penetrating gray eyes run over him.

"Shore, it's Jim. I reckoned you'd know me. Hoped you would, as I wasn't keen about raisin' your smoke."

"A-huh. What you-all doin' over heah, Jim?" asked Monty, with a glance at the three watchful riders.

"Main thing I come over for was to buy stock for Strickland. An' he said, if it wasn't out of my way, I might fetch you back. Word come that you've been seen in Kanab. An' when I made inquiry at White Sage, I shore knowed who Sam Hill was."

"I see. Kinda tough it happened to be Strickland. Dog-gone! My luck just couldn't last."

"Smoke, you look uncommon fine," said the sheriff, with another appraising glance. "You shore haven't been drinkin'. An' I seen first off you wasn't totin' no gun."

"That's all past for me, Jim."

"Wal, I'll be damned!" ejaculated Sneed, and fumbled for a cigarette. "Bellew, I just don't savvy."

"Reckon you wouldn't, Jim. I'd like to ask if my

81

name ever got linked up with that Green Valley deal two years an' more ago?"

"No, it didn't, Smoke, I'm glad to say. Your pards, Slim an' Cuffy, pulled that. Slim was killed coverin' Cuffy's escape."

"A-huh. So Slim . . . wal, wal . . . ," sighed Monty, and paused a moment to gaze into space.

"Smoke, tell me your deal here," said Sneed.

"Shore. But would you mind comin' indoors?"

"Reckon I wouldn't. But, Smoke, I'm still figgerin' you the cowboy."

"Wal, you're way off. Get down an' come in."

Monty led the sheriff into Rebecca's bedroom. She was awake, playing with the baby, and both looked lovely. "Jim, this is my wife an' youngster," said Monty feelingly. "An' Rebecca, this heah is an old friend of mine, Jim Sneed, from Arizona."

That must have been a hard moment for the sheriff—the cordial welcome of the blushing wife, the smiling mite of a baby who hung onto his finger, the atmosphere there of unadulterated joy. At any rate, when they went out again to the porch, Sneed wiped his perspiring face and swore at Monty: "God damn it. Cowboy, have you gone an' double-crossed that sweet girl?"

Monty told him the few salient facts of his romance, and told it with trembling eagerness to be believed.

"So you've turned Mormon?" ejaculated the sheriff.

"No, but I'll be true to these women. An' one thing I ask, Sneed. Don't let it be known in White Sage or anywhere over heah *why* I'm with you. I can send word to my wife I've got to go. Then afterward I'll come back."

"Smoke, I wish I had a stiff drink," replied Sneed. "But I reckon you haven't any thin'."

"Only water an' milk."

"Good Lawd! For an Arizonian!" Sneed halted at the head of the porch steps and shot out a big hand. His cold eyes had warmed. "Smoke, may I tell Strickland you'll send him some money now an' then . . . till thet debt is paid?"

Monty stared and faltered. "Jim . . . you shore can."

"Fine," returned the sheriff in a loud voice, and he strode down the steps to mount his horse. "*Adios,* cowboy. Be good to thet little woman."

Monty could not speak. He watched the riders down the lane, out into the road, and through the looming cañon gates to the desert beyond. His heart was full. He thought of Slim and Cuffy, those young firebrand comrades of his range days. He could remember now without terror. He could live once more with his phantoms of the past. He could see lean, lithe Arizona riders come into Cañon Walls, if that happy event ever chanced, and he was glad.

Black Sheep
Max Brand

Fredrick Schiller Faust (1892–1944) was born in Seattle, Washington. He wrote over 500 average-length books (300 of them Westerns) under nineteen different pseudonyms, but Max Brand—"the Jewish cowboy," as he once dubbed it—has become the most familiar and is now his trademark. Faust was convinced very early that to die in battle was the most heroic of deaths, and so, when the Great War began, he tried to get overseas. All of his efforts came to nothing, and in 1917, working at manual labor in New York City, he wrote a letter that was carried in *The New York Times* protesting this social injustice. Mark Twain's sister came to his rescue by arranging for Faust to meet Robert H. Davis, an editor at The Frank A. Munsey Company.

Faust wanted to write—poetry. What happened instead was that Davis provided Faust with a brief plot idea, told him to go down the hall to a room where there was a typewriter, only to have Faust return some six hours later with a story suitable for publication. That was "Convalescence", a short story that appeared in *All-Story Weekly* (3/31/17) and that launched Faust's career as an author of fiction. Zane Grey had recently abandoned the Munsey publications, *All-Story Weekly* and *The Argosy,* as a market for his Western serials, selling them instead to the slick-paper *Country Gentleman.* The more fiction Faust wrote for Davis, the more convinced this editor became that Faust could equal Zane Grey in writing a Western story.

The one element that is the same in Zane Grey's early Western stories and Faust's from beginning to end is that they are psycho-dramas. What impact events have on the soul, the inner spiritual changes wrought by ordeal and adversity, the power of love as an emotion and a bond between a man and a woman, and above all the meaning of life and one's experiences in the world conspire to transfigure these stories and elevate them to a plane that shimmers with nuances both symbolic and mythical. In 1920 Faust expanded the market for his fiction to include Street & Smith's *Western Story Magazine* for which throughout the next decade he would contribute regularly a million and a half words a year at a rate of 5¢ a word. It was not unusual for him to have two serial installments and a short novel in a single issue under three different names or to earn from just this one source $2,500 a week.

In 1921 Faust made the tragic discovery that he had an incurable heart condition from which he might die at any moment. This condition may have been in part emotional. At any rate, Faust became depressed about his work, and in England in 1925 he consulted H.G. Baynes, a Jungian analyst, and finally even met with C.G. Jung himself who was visiting England at the time on his way to Africa. They had good talks, although Jung did not take Faust as a patient. Jung did advise Faust that his best hope was to live a simple life. This advice Faust rejected. He went to Italy where he rented a villa in Florence, lived extravagantly, and was perpetually in debt. Faust needed his speed at writing merely to remain solvent. Yet what is most amazing about him is not that he wrote so much, but that he wrote so much so well!

By the early 1930s Faust was spending more and more time in the United States. Carl Brandt, his agent, persuaded him to write for the slick magazines since the pay was better and, toward the end of the decade, Faust moved his family to Hollywood where he found work as a screenwriter. He had missed one war; he refused to miss the Second World War. He pulled strings to become a war correspondent for *Harper's Magazine* and sailed to Europe and the Italian front. Faust hoped from this experience to write fiction about men at war, and he lived in foxholes with American soldiers involved in some of the bloodiest fighting on any front. These men, including the machine-gunner beside whom Faust died, had grown up reading his stories with their fabulous heroes and their grand deeds, and that is where on a dark night in 1944, hit by shrapnel, Faust expired, having asked the medics to attend first to the younger men who had been wounded.

Faust's Western fiction has nothing intrinsically to do with the American West, although he had voluminous notes and research materials on virtually every aspect of the frontier. *The Untamed* (Putnam, 1919) was his first Western novel and in Dan Barry, its protagonist, Faust created a man who is beyond morality in a Nietzschean sense, who is closer to the primitive and the wild in nature than other human beings, who is both frightening and sympathetic. His story continues, and his personality gains added depth, in the two sequels that complete his story, *The Night Horseman* (Putnam, 1920) and *The Seventh Man* (Putnam, 1921).

Those who worked with Faust in Hollywood were amazed at his fecundity, his ability to plot stories. However, for all of his incessant talk about plot and plotting, Faust's Western fiction is uniformly character-driven. His plots emerge from the characters as they are confronted with conflicts and frustrations. Above all, there is his humor—the hilarity of the opening chapters of *The Return of the Rancher* (Dodd, Mead, 1933), to give only one instance, is sustained by the humorous contrast between irony and naïveté. So many of Faust's characters are truly unforgettable, from the most familiar, like Dan Barry and Harry Destry, to such marvelous creations as José Ridal in *Blackie and Red* (Chelsea House, 1926) or Gaspar Sental in *The Return of the Rancher.*

Too often, it may appear, Faust's plots are pursuit stories and his protagonists in quest of an illustrious father or victims of an Achilles' heel, but these are premises and conventions that are ultimately of little consequence. His characters are in essence psychic

forces. In Faust's fiction, as Robert Sampson concluded in the first volume of *Yesterday's Faces*
(Bowling Green University Popular Press, 1983),
"every action is motivated. Every character makes
decisions and each must endure the consequences of
his decisions. Each character is gnawed by the con-
flict between his wishes and the necessities of his
experience. The story advances from the first interac-
tions of the first characters. It continues, a fugue for
full orchestra, ever more complex, modified by decisions of increasing desperation, to a climax whose
savagery may involve no bloodshed at all. But there
will be psychological tension screaming in harmonics
almost beyond the ear's capacity."

Faust's finest fiction can be enjoyed on the level of
adventure, or on the deeper level of psychic meaning.
He knew in his heart that he had not resolved the psychic conflicts he projected into his fiction, but he held
out hope to the last that the resolutions he had failed
to find in life and in his stories might somehow,
miraculously, be achieved on the higher plane of the
poetry that he continued to write. Yet Faust is not the
first writer, and will not be the last, who treasured
least what others have come to treasure most. It may
even be possible that a later generation, having read
his many works as he wrote them (and they are now
being restored after decades of inept abridgments and
rewriting), will find Frederick Faust to have been,
truly, one of the most significant American literary
artists of the 20th Century. Much more about Faust's

life, his work, and critical essays on various aspects of his fiction of all kinds can be found in *The Max Brand Companion* (Greenwood Press, 1996).

I

The barb of the cactus goes easily in, but it is difficult to get out. The minister was fond of saying that the thorn resembled sin, so easy in the commission with consequences that cling like a part of the flesh. It was about the minister, his thin face, his puckered mouth, his pale and enthusiastic eyes, that Mary Valentine was thinking, as she sat upon the ground and regarded the root of the thorn that was buried in her flesh. The intensity of the sting was like an ache, and yet it was some time before she could summon the courage to seize the little dagger and pluck it forth with an involuntary cry. She regarded the crimson point for an instant, and then flung it from her in loathing, just as the minister said one should fling away temptation.

After that, she took hold on the flesh near the wound and pressed out a generous drop of blood, for her mother, years before, had told her that it was good to make a new cut bleed in order to wash out the poison. Finally she stood up and tried her weight on the bare foot. Although she had to turn the foot far to one side for a while, in ten steps she was walking as boldly and freely as ever, and the dust was squirting up between her toes. To be sure, every step hurt her, but even at the age of nine Mary Valentine had come to realize that pain is the commonest portion in the world. Since she stepped out bravely and freely, all in a moment the bleeding ended, and the hot dust burned away the sense of pain, so that her breath was no longer shortened, and she walked erect again.

She was as straight, as supple, and as strong as a boy; she had a boy's keen glance and a boy's half-mocking, half-appealing smile; she had a boy's leanness of face, and the windy bits of sun-faded hair, which blew about it, made her seem only wilder and not more feminine. Yet somewhere the girl had to show forth, and, although boys might possibly have feet and hands so slim and small, certainly no boy since the beginning of time ever had knees so delicately and so truly made. They were exposed now because she had been in wading, and her overalls had been turned up. But for that matter, her legs were as tough a brown as the brown of her hands or her feet. She had been weathered and burned to a single rich tan, from head to foot, by the sun at the swimming pool.

Such was Mary Valentine, as she came up from the creek, vaulted over half a dozen fences which framed the corrals at the back of her uncle's house, and finally stood just inside the door of the kitchen. Uncle Marsh Valentine had tilted his chair back against the wall. All night he had been sitting at the table, facing his two sons, and all night the deep voices of the sons had rumbled on. To Mary, in the upper story of the old building, it had seemed like a strong murmuring of storm far away, and half a dozen times she had wakened and listened, and then turned in her bed and fallen asleep once more, lulled by that rumbling of words. It was three years since Jack and Oliver had fled, when they were charged with the Dinsmore killing. Since the confession of a dying criminal in the state prison had freed them of that charge, they were but just returned, and naturally there was much for them to talk over with their father. They had talked since late in the evening. It was now mid-morning. But still their themes seemed as inexhaustible as the five-gallon jug of moonshine from which they poured their drinks now and again, for they disdained a pitcher. Jack was filling the glass of his brother Oliver at that moment. He picked up the heavy jug up with one hand, and then, with a mere twist of the wrist, rolled it over his arm and tilted a thin stream into the glass. They had been drinking and talking all night, and yet their hands were as strong and steady and their eyes as bright as when that conference began. Mary Valentine would have sold the hopes of the next ten years of her life if she could have enjoyed the privilege of hearing one of the stories that these big and fierce men must have brought home.

They were more attractive than her uncle. For great physical strength and native fierceness of disposition in an older man is merely terrible, whereas in a youth it is both awful and beautiful. In sheer bulk of might, Marsh Valentine was still probably not far behind either of his boys, for time seemed to have seasoned and hardened him more than it weakened, and every one of the three was born strong and remained strong without paying any price of labor or even of exercise. They were all of a height. How many inches they were above six feet Mary Valentine did not exactly know. They were all of a weight; yet she had not the slightest idea how many pounds they weighed. She only knew that other men walked with ease through the narrow front door of the Valentine house, but that her uncle and his two sons brushed the jamb on either side with their spread of shoulders.

But the shining black hair of Marsh Valentine was now turning gray, and the piercing black eyes were shadowed by steeply overhanging brows, and the throat of the man had thickened to a neck like the neck of a wild boar. Moreover, he seemed stodgier and less active than his boys, and, although they were not a hair's breadth taller than he, they seemed to have an advantage of inches. They might have stood for the young Hercules, but he was the very spirit of the older, with the shadow of doom already fallen upon him, one might have said.

He faced Mary at the table now, and it seemed to her that he had been drinking at the fountain of youth in listening to the tales of his sons' exploits. What those adventures had been, Mary herself had heard at secondhand through the rumors of one kind and another that had often floated through the village. Those rumors related how the two had gone abroad among the mountains and had done many a wicked and many a cruel deed. But all had been forgiven by the governor, who declared that the false accusations had driven these two away from home and fairly forced them into careers of crime. Mary Valentine, watching them from the doorway, did not know whether to think them more formidable or more glorious, so handsome, so huge, so fearless were they. Suddenly they spied her, for she had been sent to bed before their arrival the night before, since Uncle Marsh could not be bothered by the "brat" when his two boys came home for their first evening.

"Well, by guns," roared Jack Valentine, "if it ain't Mary!"

"Mary all growed up and looking more tomboy than ever!" thundered Oliver. "Come here, kid!"

Mary would have desired nothing better than to sit on his broad knee and hear strange stories of a thousand things about which she yearned to ask. But, when she glanced at her uncle, she saw instantly by his dark brow that he was not ready for an interruption. So she skirmished from a distance, to try out the enemy's disposition.

"I can't stay," said Mary.

"The dickens you can't!"

"Why not?" bellowed Oliver.

"Because Uncle Marsh doesn't want me to."

"He ain't said a word."

"But he's looking a whole heap of 'em."

"Come here, kid, and don't start trying to read

Dad's mind. Come here and sit on my knee. I got something here to. . . ."

She looked at Uncle Marsh. He was staring down to the floor, apparently lost in thought, and therefore she decided that he was harmless. So she advanced with caution toward Oliver, and she had almost reached him when a hand flicked out like the lightning flip of a grizzly's forepaw and knocked her head over heels back to the door through which she had just stepped.

"You've killed her!" shouted Oliver.

"Her head's busted!" began Jack, glaring at his father in horror.

They both rushed to lift that slender, little, motionless body that now lay on the floor, but the sudden thunder of their father's voice stopped them in their tracks.

"Who's raisin' that kid?" he roared at them.

They turned upon him, growling.

"You'd like to have killed her, hitting her that hard," said Oliver.

"If I do the killing, I'll do the hanging," said the father, "and I'll take no back talk from a spindle-legged, wall-eyed, rattle-headed, half-growed-up brat like you. Keep your hands out of this little business, both of you!"

They stared at one another, their color rising, their eyes fierce, for they had been away from the parental roof for many a month and their spirit of independence had swelled great in them. Yet the old habit of obedience conquered them—that and the fierce glare of Marsh Valentine, as he confronted them, so that he seemed in his chair bigger and more formidable than they appeared standing straight. They slinked back into their seats, and, as they did so, Mary recovered her senses and came staggering to her feet. As a matter of fact, there had been more accidental than intentional violence in the blow that had felled her. Uncle Marsh had struck her many times and heavily. But this morning he misgauged the weight of his hand and the strength of his wrist and the lightness of her slender, little body. The cuff fell like the stroke of a bear's paw, and he had winced as he saw her fall. Yet, having done the thing, he determined to bluster it through, which is typical of all undisciplined natures.

She drew herself up, clinging to the side of the door. The faces of Jack and Oliver burned with shame that they should have sat by and watched such a thing. Yet they thrust out their jaws and determined that they should not lose face. She stood by the door now, swaying a little and blinking. But she uttered not a word of complaint, and presently her eyes cleared.

Then said Uncle Marsh: "Mary, if you knowed that I wanted you not to come in, why the devil didn't you keep out?"

He spoke as kindly as he could, although even at the best his voice was rough. Mary merely watched him for an instant, saying nothing, but fumbling on the kitchen table, which stood beside the door, until her hand had closed upon a heavy tumbler. This she suddenly threw and not with an awkward and wobbling arm, as most girls throw, but whipping her hand over her shoulder in true boy fashion. With an upflung arm, Uncle Marsh barely avoided the flying peril. Otherwise his forehead would have shattered the glass that now crashed upon the floor as Uncle Marsh lurched forward.

Mary, however, was gone through the door, with the speed of the cracker on the end of the lash of a four-horse whip. Uncle Marsh paused at the door to threaten her with an upraised hand and a word of thunder that went pealing away among the barns and the sheds.

"Why didn't you catch her?" asked Oliver, as their father turned back into the room.

"Why don't I catch a swallow?" grumbled the big man, and sat down again.

II

Mary sauntered on until she stood in the street, squirting the dust through the interstices between her toes, by a dexterous movement of which she alone was master and that was the passionate envy of every boy in the village. The twisting street was the intolerable white of molten steel. The reflection from it was almost as withering as the direct blast from the face of the sun, but Mary Valentine made a sufficient shade for her eyes by jerking down over them the brim of her black felt hat. At least it had at one time been black, but it was now a rich and ripening green.

To another that sun-beaten line of houses would have been blasted by monotonous familiarity, but not so with Mary Valentine. There was not a fence or a front gate, there was not a porch or a pane of glass, which did not call up some worthy recollection in her mind. Yonder was the steeple of the church, upon the hot top of whose stove she had dropped the cat and rent the singing of the choir in twain with a burst of superlative caterwauling. Yonder was the fence over which she had leaped in time to escape the snaky lariat of Deputy Sheriff Walters, and there was the big bay window of Judge Thompson's house, which with a well-aimed stone she had shattered to bits.

Uncle Marsh had had to pay for that, and he had flogged her in such ample recompense that her flesh still burned deeply at the very memory. The thought spurred her on down the street. Under the cluster of willows around the corner she found the two Davis boys and Chet Smith, with Chet's little cousin.

"Hello, Skinny," said Sam Davis.

"Hello, Four Eyes," greeted Mary Valentine.

Her smile was perfectly nonchalant, but she stole a glance down at her legs. It was perfectly true that she was more slenderly made than the boys. It had irked her more than once. They had a burly mass of bone and brawn against which she could not stand, if she were cornered. But in the open, where activity counted, the matter was entirely different.

"I ain't wore glasses for a month," said Sam in stout defense.

"You got a batty look to your eyes, just the same."

"It's a lie," said Sam. "Ain't it, Chet?"

"Hello, Chet!" said Mary gaily. "How you been feeling since Hal McCormack licked you?"

"He didn't lick me," said Chet, pale with shame and anger. "I just stumbled and, when I fell, I hit. . . ."

"There was some that said when your nose began to bleed you started bawling and run for home," remarked Mary.

"Do you believe that sort of a . . . ?"

"I dunno," said Mary. "You don't look like much to me."

Chet was speechless. Mary was famous for the cruelty of her tongue, but this was simply outrageous. How could Chet know of the undeserved blow that had fallen upon her at her uncle's house? "Let's take her down to the creek and duck her!" he cried at last. "Let's teach her a little politeness!"

The Davis boys had been victimized a hundred times by the vixen. They uttered a wild whoop of joy and threw themselves at Mary. How it happened none of them could exactly tell, but their hands missed her. She stooped under the sweeping arms of the Davis boys as they closed on her. She rose with a handful of sand and blinding dust that she threw fully into the face of Chet, and, then, because her retreat was cut off by a barbed-wire fence on the one side and by the Davis boys on the other, she went up a big willow, like a cat, and sat in the branches, laughing at Chet Smith who was still coughing dust out of his lungs and wiping it out of his eyes. But when he was able to speak, he called hoarsely to the Davis boys to help him rout the enemy from the stronghold, and the three plunged up among the branches.

But alas, they had not counted upon their host! From capacious pockets she brought out rough-edged rocks, not pretty pebbles picked up at the creek, but jagged missiles meant for warfare. Then she wrapped her legs around the branch on which she was sitting and swung to the side with both hands free. Never were better targets; never was better marksmanship! Her first shot landed on the head of Sam Davis. Had it been centered a bit more, it would have knocked him out of the tree, but, as it was, it glanced off and merely raised a bump and a yell from him. Her second shot, aimed fairly for the face of Chet, was intercepted by a raised arm that was cut by the sharp edge of the stone, and the pain caused him to lose his grip. The result was that he slipped down through the branches, with a scream of fear, and, having managed to clutch a lower limb in time to break his fall, landed, weak and trembling, upon the ground beneath. The two Davis boys instantly dropped down to his side, and the three heroes beat a retreat. But, if they could not carry the enemy by boarding, they still had an advantage at long bowls. They stood off and began a shower of rocks from three points at the victim in the tree. But it was a hard target to hit. She was never still, twisting out of sight around the trunk, climbing up and down from branch to branch. Although one or two rocks struck her glancing blows, she was practically unharmed. However, she had no desire to remain a target. They were crowding in, getting the range, and throwing straighter and faster. Sooner or later she might be knocked from the branches, and then would follow a ducking at the creek that she could never forget.

Presently she slipped out to the end of a branch and concentrated her fire upon Joe Davis, immediately before her. Speed was not what she wanted, but accuracy. She nailed him in the leg with one rock and rapped his ribs with another, and, when he turned about with a yell of pain and anger, she planted a third fairly in the small of his back. It was too much for Joe. When a fourth rock missed his ear by an inch, he fled to the side and out of danger. That was all the opening Mary Valentine asked for. She dropped down through the tree—a brown streak—hardly seeming to touch the branches as she flew past. She hit the ground, running, and darted out through the gap that the desertion of Joe had made. There was a spirited pursuit, but in five minutes she was safe. Not one of the three could match his speed of foot against the flashing lightness of her legs.

She dropped them behind her in a copse and doubled straight back to the village. She was not even panting when she reached the street again, but her eye was like the eye of a hawk. She had not yet extracted from humanity sufficient payment for that blow her uncle had given her. So she went like a poacher among the back yards, and what should she find in the yard of the blacksmith but an imitation tea in progress—a great bowl of lemonade, standing in the shade of a tree near the carriage shed, and a dozen little girls surrounding it, all in dainty little frocks, with dainty little faces, and sweet, chirping little voices.

The nose of Mary Valentine wrinkled with disdain. If there was a pang in her inmost spirit, it was quickly banished from consciousness. One sharp glance showed her the point of strategic weakness. In an instant she was up the rear of the shed with a chunk of wood tucked under her arm. Like an Indian she stole to the front of the little building and leaned out. The shadow of the chunk of wood fell upon the bowl of lemonade beneath. Too late the destined victims looked up and shrieked at the sight of the marauder— for the chunk fell. The lemonade was splashed stickily over a dozen best dresses, and the marauder fled with a whoop of joyous content.

Now there would be twelve complaints lodged by irate fathers with Uncle Marsh before the day was over, and that meant a whipping at dark and supper- time, but for that matter she would receive one because of the glass she had thrown at her uncle's head, and why not be thrashed for two offenses as well as one? She shrugged her shoulders and went looking for more adventure. She crossed from the vil- lage. She climbed the hill to the west. She looked down to the creek, winding, long and lazy, through the hollow, with a dense forest crowded on its banks. She looked beyond to the red cattle on the brown hills, to the blue of the horizon sky, to the white sheen of the clouds, which the wind was blowing raggedly above her head. No breath of that wind touched the face of the earth, but, although the sun pressed, hot and heavy, down upon her, Mary Valentine did not care. Her soul was at rest, since she had extracted from society at large as much pain as she had suffered. Since she had her fill of adventure, she told herself that the next wise step would be to find a shady place by the creek, there to rest, and there, perhaps, to strip off her clothes and slide into the black, silent waters of some pool.

She found the right place. Indeed, there was not an inch along the winding waters of the creek within five miles of the village that she did not know by heart, and she longed above all things to wander down its course someday to the great river into which it disappeared. She found the right place near a strip of fresh grass. The sifted sunlight fell upon her through the thin leaves of a willow, so that she could see the blue-white heart of the sky, when the wind stirred the head of the tree. The breeze rose, grew steady, pushed back a large branch, and she was lost in the contemplation of a buzzard hanging in the keen distance. Suddenly she heard a noise beside her. It was a faint rattling, and then she heard the weight of a footfall pressing the earth. Perhaps Chet and the Davis boys had trailed her, after all. She leaped to her feet and confronted a stranger, an armed man, who at that instant stepped into the little clearing.

There was something about this stranger, armed though he was, that reassured her as to his character. Mary drew a breath of relief, but the instant her shadow rose, the newcomer had whirled upon her, and in whirling, as though automatically, he brought out the shining length of a Colt revolver and pointed it in her direction. It sent a little shock through Mary. When the muzzle of the gun passed across the line of her body, it was as though a knife had whipped across her. The stranger was trying to smile, as he put up the gun again, but the shadow of seriousness was still behind his eyes, and something told Mary—perhaps it was a sudden pallor that was showing in his cheeks—that he had come within a hair's breadth of planting a bullet in her heart, before he distinguished her as a child—and as a girl.

III

"Well," said Mary, with her usual nonchalance, "the gent that says I'm not born lucky, lies!"

He was drumming on the handle of his gun, as he examined her, and it seemed to Mary that he started a little as she spoke.

"Why lucky?" he asked her.

"How close," said Mary, "did you come to drilling me just then?"

He flushed. "No danger of that," he said, but the flush meant more than the words.

"Maybe not," she said, "if you shoot like most left-handed men that I know of."

He laughed, and, when he laughed, he threw back his head and let the merriment flow freely out from his throat. She liked that about him very much. Uncle Marsh, for instance, never took his eyes from another's face when he laughed.

"What are you doing here?" he asked her.

"Resting," said Mary.

"From what?"

She looked at him closely. He was very, very brown. He was browner, indeed, than she was, and that very brown skin made the blue of his eyes wonderfully intense. He had a thin face, very much drawn of cheek and marked about the eyes, so that Mary thought she had never seen so weary a face. He looked as though he had not slept for a fortnight, and yet there was no seeking for rest in his eyes. She could see at a glance that he was brave. In fact, she was a judge of courage, for she had spent her life surrounded by it, and, although this was hardly the type of fearlessness that showed in the faces of her uncle and her cousins, yet she felt its presence most distinctly. He seemed small, too, compared with those burly giants, yet, when she estimated him with an accurate glance, she knew that he was close to six feet in height, and, although his lower body was wiry and lean, there was presence of great strength in the width of his shoulders.

"I guess I got tired doing the same thing that you been doing," said Mary.

He started again.

"What do you mean by that?" he asked.

"Running away," said Mary.

He could not help flashing a glance over his shoulder, then he centered his stare upon her. "You're a queer kid," he said. "Suppose we sit down and talk it over."

"Sure," said Mary, and they slumped down upon the turf, side-by-side.

"What do you mean by me running away?" he asked, rolling his cigarette.

"You might offer me the makings," said Mary.

Once more he seemed surprised. But at length he passed the package of brown papers and the sack of tobacco to her. She made her cigarette with a swift exactness, sifting in the correct amount of tobacco with a single flick of the bag and rolling the paper with one twist of the fingers. She lighted the sulphur match with equal skill by whipping the nail of her thumb across its head. Then she shot a thin stream of smoke at the branches above her, and leaned back against the trunk of the willow tree with a sigh of content.

"How long have you been smoking?"

"I dunno that I just exactly remember," said Mary.

"And what have you been running away from?"

"Uncle Marsh."

"What's he done to you?"

"He'll whale me tonight."

"Why?"

"I've been raising ructions."

"Ah," said the stranger, "you have?"

"Ah," mocked Mary, "I have. You talk like a preacher, stranger. What are *you* running away from?"

"I haven't said that I'm running away."

"I can tell, though."

"How?"

"You look twice at everything. Once to see that it's there, and once to see that it ain't sneaking up on you. 'Most like you've plugged somebody."

The stranger smiled. "You have me stopped," he declared, shifting his holster so that he could sit more comfortably. "Smoking and raising ructions at your age, what'll you be when you grow up?"

"Into a woman?" asked Mary.

"Yep."

"I sure hate to think of that bad time coming."

He laughed again in the hearty way that she liked so much.

"You don't want me to grow up, then?"

"Do I look as if I did? You seem contented. When you look over the town, I suppose that there isn't a single grown girl that you'd care to be like."

"Only one," said Mary, "and it ain't any use to want to be like her."

"How come?" asked the stranger.

"You're fuller of questions," said Mary, "than a prickly pear is full of stickers, Lefty."

"I carried over being curious out of time when I was

107

a kid. Bad habit I can't get rid of. But why can't you be like the girl you admire?"

Mary sighed. "Look yonder," she said, pointing up to the sky beyond the branches. "Can you tell how that there blue is mixed up with sunshine and things so's you can look a million miles into it?"

"No, I can't."

"She's as different from me," said Mary, "as that blue sky up yonder is different from the blue of these here overalls. Both are kind of faded-looking, but they ain't the same!"

He chuckled again. "I suppose she's pretty?"

"Nothing to tell the church about, she ain't. She's got red hair and a stub nose."

"Ah," said Lefty, "red hair?"

"She's got a big mouth, too. And her eyes look like they was pinned on her head mighty quick and careless."

"As bad as all that?"

"Yep . . . worse!"

"What do you like about her?"

"Old son," said Mary, "she's got a voice that's the pure quill! I could sit here the rest of my life if she'd just stay and read to me. She's the teacher over to the school. You see?"

"God bless me!" said Lefty.

"D'you know her?"

"I'd like to, if she's as fine as that."

"I ain't got the words for her," she assured him.

"What's her name?"

"Nancy Pembroke."

"It's a good name," said Lefty. "I'll bet she'd be a pal."

"She wouldn't," said Mary. "She's got no use for men."

"How come?"

"She was about to tie up to a gent some three or four years back, but he busted loose and bumped off a man just before the ceremony. He had to run for it, and ever since that time she's been thinking about nobody but him."

Lefty leaned forward upon his hands and stared at Mary, as though she were a ghost. "D'you mean that?" he asked.

"What's up?" asked Mary.

"Nothing," he said.

"You look sort of sick. Did you know Kinkaid?"

"Does she tell that name around?"

"She says that she ain't ashamed. She says that she cares more for him than ever."

"Oh, Lord," groaned Lefty, "what a woman she is!" And he let his eyes wander past Mary and far among the trees.

"Lefty," said Mary presently.

"Well?" he murmured.

"I'd like to ask you a question. Will you answer it?"

"If it ain't too long."

"One word'll answer, Lefty."

"Fire away, then."

"Is your name Kinkaid?"

IV

Having watched and talked all night and all the evening before and all the morning that followed, Marsh Valentine and his sons slept until five. When they wakened, as of one accord, they yawned the sleep out of their throats and stretched it out of their iron muscles, and so they were ready for action of any kind again. Their tremendous bodies were unimpaired by the long watch and the short sleep, but their tempers were wolfish. They cooked and ate an evening breakfast without speaking to one another. As they sat about on the verandah of the shack, smoking their cigarettes and scowling at the wind that blew hotly in their faces, Mary Valentine came home. The manner of her coming was as strange as the manner of her leaving that morning.

She appeared out of the heart of the dusk and came straight up to Uncle Marsh. She stood before him with her arms folded across her breast and her feet braced, as though against the expected shock of a heavy blow.

"Well," she said, "here I am. I'm ready to take what's coming to me!"

Uncle Marsh regarded her in silence. His hand twitched and his frown grew murderously black. He even settled a little forward in his chair, and his two sons watched anxiously. If the big man put forth even a fraction of his strength, it was certain that he would crush the frail body of the child and the life hidden within it. But finally, with a shrug of his heavy shoulders, he settled back in his chair. "Get inside," he said. Mary glided softly through the door.

"What you going to do to her?" asked Oliver.

"You couldn't guess in a thousand years."

"Couldn't?"

"No, I'm going to do nothing to her."

"What!"

"Lemme tell you something, Oliver. The gent that lays hands on that little devil will get his throat cut for his trouble."

"You're afraid of her, then." Oliver grinned.

"Ain't you?"

"I dunno but I am," said Oliver. "But I thought that you was going to bust her in two when she stood up to you."

"I was ashamed for what I done this morning," said Uncle Marsh slowly. "I didn't think . . . I just hit. And it sort of did me good when she got up and threw that glass at me. If I'd caught her, I'd have told her I was sorry that I'd hit her. Believe me, I'd rather take a beating than do what I did then."

Glances were exchanged sharply between the two sons. There was no doubt at all that they were glad to hear this conclusion.

"Going to tell her that now?"

"Nope. She's been a rebel, and she's got to pay for it. There's only one way to rule a Valentine, and that's with fear. She'll be afraid now for days and days that she's about to get paid for what she done today, and that'll keep her in hand. Otherwise, there wouldn't be no living with her."

"Did you ever try kindness?" asked Jack Valentine.

"I ain't a fool. When she first come to me, I took one look at them eyes of hers, and I knew what she needed was a whip. She's a Valentine, and the Valentines make a pile better men than women. But if. . . ." Here he broke off short, for Oliver had raised his hand for silence.

"What is it?" asked the father.

"I heard a whistle."

"Keep quiet, then. If it's the whistle I expect, it'll come again."

And come again it did, with a peculiar falling note at the end, like the whistle of a bird.

"It's Markle," said the father.

It brought the two sons out of their chairs.

"Sit down," he commanded. "Are you going to act like Markle was the devil just come up from hell?"

"Ain't that what he is?"

"Pretty close to that, but I'd rather be turned to a cinder than have him know that I think him any-thing!"

"Dad, you're kind of afraid of him yourself!"

"A gent that ain't afraid of Markle is a fool. Are you afraid of poison? Are you afraid of a snake?"

"Then why work with him?"

"We ain't working with him yet. Ain't much chance

that we will. But we're just going to listen to him talking. Understand?"

There were nods from the sons. Presently straight up the slope in front of the house jogged a horseman. Even in the saddle he seemed extraordinarily short. He looked more like a mounted sack than a mounted man. He slid down to the ground and advanced. As he walked, his size was shown in a more ludicrous light, for he was not a breath over five feet in height, and yet the horse that he bestrode was a monster, even larger than those huge animals that were now munching hay in the Valentine barn, animals capable of supporting all the Valentine bulk. This magnificent beast was perhaps a shade under seventeen hands and gloriously muscled. He was as huge and as statuesque among horses as his rider was blunt and misshapen among men.

He came squarely into the range of the light that shone through the open doorway from the interior of the house, where Mary was foraging for supplies in the kitchen, sending out a faint chiming of pans now and again. It seemed very strange that this outlawed man should have come up so boldly, without waiting to reconnoiter, and should now stand where the light fell full upon a head worth thousands and thousands of dollars to the man whose lucky bullet should bring him down to the earth.

Grotesque he certainly was. His head was a pyramid, of which a wide, bulging jaw was the base, and the narrowing forehead was the blunt apex. His nose was as fat as that of a pugilist who had been hammered to a pulp a hundred times. His little eyes peered out from beneath great flabby lids that seemed to be raised only with a pronounced effort. His head was placed upon his shoulders without the support of a neck, and his body was a rounded barrel. His legs were two diminutive pipe stems utterly inadequate to support such a burden, and therefore they sagged in sadly at the knees.

For a moment he remained in the shaft of light as though he wished each of the three shadowy giants to see his face distinctly. Then he advanced to Marsh, who had risen to meet him. They shook hands in silence, and then the sons were presented. To them Markle spoke freely enough.

"I've been waiting to see you for three years," he said. "I've tried a dozen times to get in touch with you, but you been moving so fast that I ain't ever come up with you. But now that I'm here, I'll say that I'm mighty glad to see you both. It ain't the last that we're going to meet."

"Maybe not," said Marsh Valentine, "but the boys don't take to the job that you got in mind. I ain't been able to tell them no particulars, but they don't cotton to the idea."

"They're figuring on going straight, I guess," said Markle, looking from one young giant to the other.

"That's it."

"Do they think they can do it?"

"They do."

"All young men are blockheads," said Markle, and he took a chair and tilted it back against the wall.

There was no answer. Neither of them would have taken so much from any other human being, but Markle was different. To challenge him meant to challenge his gun, and to challenge his gun was to flirt with death. Besides, he was rolling a cigarette, and his manner was far more amiable than his words. The other three sat down.

"I dunno," said Marsh. "I can't say that I'm trying to persuade 'em any, Markle."

"How d'you figure on going straight?"

"Starting in cowpunching," said Oliver.

"Have you hunted for a job yet?"

"Only asked a couple."

"Had any luck?"

"Both outfits was full up."

Markle snorted. "There ain't a big outfit in the mountains that's too full up not to need a Valentine," he said. "There ain't an outfit in the range that don't know that any Valentine can do two men's work. Why, Oliver, ain't it said that you never been throwed from a hoss, and that you can break six bad 'uns a day and keep it up for a month?"

"I dunno that I'm as good as all that," said Oliver, "but I have a way with hosses."

"You're as good as that and better. I've heard about your work. And there's Jack, that's sure death with a rope. Jack knows the points of a cowpuncher's work like it was all wrote down in a book that he knowed by heart. No, partners, there ain't a bunch on the range that wouldn't be glad to have you."

"But they're full-handed, the two we asked."

"They lied. Everybody's short-handed this season. Everybody's looking for more men."

"Why should they turn us down, then?"

"Because they don't trust you."

"The governor gave us a pardon."

"The governor pardoned you, but the gents around these parts ain't the governor."

"What do you mean by that?"

"They all think that you're crooked. I've heard 'em talk. They think that every Valentine is a crook. And they'll never hire you."

There was a growl from the two.

"We'll prove that we're straight, though," said Jack.

"How much money have you got laid by?" asked Markle of the father.

There was no answer for a moment. "I've been in bad luck. I ain't got any money laid by."

"Son," said the outlaw to Jack, "you'll starve before you get through proving your point. You'll starve, I say, and, when you got to have food to put inside of you, you'll have to go out and take it. That's the way always. You done a thing you were blamed for. They hunted you for three years, and they'll keep on hunting you, no matter what the governor says. You ain't got a chance!"

Silence came heavily upon the group for a time.

"Is that right, Dad?" asked Oliver.

"I dunno," said Marsh miserably. "I dunno what to say to you."

"Ask yourselves," said Markle.

"We have been asking ourselves."

"And even if you got a job, would you be able to hold it down? For three years you been free. Can you settle down and take the orders of a foreman that you could bust in two between your hands?"

"It'd be hard," admitted Oliver.

"It ain't possible, son. I'm talking because I want you with me, but I'm telling you the truth at the same time."

"We can test things out."

"If you wait for that time, I won't be here. I've come to offer you a fine chance, Oliver and Jack."

"Tell us the game."

"There's a hundred thousand of the long green in the bank right this here minute."

"Bank robbery!" exclaimed Jack.

"Wait a minute," said Oliver. "Might as well be something big as something little. What's the plan?"

"A mighty easy one. I got six men with me. They're all hard-boiled. They're all hard riders and straight shooters and they all would stick close together. There ain't a one of the six that ain't killed his man. There ain't a one of the six that wouldn't hang if he was captured. So they'll fight till they drop. That's the kind of men that I like to have around me. These six and you two and me make nine men. I'd come straight into town tomorrow afternoon about the middle of the. . . ."

"And let people see you?"

"They'd never recognize me. They might know my picture, but they won't believe their eyes when they see me riding into town. And they'll go right on about their business and leave me to mine. Then I put five men around the bank to watch the horses and keep away the crowd, when folks start to coming. With the other four we go into the bank, and I walk up to the cashier's window and shove a gun under his nose. The other three keep the boys in the bank covered, and I make them dish out the stuff that's in the safe. Ain't that simple?"

"Simple," said Oliver, "but it means a killing."

"Of who . . . the cashier?"

"I know the cashier."

"So do I, and I got him fixed. He's working with me. You'd say that cashier would get himself killed rather than give up, but I knowed that, and I fixed him right. He'll do what me and the gun tell him to do."

"Are you sure?"

"Absolute."

"But what if old man Preston is around?"

"He's a fighter, but he's ready for a funeral, anyway. He's done his killings in his day, and it's turn and turn about. He's got to take his medicine if he asks for it tomorrow!"

Oliver shook his head. "It won't do," he said. "I can't do the work. I go straight, or I go bust. That's all there is to it!"

"Wait!" said Markle suddenly, raising his hand. After a moment he added: "Somebody's coming. I'll just go inside." And he walked deliberately into the house.

V

He had disappeared through the door and settled himself quietly before they heard the noise that the keen ear of the outlaw had detected. Then they made out the steady and muffled beating of the hoofs of a horse in the dust that led up from the village street.

"How could he have heard it?" asked Oliver, touched with awe by the acute senses of the outlaw.

"Living wild and free for half the years of his life is what made him sharp at hearing," said the father. "They say that Markle can hear a whisper clear across a room while he's sound asleep."

"They say that he can shoot a knothole out of a board at fifty yards, while his hoss is galloping, too," said Oliver scornfully.

"He can," said the father, "because I seen him do it."

This amazing announcement caused a gasp of interest but there was no further opportunity for talk. The horseman took shape in the night, halted his animal, and dismounted just before them. He called before he approached.

"Are you there, Marsh?"

"Here!" answered Valentine, and he added in a

swift whisper to his sons: "It's Sheriff Aldridge!"

The two big men stiffened in their places. For three years the famous sheriff had trailed them, and, indeed, he had been about to bag them when the pardon of the governor cut the knot that he had tied about them. Now the sheriff approached and stood near the verandah.

"Sit down," invited Marsh Valentine.

The sheriff dismissed the invitation with a wave of his hand. "I'll stand," he asserted. "I been sitting on my saddle till my legs are sort of cramped. Marsh, is this Oliver, and is that Jack?"

"Right."

"I'm glad I found you all three together. I got something to say that you'll all have to hear sooner or later."

"Come right out with it, Aldridge."

"Marsh, I got to talk pretty straight to you."

"Fire away. Everybody knows that you ain't got any store of soft words, Sheriff."

The sternness of the sheriff was known and dreaded for a thousand miles among the mountains. He was as keen as a ferret upon the trail and almost as relentless. "I came up here to say that Markle ain't far away."

It was a stunning blow. None of the three could speak for an instant, and each one of them covertly strained his eyes toward the trees that encircled the house at a little distance. For, if the sheriff had guessed at the coming of Markle, he would certainly not attempt to make that capture without assistance.

The woods must be full of the men he had brought to assist in the great work. Although it was ordinarily to be expected that one sheriff was equal to one criminal, it was foolhardy to presume that any one man was the match of Markle.

The sheriff went on speaking: "Maybe you've seen him."

"I ain't flush," said Marsh Valentine, answering indirectly. "I guess that I could use the money on Markle's head as good as the next man."

"Well," said the sheriff, "I'm not a mind-reader. All I can say is that Markle has sneaked into the mountains near here, and that we're watching for him. I can swear to that, and the game ain't running very thick in the mountains. That means he'll be drawing on somebody for supplies, if he can, and I sure hope that he ain't drawing on you, Valentine."

Marsh Valentine shrugged his wide shoulders. "I ain't a fool, Sheriff. I've had trouble enough with the law without wanting to get burned again."

"If I could be sure of that . . . but I can't be sure of anything, Marsh. I ain't saying that you lie. All I say is that you and me have never had a real brush, and that I'm hoping that we never do have one. But if I find out anybody's having dealings with Markle, it'll go hard with him. Markle ain't a man. He's a beast. And them that deal with him is the same as him. I'll treat 'em that way!"

Here Jack Valentine could bear it no longer. "Are you aiming that talk at me and Oliver?" he asked.

"I'm aiming it at nobody, Jack," said the sheriff. "But I sure want you and Oliver to watch yourselves half as close as I'm watching you. You had luck with me once, but you ain't going to have no luck the second time."

"You've talked enough for me to know your drift," said Oliver. "You can move on, Sheriff. I'll ride clean into your office and give you a call when I want your helping words. Understand?"

"Trouble breeds trouble," said the sheriff darkly. "I been waiting for it to crop up out here in this house for a good long time, and I guess it's about due to arrive. If there's a sign of Markle having got a grubstake from you, I'll come out here, raising more trouble than you ever dreamed of seeing. So long."

Swinging with graceful ease back into the saddle, he made off through the night once more. The quiet was thick and heavy that he left behind him, and into it stepped the pudgy figure of Markle. He was laughing softly, and at every wave of his laughter the two big men winced.

"Well, boys," he said, "there's the start of the square deal that you're waiting for. How'd you like it?"

Jack Valentine sprang to his feet. "I'm with you, Markle!" he cried. "I've sat here and listened to myself being insulted. If they already think that we're men of your gang, why shouldn't we go ahead and be what they think? But when we get into your harness, we're going to move such a load that they'll wish we were on the other side of the sun. Oliver, are you with me?"

"Wait a minute before you answer!" broke in Marsh. "Boys, you got to take this here thing sober. What you decide now is going to make the rest of your lives."

"I'm ready to decide," answered Oliver. "I want to wring the neck of Aldridge. After that I don't much care what happens to us."

"Leave Aldridge out of it," said Marsh Valentine. "He ain't as bad as you think. Never framed a gent in his life. I'll say that for Aldridge. Besides, it was sort of honest for him to come right up here and give us a warning."

"Honest? What he wanted was a chance to insult us, knowing that we wouldn't tackle the sheriff unless we had to."

"Maybe not, boys. Aldridge ain't any smooth talker, but there ain't nobody ever accused him of lying."

"I accuse him now. Markle, I'm with you!"

Markle shook that great hand and the hand of the other brother, while Marsh sank back in his chair with a groan, as he saw that the compact was made.

"What's the matter?" queried Markle. "I didn't ask you to let me at 'em?"

"I thought that they'd stand up ag'in' the gaff," muttered Marsh Valentine. "But they buckled up. They couldn't hold out ag'in' temptation."

"Well," said Markle, "it's only them that are in it. You'll be safe enough out of the game tomorrow."

"Me out? You couldn't keep me out. Me out with my two lads in?"

"You'll come in, Marsh?"

"To the limit."

"Will you shake on the deal?"

"I will, but no thanks to you." Their hands closed. "You've sold the whole family," said Marsh Valentine. "And now get out, Markle, before we change our minds."

Markle waited for no second invitation. He waved his hand to them and strolled off into the dark. Then they heard him talking to himself, as he dragged himself onto the saddle. "We'll come by this way and pick you up tomorrow!" he called. "By the way, old Aldridge is kind of partial to me, eh?"

He was still laughing at his jest, as he rode away in the night.

"Dad," said Oliver.

"Well?" asked the old man, lifting his head slowly from the hand upon which he had dropped it.

"I got an idea that Markle was doing all that talking to us just to pull you into his gang."

"Did you figure that out, too? Then you're wiser than I took you to be, Oliver. Yep, that's what the hound wants. And he's got it."

"But we," cried Jack, "will get in our crack at Aldridge!"

"And the hundred thousand!" said Oliver.

VI

On the steep roof above the verandah Mary Valentine uncurled herself from the cramped position in which she had been lying. She had overheard everything that had passed beneath her, and she had understood. That is, she had heard everything since the arrival of the sheriff, and her mind was humming with the new information. What Markle was she knew partly by rumor, which had touched her attention, and still more by the sound of his voice and the words he had spoken. She realized that here was one who was as formidable as either her uncle or her two great cousins.

She went slowly, slowly up the incline of the roof. It had been comparatively simple to make the descent without a noise, but it was painfully hard to make the ascent, and, indeed, just before she reached the window, a shingle creaked and then cracked beneath her weight. There was an exclamation from the verandah beneath her, and then a rush up the stairs.

Through the window went Mary with the agility of a cat, and into her room she raced and flung herself on the bed. Footfalls rushed swiftly past her door and then to the window overlooking the verandah roof.

"Nothing here!"

"Look in Mary's room. Maybe it was her."

At the door presently loomed the great form of Oliver. He strode into the room, none too lightly, scratched a match, and, as the flame spurted blue from the sulphur head, he looked down and surveyed her.

She could only pray that her eyelids would not quiver, or that the heaving of her bosom would not betray that she was panting for breath. Indeed, in the struggle to control that breathing, she was almost stifled. But presently the big hand of Oliver gripped her shoulder and raised her to a sitting posture. She blinked her eyes at him rapidly and yawned.

"What's up?" she asked. "Got the makings, Ollie?"

"Forget the makings," grunted Oliver. "What I want to know is how long you been asleep here?"

"I dunno," said Mary. "I was plumb beat. I went to sleep without undressing. Is it midnight, Ollie?"

"It ain't," said Oliver, and he let her fall back upon the bed.

Then he left the room, and, as he went back to the verandah, Mary slipped to the front upstairs window again. She could hear them talking, at first very softly and then with more confidence, as they heard the report of Oliver.

"She was asleep," said Oliver.

"How did you know?" asked his father. "She could play dead like a rabbit, the little fox!"

"She had all the look of it in her eyes," said Oliver. "She'd been sound asleep, all right. She wanted to know if it was midnight." He chuckled.

"If you start in believing what she says," declared Uncle Marsh, "she'll give you enough inside of a day for a whole book. There's some that got to study lying. But Mary was just born with a lot of talent for saying things that ain't true. She can make up lies faster'n Markle can fan a gun."

"Does Markle fan a gun?"

"He does."

"I've heard talk about fanning, but I ain't never seen it done."

"Markle does it."

"But can he hit anything when he fans his gun?"

"I've seen him knock over a rabbit."

There was a groan of astonishment from the two boys, and Mary went back to her room. There she took the parcel of food that she had prepared in the kitchen. There was a loaf of bread and a liberal chunk of ham, a pound of coffee, and a small portion of salt. She wrapped the package in an outer layer of paper, and then made her exit through the window. A drainage pipe ran down from the eaves near her window, and she held the package with her teeth and lowered herself, hand over hand, to the ground with the easy agility of a monkey.

As she went toward the village, she bumped her toe on a stump and recalled that one calamity had been spared her that day; this was the news of her exploit with the bowl of lemonade and the splashed dresses. That escapade had not been revealed to Uncle Marsh. Otherwise there would have been a whipping. But, perhaps, this punishment, as well as that for her revolt of the morning, was being saved against a time when

Uncle Marsh should have conceived a torment great enough to balance against her misdeeds.

However, before that time of punishment came, Uncle Marsh and both of her cousins would be far away from her. They would be hounded across the county as bank robbers. Mary stopped short and shook her head, as that awful thought came home to her again. Markle, she knew, was charged with a score of murders that were known and proved, and there were others which were guessed at. Perhaps Uncle Marsh and his sons would soon be in the same category with the famous outlaw!

At this she rubbed the shin of her left leg with the toes of her right, standing balanced, with the surety of a crane on one foot. No doubt such a calamity would free her from the strict government of Uncle Marsh, but it was also to be considered that Uncle Marsh was not altogether to be despised or hated. That he was strict had to be admitted, but he could also be kind. Ordinarily he paid not the slightest attention to her, but on that grim day when her father died, she could not forget how the giant had come to her and taken her tenderly in his arms and promised her a home. She could not forget, also, that, when she had been sick on two occasions, Uncle Marsh would allow no one to nurse her but himself, that he had remained day and night beside her bed, and that the strength of his great hands had seemed to bring her back to life. It was no wonder, therefore, that her opinion of Uncle Marsh was a mixed one. If on the one hand she dreaded him like death, on the other hand she respected him with a mighty reverence.

Above all, she had a pride in her clan, a pride that was like a fire burning in her breast. She had walked the village street, straighter and prouder, because her uncle was the strongest old man in the mountains, and her two cousins the strongest of the younger men. She rejoiced in the awe with which others looked upon the three. But to be known as members of a gang of robbers—to serve under the leadership of a murderer, a stone-hearted killer who had taken lives for hire—this was too much! Solemnly she resolved the problem of how she should stave off the calamity. For, after it happened, she could never again lift her head. She would be shamed for the rest of her days.

When she started on her way, it was at a swift jig, so great was her haste, and so sudden the inspiration that had startled her. She headed straight into the village and did not slacken her gait until she had arrived at a deserted shack on the outskirts of the town, upon the farther side. Its age was presumably not very great, but paint had never shielded its boards from the cruel weather, and rains and winds and warping suns had wrenched it askew and made all of its cracks gape. It staggered to one side away from the northern winds that came combing down the valley, and the ruins of a shed nearby seemed to prophesy the collapse of the house itself. It was the handwriting upon the wall.

Yet it was at this house that Mary Valentine stopped

and rapped faintly at the door. The door, after a chair had been pushed noisily back, was opened by the sheriff. For this was his home. He tamped down the burning tobacco in his pipe with a calloused forefinger, and Mary wondered the hot coal did not singe him to the very flesh. But he removed his fingertip, snapped the ashes from it, wiped it upon his hip, and finally spoke.

"Well, Mary," he said, "what in tarnation have you been up to now?"

She was by no means unhappy to postpone the statement of her real errand, and she welcomed this oblique opening.

"How come," said Mary, "that you figure that I been doing something wrong, Sheriff?"

The sheriff sighed. "When folks do little things," he said, "they let other people tell about it. But when they're pretty deep stuck in the mud, they snoop around to see what the law is going to do to them."

"Well," said Mary, "maybe you're wrong."

"Well," said the sheriff, "maybe I ain't. By the way, Mister and Missus Thomas came up and called on me today."

"Has that got something to do with me?" asked Mary, cocking her head anxiously on one side.

"Nothing much. They figure you ought to be sent some place where you can be looked after, if your uncle can't handle it. And I guess that Marsh Valentine would admit that you're more than a handful."

"I dunno what you mean," said Mary, "unless it's

because that freckle-faced Thomas girl got splashed with a little lemonade today. Is that it?"

"Why did you do it?" asked the sheriff curiously. "Those girls weren't bothering you, Mary."

"They looked plumb silly," said Mary, "standing around and trying to talk like growed-ups. It made me so tired I ached. I had to bust up that party, so I took the shortest way to the finish. Wouldn't you have wanted to do the same thing?"

"Maybe," said the sheriff, but he remained very grave.

She studied him as fixedly as he studied her. "I know what you think," she said. "You figure that all the Valentines are bad, and that I'm as bad as the rest. Is that it?"

"Of course not!"

"You're sort of polite, but I know what's behind your eyes. Well, Mister Sheriff, you're all wrong. Look here, the Valentines were as good as any people in the world. Then along came Uncle Marsh and his two sons, and they're so dog-gone big that everybody expects them to bust heads. And because everybody stands around plumb *expecting* trouble from Uncle Marsh and Ollie and Jack, they get trouble . . . and a whole fistful of it, too! Ain't that reasonable?"

"Mary," said the sheriff, "where did you hear that?"

"Look here," said Mary, "if I act like I was afraid of Sammy Davis in the school yard, Sammy's going to start bothering me and trying to pull my hair and a whole lot of other fool things. But if I act like Sammy

Davis was a worm I could squash with a look, he don't bother me at all. Ain't I right, Sheriff Aldridge?"

The sheriff coughed, and then rubbed his knuckles across his chin. "Come inside and set yourself down, Mary," he said. He stood back from the door to let her pass.

VII

Only those who lived in that county could appreciate the honor that had been bestowed upon Mary, for the sheriff had no friends near and dear enough to ask into his house. He lived resolutely alone, and he had done so since the landslide carried away his wife and his son, eight years before. That had made him an old man at a stroke, and it had also made him a misanthrope and a hermit. If he was elected sheriff, it was not that people were fond of him, but because he was infinitely respected. They were too much afraid of him to pity him, but he was elected because he was needed.

Among the mountains that surrounded the town there were a thousand nests where outlaws could secret themselves, to issue forth like storms at times of advantage and harry the countryside. Many an industrious rancher had been ruined by the constant rustling of his cows, and many a hard-working miner had been cleaned out of his season's gold dust by a stick-up artist with a gun. So the district needed a sheriff who was something more than a name and a badge, and Sheriff Aldridge was the man. He had thrown his blanket in this wretched shack. In the ramshackle barn there was room for his three fine horses, whose color was known five hundred miles on every side. And the sheriff was as firmly fixed in his office as a man who is lashed into the saddle.

The room in which Mary found herself lived up to what tradition had said about the sheriff. It was a long and narrow apartment, which was used by him for the three purposes of cooking, eating, and sleeping. The rest of the house was absolutely abandoned. But there was a stove in one end of the room, with a bunk against the wall at the other end, and two old saddles, bridles, all manner of riding gear, spurs, guns, boots, belts, hats, hanging from the pegs which went down either wall.

As for his official correspondence, he had a little lame-legged desk in one corner. This, then, was the habitation of the most efficient sheriff along the entire range. As for what he spent his money on, Mary could not imagine, although rumor said that he simply put it in the bank and let it lie there, accumulating interest simply because he did not know what to do with it. The cost of his horses and their feed, the price of his guns and their ammunition, of which he consumed enough for an hour's practice every day, the price of his provisions, which were of the simplest imaginable, these were the only objects on which he expended a penny with the exception of his tobacco.

For he had worn the same clothes for a dozen years, and, although they were ingrained of dust and dirt, the sheriff paid no heed. "The slicker they are, the slicker they fit in the saddle," he was fond of saying.

He pointed to a chair—it was the only one in the room—and, when Mary sat down in it, he slouched down upon the bunk and rolled a cigarette.

"Got enough for another?" asked Mary.

He hesitated, just so long as a man hesitates before he draws a gun, then, perfectly grave, he passed the makings to her.

"I forgot that you smoke," said the sheriff, and, having waited for her to make her smoke, he lighted them both with the same match. "Now," he said, "the way I make it out is that the Valentines are good, honest, law-fearing gents. Is that it, Mary?"

"That's it," she answered calmly. "Except that they don't fear nothing, and you know it."

A shadow of a grin appeared at the corners of the sheriff's mouth. "What's that?" he asked, pointing to the bundle of food she carried.

"A present," said Mary.

"Ah?" said the sheriff.

"If I show it to you, will you keep the secret of who it's meant for?"

"Why is it a secret?"

"You'd be glad to know," said Mary who now had the conversation back on the track in which she wished it.

"Fire away, then."

"I'll have to have your promise."

"Is it for Markle?"

She started to answer, then sat back in her chair with a smile.

"Very well," said the sheriff, grinning at the adroitness with which she had avoided his remark. "But I give no promises till I know what they're about."

Mary bowed her head in thought. She had not expected that the way would be quite as hard as this, but, as she listened, she heard a voice singing in the distance, a voice that pierced, small and sharp, through the walls of the shaky house, a voice infinitely sweet and tender. Mary, raising her small head, heard and recognized the singing of Nancy Pembroke.

"D'you know who's singing?" she asked.

"Yes," said the sheriff, "it's Nancy, of course."

Mary blinked at him, but after all there was nothing strange in the ease with which he recognized Nancy's voice, for her sweet singing was known to the whole village. Yet who could have expected the iron sheriff to have opened his mind to such a thing as music?

"Well," said Mary, "this has something to do with Nancy."

"Of course," said the sheriff, "if it has anything to do with her, I'll give you my promise. I won't use nothing that you may tell me."

Mary breathed a great sigh, so keen was her relief. "I'll put it to you this way," she said. "Suppose that a gent was overdue to go to meet a girl that he loved . . . suppose that while he was riding, he comes acrost a man he'd had trouble with before . . . suppose the other man tries to start a fight and finally gets what he wants . . . suppose the first man drops him and kills him in a square fight. Now suppose that a crooked pal of the dead man seen the fight from a distance and rides into town and tells a lie about how his partner was *murdered.*"

"Ah," said the sheriff.

"Well," said Mary, "that's what happened with Lefty Kinkaid."

The sheriff started up from the bunk. "Is Kinkaid near here?" he asked with fire in his eye.

"Sure," said Mary. "I'm taking this chuck to him down by the creek."

The sheriff, in place of answering with words, merely scooped up his hat and jammed it on his head.

"You gave me a promise," said Mary.

"What's Kinkaid got to do with Nancy Pembroke?"

"He was going to marry her, that's all, and he's come back to these parts just to see her. I'll bet you that Nancy has come back from seeing him right now. Listen!"

The singing had been drawing steadily closer and closer; now it turned a corner and swelled suddenly beside them. It passed; it turned another corner and was suddenly dimmed.

"My sakes," said Mary, as she twisted her feet under her and sat cross-legged in the chair, "ain't Nancy happy?"

The sheriff was chewing his lips savagely, his eyes

glancing from one side to the other. "Very well," he said at last, "you may be right. You may be right . . . and you're a clever little demon, Mary." He turned upon her again, jerking his sombrero lower over his eyes. "What, in the name of sin, do you want out of me?" he asked her point-blank.

"Would you listen to me?"

"Yes," said the sheriff softly, for his head was still raised to hear the last and dying notes of Nancy's song in the distance. "But why are you so much interested in Nancy's affairs?"

"She's treated me white," said Mary, half-choked with emotion. "She's been square with me!"

"And Kinkaid?"

"Look here," said Mary, "what'd you rather do than anything in the world?"

"You make that guess for me, Mary."

"You'd rather catch Markle."

"What d'you know about him?" asked the sheriff, changing color.

"Suppose that Lefty was to nail him?" asked Mary. "Would Lefty be pardoned?"

"A dozen like Kinkaid would be pardoned if they got rid of one like Markle!"

"Would you shake on that?"

"Maybe I would."

"Here's my hand," said Mary.

The sheriff took it, still hesitating, still studying her rather desperately and not able to make out what he wished to understand. "But you know that one man could never nail Markle," he told her. "You know that Markle may have a dozen hard ones all around him, and every man able to fight like a tiger?"

"I know that," said Mary. "If Markle was cleaned out and his gang with him, there'd be reputations made, eh?"

"Reputation enough for twenty men."

Mary uncrossed her legs and stood up, yawning. "I got to be going," she said.

"So long," said the sheriff, "and good luck, Mary!"

"Thanks!" she answered, and sauntered to the door.

"But what if your man don't win out?" asked the sheriff.

"There ain't a chance of him losing," said Mary.

"Why not?"

"Didn't you hear Nancy Pembroke singing?"

"Well," said the sheriff, "even a pretty voice can't do everything in the world."

"There's another reason Lefty can't lose," said Mary.

"Let me hear that one."

"Because I'm going to be there to put the business through."

She disappeared through the doorway. As for the sheriff, he threw back his head and broke into laughter that stopped very short in the middle. He had listened to his own mirth and realized, with amazement, that he had not laughed like this for eight years.

VIII

"There's only one way that you can get back on your feet as an honest man," said Mary.

Lefty, his mouth too full of the provisions she had brought him to answer at once, stopped chewing and stared at her, as though his eyes would pop out from their sockets. When he had finally swallowed and could speak, he gasped: "What do you mean, Mary?"

"I mean Markle. If you was to get Markle, everything would be squared up. The sheriff would get your pardon from the governor. What's more, everybody would figure that you was a sort of a hero, Lefty."

"If I beat Markle and his gang, I would be." Lefty grinned. "There ain't a chance, Mary. I'd need a dozen men to back me."

"Any Valentine," said Mary, "is as good as three other men. Suppose you have my uncle and his two sons behind you?"

"Count them each for three," said Lefty, still grinning. "That's only nine men. Where are the other three, Mary?"

"I'm a Valentine," said Mary, "and I'd come along."

So they laughed together.

"Do you mean that I could get your uncle and your two cousins to work with me?" asked Lefty more seriously.

"Wait a minute," said Mary, "because I'm sure thinking hard."

She lifted her head. Above her the trees swayed like smoke above the small light of the campfire. Past the trees a star or two looked down at her.

"Lefty," she said, "you'll win, or you'll die. D'you love Nancy enough for that?"

"To win her, or else die trying? I do, partner."

"She sure loves you, Lefty."

"I dunno why," said Lefty, "but it really looks as though she does."

"Well," said Mary, "dog-goned if it don't look as though I got to find a way to pull you right out of the fire."

So she stood up and began to pace rapidly back and forth, smoking at a great rate and scowling at the shaking flames of the fire and the unearthly bodies of the trees half buried in the night around her. Then, under the weight of an inspiration, she paused. The idea grew large; she clasped her hands together.

"Lefty," she cried, "have you got a hoss?"

"I have."

"Will you loan him to me?"

"Partner," said Lefty, "ask me for my right arm and my right hand, and throw in my left, too . . . but don't ask me for my hoss. Can't you use one of your uncle's?"

"He ain't got any hosses," said Mary. "He's got a bunch of mountains. They're strong enough to hold up the sky, but they ain't fast enough to catch up with a fat pig. I need some speed tonight."

"How do you know that my hoss is fast?" asked Lefty curiously. "You've never seen her."

"If she wasn't fast, you'd have been stretching a rope a long time back," said Mary. "Make up your mind quick, Lefty. Are you going to take a long chance and lemme have the hoss, or are you going to admit you're beat before the game begins?"

"How am I beat so long as Nancy stays by me?"

"What good can you do for her unless you got a pardon? Will you tell me that? All you can do is to spoil her life by keeping her from marrying somebody else!"

Lefty sighed as the truth of these remarks pressed grimly home in him. "What's your plan, Mary?"

"I ain't talking till I can show some results."

"Not a word?"

"Not a word!"

Without further comment, he rose, disappeared among the trees, and in five minutes returned with a gray mare, like a lovely ghost of a horse in the pale light. She tossed her head, looked this way and then that, and finally walked up to the fire and sniffed at it, crouching like a great cat, ready to spring away to safety.

"I got her when she was a little filly hardly up to your hip," said Lefty gently. "I raised her by hand till I got her to what you see her now. It ain't easy to hand her over, Mary."

"I'll treat her like she was mine," she assured him. "Will you shorten up the stirrups?"

Advancing toward the mare, Lefty went forward hesitantly to do as she bade, still doubtful. The careless assurance of Mary's approach seemed to carry him before her. Mary scrambled into the saddle and shortened the stirrup upon one side, while Lefty shortened the other, and then she gathered the reins.

"Start straight on for the Valentine house," she advised him. "And when you get there, wait. No, you can do better than that. You can go straight into the house and start making friends with Uncle Marsh. You show him that you need him, and tell him what for and why. Before you get through talking, I'll be back. If he's got any doubt about tying up with you, he'll get over it before I'm through with my game. So long, Lefty."

"Wait!" cried Lefty. "I don't know that I'm going through with this deal. I dunno what. . . ."

Lefty reached for the bridle of the gray, but she was away as smoothly as running water and as smoothly as a bullet from a gun. Although Lefty shouted after her, Mary was already out of sight under the trees and the dark and he could only hear the noise of the mare, as she tore through the wood.

Her plan, so quickly born, had seemed to the girl a foolish thing at first, but when she sat in the saddle upon the mare and felt all that strength and that speed poured forth according to her touch upon the reins, she began to think that there must be some power in her worth considering, and the plan, which had appeared such an airy phantasm, now was a solid possibility. On the back of the gray mare one could not ride forth to a failure.

She went straight as an arrow back to the Valentine house. After she tethered the mare in the woods, she entered with the softness of a shadow. On the way up to her room she looked in upon the conclave of the three. The adventures of years could not be all told in a single sitting, no matter how prolonged, and therefore the boys were still talking, and the old man was still listening and drinking. Mary regarded him with wonder. She knew that when ordinary men drank so much their tongues began to stumble and grow weak. But Marsh Valentine showed no effect. Perhaps his eyes were a little brighter and his color a little higher, but his hand was still as steady and as strong as steel.

Making her way to her room, Mary there took out the board that during the winter months of school served her as a desk. She produced a pencil and chewed the end of it, waiting for ideas. Of course they came slowly. Inspirations do not spring forth like magic; if there is water in the well, it must nevertheless be pumped out.

There was a fragment of her uncle's writing in a corner of the room, in the flyleaf of an old book. She brought it out and studied it. If she had infinite time, she might be able to duplicate that writing easily enough, but in the meantime she must act with haste, and so she began to compose her epistle, writing swiftly and in a general style not unlike that of Marsh Valentine.

Dear Markle:

After you left we talked things over. And when we'd argued it back and forth, whether it'd be better to work with you against the law, or with the law against you, we finally decided that there'd be more fun in hunting you than in being hunted with you. Besides, me and the boys all feel that if we ever got to run for cover, we don't want to do it with a skunk.

So we decided that we'd go after your scalp, Markle, and that we'd get the reward that's offered. All we can't understand is how they came to put so much money on the hide of a rat like you.

This letter is to get you ready to run. Before you've had it long, I'll be along on its heels. Do some fast thinking and you'd better ride even faster than you think. Here's wishing you better luck than I think you're going to have.

Marsh Valentine

She regarded this letter with the greatest pride. It was very much as her uncle would have spoken, if he felt violently upon any subject. What the effect would be on Markle she could surmise vividly enough when she recalled the hideous face and the animal eyes of the little outlaw.

The second letter, however, presented far greater difficulties. She had heard Markle speak only a few words. As for his handwriting, she had not the slightest conception what it might be. All had to be created from nothing; the storm had to be announced into a sky of the purest blue. Finally she wrote in a pudgy, heavy hand:

Dear Valentine:

I've thought it over since I seen you, and I've talked it over with some of my men. Seems like I didn't know much about you. They tell me that you've got fat and lazy, and that you ain't worth much in a fight. If that's the way of it, you ain't going to be no good to me. You can stay at home and sleep. I won't be calling for you.

A couple of the boys, though, have a grudge against you. They're playing poker now to see whether or not they'll go down and clean up on you and your two kids. This is just to let you know.

Markle

The more she regarded this second letter, the more pleased she was. She was confident that she had struck a note that would start the inflammable nature of her uncle into a fire of rage. Once that fire was kindled, he could not help but wish the death of Markle.

It only required that the message should be brought to him before he went to bed and before the exciting tales, that his sons were telling to him, had lost their effect through the passage of ever so slight an amount of time.

IX

She knew where Markle and his men would be hiding for she knew the hills near the town as well as she knew the course of the river and the woods that grew along its banks. If the sheriff and his men suspected that Markle was near the town and went out to hunt for him, they would be searching along the hollows and in the obscure nooks and corners of the hills. But Mary knew well enough that the outlaw would not hide in any such place. He would look for only one thing, and that would be a region where he could see a foe at a distance and be prepared either to attack or flee, according to the strength of the enemy. And there was one ideal place for that location.

Far back from the town, where the hills rolled up to the size of small mountains, there was a plateau shaped like the hump on a camel's back. There were two sharp walls to the north and to the south, precipices that a man could not mount without difficulty, and that a horse could not climb at all. But to the east and the west the slopes were more practicable. On the top of this plateau, as Mary was reasonably certain, the great outlaw would take up his quarters; his controlling reason would be that no one could expect him to try to find a hiding place in a spot as bare as the palm of one's hand.

He would be protected by the very unexpectedness of his location. It was too large a district to be surrounded by anything less than a regiment, and yet it was so small that a pair of lookouts could take precautions against any party attempting to steal in. Mary had often wondered why that plateau was not combed by a searching squad. Now she made the place the goal of her journey.

It meant a brisk ride, and she put the gray mare mercilessly over the road. Where there was no road, she went a twisting way along cow paths, and where the cow paths vanished, she struck across country in an arrow-straight flight. Up the eastern grade toward the top of the plateau she rode without the slightest slowing of her horse. If the outlaw were, indeed, in refuge in this place, it would be watched by a sentinel at the head of either end of the upper level. But if she went boldly in, she might be taken in the darkness for a member of the gang returning, or for some friend of the gang approaching with news.

In fact, she had barely gone halfway up the slope when someone whistled from the clump of trees that stood on the top of a little knoll. She pressed on the faster. The whistle came again, and this time shrill and high-pitched, as though in alarm. This time she replied with the very phrase that the whistler had used, running the notes out as fluidly as though she had practiced the air a thousand times. She rode on, swaying a little to one side in the saddle in her eagerness to watch and to hear, but there was no other sound, and it was patent that her whistle had been the appointed sign. Hastily she conned it again in her mind and whistled it in a soft rehearsal to herself. If there were a second sentinel, she would be prepared!

But, without the sign of a shadow, she reached the top of the slope, and there was the long and narrow stretch of the plateau before her, with pointed rocks thrusting up on its face, and massive clusters of trees here and there. If the whistle down the slope had prepared her to find that her guess had been correct, she could not have dreamed that she would discover the whole camp left so open to approach. She felt something that was almost akin to shame, as she looked upon it. One good rifleman, quick on the trigger, could do much damage in this place before the remnant of the gang reached safety.

The last of a big fire burned in the center of a great circle of rocks. The glow of the half-dead embers and the reflection of the light from the polished surfaces of the rocks showed half a dozen figures asleep between the fire and the outer rim of the rocks. In fact, it was a perfect retreat. The great fire would serve to cook the food of the gang and to keep them warm at night; the immense boulders would shut away the major force of even a storm wind, and, above all, the big rocks would keep the light from showing from the top of the plateau upon the plain beneath. They had only to take care that no smoke rose during the day. At night they could heap up as huge a pyre as they chose, for the flames could never become visible.

Suppose that Uncle Marsh had been in her place? He could have shouted an alarm, to give the outlaws a fighting chance, and then, when they bolted for cover, he could have picked off half their number. So thought Mary, as she reined her horse on the verge of the circle of the rocks. Her own work must be just as spectacular, but of a different kind. A gust of wind tossed up half a dozen points of flame and showed her the face of Markle, as he lay asleep, and, although she had never seen him, she could recognize him at once by the descriptions she had heard of him. For his features, as he slept, were almost as brutal as though he were waking. She sent the gray mare ahead, and the fine horse, as though realizing that a light step was necessary here, stole forward without making a sound until it stood directly by the side of the sleeping chief. Then the letter fluttered from the hand of Mary and struck the face of Markle. At the same instant she uttered a piercing yell and touched the mare with her heels.

The result was pandemonium. Half a dozen forms rose to their feet, shouting, while the mare darted away through them, leaped through a gap in the rocks on the farther side of the circle, and was gone into the outer darkness before a single bullet had been sent after her.

Once in the open, she swung the gray sharply around and sped back along the same course by which she had climbed. A horseman grew up out of the gloom before her. She swerved the mare to one side, and, as she flattened herself along the neck of the flying animal, a bullet hissed above her. Then she was past that outer guard and racing down the slope. Other bullets combed the air above her and about her. Behind the sentinel, who was vainly rushing after her and shooting as he went, there arose a vague hubbub. But with every moment she left that noise farther behind. The shooting ceased, and presently she was galloping beyond danger. There was nothing to accompany her, saving the wild beating of her heart and a fierce sense of exultation.

She cut back for the house of the Valentines. What remained of her work must be done very quickly, for, unless she was very mistaken, the men of Markle would be soon riding hard and fast to avenge the insult to their leader. The house was as she left it, dark, save for the one light in the one window. She made that out, and then she reached the barn and put up the gray mare. Coming back toward the house, she picked up a large rock, and to the rock she tied the letter that she had written in the name of Markle.

Pausing at the window, she looked in. There sat Uncle Marsh, and his two sons were with him. Facing the trio was Lefty Kinkaid. He had argued in vain, it seemed, for the three faces were utterly hostile as they regarded him. Indeed, he was on the very point of taking his departure and had picked up his hat.

Now, or never, was the time for Mary. Straight through the window she hurled the rock. There followed a crashing of the glass of the pane and the tinkling of the broken fragments upon the floor inside. There followed the shouts of the men, also, and the deep roar of Uncle Marsh, telling Oliver to guard the front door and Jack the rear, while he himself took care of the window.

She saw and heard this much. Then she was up the drainage pipe leading to the window of her room. It was a strain even for her wiry arms and her bare, active feet, but she reached the window at last, swung herself through, and lay at last huddled beneath the bedclothes. But, since they did not immediately come up to search for her, she decided that there was a logical course open that would enable her to see with her own eyes what was going on downstairs. So she jumped up from the bed again and sped down the stairs. At the door of the dining room she paused, yawning wide and pretending to rub the sleep out of her eyes. As a matter of fact, she was alert in every sense to what was happening before her.

X

When Lefty Kinkaid started for the Valentine house, it had been half unwillingly, half in rage. He felt that he had been bewitched by a child, and he was accordingly half bewildered and half furious. His fine mare was gone. Upon the back of the horse, that had given him his safety for all the period during which he had been a stranger to the law, the girl had ridden away, and here he was left almost as helpless as a fish out of water!

Having committed himself so far in the ways of folly, there seemed nothing left but to march ahead in the same course. So he went on to the house of the Valentines. There his reception was typical of Uncle Marsh. He was greeted heartily and cordially, although they had never been good friends before the killing that had made Lefty flee for his life. He was given the most comfortable chair. Food was warmed for him by Oliver and Jack while Uncle Marsh poured forth the drinks. Even when he had finished what he could eat of the meal they placed before him, there was still not a question asked about his errand to them that night, nor was there a word about his wanderings during the period since Uncle Marsh had last seen him.

The courtesy of Marsh Valentine had rough edges, but his heart was right—there could be no doubt of that—and something fine under an odd exterior. The same thing that Lefty had sensed in Mary Valentine, it seemed to him was in her uncle. As for the two younger Valentines, they were as yet not developed enough to show their real characters, and they had wandered so far and so long that a wolfish air sat upon them and gleamed out of their eyes.

When he broached his business, Uncle Marsh said

not a word. He was busy looking down to his clasped hands in his lap, where he was twining and untwining his thick fingers. But the two sons were black of brow at once. They pushed back their chairs a little. Their scowls dwelt heavily upon him, and it seemed to Lefty Kinkaid that their big hands were lingering suspiciously near their guns. At last Jack could endure it no longer.

"Looks to me," he said, "like it would be a god-damned strange thing for a Valentine to foller the lead of any other man. What work we got to do, I guess could be done with our own planning and our own hands. Ain't I right, Dad?"

His father grunted.

"Ain't I right?" asked Jack more eagerly. "You ain't going to listen to what this here Kinkaid has got to say?"

This was sufficiently irritating to have brought a sharp response from Lefty, but, since that fatal day on which he had given loose rein to his temper, he had kept it carefully under check. He checked it now. Moreover, the heavy voice of the father rolled over his son's remarks at once.

"Shut up, Jack," he said. "You dunno nothing. And the talking that needs to be done, I guess that I can do it." Now he turned upon Kinkaid. "The way I size it up, Kinkaid," he said, "you want to clean up on Markle and his gang so's you can get back in good standing with the sheriff. Is that it? Has old Aldridge got under your skin a bit?"

153

"I'm afraid of the law," admitted Lefty with such frankness that the two younger men started. "Besides, I want what the law won't let me have."

"All right," said Marsh Valentine, "you would get a pardon out of cleaning up Markle's gang, but what would we get? Fame?"

"Fame," said Lefty, nodding. "You'd be knowed all over the range. . . ."

"As the gents that Lefty Kinkaid used for cleaning up Markle."

"I'm not the leader. I'll work under your orders, Valentine. All I want is a chance to tackle this job along with you and Oliver and Jack."

Marsh growled, but it was evident that he was a little moved by this thought. "I used to have a lot of fool ideas," he declared, "when I was a kid. But now that I'm pretty close to being called a man, I ain't hankering after no fame, with a bunch of lead inside of my skin. No thank you, Lefty!"

"There's a better reason than that," said Lefty. He had saved the vital pressure only for the case of the strictest necessity. He saw that necessity now, and reluctantly he used his last weapon. "Since Jack and Oliver ran amuck," he said, "how many folks trust you or them? How many are just waiting for you to make one slip before they jump on you? If anything goes wrong within a hundred miles, ain't you going to be blamed for it? Ain't you going to be hunted and shadowed like three crooks? What I'm offering you is the same thing I'm trying for myself . . . and that's a chance to get all square before the law!"

"Curse the law!" roared Marsh Valentine and beat upon the table before him. "Curse the law! I don't need nobody patting me on the back to tell me what's right and what's wrong! The law has got along without me, and now I'll get along without the law!"

There were heavy growls of approval from his sons; their hearts were already fast on the side of Markle, and they had dreaded lest their father should slip from his first resolution to fight on the side of the famous outlaw. Not that they loved bloodshed and cruelty, but they *did* love adventure, and it was adventure that they expected to find when they rode at the side of the peerless leader. It was at this point that Lefty Kinkaid gave up the battle and turned to pick up his hat. It was at this point, also, that a stone crashed through the window.

There followed a few seconds of pandemonium, during which Lefty found himself looking down the muzzle of a gun held in the hand of old Valentine—a gun that had been produced with magic speed.

"If there's someone about to be double-crossed, and you're in it, you go first, Lefty," he said to his guest.

He sent his sons to guard the front and the rear of the house, and in the meantime he jerked the gun out of Lefty's holster. He had proceeded thus far, however, when he noted the paper tied to the rock that had been thrown through the pane of glass. He snatched it up, unrolled it, read it, and called to his boys in a voice of thunder that brought them running. It was this tableau that Mary witnessed from the door as she stood, rubbing her eyes in pretended sleepiness. She heard Uncle Marsh read the letter. Twice he read it. The first time rapidly, only pausing to exclaim now and again, the second time with great slowness, waiting for comments, as he completed every phrase. The comments came in the greatest abundance. There were roars of execration from the two boys. Only Lefty was silent.

"But it ain't possible!" cried Marsh at last. "It ain't possible that I've got so old that folks should begin to talk down to me. The only thing that it looks like to me is that this letter is a joke, and that somebody must have wrote it out and just signed the name of Markle to it!"

"D'you want Kinkaid to stand around and hear all of this?" asked Jack.

"Kinkaid and the rest of us are going on the trail of that skunk," said Marsh Valentine. "What he knows don't make no difference. But is this letter square? Don't nobody know what the handwriting of Markle is like?"

He showed the letter around the room, and it was eagerly scanned. But the general opinion was that, in the absence of exact information, the handwriting was, indeed, exactly such as might be expected to come from the blunt fingers and the heavy wrist of the outlaw.

"And it's like Markle to send the letter in that way . . . crashing it through the window," said Marsh slowly. "There ain't any doubt about that. No, this here letter come from Markle, and now. . . . What are *you* doing down here?"

He reached the door with a stride, seized Mary by the neck, and dragged her into the light.

"I heard a bunch of shouting and a crash down here," said Mary, "and I just come to find out what might be happening."

"Hmm," said her uncle, "there's some kind of an instinct in me that tells me that you're a-lying, Mary. And you got some trouble ahead for you, if you are."

"I'm telling you the honest truth," said Mary, shaking her head as if to deprecate his doubt.

"Where you been?"

"In bed, of course!"

"How come you got your overalls and your shirt on? Been sleeping in them?"

"I seen her asleep in 'em," said Oliver, rather kindly coming to her rescue.

"Shut up," snapped the old man over his shoulder. "You don't see nothing. Mary, where you been?"

"In bed."

"That's a lie."

She shrugged her shoulders.

"How come you been in bed, when I can smell hoss on you. You been riding?"

She blinked. What could she invent that would satisfy the old judge? "I'll tell you honest, Uncle Marsh."

"Fire away."

"I couldn't sleep very well. I just woke up with a bad dream in the middle of the night and couldn't go to sleep again."

"Bad dream? Bad conscience," grunted her uncle.

"Well," continued Mary, "when I seen that I couldn't get to sleep, I thought I'd have a ride. So I went out to the stable. . . ."

"How did you get downstairs with us sitting right in here all the time?"

A precious secret must be sacrificed now! But she gave it up instantly. "I went down the drain right outside of my window."

"Ah!" exclaimed her uncle, but he said no more.

"Then I went to the stable and caught up old Barney hoss. . . ."

"You rode Barney?"

"Yes."

"Mary, since when has Barney got gray hairs?"

She looked down. Yes, on the roll of her overalls, where they were turned up to the knee around her bare legs, there were some unlucky gray hairs from the mare.

"Now," said her uncle, rather more curious than in a passion, "how you going to get out of this hole, Mary? Where can you wriggle out?"

But Mary threw up her head suddenly. "Markle'll save me!" she said with a ring to her voice. "Listen!"

As she raised her head, they heard the rushing of many horses sweeping straight on through the night toward the ranch house. Sudden surmises of what this strange child might know and had done leaped into every eye. Even her uncle drew back from her. Then a yell tingled across the night air, and Marsh Valentine groaned with excitement.

"It *is* Markle," he said, "and now we got our work before us!"

XI

"It ain't possible!" cried Oliver Valentine. "Even Markle ain't got the nerve to try to rush this here house, with the village so close to it!"

"You dunno Markle!" answered his father. "But I *do* know him, and I know that nothing is too much of a chance for him to take. There's four walls to this here house, and there's only three men. Maybe that's one thing he figures on. He'll come at us from all four sides and get through on one of 'em . . . unless we can count on you, Lefty Kinkaid?"

Kinkaid wrung Marsh Valentine's hand. "I'm here to the finish," he said. "Let me have the gun again!"

It was passed to him, and Valentine's stentorian voice assigned the places for each of the combatants. There was a man for the front door and the rear; there was another for a window on each of the other sides of the house. Then he caught Mary by the shoulder, as she strove to dart out of the room.

"Where are you going?" he shouted.

"To get to the village and find the sheriff!" she said.

"To bring help? Forget the sheriff! There never was

159

a crook and a gang of crooks in the world that could beat four honest men!"

Mary, numb with wonder and with happiness, stood back and smiled up to him. No matter if it were her work, and if the end of that work brought destruction upon the Valentines, in the meantime it was also her work that had roused them to the truth and made them see that it was better to die as honest men than to live as rogues. Her own blood felt cleaner and her heart stronger.

Then the storm broke suddenly, as the thunder-shower sometimes drops out of a black sky, one or two distant rumbles, and then a rattling flood of water, crashing upon the roof. A chorus of yells besieged the house and poured around it from every side. Then guns began to crack, as volleys of shots smashed through the house, and all the time came that wild Indian yelling that was characteristic of the Markle gang, as though they wished to give proof that they were savages, devoid of the kindness of other men. She had heard of their battle cries, but she had never been able to conjure up a mental image of such wolfish wails proceeding from human throats. They stopped her heart and made her nerves jangle. She knew that, as those cries swung down over the village, the horror of them would stop the hearts of the villagers, just as they had stopped hers. The crowd of rescuers would assemble slowly, very slowly, and push at a snail's pace up the slope to the house of the Valentines. Before they arrived, the torrent would have washed away the defenders and left them dead.

She crouched in the dining room and listened. She found herself saying over and over: "It's terrible . . . I'm afraid! It's terrible! I'm afraid!"

But she was not afraid, and it seemed to her more glorious than terrible. Indeed, she could not feel what she might be expected to feel. All of her young life she had loved thunderstorms. When the sky was black, and the rain whipped down, and the thunder burst in drenching waves of noise, and the lightning ripped the fabric of the world in twain, then she was happiest, spurring a frightened horse down a wild mountain road alone. Or, she would stand still, with her hands flung out, palms out, and her face turned upward. This breaking of the battle was like the breaking of the storm, except that men became more wonderful and more beautiful to her than the powers of the elements.

It was the central room of the house and the largest, this room in which she stood, and from it she could look through the open doors and see each of the defenders at his work. For lights there were small flashes, like the leap of miniature thunderbolts, with this sinister distinction: the lightning was aimed blindly at the whole round earth, but the bullets were impelled by cunning hands.

By those darting tongues of fire it seemed to Mary that she saw enough to read the character of each of the fighters. There was Marsh Valentine, walking steadily up and down past two windows. He carried a long-barreled rifle that spoke more seldom than the weapons of any of the others, but when it did speak, it appeared to Mary that one of the assailants must surely fall. There were Jack and Oliver, shouting and calling to their father, who called back to them with a voice even louder than theirs. They were like demons enjoying a scene in hell.

But there was not a sound from Lefty Kinkaid. He had no rifle. Instead, he had taken another revolver to be used with his own gun. He had one in either hand, and he slunk from window to window along his side of the house, a form as secret and as deadly as a hunting panther. The crackle of his weapons seemed lost in the louder roaring of the rifles of the other three, and so he appeared to be shooting silently. She wondered at him. He had seemed strangely gentle before. Now he seemed more terrible than all the others.

It was amazing that with such defenders the assailants could endure the fire for a single instant. There could not be more than seven or eight of them, and enough bullets had already been fired by expert hands to have laid low three dozen fighters. Yet still there seemed greater and greater need of battle. She remembered the handicaps of the defenders. They themselves fought through doors and windows, and every door and window was therefore made a target by the approaching outlaws. But the men in the house had nothing to guide their own shots. In the blackness beyond the house the enemy was invisible, except for the occasional flashes of guns, but these were illusory lights that misled rather than guided their aim.

Whatever happened on the outside, the roar of their guns did not diminish, but there was a sudden cry from Jack Valentine. He reeled back into the dining room, holding his right hand with his left. He seemed infuriated, not in pain.

"Any other place but this!" he shouted. "Right through the right forearm . . . and me with no chance to handle a gun now!" He sank into a chair and shook his left hand at the roar of the battle. "Curse them!" he said. "If I can get this one hand on one of 'em . . . if I could sink my fingers in the fat throat of that Markle, I'd tear his windpipe out!"

"Gimme your hand!" said Mary. "You gotta have it fixed up."

"What d'you know about putting on a bandage . . . in the dark?"

"Shut up . . . stop talking. You're bleeding mighty fast. Gimme that arm and keep quiet!"

She did not know herself, but wondered at the firm-nerved spirit that had taken possession of her body. She took the hand, felt the hot crimson sweeping down it. She used Jack's knife and with it slashed strips from his shirt. These she bound around his arm.

"It ain't much," she told him, as she worked. "It must have been a rifle bullet. A revolver slug would have tore you up pretty bad, Jack. But the rifle bullet just slipped right through and didn't do you much harm to speak about." She finished the bandage. "Go sit over there ag'in' the wall," she commanded, pushing his great bulk before her, as he rose from the chair. "Sit right down here with your back ag'in' the wall, and . . . here's your rifle!" She ran back and brought it. The barrel was so hot that it singed the skin of her hands. Yet she loved that pain. It was a small contribution that she could make to the great cause, that little agony of the burned hands. "Take this here gun and balance it across your knees. You can't fight steady, but if they bust in, you could get in one shot . . . you could kill one of 'em, Jack!"

"Mary . . . you're a wonder! If you was a man, you'd be the best ever!"

She had hardly turned from him when Oliver Valentine fell with a groan. He had run for an instant to the front of the house to take the place of his brother, quitting his own station for an instant. He had hardly arrived before the door when he was felled, as though there were stationed opposite that place of vantage a destroyer able to see in the dark. Mary raced to Oliver.

"They got me," he gasped to her. "They got me good!"

"Where, Oliver? Where?"

"You wouldn't understand. It ain't nothing. I ain't whining, am I? Run along, Mary! Get down into the cellar! What d'you mean by being up here where one of them bullets might . . . ?" He stopped with a stifled groan.

"Where? When?" she begged him, as she fumbled

at his body. She had never known before how she loved that great, rough-handed fellow. He had really taught her the fine points of riding, and for that alone she would have owed him a deathless gratitude. She found the place where his shirt was wet with crimson. He winced at her touch.

"Leave me be!" he told her. "There ain't nothing can be done for me. It landed me square in the breast."

"But here's where it came out! Your side is all soaking with crimson, Oliver. That slug must have glanced off the ribs and come around out here. It don't amount to nothing. You see, all you need is patching!"

"All I need is water. Say, Mary, I'm burning up inside."

"I've heard 'em tell why. It's the loss of the blood that gives you a fever inside. But you'll be a pile better right *pronto*. Wait till I get this plugged up, and then you can have all the water that you can drink."

"God bless you, honey."

"Just help me by trying to lift yourself when I say, so's I can get the bandage around you."

While she spoke, she was ripping his shirt away. His naked chest, hot, rippling with giant muscles, was under her hands. If God could give her a sense of touch equal to sight for one minute, she might stop that flow of crimson. In an instant she was at work, and he obediently shifted the bulk of his body at her command. So the bandage was made and drawn taut with all her strength, until he groaned and groaned again under the agony of it. Then, as she made the knot fast, certain that her work had failed, but still with a blind hope that the flowing of the crimson might have been checked a little, she heard a shout from his lips, a shout echoed by Jack against the wall.

She turned and saw the huge bulk of Uncle Marsh, lighted by the flashes of his rifle that he was still blindly firing through the window, stagger back into the center of the room and crumple upon the floor.

XII

It was like the fall of an Atlas who had upheld their little world from destruction. Oliver began to drag his half-wrecked body toward his father. Jack threw away the rifle, as though mere weapons could be of no more use, now that the keystone of the arch had fallen.

"Get away from me," snarled Marsh Valentine. "They've drilled me clean through the right leg. It ain't nothing. I can still sit and fight 'em. Get back to your guns and start shooting. I can bandage myself. I'll wring necks for this!"

But, for all his defiance, the battle was plainly lost to the defenders. All that Mary could wonder about and wish for was the coming of succor from the village. Certainly they must have heard the sounds of the firing long before, and they must have begun gathering a mob of armed men to go to the assistance of their companion on the hill. Yet she remembered two things with a sinking heart. After all, the battle had only lasted a few minutes, and those men in the village, brave though they were, would not hurry so fast to the assistance of men in such repute as the Valentines. There was still time, there was still ample time for the enemy to discover the weakness of the defense and to rush the place. For here were walls undefended upon three sides, and Marsh Valentine was down for the time being. He must bandage that leg before he could fight; otherwise, it simply meant bleeding to death.

"It's all Kinkaid now," said Marsh Valentine. "It's all up to him and what he can do!"

Kinkaid was doing his best, and his best was a very great deal. He squatted in the dining room, at a point where his revolvers could sweep every room of the lower floor of the house. If the enemy could gain the upper story, the game was over, of course. In the meantime, from the central vantage point, Kinkaid might be able to keep off the assailants. But in a position that commanded the other rooms, he was also exposed to a torrent of lead that, entering the house from every angle, swept across it toward the center. Hard-shooting rifles whipped their slugs through the flimsy walls of the shack, as though they were paper. Something stung the throat of Mary. She touched her breast; red was running from a wound. It was not serious, but it would mark her for life.

Well, it was worth being marked, this night of

nights! It was worth dying for! All the thunderstorms of the world rolled together were not worth one second of this terror, this cold presence of death, this thrilling, hot presence of courage that defied death! She could have sung, but her throat was choked with something that had never been in it before. If Kinkaid could hold out long enough to allow the help to come from the village. . . .

She had run in from the kitchen with water for Oliver, when she heard a voice wail from the outside of the house. "Close in! Close in! You fools, have I got to do it all? They're almost finished!"

That was Markle. No other human throat could have given utterance to sounds so beast-like, so compact with horrible desire to destroy.

There was an answering shout. Surely the shout came from twenty throats, then a smashing volley. No, it was not one discharge, but a concentration of gunpowder from many hands, all working at rapid fire. Kinkaid sank to the floor; the last of the defenders was down. She raced to him and dropped to her knees beside him.

"You've got the say," she said. "You're the last to go down. If you say the word, I'll tell 'em that we've surrendered!"

"Get away from me," groaned Kinkaid, and swayed to his knees. "Get away and grab two guns . . . these things . . . they're empty, and my cartridges are gone! Firing at shadows. Oh, for one glimpse of a target, and then I'll show 'em!"

Mary's brain went numb with joy in his courage. She turned half blindly. She found Oliver. From his holsters she carried back his two revolvers. Poor Oliver! He was lying on the side of his father, reaching out a hand to touch Marsh Valentine. Pray heaven that he was not done for! But with the new guns in his hand she heard a faint moan of joy from the lips of Kinkaid.

"Where are you hurt?" she said to him. "Let me try to bandage. . . ."

"You little fool! Get away from here. The bullets are coming too fast in this place."

"They'll murder you, Lefty!"

"It's for her, Mary. And if they get me, you'll tell her that it was for her sake?"

"Yes, yes!"

"God bless you, honey! If you were a man, you'd be worth a million!"

The very words that someone else had said to her on this wild night. Who it was she could not for the instant remember. Leave him here? She could have laughed at the thought. He was still swaying a little upon his knees, but she knew without asking that it was not weakness, but the battle fury that swung him back and forth.

Something was in the doorway. Yes, they were charging toward the house, yelling. A hundred fiends were shrieking as they raced toward the old house, and there was someone who had leaped into the doorway.

"Ah!" She heard Lefty gasp the word with satisfaction, and she knew what it meant. This was the real target for which he had wished. Here it was, fully before his eyes. Only a target for an instant, however, and then it swerved into darkness, but that instant had been enough. Lefty had located his mark, and, as the darkness inside the door swallowed the figure, he fired. A gun flashed twice in response: once at breast height, and once again from the level of the floor. There were the sound and the shock of a heavy body that had crashed down. The gun flashed no more. Something told Mary that yonder outlaw who had died shooting would never again pull a trigger.

Lefty had swerved around. He was facing the stairs. What he saw, she could not dream. All was deep dark to her. But he fired, and there was a yell, then the thundering fall of an inert body down the steps. It struck a chair in the room. The chair was turned to a limp wreck. The body skidded a man's length beyond, and then lay without a quiver.

Two were gone. How many more? Then a voice, somewhere in the house—somewhere not far away— was crying: "Close in! There's only one of 'em. Blow him to bits!"

It was Markle again! It was that same tremendous, animal wail. But where was he? The voice seemed to press in from every direction upon them. It beat against them like a hundred hands of fear in the darkness. Mary saw Kinkaid buckle closer to the floor, with a gasp. He was afraid; just as fear had taken her by the throat, so it had taken him. A cold perspiration of shame for him stood upon her forehead. It was worse than death to find fear in such a man as Lefty Kinkaid.

It was only the flinching of an instant, however. The shadowy form of Kinkaid rose again. She saw the dim form of the guns glimmering in his hands. Now, in the parlor and rushing straight toward them, she made out a squat, bulky figure. It was Markle, she knew instantly. A little angry tongue of flame darted out. A gun loomed that seemed louder than the report of other guns, and Kinkaid went down, as though a weight had crushed him to the floor.

"He's down!" thundered Markle. "We've got 'em! Lights! Finish 'em off!"

He could see in the dark, then? But there was a stir at her feet. It was Kinkaid, turning with an effort upon his side. A gun spat from his hand, and it was answered by a sharp howl from Markle. Yet it seemed incredible to her that the charge of the squat form could have been stopped. Instinctively she knew that the adroit fighter, who had brought down Jack and Oliver, was the leader of the gang, but yonder he was, on the floor like Kinkaid, but now pouring forth a double stream of bullets. Something stung her again, this time on the shoulder. But she felt no desire to flee; there was only a thrust of hot joy that proved to her that the bullets of the leader were flying wild. She saw Kinkaid writhe still higher. She saw the gleam of his gun as he steadied himself. Oh, nerve of iron that could brace him to take time for deliberate aim in the face of that avalanche of bullets!

The gun exploded. There was a roar of agony in the black darkness, and the shadow that was Markle disappeared on the black floor. Then, in the great distance, so it seemed to Mary, there were voices calling. Did she recognize the call of the mighty sheriff? But what she did hear with certainty was the calling of other voices in the house itself.

"They're cutting us off. Get back to the horses!"

Now the trampling of feet began. So much she heard. Then something snapped in her. Or, rather, it was as though a great hand that had been supporting her was now removed, and she was allowed to slump down. She stumbled. Her mind was blacker than the darkness around her.

"Lefty," she murmured, "I'm kind of sick. I . . . I'm dying, Lefty."

But it had been only a swoon. When she wakened, the dream of darkness was gone. She found herself lying on a bed in the best room in the best house in town. Beside her bed was Nancy Pembroke. She watched Nancy with a strange and quiet interest. It seemed to her that she could read a whole long story in the face of the teacher.

"Miss Pembroke," she said at last.

There was a cry of happiness from Nancy. Her gentle arms went around the body of her patient.

"Miss Pembroke, I guess Lefty's pulled through all right."

"He'll be walking in a week."

"And Uncle Marsh and . . . ?"

"All three of them are going to get well. And the whole town knows that they are heroes now, and not simply black sheep, dear. You've opened the eyes of everyone."

"Me? I didn't do nothing. I just gave 'em a chance," said Mary.

"Oh, my dear!" cried Nancy Pembroke. "But I know the truth, and so does Lefty. *You* wrote the letters . . . and *you* carried them. Lefty guessed it first. And, oh, Mary, when you grow up, you'll be a woman in a million!"

"These left-handed gents," said Mary, "they sure got a funny way of thinking things out, eh?" She added after a time: "Say, Miss Pembroke, have you got the makings?"

Showdown on the Hogback
Louis L'Amour

Louis Dearborn LaMoore (1908–1988) was born in Jamestown, North Dakota. He left home at fifteen and subsequently held a wide variety of jobs although he worked mostly as a merchant seaman. From his earliest youth, L'Amour had a love of verse. His first published work was a poem, "The Chap Worth While," appearing when he was eighteen years old in his former hometown's newspaper, the *Jamestown Sun*. It is the only poem from his early years that he left out of *Smoke from This Altar* that appeared in 1939 from Lusk Publishers in Oklahoma City, a book that L'Amour published himself; however, this poem is reproduced in *The Louis L'Amour Companion* (Andrews and McMeel, 1992) edited by Robert Weinberg. L'Amour wrote poems and articles for a number of small circulation arts magazines all through the early 1930s and, after hundreds of rejection slips, finally had his first story accepted, "Anything for a Pal" in *True Gang Life* (10/35). He returned in 1938 to live with his family where they had settled in Choctaw, Oklahoma, determined to make writing his career. He wrote a fight story bought by Standard Magazines that year and became acquainted with editor Leo Margulies who was to play an important role later in L'Amour's life. "The Town No Guns Could Tame" in *New Western* (3/40) was his first published Western story.

During the Second World War, L'Amour was drafted and ultimately served with the U.S. Army Transportation Corps in Europe. However, in the two years before he was shipped out, he managed to write a great many adventure stories for Standard Magazines. The first story he published in 1946, the year of his discharge, was a Western, "Law of the Desert Born", in *Dime Western* (4/46). A call to Leo Margulies resulted in L'Amour's agreeing to write Western stories for the various Western pulp magazines published by Standard Magazines, a third of which appeared under the byline Jim Mayo, the name of a character in L'Amour's earlier adventure fiction. The proposal for L'Amour to write new Hopalong Cassidy novels came from Margulies who wanted to launch *Hopalong Cassidy's Western Magazine* to take advantage of the popularity William Boyd's old films and new television series were enjoying with a new generation. Doubleday & Company agreed to publish the pulp novelettes in hard cover books. L'Amour was paid $500 a story, no royalties, and he was assigned the house name Tex Burns. L'Amour read Clarence E. Mulford's books about the Bar-20 and based his Hopalong Cassidy on Mulford's original creation. Only two issues of the magazine appeared before it ceased publication. Doubleday felt that the Hopalong character had to appear exactly as William Boyd did in the films and on television, and thus even the first two novels had to be revamped to meet with this requirement prior to publication in book form.

L'Amour's first Western novel under his own byline was *Westward the Tide* (World's Work, 1950). It was rejected by every American publisher to which it was submitted. World's Work paid a flat £75 without royalties for British Empire rights in perpetuity. L'Amour sold his first Western short story to a slick magazine a year later, "The Gift of Cochise", in *Collier's* (7/5/52). Robert Fellows and John Wayne purchased screen rights to this story from L'Amour for $4,000, and James Edward Grant, one of Wayne's favorite screenwriters, developed a script from it, changing L'Amour's Ches Lane to Hondo Lane. L'Amour retained the right to novelize Grant's screenplay, which differs substantially from his short story, and he was able to get an endorsement from Wayne to be used as a blurb, stating that *Hondo* was the finest Western Wayne had ever read. *Hondo* (Fawcett Gold Medal, 1953) by Louis L'Amour was released on the same day as the film, *Hondo* (Warner, 1953), with a first printing of 320,000 copies.

With *Showdown at Yellow Butte* (Ace, 1953) by Jim Mayo, L'Amour began a series of short Western novels for Don Wollheim that could be doubled with other short novels by other authors in Ace Publishing's paperback twofers. Advances on these were $800, and usually the author never earned any royalties. *Heller with a Gun* (Fawcett Gold Medal, 1955) was the first of a series of original Westerns L'Amour had agreed to write under his own name following the success of *Hondo* for Fawcett. L'Amour wanted even this early to have his Western novels published in hard cover editions. He expanded "Guns of the Timberland" by Jim Mayo in *West* (9/50) to make *Guns of the Timberlands* (Jason Press, 1955), a hard cover Western for which he was paid an advance of $250. Another novel for Jason Press followed and then *Silver Cañon* (Avalon Books, 1956) for Thomas Bouregy & Company. These were basically lending library publishers, and the books seldom earned much money above the small advances paid.

The great turn in L'Amour's fortunes came about because of problems Saul David was having with his original paperback Westerns program at Bantam Books. Fred Glidden had been signed to a contract to produce two original paperback Luke Short Western novels a year for an advance of $15,000 each. It was a long-term contract, but, in the first ten years of it, Fred only wrote six novels. Literary agent Marguerite E. Harper then persuaded Bantam that Fred's brother, Jon, could help fulfill the contract, and Jon was signed for eight Peter Dawson Western novels. When Jon died suddenly before completing even one book for Bantam, Harper managed to engage a ghost writer at the Disney studios to write these eight "Peter Dawson" novels, beginning with *The Savages* (Bantam, 1959). They proved inferior to anything Jon had ever written, and what sales they had seemed to be due only to the Peter Dawson name.

Saul David wanted to know from L'Amour if *he* could deliver two Western novels a year. L'Amour said he could, and he did. In fact, by 1962 this number was increased to three original paperback novels a year. The first L'Amour novel to appear under the Bantam contract was *Radigan* (Bantam, 1958). It seemed to me, after I read all of the Western stories L'Amour ever wrote in preparation for my essay, "Louis L'Amour's Western Fiction" in *A Variable Harvest* (McFarland, 1990), that by the time L'Amour wrote "Riders of the Dawn" in *Giant Western* (6/51), the short novel he later expanded to form *Silver Cañon,* he had almost burned out on the Western story, and this was years before his fame, wealth, and tremendous sales figures. He had developed seven basic plot situations in his pulp Western stories, and he used them over and over again in writing his original paperback Westerns. *Flint* (Bantam, 1960), considered by many to be one of L'Amour's better efforts, is basically a reprise of the range-war plot which, of the seven, is the one L'Amour used most often. L'Amour's hero, Flint, knows about a hide-out in the badlands (where, depending on the story, something is hidden: cattle, horses, outlaws, etc.). Even certain episodes within his basic plots are repeated again and again. Flint scales a sharp V in a cañon wall to escape a tight spot as Jim Gatlin had before him in L'Amour's "The Black Rock Coffin Makers" in *.44 Western* (2/50) and many a L'Amour hero would again.

Basic to this range-war plot is the villain's means for crowding out the other ranchers in a district. He brings in a giant herd that requires all the available grass and forces all the smaller ranchers out of business. It was this same strategy Bantam used in marketing L'Amour. *All* of his Western titles were continuously kept in print. Independent distributors were required to buy titles in lots of 10,000 copies if they wanted access to other Bantam titles at significantly discounted prices. In time L'Amour's paperbacks forced almost everyone else off the racks in the Western sections. L'Amour himself comprised the other half of this successful strategy. He dressed up in cowboy outfits, traveled about the country in a motor home, visiting with independent distributors, taking them to dinner and charming them, making them personal friends. He promoted himself at every available opportunity. L'Amour insisted that he was telling the stories of the people who had made America a great nation, and he appealed to patriotism as much as to commercialism in his rhetoric.

His fiction suffered, of course, stories written hurriedly and submitted in their first draft and published as he wrote them. A character would have a rifle in his hand, a model not yet invented in the period in which the story was set, and, when he crossed a street, the rifle would vanish without explanation. A scene would begin in a saloon and suddenly the setting would be a hotel dining room. Characters would die once and, a few pages later, die again. An old man for most of a story would turn out to be in his twenties.

Once, when we were talking and Louis had showed me his topographical maps and his library of thousands of volumes that he claimed he used for research, he asserted that, if he claimed there was a rock in a road at a certain point in a story, his readers knew that, if they went to that spot, they would find the rock just as he described it. I told him that might be so, but I personally was troubled by the many inconsistencies in his stories. Take *Last Stand at Papago Wells* (Fawcett Gold Medal, 1957). Five characters are killed during an Indian raid. One of the surviving characters emerges from seclusion after the attack and counts six corpses.

"I'll have to go back and count them again," L'Amour said, and smiled. "But, you know, I don't think the people who read my books would really care."

All of this notwithstanding, there are many fine, and some spectacular, moments in Louis L'Amour's Western fiction. I think he was at his best in the shorter forms, especially his magazine stories, and the two best stories he ever wrote appeared in the 1950s, "The Gift of Cochise" early in the decade and "War Party" in *The Saturday Evening Post* in 1959. The latter was later expanded by L'Amour to serve as the opening chapters for *Bendigo Shafter* (Dutton, 1979). That book is so poorly structured that Harold Kuebler, senior editor at Doubleday & Company to whom it was first offered, said he would not publish it unless L'Amour undertook extensive revisions. This L'Amour refused to do, and, eventually, Bantam started a hardcover publishing program to accommodate him when no other hardcover publisher proved willing to accept his books as he wrote them. Yet the short novel that follows possesses several of the characteristics in purest form that, I suspect, no matter how diluted they ultimately would become, account in largest measure for the loyal following Louis L'Amour won from his readers: a strong male character who is single and hence marriageable; and the powerful, romantic, strangely compelling vision of the American West that invests L'Amour's Western fiction and makes it such a delightful escape from the cares of a later time—in this author's words: "It was a land where nothing was small, nothing was simple. Everything, the lives of men and the stories they told, ran to extremes."

I

Everything was quiet in Mustang. Three whole days had passed without a killing. The townsfolk, knowing their community, were not fooled, but rather had long since resigned themselves to the inevitable and would, in fact, be relieved when the situation was back to normal with a killing every day, or more on hot days. When there had been no killing for several days, pressure mounted because no one knew who would be next. Moreover, with Clay Allison, who had killed thirty men, playing poker over at the Morrison House, and Black Jack Ketchum who richly deserved the hanging he was soon to get, sleeping off a drunk at the St. James, trouble could be expected.

The walk before the St. James was cool at this hour, and Captain Tom Kedrick, a stranger in town, sat in a well-polished chair and studied the street with interested eyes. He was a tall young man with rusty brown hair and green eyes, quiet-mannered and quick to smile. Women never failed to look twice, and, when their eyes met his, their hearts pounded, a fact of which Tom Kedrick was totally unaware. He knew women seemed to like him, but it never failed to leave him mildly astonished when they liked him very much, which they often did.

The street he watched was crowded with buckboards, freight wagons, a newly arrived stage and one about to depart. All the hitch rails were lined with saddled horses wearing a variety of brands. Kedrick was suddenly aware that a young man stood beside him, and he glanced up. The fellow was scarcely more than a boy and he had soft brown eyes and hair that needed cutting. "Cap'n Kedrick?" he inquired. "John Gunter sent me. I'm Dornie Shaw."

"Oh, yes!" Kedrick got to his feet, smiling, and thrust out his hand. "Nice to know you, Shaw. Are you working for Gunter?"

Shaw's soft brown eyes were faintly ironic. "With him," he corrected. "I work for no man."

"I see."

Kedrick did not see at all, but he was prepared to wait and find out. There was something oddly disturbing about this young man, something that had Kedrick on edge and queerly alert. "Where's Gunter now?"

"Down the street. He asked me to check an' see if you were here, an', if you were, to ask you to stick around close to the hotel. He'll be along soon."

"All right. Sit down, why don't you?"

Shaw glanced briefly at the chairs. "I'll stand. I never sit in no chair with arms on them. Apt to get in the way."

"In the way?" Kedrick glanced up, and then his eyes fell to the two guns Shaw wore, their butts hanging wide. "Oh, yes! I see." He nodded at the guns. "The town marshal doesn't object?"

Dornie Shaw looked at him, smiling slowly. "Not to me, he don't. Wouldn't do him no good if he did." He added after a minute: "Anyway, not in Mustang. Too many hardcases. I never seen a marshal could make it stick in this town."

Kedrick smiled. "Hickok? Earp? Masterson?"

"Maybe"—Dornie Shaw was openly skeptical—"but I doubt it. Allison's here. So's Ketchum. Billy the Kid's been around, and some of that crowd. A marshal in this town would have to be mighty fast, an' prove it ever' day."

"Maybe you're right." He studied Shaw surreptitiously. What was it about him that was so disturbing?

Not the two guns, for he had seen many men who wore guns, had been reared among them, in fact. No, it was something else, some quality he could not define, but it was a sort of lurking menace, an odd feeling with such a calm-eyed young man.

"We've got some good men," Shaw volunteered, after a minute. "Picked up a couple today. Laredo Shad's goin' to be one of the best, I'm thinkin'. He's a tough hand, an' gun-wise as all get out. Three more come in today. Fessenden, Poinsett, an' Goff."

Obviously, from the manner in which he spoke, the names meant much to Shaw, but they meant exactly nothing to Kedrick. Fessenden seemed to strike some sort of a responsive note but he could not put a finger on it. His eyes strayed down the street, studying the crowd. "You think they'll really fight?" he asked, studying the crowd. "Are there enough of them?"

"That bunch?" Shaw's voice was dry. "They'll fight, all right. You got some tough boys in that outfit. Injun scrappers, an' such like. They won't scare worth a damn." He glanced curiously at Kedrick. "Gunter says you're a fighter."

Was that doubt in Shaw's voice? Kedrick smiled, then shrugged. "I get along. I was in the Army, if that means anything."

"Been West before?"

"Sure! I was born in California, just before the rush. When the war broke out, I was sixteen, but I went in with a bunch from Nevada. Stayed in a couple of years after the war, fighting Apaches."

Shaw nodded, as if satisfied. "Gunter thinks well of you, but he's the only one of them, an' not the most important one."

A short, thick-set man with a square-cut beard looking enough like General Grant to be his twin was pushing through the crowd toward them. He even smoked a thick, black cigar. The man walking beside him was as tall as Kedrick, who stood an easy inch above six feet. He had a sharply cut face and his eyes were cold, but they were the eyes of a man born to command, a man who could be utterly ruthless. That would be Colonel Loren Keith. That meant there was one yet, who he must meet. The man Burwick. The three were partners, and of the three only Burwick was from the area.

Gunter smiled quickly, his lips parting over clenched white teeth that gripped his cigar. He thrust out his hand. "Good to see you, Kedrick! Colonel, this is our man! If there ever was a man born to ramrod this thing through, this is the one. I told you of that drive he made for Patterson. Took those cattle through without losing a head, rustlers an' Comanches be damned."

Keith nodded, his cold eyes taking in Kedrick at a glance. "Captain . . . that was an Army title, Kedrick?"

"Army. The War Between the States."

"I see. There was a Thomas Kedrick who was a sergeant in the fighting against the Apaches."

"That was me. All of us went down some in rank after the troops were discharged."

"How much time in the war?" Keith's eyes still studied him.

"Four years, and two campaigning in the Southwest."

"Not bad. You should know what to expect in a fight." His eyes went to Kedrick's, faintly supercilious. "I have twelve years, myself. Regular Army."

Kedrick found that Keith's attitude irritated him. He had meant to say nothing about it, but suddenly he was speaking. "My American Army experience, Colonel, was only part of mine. I was with Bazaine, at the defense of Metz, in the Franco-Prussian War. I escaped, and was with MacMahon at the Battle of Sedan."

Keith's eyes sharpened and his lips thinned. Kedrick could feel the sharp dislike rising in the man. Keith was defiantly possessed of a strong superiority complex.

"Is that all?" he asked coolly.

"Why, no. Since you ask, it was not. I was with Wolseley, in the Second Ashanti War in Africa. And I was in the two-year campaign against the Tungans of northern T'ien Shan . . . with the rank of general."

"You seem to get around a good bit," Keith said dryly, "a genuine mercenary."

Kedrick smiled, undisturbed. "If you like. That's what you want here, isn't it? Men who can fight?

Isn't it customary for some men to hire others to do their fighting for them?"

Colonel Keith's face flamed, then went white, but before he could speak, a big, square-faced man thrust himself through the crowd and stopped to face them. "You, is it, Gunter? Well, I've heard tell the reason why you're here, an', if you expect to take from hard-workin' men the land they've slaved for, you better come a-shootin'!"

Before anyone could speak, Dornie slid between Keith and Gunter and fronted the man. "You lookin' for trouble? You want to start your shootin' now?"

His voice was low, almost a purr, but Kedrick was startled by the shocked expression on the man's face. He drew back, holding his hands wide. "I wasn't bracin' you, Dornie. Didn't even know you was around."

"Then get out!" Shaw snarled, passion suddenly breaking through his calmness, and something else, something Kedrick spotted with a shock—the driving urge to kill!

"Get out!" Shaw repeated. "An' if you want to live, keep goin'!"

Stumblingly the man turned and ducked into the hastily assembled crowd, and Tom Kedrick, scanning their faces, found hard indifference there, or hatred. In no face did he see warmth or friendly feeling. He frowned thoughtfully, then turned away.

Gunter caught his arm, eager to take advantage of the break the interruption had made to bring peace between the two. "You see what we're up against?" he began. "Now that was Peters. He's harmless, but there's others would have drawn, and drawn fast. They won't be all like that. Let's go meet Burwick."

Kedrick fell in beside Gunter who carefully interposed himself between the two men. Once, Tom glanced back. What had become of Dornie Shaw he did not know, but he did know his second in command, which job was Shaw's, was a killer. He knew the type from of old.

Yet he was disturbed more than he cared to admit by the man who had braced them. Peters had the look of an honest man, even if not an intelligent one. Of course, there might be honest men among them, if they were men of Peters's stripe. He was always a follower, and he might follow where the wrong men led. Certainly, if this land was going to Gunter, Keith, and Burwick through a government bill, there could be nothing wrong with it. If the government sold the land to them, squatters had no rights there. Still, if there were many like Peters, the job was not going to be all he had expected.

Gunter stopped before a square stone house set back from the street. "This here's headquarters," he said. "We hole up here when in town. Come on in."

A wide verandah skirted the house, and, as they stepped upon it, they saw a girl in a gray skirt and white blouse sitting a few feet away with an open book in her lap. Gunter halted. "Colonel, you've met Miss Duane."

"Cap'n Kedrick, my niece, Consuelo Duane."

Their eyes met—and held. For a breathless moment, no voice was lifted. Tom Kedrick felt as though his muscles had gone dead, for he could not move. Her own eyes were wide, startled.

Kedrick recovered himself with a start. He bowed. "Miss Duane!"

"Captain Kedrick"—somehow she was on her feet and moving toward him—"I hope you'll like it here!"

His eyes had not left hers, and now color was coming into her cheeks. "I shall," he said gently. "Nothing can prevent me now."

"Don't be too sure of that, Captain." Keith's voice was sharp and cold. "We are late for our visit. Let's be going. Your pardon, Connie. Burwick is waiting."

Kedrick glanced back as he went through the door, and the girl was still standing there, poised, motionless.

Keith's irritation was obvious, but Gunter seemed to have noticed nothing. Dornie Shaw, who had materialized from somewhere, glanced briefly at Kedrick, but said nothing at all. Coolly he began to roll a smoke.

II

Burwick crouched behind a table. He was an incredibly fat man, and incredibly dirty. A stubble of graying beard covered his jowls and his several chins, yet the eyes that measured Kedrick from beneath the

190

almost hairless brows were sharp, malignant, and set close alongside a nose too small for his face. His shirt was open, and the edge of the collar was greasy. Rims of black marked each fingernail.

He glanced at the others, then back at Kedrick. "Sit down!" he said. "You're late! Business won't wait!" His bulbous head swung from Kedrick to Gunter. "John, this the man who'll ramrod those skunks off that land? This him?"

"Yes, that's Kedrick," Gunter said hastily. Oddly enough, he seemed almost frightened of Burwick. Keith had said nothing since they entered the room. Quietly he seemed to have withdrawn, stepped momentarily from the picture. It was, Kedrick was to discover, a faculty he had when Burwick was near. "He'll do the job, all right."

Burwick turned his eyes on Kedrick after a moment and nodded: "Know a good deal about you, son." His voice was almost genial. "You'll do, if you don't get too soft with them. We've no time to waste, you understand. They've had notice to move. Give 'em one more notice, then get 'em off or bury 'em! That's your business, not mine. I'll ask the questions," he added sharply, "an' I'll see nobody else does. What happens here is our business."

He dismissed Kedrick from his mind and turned his attention to Gunter. "You've ordered like I told you? Grub for fifty men for fifty days? Once this situation is cleaned up, I want to get started at once. The sooner we have work started, the sooner we'll be all set. I want no backfiring on this job."

Burwick turned sharply to Tom Kedrick. "Ten days! I give you ten days! If you need more than five, I'll be disappointed. If you've not the heart for it, turn Dornie loose. Dornie'll show 'em." He cackled suddenly. "That's right! Dornie'll show 'em!" He sobered down, glanced at the papers on his desk, then without looking up: "Kedrick, you can go. Dornie, you run along, too."

Kedrick hesitated, then arose. "How many of these men are there?" he asked suddenly. "Have any of them families?"

Gunter turned on him nervously: "I'll tell you all you need to know, Tom. See you later."

Kedrick shrugged and, picking up his hat, walked out. Dornie Shaw had already vanished. Yet when he reached the verandah, Connie Duane still sat there, only now she was not reading, merely staring over the top of her book at the dusty, sun-swept street.

He paused, hat in hand. "Have you been in Mustang long?"

She looked up, studying him for a long minute before she spoke. "Why, no. Not long. Yet long enough to learn to love and hate." She turned her eyes to the hills, then back to him. "I love this country, Captain, can you understand that? I'm a city girl, born and bred in the city, and yet when I first saw those red rock walls, those lonely mesas, the desert, the Indian ponies . . . why, Captain, I fell in love! This is my country! I could stay here forever!"

Surprised, he studied her again, more pleased than he could easily have admitted. "That's the way I feel about it. But you said to love and to hate. You love the country. Now what do you hate?"

"Some of the men who infest it, Captain. Some of the human wolves it breeds, and others, bred somewhere, who come to it to feed off the ones who came earlier and were more courageous but are less knowing, less tricky."

More and more surprised, he leaned on the rail. "I don't know if I follow you, Miss Duane. I haven't been here long, but I haven't met any of those you speak of."

She looked up at him, her eyes frank and cool. Slowly she closed her book and turned toward the door. "You haven't, Captain?" Her voice was suddenly cool. "Are you sure? At this moment, I am wondering if you are not one of them." She stepped through the door and was gone.

Tom Kedrick stood for a moment, staring after her. When he turned away, it was with a puzzled frown on his face. Now what did she mean by that? What did she know about him that could incline her to such a view? Despite himself, he was both irritated and disturbed. Coupled with the anger of the man Peters, it offered a new element to his thinking. Yet, how could Consuelo Duane, John Gunter's niece, have the same opinions owned by Peters? No doubt they stemmed from different sources.

Troubled, he walked on down to the street of the

town and stood there, looking around. He had not yet changed into Western clothes, and wore a flat-crowned, flat-brimmed black hat, which he would retain, and a tailored gray suit with black Western-style boots. Pausing on the corner, he slowly rolled a cigarette and lighted it. He made a dashing, handsome figure as he stood there in his perfectly fitted suit, his lean, bronzed face strong, intelligent, and interesting. Both men and women glanced at him, and most of them twice. His military erectness, broad shoulders, and cool self-possession were enough to mark him in any crowd. His mind had escaped his immediate problem now and was lost in the never-ending excitement of a crowded Western street. Such places held, all jammed together without rhyme or reason, all types and manner of men.

For the West was of all things a melting pot. Adventurers came to seek gold, new lands, excitement. Gamblers, women of the oldest and most active profession, thugs, gunmen, cow rustlers, horse thieves, miners, cowhands, freighters, and just drifters, all crowded the street. That bearded man in the sun-faded red wool shirt might, if prompted, start to spout Shakespeare. The slender young man talking to the girl in the buckboard might have graduated from Oxford, and the white-faced gambler might be the scion of an old Southern family.

There was no knowing in this strangest, most exciting, and colorful of countries, during its most exciting time. All classes, types, and nationalities had come West, all looking for the pot of gold at the foot of any available rainbow, and most of them were more engrossed in the looking than the finding. All men wore guns, most of them in plain sight. Few of them would hesitate to use them if need be. The man who fought with his fists was a rarity, although present.

A big man lurched from the crowd. Tom glanced at him, and their eyes met. Obviously the man had been drinking and was hunting trouble, and, as their eyes met, he stopped. Sensing trouble, other passersby stopped, too.

"So?" The big man stood, wide-legged, his sleeves rolled above thick, hairy forearms. " 'Nother one of them durn thieves. Land stealers!" He chuckled suddenly. "Well, your murderer ain't with you now to save your bacon, an' I aim to git my share of you right now. Reach!"

Kedrick's mouth was dry, but his eyes were calm. He held the cigarette in his right hand near his mouth. "Sorry, friend, I'm not packing a gun. If I were, I'd still not kill you. You're mistaken, man, about that land. My people have a rightful claim to it."

"Have they, now?" The big man came a step nearer, his hand on the butt of his gun. "The right to take from a man the land he's sweated over? To tear down his home? To run his kids out on the desert?"

Despite the fact that the man was drunk, Tom Kedrick saw beyond it a sullen and honest fury— and fear. Not fear of him, for this man was not afraid, nor would he be afraid of even Dornie Shaw. He was afraid for his family. The realization of that fact struck Kedrick and disturbed him anew. More and more he was questioning the course he had chosen.

The crowd murmured and was ugly. Obviously their sympathies were with the big man, and against Kedrick. A low murmur, then a rustling in the crowd, and suddenly, deathly silence. Kedrick saw the big man's face pale, and heard someone whisper hoarsely: "Look out, Burt. It's Dornie Shaw."

Kedrick was suddenly aware that Shaw had moved up beside him. "Let me have him, Cap'n." Shaw's voice was low. "It's time this here was stopped."

Kedrick's voice was sharp, cold. "No! Move back, Shaw! I'll fight my own battles!"

"But you ain't got a gun!" Shaw's voice was sharper in protest.

Burt showed no desire to retreat. That the appearance of Shaw was a shock was evident, but this man was not Peters. He was going to stand his ground. His eyes, wary now but puzzled, shifted from Shaw to Kedrick, and Tom took an easy step forward, putting him almost within arm's length of Burt.

"Shaw's not in this, Burt," he said quietly. "I've no quarrel with you, man, but no man calls me without getting his chance. If you want what I've got, don't let the fact that I'm not armed stop you. I wanted no quarrel, but you do, so have at it!"

Suspicion was in the big man's eyes. He had seen

guns come from nowhere before, and especially from men dressed as this one did. He was not prepared to believe that Kedrick would face him unarmed. "You got a gun!" he snapped. "You got a hide-out, you damned coyote!"

He jerked his gun from the holster and in that instant Tom Kedrick moved. The edge of his left hand chopped down on the rising wrist of the gun hand, and he stepped in, whipping up his right in an uppercut that packed all the power in his lean, whip-cord body. The punch was fast and perfectly timed, and the crack of it on the corner of Burt's jaw was like the crack of a teamster's whip. Burt hit the walk just one split second after his gun, and hit it right on his shoulder blades.

Coolly then Kedrick stooped and picked up the gun, an old 1851 Model Navy revolver. He stood over the man, his eyes searching the crowd. Wherever he looked, there were hard, blank faces. He glanced down at Burt, and the big man was slowly sitting up, shaking his big head. He darted to lift his right hand and gave a sudden gasp of pain. He stared at it, then looked up. "You broke my wrist!" he said. "It's busted! An' me with my plowin' to do!"

"Better get up," Kedrick said quietly. "You asked for it, you know." When the man was on his feet, Kedrick calmly handed him his six-shooter. Their eyes met over the gun and Kedrick smiled. "Take it. Drop it down in your holster an' forget it. I'm not worried. You're not the man to shoot another in the back."

Calmly he turned his back and walked slowly away down the street. Before the St. James he paused. His fingers trembled ever so slightly as he took out a paper and shook tobacco into it.

"That was slick." It was Dornie Shaw's soft voice. His brown eyes probed Kedrick's face curiously. "Never seen the like. Just slapped his wrist and busted it."

With Keith, John Gunter had come up, smiling broadly. "Saw it all, son. That'll do more good than a dozen killings. Just like Tom Smith used to do. Old Bear Creek Tom who handled some of the toughest rannies that ever came over the trail with nothin' but his fists."

"What would you have done if he had jerked that gun back and fired?" Keith asked.

Kedrick shrugged, wanting to forget it. "He hadn't time," he said quietly, "but there are answers to that, too."

"Some of the boys will be up to see you tonight, Tom," Gunter advised. "I've had Dornie notify Shad, Fessenden, and some of the others. Better figure on a ride out there tomorrow. Makin' a start, anyway. Just sort of ride around with some of the boys to let 'em know we ain't foolin'."

Kedrick nodded, and after a brief discussion went inside and to his room. Certainly, he reflected, the West had not changed. Things still happened fast out here.

He pulled off his coat, waistcoat, and vest, then his

boots. Stripped to the waist, he sat down on the bed and dug into his valise. For a couple of minutes he dug around and then drew out two well-oiled holsters and gun belts. In the holsters were two .44 Russian pistols, a Smith & Wesson gun, manufactured on order for the Russian Army, and one of the most accurate shooting pistols on the market up to that time. Carefully he checked the loads, then returned the guns to their holsters and put them aside. Digging around, he drew out a second pair of guns, holsters and belts. Each of these was a Walch twelve-shot Navy pistol, caliber .36, and almost identical in size and weight to the Frontier Colt or the .44 Russian. Rarely seen in the West, and disliked by some, Kedrick had used the guns on many occasions and found them always satisfactory. There were times when the added firepower was a big help. As for stopping power, the .36 in the hands of a good marksman lacked but little offered by the heavier .44 caliber.

Yet, there was a time and a place for everything, and these guns had an added tactical value. Carefully he wrapped them once more and returned them to the bottom of his valise. Then he belted on the .44 Russians and, digging out his Winchester, carefully cleaned, oiled, and loaded it. Then he sat down on the bed and was about to remove his guns again and stretch out, when there was a light tap at the door.

"Come in," said Kedrick, "and, if you're an enemy, I'll be pleased to know you."

The door opened and closed all in a breath. The

man that stood with his back to it, facing Kedrick, was scarcely five feet four, yet almost as broad as he was tall, but all of it sheer power of bone and muscle and not an ounce of fat anywhere. His broad, brown face might have been graved from stone, and the bristle of short-cropped hair above it was black as a crow's wing. The man's neck spread to broad, thick shoulders. On his right hip he packed a gun. In his hand he held a narrow-brimmed hard hat.

Kedrick leaped to his feet. "Dai!" The name was an explosion of sound. "Dai Reid! And what are you doing in this country?"

"Ah? So it's that you ask, is it? Well, it's trouble there is, bye, much of trouble! An' you that's by way of bringin' it!"

"Me?" Kedrick waved to a chair. "Tell me what you mean."

The Welshman searched his face, then seated himself, his huge palms resting on his knees. His legs were thick-muscled and bowed. "It's the man Burwick you're with? An' you've the job taken to run us off the land? There is changed you are, Tom, an' for the worse."

"You're one of them? You're on the land Burwick, Keith, and Gunter claim?"

"I am that. And a sight of work I've done on it, too. An' now the rascals would be puttin' me off. Well, they'll have a fight to move me, an' you, too, if you're to stay one of them."

Kedrick studied the Welshman thoughtfully. All his

doubts had come to a head now, for this man he knew. His own father had been Welsh, his mother Irish, and Dai Reid had been friend to them both. Dai had come from the old country with his father, had worked beside him when he courted his mother, and, although much younger than Gwilym Kedrick, he had come West with him, too.

"Dai," he said slowly, "I'll admit that today I've been having doubts of all this. You see, I knew John Gunter after the war, and I took a herd of cattle over the trail for a friend of his. There was trouble that year, the Indians holding every herd and demanding large numbers of cattle for themselves, the rustlers trying to seal whole herds, and others demanding money for passage across land they claimed. I took my herd through without paying anything but a few fat beefs for the Indians, who richly deserved them. But not what they demanded . . . they got what I wanted to give. Gunter remembered me from that and knew something of my war record, so when he approached me in New Orleans, his proposition sounded good. And this is what he told me.

"His firm . . . Burwick, Keith, and Gunter . . . had filed application for the survey and purchase of all or parts of nearly three hundred sections of land. They made oath that this land was swampland or over-flowed and came under the General Land Office ruling that it was land too wet for irrigation at seeding time, though later requiring irrigation, and therefore subject to sale as swamp. He went on to say that they had arranged to buy the land, but that a bunch of squatters were on it who refused to leave. He wanted to hire me to lead a force to see the land was cleared, and he said that as most of them were rustlers, outlaws, or renegades of one sort or another, there would be fighting and force would be necessary."

Dai nodded. "Right he was as to the fighting, but renegades, no. Well,"—he smiled grimly past his pipe—"I'd not be saying that now, but there's mighty few. There are bad apples in all barrels, one or two, but most of us be good people, with homes built and crops in. An' did he tell you that their oath was given that the land was unoccupied? Well, given it was! And let me tell you. Ninety-four sections have homes on them, some mighty poor, but homes. Shrewd they were with the planning. Six months the notices must be posted, but they posted them in fine print and where few men could read, and three months are by before anything is noticed, and by accident only. So now they come to force us off, to be sure the land is unoccupied and ready. As for swamp, 'tis desert now, and always desert. Crops can only be grown where the water is, an' little enough of that." Dai shook his head and knocked out his short-stemmed pipe. "Money we've none to fight them, no lawyers among us, although one who's as likely to help, a newspaper man, he is. But what good without money to send him to Washington?" The Welshman's face was gloomy. "They'll beat us, that we know. They've money to fight us with, and tough men, but some of them will die on the ground and pay for it with their red blood, and those among us there are who plan to see 'tis not only the hired gunners who die, but the high an' mighty. You, too, lad, if among them you stay."

Kedrick was thoughtful. "Dai, this story is different from the one I've had. I'll have to think about it, and tomorrow we ride out to look the land over and show ourselves."

Reid looked up sharply. "Don't you be one of them, bye! We've plans made to see no man gets off alive if we can help it."

"Look, man." Kedrick leaned forward. "You've got to change that. I mean, for now. Tomorrow it's mainly a show of force, a threat. There will be no shooting, I promise you. We'll ride out, look around, then ride back. If there's shooting, your men will start it. Now you go back to them and stop it. Let them hold off, and let me look around."

Dai Reid got slowly to his feet. "Ah, lad, 'tis good to see you again, but under happier circumstances I wish it were! I'd like to have you to the house for supper and a game, as in the old days. You'd like the wife I have."

"You? Married?" Kedrick was incredulous. "I'd never believe it!"

Dai grinned sheepishly. "Married it is, all right, and happy, Tom." His face darkened. "Happy if I can keep my ground. But one promise I make. If your bloody riders take my ground, my body will be there where they ride past, and it will be not alone, but with dead men around."

Long after the Welshman had gone, Tom Kedrick sat silently and studied the street beyond the window. Was this what Consuelo Duane had meant? Whose side was she on? First, he must ride over the land, see it for himself, and then he must have another talk with Gunter. Uneasily he looked again at the faces of the men in his mind. The cold, wolf-like face of Keith, the fat, slobby face of Burwick, underlined with harsh, domineering power, and the face of Gunter, friendly, affable, but was it not a little—sly?

From outside came the noise of a tinny piano and a strident female voice, singing. Chips rattled, and there was the constant rustle of movement and of booted feet. Somewhere a spur jingled, and Tom Kedrick got to his feet and slipped into a shirt. When he was dressed again, with his guns belted on, he left his room and walked down the hall to the lobby.

From a room beside his, a man stepped and stared after him. It was Dornie Shaw.

III

Only the dweller in the deserts can know such mornings, such silences, drowsy with warmth and the song of the cicadas; nowhere but in the desert shall the far miles stand out so clearly, the mesas, towers, and cliffs so boldly outlined. Nowhere will the cloud shadows island themselves as on the desert, offering their brief respite from the sun.

Six riders, their saddles creaking, six hard men, each lost in the twisted arroyos of his own thoughts, were emerging upon the broad desert. They were men who had used their guns to kill and would use them so again. Some of them were already doomed by the relentless and ruthless tide of events, and to the others their time, too, would come. Each of them was alone, as men who live by the gun are always alone, each man a potential enemy, each shadow a danger. They rode jealously, their gestures marked by restraint, their eyes by watchfulness.

A horse blew through his nostrils, a hoof clicked on a stone, someone shifted in his saddle and sighed. These were the only sounds. Tom Kedrick rode an Appaloosa gelding, fifteen hands even, with iron-gray forequarters and starkly white hindquarters splashed with tear-shaped spots of solid black—a clean-limbed horse, strong and fast, with quick, intelligent eyes and interested ears.

When they had bunched to start their ride, Laredo Shad had stopped to stare at the horse, walking around it admiringly. "You're lucky, friend. That's a horse! Where'd you find him?"

"Navajo remuda. He's a Nez Percé war horse, a long ways off his reservation."

Kedrick had noticed the men as they gathered and how they all sized him up carefully, noting his Western garb, and especially the low-hung, tied-down guns. They had seen him yesterday, in the store clothes he had worn from New Orleans, but now they could size him up better, judge him with their own kind.

He was tall and straight, and of his yesterday's clothing only the black, flat-crowned hat remained, the hat, and the high-heeled rider's boots. He wore a gray wool shirt now and a black silk kerchief around his neck. His jeans were black, and the two guns rode easily in position, ready for the swing of his hand.

Kedrick had seen them bunch, and, while they all were there, he had said simply: "All right, let's go!"

They had mounted up. Kedrick had noted slender, wiry Dornie Shaw, the great bulk of Si Fessenden, lean, bitter Poinsett, the square, blond Lee Goff, sour-faced Clauson, the oldest of the lot, and the lean Texan, Laredo Shad. Moving out, he had glanced at them. Whatever else they might be, they were fighting men. Several times Shaw had glanced at his guns.

"You ain't wearin' Colts?"

"No, Forty-Four Russians. They are a good gun, one of the most accurate ever built." He had indicated the trail ahead with a nod. "You've been out this way before?"

"Yeah, we got quite a ride. We'll noon at a spring I know just over the North Fork. There's some deep cañons to cross, then a big peak. The Indians an' Spanish called it The Orphan. All wild country. Right behind there we'll begin strikin' a few of 'em." He grinned a little, showing his white, even teeth. "They are scattered all over hell's half acre."

"Dornie," Goff had asked suddenly, "you figure on ridin' over to the *malpais* this trip?"

Clauson had chuckled. "Sure, he will! He should've give up long ago, but he's sure hard to whip! That girl has set her sights higher'n any west-country gun-slinger."

"She's shapely, at that!" Goff was openly admiring. "Right shapely, but playin' no fav'rites."

"Maybe they're playin' each other for what they can git," Poinsett had said wryly. "Maybe that's where he gets all the news he's tellin' Keith. He sure seems to know a sight o' what's goin' around."

Dornie Shaw had turned in his saddle, and his thin features had sharpened. "Shut up!" he had said coldly.

The older man had tightened and his eyes had blazed back with genuine hate, yet he had held his peace. It was educational to see how quickly he quieted down; for Poinsett, a hard, vicious man with no love for anybody or anything obviously wanted no part of what Shaw could give him.

As the day drew on, Kedrick studied the men, and noticed they all avoided giving offense to Shaw, even the burly Fessenden who had killed twenty men and was the only one of the group Kedrick had ever seen before. He wondered if Fessenden remembered him and decided he would know before the day was out.

Around the noon camp there was less friendly

banter than in a cow camp. These men were surly and touchy. Only Shaw seemed to relax much, and everything came easily for him. Clauson seemed to take over the cooking job by tacit consent, and the reason was soon obvious. He was really an excellent cook.

As he ate, Tom Kedrick studied his situation with care. He had taken this job in New Orleans, and at the time had needed money badly. Gunter had put up the cash to get him out here, and, if he did back out, he would have to find a way to repay him. Yet the more he looked over this group, the more he believed that he was into something that he wanted out of, but fast.

He had fought as a soldier of fortune in several wars. War had been his profession, and he had been a skilled fighting man almost from the beginning. His father, a one-time soldier, had a love for tactics, and Tom had grown up with an interest in things military. His education had mostly come from his father and from a newspaperman who lived with them for a winter and helped to teach the boy what he could.

Kedrick had grown up with his interest in tactics, and had entered the Army and fought through the War Between the States. The subsequent fighting had given him a practical background to accompany his study and theory, but with all his fighting and the killing it had entailed, he had not become callous. To run a bunch of renegades off the land seemed simple enough and it promised action and excitement. It was a job he could do. Now he was no longer sure it was a job he wanted to do, for his talk with Dai Reid as well as the attitude of so many people in Mustang had convinced him that all was not as simple as it had first appeared. Now, before taking a final step, he wanted to survey the situation and see just who he would be fighting, and where. At the same time he knew the men who rode with him were going to ask few questions. They would do their killing, collect their money, and ride on.

Of them all, only Shad might think as he did, and Kedrick made a mental note to talk with the Texan before the day was over, find out where he stood and what he knew. He was inclined to agree with Shaw's original judgment, that Shad was one of the best of the lot with a gun. The man's easy way was not only natural to him, he was simply confident with that hard confidence that comes only from having measured his ability and knowing what he could do when the chips were down.

After he finished his coffee, he got to his feet and strolled over to the spring, had a drink, then arose and walked to his horse, tightening the cinch he had loosened when they stopped. The air was clear, and despite their lowered voices he could catch most of what was said.

The first question he missed, but Fessenden's reply he heard. "Don't you fret about him. He's a scrapper from way back, Dornie. I found that out. This here ain't our first meetin'."

Even at this distance and with his horse between

him and the circle of men, Kedrick could sense their attention.

"Tried to finagle him out of that Patterson herd, up in Injun Territory. He didn't finagle worth a damn."

"What happened?" Goff demanded. "Any shootin'?"

"Some. I was ridin' partners with Chuck Gibbons, the Llano gunman, an' Chuck was always on the prod, sort of. One, two times I figured I might have to shoot it out with him my own self, but wasn't exactly honin' for trouble. We had too good a thing there to bust it up quarrelin'. But Chuck, he was plumb salty, an', when Kedrick faced him an' wouldn't back down or deliver the cattle, Chuck called him."

Fessenden sipped his coffee, while they waited impatiently. When they could stand the suspense no longer, Goff demanded: "Well, what happened?"

The big man shrugged. "Kedrick's here, ain't he?"

"I mean . . . what was the story?"

"Gibbons never cleared leather. None of us even seen Kedrick draw, but you could have put a half dollar over the two holes in Chuck's left shirt pocket."

Nobody spoke after that, and Tom Kedrick took his time over the cinch, then with his horse between them he walked away farther and circled, scouting the terrain thoughtfully.

He was too experienced a man to fail to appreciate how important is knowledge of terrain. All this country from Mustang to the territorial line would become a battleground in the near future, and a man's life might depend on what he knew, so he wanted an opportunity to study the country or ask questions. He had handled tough groups before, and he was not disturbed over the problem they presented, although in this case he knew the situation was much more serious. In a group they would be easier to handle than separately, for these men were individualists all, and without any group loyalty. They had faith in only two things in the last analysis: six-gun skill and money. By these they lived and by these they would die. That Fessenden had talked was pleasing, for it would settle the doubts of some of them, at least. Knowing him for a gun hand, they would more willingly accept orders from him, not because of fear, but rather because they knew him for one of their own, and not some stranger brought in for command.

When they moved out, taking their time, the heat had increased. Not a thing stirred on the wide, shallow face of the desert but a far and lonely buzzard that floated, high and alone, over a far-off mesa. Tom Kedrick's eyes roamed the country ceaselessly, and yet from time to time his thoughts kept reverting to the girl on the verandah. Connie Duane was a beautiful girl—Gunter's niece, but apparently not approving all he did. Why was she here? What was her connection with Keith? Kedrick sensed the animosity of Keith and welcomed it. A quiet man, he was slow to anger, but tough, and, when pushed, a deep-seated anger arose within him in a black tide that made him a driving fury. Knowing this rage that lay dormant within him, he rode carefully, talked carefully, and held his temper and his hand.

Dornie Shaw drew up suddenly. "This here is Cañon Largo"—he said, waving his hand down the rift before them—"that peak ahead an' on your right is The Orphan. Injuns won't let no white man up there, but they say there's a spring with a good flow of water on top. Yonder begins the country in the Burwick, Keith, and Gunter buy. They don't have the land solid to the Arizona border, but they've got a big chunk of it. The center of the squatters is a town called Yellow Butte. There's maybe ten, twelve buildin's there, among 'em a store, a stable, corrals, a saloon, an' a bank."

Kedrick nodded thoughtfully. The country before him was high desert and could under no circumstances be called swamp. In the area where he stood there was little growth, a few patches of curly mesquite grass or black grama, with prickly pear, soap-weed, creosote bush, and catclaw scattered through it. In some of the washes he saw the deeper green of piñon or juniper.

They pushed on, entered the cañon, and emerged from it, heading due west. He rode warily, and once, far off on his left, he glimpsed a horseman. Later, seeing the same rider, nearer than before, he deduced they were under observation and hoped there would be no attack.

Dornie Shaw said: "The country where most of the squatters are is right smack dab in the middle o' the range the company is after. The *hombre* most likely to head 'em is Bob McLennon. He's got him two right-hand men name of Pete Slagle an' Pit Laine. Now, you asked me the other day if they would fight. Them three are shinnery oak. Slagle's an oldish feller, but McLennon's in his forties an' was once a cow-town marshal. Laine, well, he's a tough one to figure, but he packs two guns an' cuts him a wide swath over there. I hear tell he had him some gun trouble up Durango way an' he didn't need no help to handle it."

From behind him Kedrick heard a low voice mutter: "'Most as hard to figure as his sister!'"

Shaw's mouth tightened, but he gave no other evidence that he had heard, but the comment added a little to Kedrick's information. Obviously Dornie Shaw had a friend in the enemy's camp, and the information with which he had been supplying Keith must come from that source. Was the girl betraying her own brother and her friends? It could be, but could Shaw come and go among them without danger? Or did he worry himself about it? There had been no mention of Dai Reid, yet the powerful little Welshman was sure to be a figure wherever he stood, and he was definitely a man to be reckoned with.

Suddenly a rider appeared from an arroyo not thirty yards off and walked her horse toward them. Dornie Shaw swore softly and drew up. As one man, they all stopped.

213

The girl was small, well-made, her skin as brown as that of an Indian, her hair coal black. She had large, beautiful eyes and small hands. Her eyes flashed from Dornie to the others, then clung to Tom Kedrick, measuring him for a long minute. "Who's your friend, Dornie?" she said. "Introduce me."

Shaw's eyes were dark and hard as he turned slightly. "Cap'n Kedrick, I want you to meet Sue Laine."

"Captain?" She studied him anew. "Were you in the Army?"

"Yes," he said quietly. Her pinto was not the horse of the rider who had been observing them; therefore, there was another rider out there somewhere. Who was he?

"You're ridin' quite a ways from home, Sue," Shaw interrupted. "You think that's wise?"

"I can take care of myself, Dornie!" Her reply was cool, and Kedrick saw blood rise under Shaw's skin. "However, I came to warn you, or Captain Kedrick, if he is in charge. It won't be safe to ride any farther. McLennon called a meeting this morning and they voted to open fire on any party of surveyors or strange riders they see. From now on, this country is closed. A rider is going to Mustang tonight with the news."

"There she is," Goff said dryly. "They are sure enough askin' for it! What if we ride on, anyway?"

She glanced at him. "Then there will be fighting," she said quietly.

"Well," Poinsett said impatiently, "what are we talkin' for? We come here to fight, didn't we? Let's ride on an' see how much battle they got in them."

Tom Kedrick studied the girl thoughtfully. She was pretty, all right, very pretty. She lacked the quiet beauty of Connie Duane, but she did have beauty. "Do they have scouts out?" he asked.

She glanced at him. "Not yet, but they will have." She smiled. "If they had, I'd never have dared ride to warn you."

"Whose side are you on, Miss Laine?" Kedrick asked.

Dornie Shaw's head came around sharply and his eyes blazed. Before he could speak, Sue Laine answered for herself: "That decision I make for myself. My brother does not make it for me, nor any one of them. They are fools! To fight over this desert!" Contemptuously she waved a hand at it. "There's no more than a bare living on it, anyway! If they lose, maybe we can leave this country." She swung her horse abruptly. "Well, you've had your warning. Now I'll go back."

"I'll be ridin' your way," Shaw interposed.

Her eyes swung back to him. "Don't bother!" Then she turned her attention deliberately to Kedrick and measured him again with her cool eyes, a hint of a smile in them now. "If anybody comes, let Captain Kedrick come. They don't know him!"

Somebody in the group chuckled, and Dornie Shaw swung his horse, his face white as death. His teeth were bared, his right hand poised. "Who

215

laughed?" he said, his voice almost trembling.

"Miss Laine," Kedrick said quietly, "I think Dornie Shaw could make the trip better than I. He knows the country."

Shaw's eyes glittered. "I asked . . . *who laughed?*"

Kedrick turned his head. "Forget it, Shaw." His voice was crisp. "There'll be no fighting with other men in the outfit while I'm in command!"

For an instant, Dornie Shaw held his pose, then his eyes, suddenly opaque as a rattler's, swung toward Kedrick. "You're tellin' *me?*" Incredulity was mixed with sarcasm.

Tom Kedrick knew danger when he saw it, but he only nodded. "You, or anybody, Dornie. We have a job to do. You've hired me for that job as much as any man here. If we begin to fight among ourselves, we'll get nothing done, and right now we can't afford to lose a good man. I scarcely think," he added, "that either Keith or Burwick would like the idea of a killing among their own men."

Shaw's eyes held Kedrick's and for an instant there was no sound. A cicada hummed in the brush, and Sue Laine's horse stamped at a fly. Tom Kedrick knew in that instant that Dornie Shaw hated him, and he had an idea that this was the first time Shaw had ever been thwarted in any purpose he held.

Then Shaw's right hand slowly lowered. "You got me on that one, Cap'n." His voice was empty, dry. "I reckon this is too soon to start shootin' an' old man Burwick is right touchy."

Sue Laine glanced again at Kedrick, genuine surprise and not a little respect in her eyes. "I'll be going. Watch yourselves!"

Before her horse could more than start, Kedrick asked: "Miss Laine, which of your outfit rides a long-legged grulla?"

She turned on him, her face pale as death. "A . . . a grulla?"

"Yes," he said, "such a rider has been watching us most of the morning, and such a rider is not over a half mile away now. Also," he added, "he has a field glass!"

Fessenden turned with an oath, and Poinsett glared around. Only Shaw spoke. His voice was strained and queer. "A grulla? Here?"

He refused to say more, but Kedrick studied him, puzzled by the remark. It was almost as if Shaw knew the grulla horse, but had not expected it to be seen here. The same might be true of Sue Laine, obviously upset by his comment. Long after they rode on, turning back toward the spring on the North Fork, Kedrick puzzled over it. This was an entirely new element that might mean anything or nothing.

There was little talking on the way back. Poinsett was obviously irritated that they had not ridden on in, yet he seemed content enough to settle down into another camp.

IV

Dornie Shaw was silent, saying nothing at all. Only when Tom Kedrick arose after supper and began to saddle his horse did he look up. Kedrick glanced at him. "Shaw, I'm ridin' to Yellow Butte. I'm going to look that set-up over at first-hand. I don't want trouble, an' I'm not huntin' any, but I want to know what we're tacklin'."

Shaw was standing, staring after him, when he rode off. He rode swiftly, pushing due west at a good pace to take advantage of the remaining light. He had more than one reason for the ride. He wanted to study the town and the terrain, but also he wanted to see what the people were like. Were they family men? Or were they outlaws? He had seen little thus far that tended to prove the outlaw theory.

The town of Yellow Butte lay huddled at the base of the long, oval-shaped mesa from which it took its name. There, on a bit of flat land, the stone and frame buildings of the town had gathered together. Most of them backed against the higher land behind them, and faced toward the arroyo. Only three buildings and the corrals were on the arroyo side, but one thing was obvious. The town had never been planned for defense.

A rifleman or two on top of Yellow Butte could cover any movement in the village, and the town was exposed to fire from both the high ground behind the town, and the bed of the arroyo where there was shelter under its banks. The butte itself was scarcely one hundred and fifty feet higher than the town and looked right down the wide street before the buildings.

Obviously, however, some move had been made toward defense, or was in the process of being made, for there were some piles of earth, plainly from recent digging, near several of the buildings. He studied them, puzzled over their origin and cause. Finally he gave up and scouted the area.

He glanced at the butte thoughtfully. Had they thought of putting their own riflemen up there? It would seem the obvious thing, yet more than one competent commander had forgotten the obvious at some time during his career, and it might also be true of these men. The top of the butte not only commanded the town, but most of the country around, and was the highest point within several miles.

That could come later. Now Kedrick turned his Appaloosa down the hill toward the town, riding in the open, his right hand hanging free at his side. Yet, if he was seen, nothing was done to disturb him. How would it have been if there were more than one rider?

He swung down before the Butte Saloon, and tied his horse at the rail. The animal was weary, he knew, and in no shape for a long ride, but he had made his own plans and they did not require such a ride. The street was empty, so he stepped up on the walk and pushed through the swinging doors into the bright lights of the interior. A man sitting alone at a table saw him, scowled, and started to speak, then went on with his solitaire. Tom Kedrick crossed to the bar. "Rye," he said quietly.

The bartender nodded and, without looking up, poured the drink. It was not until Kedrick dropped his coin on the bar that he did raise his glance. Instantly his face stiffened: "Who're you?" he demanded. "I never saw you before!"

Kedrick was aware that men had closed in on both sides of him, both of them strangers. One was a sharp-looking, oldish man, the other an obviously belligerent redhead. "Pour a drink for my friends, too," he said, and then he turned slowly, so they would not mistake his intentions, until his back was to the bar. Carefully he surveyed the room. There were a dozen men here, and all eyes were on him. "I'm buying," he said quietly. "Will you gentlemen join me?"

Nobody moved, and he shrugged. He turned back to the bar. His drink was gone.

Slowly he lifted his eyes to the bartender. "I bought a drink," he said quietly.

The man stared back at him, his eyes hard. "Never noticed it," he said.

"I bought a drink, paid my money, and I want my drink."

All was still. The men on either side of him leaned on the bar, ignoring him.

"I'm a patient man," he persisted, "I bought a drink, an' I want it . . . now."

"Mister"—the bartender thrust his wide face across the bar—"we don't serve drinks to your kind here. Now get out before we throw you out!"

Kedrick's forearms were resting on the edge of the bar, and what happened was done so swiftly that neither man beside him had a chance to move. Tom Kedrick's right hand shot out and grabbed the bartender by the shirt collar under his chin, then he turned swiftly back to the bar, and heaved! The bartender came over the bar as if greased and hit the floor with a crash. Instantly Kedrick spun away from the two men beside him and stood facing the room, gun in hand.

Men had started to their feet, and several had moved toward him. Now they froze where they were. The .44 Russian had appeared as if materialized from thin air.

"Gentlemen," Kedrick said quietly, "I did not come here hunting trouble. I have been hired for a job as all of you, at some time or another, have been hired for a job. I came to see if you were the manner of men you have been represented as being. Evidently your bartender is hard of hearing, or lacking in true hospitality. I ordered a drink. You"—Kedrick gestured at the man playing solitaire—"look like a man of judgment. You pour my drink and pour it on the end of the bar nearest me. Then"—his eyes held the room—"pour each of these gentlemen a drink." With his left

221

hand he extracted a gold eagle from his pocket and slapped it on the bar. "That pays."

He took another step back, then coolly he holstered his gun. Eyes studied him, but nobody moved. The redhead did not like it. He had an urge to show how tough he was and Kedrick could see it building. "You!" Kedrick asked quickly. "Are you married? Children?"

The redhead stared at him, then said, his voice surly: "Yeah, I'm married, and I got two kids. What's it to you?"

"I told you," Kedrick replied evenly. "I came to see what manner of men you are."

The man who was pouring the drinks looked up. "I'll answer your questions. I'm Pete Slagle."

"I've heard of you."

A slight smile came to Slagle's mouth. "Yeah," he said, "an' I've heard of you."

Nobody moved or spoke while Slagle calmly poured the drinks, then he straightened and glanced around the room. "Men," he said, "I reckon there's no use goin' off half-cocked an' getting' somebody killed. Let's give this man a chance to speak his piece. We sure don't have to buy what he wants to sell us if we don't like his argument."

"Thanks, Slagle." Kedrick studied the room. Two of the faces seemed hard, unrelenting. Another was genuinely interested, but at the door in the rear a man loitered who had shifty eyes and a sour face. He could have been, in disposition at least, a twin brother to the former outlaw, Clauson.

"The land around here," Kedrick said quietly, "is about to be purchased from the government by the firm who has employed me. The firm of Burwick, Keith, and Gunter. In New Orleans, where I was hired, I was told that there were squatters on the land, a bunch of outlaws, renegades, and wasters, that they would resist being put off, and would aim to keep the badlands for themselves. My job was to clean them out, to clear the land for the company. I have come here for that purpose."

There was a low murmur from the back of the room. Kedrick took time to toss off his drink, and then calmly begin to roll a smoke. To his right, the door opened and two men came in. One of these was as tall as himself with coal-black hair turning gray at the temples. His eyes were gray and cold, his face firmly cut. He glanced sharply around the room, then at Kedrick.

"Cap'n Tom Kedrick, Bob," Slagle said quietly, "speakin' his piece. He's just explained that we've been represented as a bunch of renegades."

"That sounds like Burwick," McLennon said. "Get on with it, Kedrick."

"I've little to say but this. Naturally, like any good fighting man, I wanted to look over the terrain. Moreover, since arriving in Mustang, certain rumors and hints have reached me that the picture is not one-sided. I have come out here to look you over, to see exactly what sort of people you are, and if you are the outlaws and wasters you have been repre-

223

sented to be. Also, I would like to have a statement from you."

Red's face was ugly. "We got nothin' to say to you, Kedrick," he said harshly, "nothin' at all! Just you come down here with your killers an' see how many get away alive!"

"Wait a minute, Red!" Slagle interrupted. "Let Tom have his say."

"Aw, why bother?" Red said roughly. "The man is scared or he'd never have come huntin' information!"

Kedrick's eyes held Red's thoughtfully, and he said slowly: "No, Red, I'm not scared. If I decide the company is right and you are to be run off, that is exactly what I'll do. If the men I have are not enough, I'll get more. I'm used to war, Red. I've been at it all my life, and I know how to win. I'm not here because I'm scared. I have come simply because I make a pass at being a just man. If you have a just claim to your places here, and are not as represented, I'll step out of this.

"Naturally," he added, "I can't speak for the others, but I will advise them as to my conclusions."

"Fair enough," McLennon agreed. "All right, I'll state our case. This land is government land like all of it. The Navajos an' Utes claim some of it, an' some of us have dickered with them for land. We've moved in an' settled on this land. Four or five of us have been here upwards of ten years, most of us have been here more than three. We've barns built, springs cleaned out, some fences. We've stocked some land, lived through a few bad summers and worse winters. Some of us have wives, an' some of us children. We're makin' homes here. The company is tryin' to gyp us. The law says we were to have six months' notice. That is, it was to be posted six months before the sale by the government to the company. This land, as we understand it, is supposed to be unoccupied. Well, it isn't. We live on it. Moreover, that notice was posted five months ago, stuck in out-of-the-way places, in print so fine a man can scarcely read it without a magnifyin' glass. A month ago one of the boys read it, but it took him a few days to sort out the meanin' out of the legal phrasin', and then he hightailed it to me. We ain't got the money to send a man to the government. So all we can do is fight. That's what we figure on. If the company runs us off, which I don't figure you or nobody can do, they'll buy ever' inch of it with their blood, believe me."

A murmur of appreciation went through the room, and Kedrick scanned their faces thoughtfully. Dornie Shaw had judged these men correctly. They would fight. Moreover, with men like McLennon and Slagle to lead them, they would be hard to handle. Legally the company seemed to be in the best position; the squatters were bucking a stacked deck. From here it would take a man all of two weeks, and possibly three, even to get to Washington, let alone cut through all the government red tape to get to the men who could block the sale—if it could be blocked.

"This here's a speculation on their part," McLennon

stated. "There's rumor this here land is goin' into an Injun reservation, an', if it does, that means they'll stick the government a nice price for the land."

"Or you will," Kedrick replied. "Looks like there's two sides to this question, McLennon. The company has an argument. If the federal government does make this a reservation, you'll have to move, anyway."

"We'll face that when it comes," Slagle said. "Right now we're buckin' the company. Our folks aren't speculators. We aren't gunmen, either."

Another man had entered the room, and Kedrick spotted him instantly. It was Burt, the big man he had whipped in the street fight. The man stopped by the wall, and surveyed the room.

"None of you?" Kedrick asked gently. "I have heard some stories about Pit Laine."

"Laine's a good man!" Red burst out heatedly. "He'll do to ride any river with!"

Neither McLennon nor Slagle spoke, and the latter shifted his feet uneasily. Evidently there was a difference of opinion here. He made a note to check on Laine, to find out more about him.

"Well," Kedrick said finally, "I reckon I'll study it a little. In the meantime, let's keep the peace. I'll keep my men off, if you will do likewise."

"We aren't huntin' trouble," McLennon said. "As long as there's no shootin' at us, an' as long as the company men stay off our land, there'll be no trouble from us."

"Fact is," Slagle said, "we sent Roberts ridin' in with a message to Burwick to that effect. We ain't huntin' for no trouble."

Kedrick turned toward the door, but the bartender's voice stopped him. "You forgot your change," he said dryly.

Kedrick glanced at him, grinned, then picked it up. "Be seein' you," he said, and stepped to the door. At that instant, the door burst open and a man staggered into the room, his arm about another man, who he dropped to the floor. "Roberts!" the man said. "He's been murdered!"

All eyes stared at the man on the floor. That he had been shot many times was obvious. He had also been ridden over, for his body was torn and beaten by the hoofs of running horses. Tom Kedrick felt his stomach turn over. Sick with pity and shock, he lifted his eyes. He looked up into a circle of accusation: McLennon, shocked and unbelieving, Slagle, horrified. Red pointed a finger that trembled with anger. "While he stands an' talks to us, his outfit murders Bob!"

"Git him!" somebody yelled. "Git him! I got a rope!"

Kedrick was standing at the door, and he knew there was no reasoning with these men. Later, they might think, and reason that he might have known nothing about the killing of Roberts. Now, they would not listen. As the man yelled, he hurled himself through the swinging doors and, jerking loose his reins, hit the saddle of the Appaloosa. The startled horse swung and lined out, not down the street, but between the buildings.

Behind him men shouted and cursed. A shot rang out, and he heard a bullet clip past his head as he swung between buildings. Then he knew his escape had driven him into a *cul-de-sac,* for he was now facing, not more than two hundred yards away, the rim around the flat where the town lay. Whether there was a break in that wall he could not guess, but he had an idea both the route upstream and that down-stream of the arroyo would be covered by guards, so he swung his horse and charged into the darkness toward Yellow Butte itself.

As he had come into town, he had seemed to see a V-shaped opening near its base. Whether there was a cut through the rim there he did not know. It might only be a box cañon, and a worse trap than the one into which he had run on his first break.

He slowed his pace, knowing that silence was the first necessity now, for, if they heard him, he could easily be bottled up. The flat was small, and aside from crossing the arroyo there were but two routes of escape, and both would be watched, as he had first surmised. The butte towered high above him now, and his horse walked softly in the abysmal darkness of its foot. His safety was a matter of minutes, for they must know they had him.

The Appaloosa was tired, he knew, for he had been going all day, and the day had been warm and he was a big man. He was in no shape for a hard run against fresh horses, so the only possible escape lay in some shrewd move that would have them guessing and give him time. Yet he must be gone before daylight or he was through. By day they would comb this area and surely discover him.

Now the cañon mouth yawned before him. The walls were not high but were deep enough to allow no escape on horseback, at least. The shouts of pursuit had stopped, but he knew they were hard at work to find him. By now they would know from the guards on the stream that he was still on the flat, and had not escaped. Those guards might be creatures of his own imagination, but knowing the men with whom he dealt, he was shrewd enough to realize that, if they had not guarded the openings before his arrival, they certainly would have sent guards out at once.

The cañon was narrow and he rode on, moving with extreme caution, yet when he had gone but a short distance, he saw the end of the cañon rising above him, black and somber. His throat tightened and his mouth went dry. The Appaloosa stopped and Tom Kedrick sat silently, feeling the labored breathing of the horse and knowing this was an end. He was trapped. Fairly trapped!

Behind him, a light flared briefly, then went out, but there was a shout. That had been a struck match, somebody looking for tracks. And they had found them. In a few minutes more, for they would move cautiously, they would be here. There would be no reasoning with them now. They had him. He was trapped.

V

Captain Tom Kedrick sat very still, listening. He heard some gravel stir; a stone rattled down the cañon. Every move would count now, and he must take no unnecessary chance. He was cornered, and, while he did not want to kill any of these men, he had no intention of being killed.

Carefully he dismounted. As his boot touched the sand, he tested it to make sure no sound would result when his weight settled. Haste now was his greatest danger. There might be nothing he could do, but he was a man of many experiences, and in the past there had always been a way out. Usually there was, if a man took his time and kept his head.

Standing still beside the Appaloosa, he studied the situation. His eyes had grown accustomed to the darkness under the bulk of Yellow Butte. He stared around, seeing the faint gray of sand underfoot, the black bulk of boulders, and the more ragged bulk of underbrush. Leading his horse, he followed a narrow strip of gray that showed an opening between boulders. Scarcely wide enough to admit his horse, the opening led back for some twenty feet, then widened. These were low boulders, rising scarcely above his waist, with the brush somewhat higher. The horse seemed to sense the danger, for it, too, walked quietly and almost without sound.

Literally he was feeling his way in the dark, but that

trail of sand must come from somewhere, for water had run here, and that water might spill off the cliff edge, or might come through some opening. Walking steadily, he found himself going deeper into a tangle of boulders, weaving his way along that thin gray trail, into he knew not what.

Twice he paused and, with his hat, worked back along the path brushing out the tracks. He could not see how good a job he was doing, but the opening was narrow enough to give him a good chance of success. When he had pushed back into the tangle for all of ten minutes, he was brought up sharply by the cliff itself. He had found his way up the slope, through the talus, brush, and scattered boulders, to the very face of the rock. Above him, and apparently out of reach, was a notch in the cliff, and this was probably the source of the sandy trail he had followed. Worried now, he ground-hitched the Appaloosa and moved along the cliff, feeling his way along the face, searching each crack.

To his left, he found nothing. Several times he paused to listen, but no sound came from down the cañon. If this were a box cañon, with no exit, they would probably know it and make no attempt to close in until daylight. In the darkness a man could put up quite a fight in here. Yet, because of their eagerness to avenge the dead man, they might push on. Speaking softly to the horse, he worked his way along the face to the right, but here the pile of talus fell off sharply and he dipped into a hollow. It was cool and the air felt damp. There might even be a spring there, but he heard no water running.

Despite the coolness he was sweating, and he paused, mopping his face and listening. As he stood there, he felt a faint breath of wind against his cheek! He stiffened with surprise, then with a sudden surge of hope he turned and eagerly explored the rocky face, but could find no source for that breeze. He started on, moving more cautiously, then the talus began to steepen under his feet, so he worked his way up the cliff alone. He carried with him his rifle.

At the top he could turn and glance back down the cañon and the faint grayness in the distance that indicated the way he had come. Here the cañon turned a bit, ending in a sort of blind alley on an angle from the true direction of the cañon. There, breaking the edge of the cliff above him, was a notch, and a steep slide led to the top! It must have been some vague stirring of wind from up there on the rim that had touched his cheek, but the slide was steeper than a stairway, and might start sliding underfoot. Certainly the rattle would give away his attempt, and it would be the matter of a few minutes only for them to circle around. As far as that went, they could even now be patrolling the rim above him.

Turning, his foot went from under him and only a frenzied grasp at some brush kept him from falling into whatever hole he had stumbled upon. Scrambling back to good footing, he dropped a pebble and heard it strike some fifteen or twenty feet down.

Working his way along the edge, he reached the foot of the slide, or nearly there, and knew what he had come upon. Water, flooding down that slide during heavy rains, had struck a soft stratum of sand or mud at this point and, striking it with force, had gouged out a deep hole that probably ran back into the cañon itself. There was always a chance that deep within this crack there might be some hiding place, some concealment. Turning abruptly, he returned for his horse.

The slide continued steeply to the bottom of the crevasse scooped from the earth, and, when they reached bottom, he glanced up. He was walking, leading the horse, but the opening of the hole in which he stood was at least fifteen feet above him, and not more than seven or eight feet in width. He moved on into it, and after only a short distance it was almost covered on top by a thick growth of brush growing on the surface or from the sides near the top.

It was cool and still down here, and he pushed on until he found a spot where the rush of water had made a turn, and had gouged deeply under the bank, making a sort of cave beneath the overhang. Into this he led his horse, and here he stopped. A little water stood at the deepest part of the turn, and he allowed the Appaloosa to drink. When the horse had finished, the shallow pool was gone.

Kedrick tried the water in his canteen, then stripped the saddle from the horse, and rubbed him down with a handful of coarse grass. Then he tied the horse and, spreading his blanket, rolled up in it. He was philo-sophical. He had done what he could. If they found him now, there was nothing to do but shoot it out where he was.

Surprisingly he slept, and, when he awakened, it was the startled breathing of the Appaloosa that warned him. Instantly he was on his feet, speaking in a whisper to the horse and resting his hand on its shoulder. Day had come, and somewhere above them, yet some distance, there were voices!

The cave in which he stood was sandstone, no more than fifteen feet in depth, and probably eight feet high at the opening. Kedrick moved to the mouth, studied the crevasse down which he had come, and it was as he had supposed, a deep-cut watercourse from the notch in the cliff. Evidently during heavy rains this roared full of water, almost to the brim.

At the place where he now stood, the brush on either side almost met over the top, and at one point a fallen slab bridged the crack. Glancing back the way he had come, Kedrick saw that much of it was also covered by brush, and there was a chance that he would not be found. A very, very slim chance, but a chance. He could ask for no more.

He wanted to smoke, but dared not, for the smell of it might warn them of his presence. Several times he heard voices, some of them quite near. He glanced toward the back of the cave and saw the gelding drinking again. Evidently the water had seeped through during the night, even though not much. His canteen was over half full, and as yet water was not a problem.

His rifle across his knees, he waited, from time to time staring down the crevasse in the direction he had been going. Where did this water flow? It must flow into the arroyo below, near town, and in that case they would certainly know of it. The men and women of the town might not know of it, but the children would without doubt. Trust them to find every cave, every niche in the rock within miles!

Yet as the morning wore on, although he heard occasionally the sound of voices, nobody approached his place of concealment, nor did they seem aware of it. Once, he ventured out into the crevasse itself, and pulled a few handfuls of grass growing on a slight mound of earth. This he fed to the horse, that ate gratefully. He dug some jerky from his own pack and chewed on it, wishing for a cup of coffee.

Later, he ventured farther down the crevasse which seemed to dip steeply from where he was, and, hearing no voices, he pushed on, coming to a point where the crevasse turned sharply again, the force of the water having hollowed out a huge cave like a bowl standing on edge, and then the water turned and shot down an even steeper declivity into the black maw of a cavern!

Having come this far, he took a chance on leaving his horse alone and walked on down toward the cave. The entrance was high and wide and the cave extended deep into the mountain with several shelves or ledges that seemed to show no signs of water. There was a pool in the bottom, and apparently the water filled a large basin, but lost itself through some cracks in the bottom of the larger hollow. Although he penetrated no great distance, he could find no evidence of another outlet, nor could he feel any motion of air. Yet, as he looked around him, he realized that with some food a man might well hide in this place for weeks, and, unless they went to the foot of the slide and found the opening into the crevasse, this place might never be discovered. The run-off from the cliff, then, did not go to the arroyo, but ended here, in this deep cavern.

The day wore on slowly, and twice he walked back down to the cavern to smoke, but left his horse where it was, for he had an idea he could escape later. Yet when dusk came, and he worked his way back up the crevasse slide, he crawled out on the edge where he could look toward the entrance and saw two men, squatting there beside a fire, with rifles under their hands. They believed him concealed inside, and hoped to starve him out.

By this time Dornie Shaw must have returned to Mustang with news of his disappearance and, probably, of their murder of the messenger. For he was sure that it had been his own group who had committed the crime. It was scarcely likely that Gunter or Keith would countenance such a thing near town where it would not fail to be seen and reported upon by unfriendly witnesses.

Returning, he studied the slide to the rim. It was barely possible that a horse might scramble up there. It would be no trick for an active man, and the Appaloosa was probably a mountain horse. It was worth a gamble—if there was no one on top to greet him. Pulling an armful of grass from near the brush and boulders, he returned to the horse, and watched it gratefully munch the rich green grass.

Connie Duane was disturbed. She had seen the messenger come to her uncle and the others, and had heard their reply. Then, at almost noon the following day, Dornie Shaw and the others had come in, and they had returned without Tom Kedrick. Why that should disturb her she could not have said, but the fact remained that it did. Since he had stepped up on the verandah, she had thought of little else, remembering the set of his chin, the way he carried his shoulders, and the startled expression when he saw her. There was something about him that was different, not only from the men around her uncle, but from any man she had known before. Now, when despite herself she had looked forward to his return, he was missing.

John Gunter came out on the verandah, nervously biting the end from a cigar. "What happened?" she asked. "Is something wrong? Where's Captain Kedrick?"

"Wish I knew!" His voice was sharp with anxiety. "He took a ride to look over those squatters an' never came back. I don't trust Shaw, no matter how much Keith does. He's too bloodthirsty. We could get into a lot of trouble here, Connie. That's why I wanted Kedrick. He has judgment, brains."

"Perhaps he decided he wanted no part of it, Uncle. Maybe he decided your squatters were not outlaws or renegades."

Gunter glanced at her sharply. "Who has been talking to you?" he demanded.

"No one. It hasn't been necessary. I have walked around town, and I've seen some of these outlaws, as you call them, have wives and children, that they buy supplies, and look like nice people. I don't like it, Uncle John, and I don't like to think that my money may be financing a part of it."

"Now, now! Don't bother your head over it. You may be sure that Loren and I will do everything we can for your best interests."

"Then drop the whole thing!" she pleaded. "There's no need for it. I've money enough, and I don't want money that comes from depriving others of their homes. They all have a right to live, a chance."

"Of course!" Gunter was impatient. "We've gone over all this before! But I tell you most of these people are trash, and no matter about that, they all will be put off that land, anyway. The government is going to buy out whoever has control. That will mean us, and that means we'll get a nice, juicy profit."

"From the government? Your own government, Uncle?" Connie studied him coolly. "I fail to understand the sort of man who will attempt to defraud his own government. There are people like that, I suppose, but somehow I never thought I'd find one in my own family."

"Don't be silly, child. You know nothing of business . . . you aren't practical."

"I suppose not. Only I seem to remember that a lot of worthwhile things don't seem practical at the moment. No, I believe I'll withdraw my investment in this deal and buy a small ranch somewhere nearby. I will have no part in it."

"You can't do that!" Gunter exploded impatiently. "Your money is already in, and there's no way of getting it out until this business is closed. Now, why don't you trust me like a good girl? You always have before!"

"Yes, I have, Uncle John, but I never believed you could be dishonest." She studied him frankly. "You aren't very happy about this yourself. You know," she persisted, "those people aren't going to move without a fight. You believed they could be frightened. Well, they can't. I've seen Bob McLennon, and he's not the kind of a man who can be frightened. Even by that choice bunch of murderers Loren has gathered together."

"They aren't that. Not murderers," Gunter protested uneasily, but refused to meet her eyes. "Reckless, yes. And temperamental. Not murderers."

"Not even Dornie Shaw? The nice-looking, boyish one who has killed a dozen men and is so cold-blooded and fiendish at times that others are afraid of him? No, Uncle, there is no way you can sidestep this. If you continue, you are going to countenance murder and the killing of innocent people. Loren doesn't care. He has always been cold-blooded. You've wondered why I wouldn't marry him. That's why. He has the disposition of a tiger. He would kill anything or anyone that stood in his way. Even you, Uncle John."

He started and looked at her uneasily. "Why did you say that?"

"Because it's true. I know our tall and handsome man. He will allow nothing to come between him and what he desires. You've chosen some choice companions." She got to her feet. "If you hear anything of Captain Kedrick, let me know, will you?"

Gunter stood still for a long time after she left. He swore bitterly. Connie was like her mother. She always had the faculty for putting her finger on the truth, and certainly she was right about this. It was beginning to look ugly, but away down deep in his heart he was upset less over Keith than over Burwick. That strange, fat, and dirty man was a thing of evil, of corruption. There was some evil thing within him, something cold and vicious as a striking snake. Connie Duane was not the only person who was disturbed over the strange disappearance of Tom Kedrick.

Bob McLennon, unofficial commander of the forces for defense, sat in his rambling ranch house on the edge of Yellow Butte. Pete Slagle, Burt Williams, Dai Reid, and Pit Laine were all gathered there. With them was Sue Laine, keeping in the background. Her dark, lively eyes were stirring from one to the other, her ears were alert for every word.

"Blazes, man!" McLennon said irritably. "Where could he have gone? I'd have sworn he went into that box cañon. There was no other place for him to go, unless he took wings and flew! He had to go in there!"

"You looked yourself," Slagle said dryly. "Did you see him? He just ain't there, that's all! He got plumb away!"

"He probably did that," Dai Reid commented. "A quick man, that Tom Kedrick. Hand or mind, he's quick." He drew out his pipe and stoked it slowly. "You shouldn't have jumped him," he continued. "I know the lad, an' he's honest. If he said that was what he come for, it was the truth he told. I'd take any oath he'd no knowledge of the killin'!"

"I'd like to believe that," McLennon agreed. "The man impressed me. We could use an honest man on the other side, one who would temper the wind a bit, or get this thing stopped."

"It won't be that Shaw who stops. He's a murderin' little devil," Slagle said. "He'll kill like a weasel in a chicken pen until there's naught left to kill."

"Kedrick fought me fair," Williams said. "I'll give him that."

"He's a fair man," Dai persisted. "Since a lad I've

known him. I'd not be wrong. I'd give fifty acres of my holdin' for the chance to talk to him."

Daylight brought the first attack. It came swiftly, a tight bunch of riders that exploded from the mouth of the arroyo hit the dusty street of Yellow Butte on a dead run, pistols firing, and then the deep, heavy concussion of dynamite. As suddenly as they had come, they were gone. Two men sprawled in the street.

Peters, the man Shaw had faced down in the street of Mustang, was one of them. He had taken three .44 slugs through the chest and died before he hit the ground. He had made one final effort to win back his self-respect. He had seen Dornie Shaw in the van of the charging riders and rushed into the street to get him. He failed to get off a single shot. The second man down was shot through the thigh and arm. He was a Swede who had just put in his second crop.

The riders had planned their attack well and had worked near enough to the guards at the mouth of the arroyo, and at a time when no attack was expected. The one guard awake was knocked down by a charging horse, but miraculously suffered only bruises. Two bundles of dynamite had been thrown. One had exploded against the door of the general store, smashing it off its hinges and tearing up the porch. The sound exploded harmlessly between the buildings.

The first rattle of rifle fire brought Tom Kedrick to

an observation point. He had saddled his horse, hoping for a break, and instantly he saw it. The two guards had rushed in to the scene of action, and he led his horse out of the crevasse, rode at a canter to the cañon's mouth, and, seeing dust over the town, he swung right and, skirting close to the butte, slipped out into the open, a free man once more.

VI

Kedrick did not return to Mustang. He had come this far for a purpose, and he meant to achieve it. Turning west and north, he rode upstream away from Yellow Butte and Mustang. He wanted actually to see some of the homes of which so much had been said. By the way these people lived he could tell the sort they were. It was still and warm in the morning, and after the preliminary escape he slowed his horse to a walk and studied the terrain.

Certainly nothing could be further from swamp-land, and in that at least the company had misrepresented. Obviously they had misrepresented in maintaining that the land was vacant, but, if the squatters were a shiftless lot, Kedrick knew he would continue his job. Already he was heartily sick of the whole mess, yet he owed Gunter money, and how to pay it back was a bigger problem. And then, although the idea lurked almost unthought in the back of his consciousness, there was Connie Duane.

In his fast moving and active life he had met many

women, and a few had interested him, but none so much as this tall girl with the quiet, interested eyes. His desire to get back to Mustang had nothing to do with the company, but only with her. At the same time, Dornie Shaw had acted without his orders, had slain the messenger, and attacked the town. Of course, they might think him dead.

Turning due north, he rode though the sagebrush and catclaw toward two towering blue mountains that stood alone this side of the rim that bordered the country to the north. On his left, he saw broken land, and what was evidently a deep arroyo. He swung the Appaloosa over and headed it toward the cañon. Suddenly he reined in.

On the ground before him were the tracks of a trotting horse, and he recognized them. They were the same tracks left by the strange rider on the grulla mustang that had scouted their approach to Yellow Butte. The tracks were fresh.

Riding more slowly, he came to the edge of the cañon and looked down at a long, green meadow, fenced and watered by a small stream. At the far side, tucked in a corner, was a stone cottage, at once more attractive and better built than any other he had seen in this section. Ahead of him a trail turned down, so without delay he rode down it and walked his horse across the meadow by a narrow lane, toward the house.

It was a pleasant place of sandstone blocks and a thatched roof. Shade trees sheltered the yard, and there were a half dozen hens pecking about. In the corral there were several horses. His heart jumped as he saw the grulla, saddled and waiting.

He drew up in the courtyard and swung down, trailing his reins. The door opened and a girl came out with a pan of water. She started as she saw him, and he recognized her instantly. It was Sue Laine, the girl of the trail, the girl in whom Dornie was reported to be interested.

"You!" she gasped as she stared at him. "They told me you were dead!"

He shrugged. "Not dead, just hungry. Could you feed a man?"

She studied him a minute, then nodded. "Come in. Better tie your horse, though. He'll head for that meadow if you don't. And"—her voice was dry—"you may need him. This isn't exactly friendly country."

He tied his horse near the grulla and followed her inside. "Isn't it?" he said. "Somehow I gathered you weren't exactly an enemy to the company."

"Don't say that!" she flared. "Don't ever say that!" Her voice lowered. "Not around here, anyway. If my brother ever heard. . . ."

So Pit Laine and his sister did not see alike? That was an interesting point. He bathed his hands and face in the basin she left him, then combed his hair. Ruefully he rubbed his chin. "Your brother got a razor? I hate to go unshaven."

She brought a razor without comment, and he

shaved, then dried his face and hands and walked into the house. It was amazingly neat, and on a side table there were several books. Flowered curtains hung at the windows, and several copper dishes were burnished to brightness. He sat down and she brought him food, beef, eggs, and homemade bread with honey.

"Everybody's looking for you," she said. "Where have you been?"

He accepted the statement and ignored the question. "After that messenger was killed, I had to get out of Yellow Butte. I did. What's been happening?"

"Keith served a final ultimatum. We either move, or they run us out. McLennon refused."

"He did right."

She turned on him, her eyes questioning. "You think that? I thought you were their man?"

He looked up from his food, and shook his head. "I don't know where I stand, but I don't go for murder, nor for running people out of their homes."

"They can't stay, anyway. If this land becomes a reservation, they will all be moved off. We will, too. They are foolish to fight."

"At least, the government will buy their land and pay for their investment. In any event, the company has misrepresented things."

"Does it matter?" She sat down opposite him. "They will win. They have money, influence, and power. The settlers here have nothing." She looked around bitterly. "Perhaps you think I am going against my own people, but that's not true. These aren't my people. Pit and I don't belong here and we never have, although Pit won't see it. Do you think I want to slave my life away on this desert?" She leaned toward him. "Look, Captain Kedrick, you're one of them, not just working for them, not just a hired gunman like Dornie Shaw. You can lead the men you have to, and I wouldn't be surprised but what you could even handle Keith. You could be a big man in this country, or any country. Why be foolish and start thinking like you are? These farmers and ranchers can do nothing for you. They can't even help themselves. The company will win, and, if you are one of them, you will have a share in the winning. Don't get foolish, Captain, stay with them, do what you have to do."

"There are things more important than money. There's self-respect."

She stared at him, her eyes widening. "You don't really believe that? Try buying supplies with it, sometime. You won't get any place. But that isn't the point. You'll do what you want, but I want a man who will take me out of this desert." She got up quickly and came around the table. "You could do it, Captain. You could become rich, right here."

He smiled at her. "Ambitious, aren't you?"

"Why not? Being a rancher's wife doesn't appeal to me. I want to get away from here, go some place, be something, and enjoy life." She hesitated, studying him. "You could edge Gunter out of it, and Keith . . .

maybe even Burwick. But the first two would be easy, and I know how."

"You do?" He looked up at her. She stood very close to him, and she was smiling down at him. She was, he had to admit, a lovely girl, and an exciting one. Too exciting for comfort right now, and that was a fact she understood completely. "How?"

She shook her head. "Oh, no! That I'd tell you only if you threw in with me, joined me. But this much I'll tell you . . . John Gunter is small potatoes. They needed money, and he had that girl's money, so they roped him in. Keith is dangerous because he is ambitious and unscrupulous, but the man to reckon with is Burwick. He will be top man when this thing is over, and you can bank on it, he has a way figured, all the time!"

"You seem to know a great deal."

"I do. Men like me, and men talk. They don't have any idea how much I lead them to say, or how much I remember."

"Why tell me all this?"

"Because you're the man who can do what has to be done. You could whip that bunch into line. All of them would listen to you, even Dornie Shaw . . . and he's suspicious of you."

"Of me? Why?"

"He saw Dai Reid come from your room. He was watching you."

So that was it! He had suspected that Shaw had something on his mind. But why had Shaw been watching? What was the little gunman thinking of? And had he reported that conference to Keith?

Kedrick finished his meal and lighted a cigarette. Ever since their first meeting in the desert, this girl had puzzled him. He was inclined to doubt if any girl, reared as she must have been, could be so sincerely disdaining of all loyalty and so plainly self-seeking. And this girl was scarcely more than a child, slim, brown, and lovely, with her quick, measuring eyes and her soft lips. Now, she seemed to have selected him for the man who was to take her away from the desert. But how many others had the same idea? And then, he had no idea of leaving the desert.

"Your brother around?" he asked.

Her glance was a quick flash of alarm. "You don't want to see him, or talk to him. You'd better get out of here."

"On the contrary, Sue, I'd like to talk to Pit. I've heard about him and I'd like to know him."

"You'd better go," she warned. "He'll be back soon, and some of that Yellow Butte crowd may be with him."

"You mean he's not here? Then whose horse is that out there? That grulla?"

Her face was strange as she shook her head. "You'll think I'm a liar, but I don't know. I never saw the rider."

His eyes searched hers. He could see nothing but sincerity there, sincerity and a little fear. "You mean that horse showed up there, tied like that? And you never saw the rider?"

"That's right. I looked out this morning, shortly after Pit left, and he was tied right there. This isn't the first time! He has been here twice before, when Pit was gone, and some others have seen him, most of them women when their husbands are away. Missus Burt Williams said he was tied to her corral for three or four hours one day."

"But surely someone has seen the rider come and mount up?"

"Never. He'll be out there like he is now . . . wait! . . . he's gone!"

Kedrick came to his feet with a start and stared out the door. Sue was right. The mouse-colored horse was gone. His own Appaloosa stood where he had been left, but the grulla had disappeared.

Walking out into the yard, he looked around very carefully, but there was nothing in sight on the plain or the hills. The horse—and he was positive he had seen it only a few minutes before—was gone! He looked at her and saw the strained expression on her face, then he walked out to the Appaloosa. Pinned to his saddle was a note. He took it down and glanced at it, then passed it to Sue who had come up beside him.

STAY AWAY

Kedrick shrugged. "Your brother do this?"

"Oh, no! I told him about the horse and he knew no more about it than I. Besides, he didn't print that. He couldn't. Pit never learned either to read or write."

• • •

Long after he left the Malpais Arroyo behind, he was puzzling over the strange horse. Somebody was seriously trying either to puzzle or frighten the squatters, yet it was an action unlike the company. Moreover, it must be somebody who had a lot of time to spend.

Kedrick rode north toward Blue Hill, then swung out, crossing the old Mormon Trail and skirting the rim. This was good grazing land. There was an abundance of rough foliage here and a good herd of cattle could fatten on this range without trouble. Moreover, the herding problem was solved in part by the rim that provided a natural drift fence beyond which the cattle could not go. When he reached Salt Creek, he turned down the creek toward the river, but swung east again, and, passing near Chimney Rock, he rode southeast until he struck the Hogback Trail. Once over that ridge he headed due east for Mustang.

Yet, as always, his eyes were alive and alert. He loved this land, harsh though it might be at times. He loved the dim purples and blues, the far-flung mists and mornings and nights, the gray-green of the sagebrush, and the rust-red of the sandstone. It was a good country, and there was room for all if it were left open for settlement.

His own mind was not yet resolved. The problem of his debt to Gunter weighed heavily upon him, and there were other considerations. He wanted no trouble, and to withdraw now might mean plenty of it, particularly if he remained in the country, which he had every reason to do. He would try to talk the company into withdrawing, but knew that would fail.

Just where, in all this, did Connie Duane actually stand? Was she involved more deeply than he believed? Or was it only what had been implied, that her uncle had invested her money in the land speculation? If such was the case, it might be difficult or impossible to get out at this stage—even if they would allow it. Burwick puzzled him. Obviously the controlling power, he gave no evidence of where that power came from, aside from some native shrewdness. Yet there might be much more to the man and evidently was, for that Keith and Gunter deferred to him was obvious. Purposely Kedrick had said nothing of his hideaway near Yellow Butte when talking to Sue. That young lady already knew more than was good for her, and that spot might again become useful. It was something to know.

Mustang was asleep when he rode into the town and headed for the stable. He put his horse up and rubbed it down thoroughly, gave it a good bait of corn, and forked down some hay. Then he made his way quickly to the St. James. As he neared the hotel, a tall, lean figure arose from the chair where he himself had been sitting a few days before. The build and the broad hat, the very hang of the guns left no mistake. It was Laredo Shad.

"Cap'n?" The voice was low. "You all right?"

"Yes, and you?"

Shad chuckled. "Don't worry none about Shad! I

stay healthy." He motioned to a chair. "You better sit down. I've been hopin' you'd show up."

"What's the talk? Did they think I was dead, or skipped the country?"

"Some o' both, I reckon. Keith was fit to be tied. He wants to see you as soon as you show . . . no matter when."

"He'll wait. I'm tired."

Shad nodded, then lighted his cigarette, which had gone out. "You know, I ain't right sure about this business."

Kedrick nodded. "I know what you mean. I'm not the man to run folks out of their homes."

"You quittin'?"

"Not yet. I'll talk to 'em first."

"Won't do no good. They are mighty bloodthirsty. It was Poinsett shot that messenger. Dornie put him up to it. Poinsett killed him, an' then four, five of those rannies shot up the body. I don't think Fessenden shot any, an' maybe Goff didn't. You can lay your last *peso* I didn't shoot none. It was mighty raw, Cap'n, mighty raw."

"They'll pay for it. Were you on the Yellow Butte raid?"

"Uhn-huh, but I didn't shoot nobody. I'm no Bible packer, Cap'n, but I do figure a fightin' man shouldn't tackle folks who cain't fight back, an' I ain't the man to be firin' on no women or kids."

"What are they talkin' up now? Any plans you know of?"

Shad hesitated, then shrugged. "Reckon you'd better talk that out with them, Cap'n. I may know somethin', but I ain't tellin', not yet."

The Texan sat silently for a few minutes while both men smoked, and then he waved an impatient hand. "Cap'n, I hired on as a gun hand, an' such I am, but I didn't figure on this sort of thing. Some of those *hombres* on the other side o' this shindig look a damned sight more human than some on our own side. I'm gettin' shut o' the whole shebang."

"Uhn-huh"—surprisingly Kedrick found resolution coming to him—"I know how you feel, but my own way will be different. I think, if I can't talk Gunter an' the rest of them out of it, I'll change sides."

Shad nodded. "I've thought of it. I sure have."

Kedrick turned suddenly and found Dornie Shaw standing not twenty feet behind them. Slowly he got to his feet, and Laredo Shad did likewise. Shaw's eyes avoided Kedrick. "If you figure on leavin' us, Shad, you better figure on killin' me first."

"If I have to," Laredo said quietly, "then I reckon you can die as simple as any other man. Want to try it now?"

"That's enough, Shad!" Kedrick's voice was sharp. "I've said there would be no more fighting. Not in this outfit."

Dornie Shaw turned his head slowly and smiled at Kedrick. "Still like to give orders, do you? Maybe that'll be changed."

"Maybe." Tom Kedrick shrugged. "That will be

time enough for me to stop giving orders. I'm turning in."

"Keith wants to see you."

"He can wait. I've had a rough time. There's nothing he wants won't wait."

"Shall I tell him that?"

"If you like."

Shaw smiled again. "You must carry a lot o' weight where you come from, Kedrick, but don't forget it ain't here. Keith is a bad man to buck. So's Burwick."

Kedrick shrugged again. "I've bucked worse. But at the moment I'm bucking nobody. I need sleep, and, by the Lord Harry, sleep is what I'll get. Whatever Keith has on his mind can wait until daylight. I'll be up then."

Shaw started to go, then hesitated, unable to restrain his curiosity. "What happened to you? We figured you were dead or taken prisoner when you didn't come back."

For the first time Kedrick began to wonder. Had Shaw wanted the messenger killed for that very reason? Had he deliberately moved that way hoping the enraged settlers would kill Kedrick? It was most likely. "It doesn't matter," he said, passing off the remark casually. "I found a way to keep out of sight."

Shaw turned away, and, when he had gone only a few steps, Tom Kedrick spoke up suddenly: "By the way, Dornie. Know anybody who rides a grulla mustang?"

Shaw stopped abruptly, but he did not turn. His

whole body seemed to stiffen. Then he started on. "No," he said gruffly, "I sure don't."

Laredo Shad stared after him. "You know, pardner, you'll either kill that *hombre* someday or you'll be killed."

"Uhn-huh," Kedrick said quietly, "I've the same feeling."

VII

Keith was pacing the floor in the office at the gray stone building when Kedrick walked in. He stopped and turned swiftly. "Shaw tells me you came in after midnight. Why didn't you come to me according to my orders?"

"Frankly I was tired. Furthermore"—Kedrick returned Keith's look—"I'd nothing to report that wouldn't keep."

"You were hired to do a job, and you haven't done it." Keith stood with his hands on his hips. "Where've you been?"

Briefly and clearly Kedrick explained, omitting only the visit to Laines' and the story of the hide-out. He continued: "Having looked the situation over, I'd say you had small chance of driving those people off. Also, you and Gunter misrepresented things to me and the government. That land is occupied not by renegades and outlaws, but by good, solid people. You can't get away with running them off."

Keith smiled contemptuously. "Getting scared? You

were supposed to be a fighting man. As for what we can do or can't do, let me tell you this, Kedrick. We've started to run those people off, and we'll do it. With or without you! Hiring you was Gunter's idea, anyway."

"That's right, it was." Gunter walked into the room followed by Burwick, and he glanced swiftly from Kedrick to Keith. "If you're complainin' about his going to look over that country, you can stop. I sent him."

"Did you tell him to come back scared to death? Saying we can't swing it?"

Burwick had been silent, but now he moved to the big chair behind the desk and dropped into it. He sighed heavily and wiped the back of his hand across his mouth, then glanced at Kedrick keenly. "What did you find out?"

"That they are determined to fight. I talked to Bob McLennon and to Slagle. There's no quit in those men. They'll fight at the drop of a hat, and to the last ditch. Right now, at this minute, they are ready for anything. Your raid killed one man, wounded another. The dynamite blasted a door loose and blew a hole in the porch."

Burwick turned swiftly and glared at Keith. "You told me three men dead and a building destroyed! Hereafter, you be sure reports to me are accurate." He swung back to Kedrick. "Go on, what happened to you? You got away?"

"I'm here."

257

Their eyes met and held for a long time, Burwick's stone-cold and hard, examining, probing.

"What do you think of the deal?" he asked finally.

"The fight," Kedrick replied carefully, "will raise a stink clear to Washington. Remember the Lincoln County War? We'll have us another general down here, and you know how much profit you'll make out of that place then!"

Burwick nodded his huge head. "Sensible, that's sensible. Have to think our way around that. At least" —he glared again at Keith and Gunter—"this man can bring in some sensible ideas and make a coherent report. You two could learn from him." He looked up at Kedrick. "Anything else?"

"A couple of things. There's a mysterious rider out on those plains. Rides a mouse-colored horse, and he's got those folks more jittery than all your threats."

"Hah?" Burwick was uninterested. He shuffled papers on his desk. "What's this I hear about you quittin'?"

"I won't be a party to murder. These people aren't outlaws, but good, substantial folks. I'd say buy them out or leave them alone."

"You aren't running this affair," Keith replied coldly. "We will decide what is to be done."

"Nobody quits," Burwick said quietly, his eyes on Kedrick's, "unless I say so!"

Tom Kedrick smiled suddenly. "Then you'd better say so, because I've quit as of now!"

"Tom!" Gunter protested. "Let's talk this over!"

"What of the money you owe the firm?" Keith demanded unpleasantly. "You can repay that, I suppose?"

"There's no need."

They all turned at the voice. Connie Duane stood in the door. "You have money of mine in this project. When Uncle John got it from me, he told me it was a real estate speculation. His other activities have been honest and practical, so I did not investigate. Now I have. I shall withdraw my money, and you can pay me less the sum advanced to Captain Kedrick. He may repay me when circumstances permit it."

All in the room were still. Gunter's face was pale, and Keith looked startled, then angry. He started to protest, but he was too slow. Burwick turned on Gunter. "You!" he snorted angrily. "You told me that was your money! You fool! What do you mean, bringing a woman into a deal like this? Well, you brought her in. Now you manage her or I shall!"

"Nobody," Connie replied, "is managing me or my affairs from now on. I'll handle them myself!" She turned to Kedrick. "I'm glad, Captain, that you've made this decision. I am sure you'll not be sorry for it."

Kedrick turned to follow her from the room, but Burwick's voice stopped him. "Captain!"

He turned. Keith's eyes were ugly and Gunter's face was haunted by doubt and fear. "Captain Kedrick," Burwick said, "I believe we are all being too hasty. I like your caution in this matter. Your suggestion that cleaning out those people might make trouble and cause talk in Washington is probable. I had considered that but, not knowing McLennon, had considered the chance negligible. Slagle, I know. McLennon I do not know. Your suggestion eliminates a frontal attack. We must try some other means. Also," he added, "I believe that your presence has some claim on that of Miss Duane. Consequently, as we can brook no failure now, I have a proposition for you. How would you like to come into the firm? As a silent partner?"

Keith's face flushed angrily, but Gunter looked up, his eyes suddenly hopeful. Burwick continued. "We could give you a fifteen percent interest, which, believe me, will be adequate. I believe you could keep Miss Duane in line, and with you at the helm we might straighten this whole thing out . . . without bloodshed."

Kedrick hesitated. The money was a temptation, for he had no desire to be indebted to Connie, yet the money alone would mean nothing. It was that last phrase that gripped his attention and made him incautious. "Without bloodshed," he repeated. "On those terms, I accept. However, let's discuss this matter a bit further."

Keith spun on his heel. "Burwick, this doesn't make sense! You know the only way we'll get these people off is by driving them off! We agreed on that before. Also, this man is not reliable. I happen to know that he has friends on the other side, and has actually been in communication with them."

"So much the better." Burwick pursed his fat lips and mopped perspiration from his face. "He'll have a contact he can use then to make a deal." He chuckled. "Suppose you two run along and let me talk to Captain Kedrick?"

Hours later, Tom Kedrick paused on the street and studied it with care. Burwick had been more than reasonable, and, little as he was able to trust him, yet he thought it possible that Burwick was sincere in his agreement to buy off a few of them, and to try to convince others. Certainly, if the government moved in, they would have to move, anyway. With McLennon and Slagle out of the picture the chances were there would be no fight, for the others lacked leadership. No fighting meant no deaths, and the settlers would come out of it with a little money at least.

He paced the street irritably, avoiding company. Burwick stank of deceit, but the man was practical and he should realize that a sudden mess of killings preceding the sale of the land would create a furor that might cause them to lose out all around. At least, trouble had been avoided for the time, and even Connie was hopeful that something might be done. Tomorrow he was returning again to try to make some deal with McLennon and Slagle. A neutral messenger was leaving tonight.

"They won't come to town," Burwick had agreed,

"so why not pick some intermediate point? Meet them, say, at Largo Cañon or Chimney Rock? Have your talk there, and I'll come with you. Just you and me, McLennon and Slagle. We can talk there and maybe make peace. Ain't it worth a try?"

It was only that chance for peace that had persuaded him and helped him to persuade Connie. She had listened in silence as he explained the situation, then she had turned to him frankly. "Captain, you don't trust them, and neither do I. Uncle John has never been this way before, and I believe somehow he has fallen under the domination of those other men. However, I think that, if Burwick is willing to talk, we should at least agree. I'll stand by you in this, and we'll hope something can come of it that will prevent trouble."

Kedrick was less hopeful than he had let it appear, and now he was studying the situation from every angle. As things stood, it was a stalemate. He was confident that with McLennon and Slagle to lead them, the settlers could manage a stiff defense of their town and their homes. Certainly they could prevent the survey being completed and prevent any use being made of the lands. Yet there were fiery elements on both sides, and Keith did not like the turn things had taken. Colonel Loren Keith had from the very beginning planned on striking fast and wiping out the opposition. It would be merely another unsolved mystery of the West. Kedrick resolved to keep an eye on the man and be prepared for anything.

He returned to the St. James and to bed, yet he

awakened early and was surprised to see Keith, mounted and riding out of town at daybreak. With a bound he was out of bed and dressing. Whatever Keith had in mind he meant to know. Swiftly he descended the stairs and went to the livery stable. Mounted, he headed out of town, found Keith's tracks with ease, and followed them. Keith turned off the trail and headed west and slightly north, but after a few miles Kedrick lost the trail and took a wide swing to try and cut it again, but Keith had vanished somewhere in the vicinity of Largo Cañon.

Returning to the hotel, he found a message from Bob McLennon. He and Slagle would meet with Burwick and Kedrick at Chimney Rock at three in the afternoon on Wednesday. It was now Monday, and a whole day lay between. Yet during the remainder of Monday he saw nothing of Dornie Shaw, although Laredo Shad appeared a couple of times, then vanished into one of the saloons.

At midnight the door of his room opened slowly and Tom Kedrick sat up, gun in hand. It was Laredo Shad.

"Somethin's up," he said, dropping on the bed, "an' she looks mighty peculiar. Couple of hours ago Poinsett an' Goff showed up an' said they had quit. No fightin' here, so they were pullin' out for Durango. About a half hour later, they mounted up an took out."

"What's peculiar about that?" Kedrick inquired, building a smoke. "That's in line with Burwick's talk with me."

"Yeah," Shad replied dryly, "but both of them came in here with a good deal of gear. They lost their pack horses somewheres and went out only with what they could carry on the one horse, an' damned little o' that."

"What about Fessenden?"

"Ain't seen him."

"Any of the others gone?"

"Clauson is. At least, he ain't around in sight. I ain't seen him since morning."

That left Shaw, who had been around little himself, and Fessenden if he was still in town. Despite himself, Kedrick was disturbed, but if Burwick was getting rid of his warriors, it was a good sign, and probably, Kedrick felt, he was getting too suspicious. Nothing, Shad said, had been said to him about quitting. "In fact," he said dryly, "the Mixus boys pulled in this morning, an' they went right to Burwick."

"Who are they?"

"Killers. Dry-gulchers, mostly. Bean an' Abe Mixus. They were in that Sandoval affair. Couple of men died awful opportune in that affair, an', come to think of it, Burwick was around. Fact is, that was where I met him."

"Were you in that?"

"Uhn-uh. I was in town, though, an' had me a run-in with Roy Gangle. Roy was a mighty tough ranny who'd been ramroddin' a big spread down thataway, an', when he got into the war, he went bad, plumb bad. We'd had trouble over a steer, an' he braced me. He was a mite slow."

It made no sense—gunmen leaving, but others arriving. Of course, the Mixus boys could have been spoken to before the change of plans. That must be it. He suggested as much to Laredo, and the Texan nodded dubiously. "Maybe. I don't trust that *hombre* none. Your man Gunter is in over his head. Keith, well, he's all around bad when it comes to that, but neither of them can hold a candle to that Burwick."

Study the situation as he could, Tom Kedrick could see no answer to it, and the fact remained that they were to meet Slagle and McLennon for a peace conference. Out of that anything might come, and he had no real cause to distrust Burwick. Morning was bright and clear with the sun promising a hot day. Yet it was still cool when Kedrick appeared on the street and crossed to the little restaurant where he ate in silence. He was on his second cup of coffee when Connie came in.

Her face brightened with a smile as she saw him, and she came over to his table. "You know, you're the one bright spot in this place. I'm so tired of that old stone house and seeing that dirty old man around that I can scarcely stand it. I'll be glad when this is all over."

He studied her. "What will you do then?"

"You know, I've not really thought of that. What I want to do is to get a ranch somewhere, a place with trees, grass, and some running water. It doesn't have to be a big place."

"Cattle?"

"A few, but horses are what I want. Horses like that one of yours, I think."

"Good idea. It takes less land for horses, and there's always a market for good stock." He studied the beauty of her mouth, the quietness and humor of her eyes. "Somehow I'm glad to think you're staying. It wouldn't be the same without you. Not now."

She looked at him quickly, her eyes dancing with laughter, but with the hint of a question in their depths. "Why, Tom! That sounds almost like gallantry. Like you were trying to make love to me, like all the cowboys."

"No, Connie," he said quietly, "when I make love to you, there won't be any doubt about it. You'll know, and I won't be fooling. Over west of here, west and south, there's a great rim that stretches for miles across the country, and a splendid pine forest atop it. There's trees, water, game, and some of the finest mountain meadows a man ever saw. I know a place over there where I camped once, a good spring, some tall trees, graceful in the wind, and a long sweep of land clear to the rim's edge, and beyond it miles upon miles of rolling, sweeping range and forest."

"It sounds fascinating, like what I've been wanting ever since I came West."

He pushed back his chair. "Maybe when this is

over, you'd ride over that way with me? I'd like to show it to you."

She looked up at him. "All right, Tom. We'll look at it together."

He paused, hat in hand, staring out the door. "Together," he mused. Then he glanced down at her. "You know, Connie, that's the most beautiful word in the language . . . together."

He walked away then, pausing to pay his check and hers, before stepping outside into the warmth of the street. A buckboard had stopped and a man was getting out of it, a man who moved warily and looked half frightened. He glanced around swiftly, then ducked through the door into the store.

VIII

Two men crossed the street suddenly. One of them was a man Kedrick had never seen before; the other was the sly-looking loafer he had seen hanging around the back door in the saloon at Yellow Butte. The loafer, a sour-faced man called Singer, was talking. They stopped, and he indicated the buckboard to the man with him. "That's him, Abe," Singer was saying, "he's one of that crowd from across the way. He's brother-in-law to McLennon."

"This is a good place to start," Abe replied shortly, low-voiced. "Let's go!"

Tom Kedrick turned on his heel and followed them. As they stepped into the door, he stepped after and caught it before it slammed shut. Neither man seemed to be aware of his presence, for they were intent on the man at the counter.

"Hello, Sloan," Singer said softly. "Meet Abe Mixus."

The name must have meant something to Sloan, for he turned, his face gray. He held a baby's bottle that he was in the act of buying in his right hand. His eyes, quick and terror-stricken, went from one to the other. He was frightened, and puzzled, and he seemed to be fighting for self-control. "You in this squabble, Singer? I figured you to be outside of it."

Singer chuckled. "That's what I aim for folks to think."

Mixus, a lean, stooped man with yellow eyeballs and a thin-cheeked face, drew a paper from his pocket. "That's a quit-claim deed, Sloan," he said. "You can sign it an' save yourself trouble."

Sloan's face was gray. His eyes went to the deed and seemed to hold there, then, slowly, they lifted. "I can't do that. My wife's having a child in the next couple of days. I worked too hard on that place to give it up. I reckon I can't sign."

"I say you better." Mixus' voice was cold, level. The storekeeper had vanished, and the room was empty save for the three, and for Tom Kedrick, standing in the shadows near some hanging jeans and slickers. "I say you better sign because you don't own that prop'ty anyhow. Want to call me a liar?"

Sloan's face was gray and yet resolution seemed to

have overcome his immediate fear. He was a brave man, and Kedrick knew that whatever he said now, he would die. He spoke first.

"No, Abe," he said softly, "I'll call you a liar."

Mixus stiffened as if struck. He was a killer, and dangerous, but he was a smart, sure-thing killer, and he had believed himself alone but for Singer. Now somebody was behind him. He stood stockstill, then started to turn. Singer had fallen back against the wall, his eyes staring to locate Kedrick.

"It's Kedrick," he said. "The boss gunman."

Mixus scowled. "What's the matter?" he said irritably. "What yuh buttin' in for?"

"There's to be no more killing, Abe." Kedrick held his ground. "We're havin' a peace conference tomorrow. This killing is over."

"Got my orders," Mixus persisted. "You talk to Burwick."

There was a movement from Sloan, and he whirled on him. "You stand still!" he barked.

"You can go, Sloan," Kedrick said. "Get in your outfit an' tell McLennon that my word is good. You'd better stop thinking about him, Abe. You're in trouble, and I'm the trouble."

Mixus was confused. He knew Kedrick was ramrodding the gunmen for the company, and he was puzzled. Had he been about to do the wrong thing? But, no, he hadn't. "You fool!" His confusion burst into fury. "Keith tol' me to git him!"

"Shut up!" Singer yelled. "Damn it! You . . . !"

269

Abe Mixus was a cold-blooded killer and no heavy-weight mentally. Orders and counterorders had come to him and, worked up to such a killing pitch, he had been suddenly stopped in the middle of it and switched off into this back trail where he floundered hopelessly. Now Singer seemed to be turning on him, and he swung toward him, his teeth bared, his face vicious.

"Don't you tell me, you white-livered coyote!" he snarled.

One hand hung over a gun, and Singer, frightened, grabbed for his own gun. Instantly Mixus whipped out his .44 and flame stabbed at Singer. The renegade turned on his heel. His knees slowly buckled and he slid to the floor, his head against a sack of flour, blood welling from his mouth.

Mixus stared down at him, and then, slowly, he blinked, then blinked again. Awareness seemed to return to him, and his jittery nerves calmed. He stared down at Singer almost unbelieving. "Why, I . . . I . . . kilt Singer," he said.

"That's right." Kedrick was watching him, knowing now upon what a slender thread of irritation this man's muscles were poised. "What will Keith say to that?"

Cunning came over Abe's horse-like face. "Keith? What give you the idee he had anythin' to do with this?" he demanded.

Slowly, attracted by the shooting and made confident by its end, people were gathering in front of the

270

door. The storekeeper had come into the room and stood watching, his face drawn and frightened.

Tom Kedrick took a slow step back as Abe's eyes turned toward the front of the store. Putting the slickers between them, he moved on cat feet to the opening between the counters and slid through into the living quarters and out into the alley behind the store.

Crossing the street below the crowd, he wound up in front of the St. James, pausing there. Laredo Shad materialized beside him. "What happened?" he asked swiftly.

Kedrick explained. "I don't get it," he said. "Keith may be moving on his own, but Burwick was to hold off until we had our talk . . . and I know Keith didn't like that. He spoke right up about it."

"Ain't Singer supposed to be a settler?" Shad asked. "Won't this serve to get 'em all riled up? Who knew that Singer was with Keith an' the company?"

"You've got a point there," Kedrick said thoughtfully. "This may be the very thing that will blow the lid off. Both of them were mighty jumpy. It looked like they had Sloan marked because he was McLennon's relative. I sprung a surprise on them, an' Mixus just couldn't get himself located."

The crowd separated, then gathered in knots along the street to discuss the new event. Shad loitered there beside him, and was standing there when Loren Keith came up. He glanced sharply at Shad, then at Kedrick. "What's happened over there?"

He kept his eyes on Kedrick as he spoke, and Kedrick shrugged. "Shooting, I guess. Not unusual for Mustang from what I hear."

"Mixus was in there," Shad commented. "Wonder if he had a hand in it?"

Keith turned and looked at Laredo, suspicion in his eyes. "Who was shot?" he inquired, his eyes going from one to the other.

"Singer, they tell me," Shad said casually. "I reckon Mixus killed him."

"Mixus? Kill Singer?" Keith shook his head. "That's preposterous!"

"Don't know why," Laredo drawled. "Mixus come heah to fight, didn't he? An' ain't Singer one o' them settlers?"

Colonel Keith hesitated, his sharp, hard features a picture of doubt and uncertainty. Watching him, Kedrick was amused and pleased. The storekeeper had not seen him, and it was doubtful if anyone had but Mixus, the dead man, and the now missing Sloan.

What Abe Mixus would offer as an explanation for shooting Singer, Tom couldn't conceive, but a traitor had died, and the enemy was confounded. Little as it might mean in the long run, it was for the moment a good thing. The only fly in the ointment was the fact that Singer had been a squatter, and that few if any knew of his tie-up with Keith and the company.

Watching the crowds in the street, Tom Kedrick began to perceive a new element shaping itself. Public opinion was a force Burwick had not reckoned with, and the faces of the men talking in the streets were hard and bitter. These were mostly poor men who had made their own way or were engaged in making their way, and they resented the action of the company. Few had known Singer well, and those few had little use for the man, but the issue, from their viewpoint, was not a matter of personalities, but a matter of a bunch of hard-working men against the company, an organization largely of outsiders, seeking to profit from the work of local people. Furthermore, whatever Singer was, he was not a gunman and he was a local man. Abe Mixus was a known killer, a gunman whose gun was for hire.

Tom Kedrick nodded toward the street. "Well, Colonel," he said, "you'd better start thinking about that unless you want to stretch hemp. That bunch is sore."

Keith stared at them nervously, then nodded and hurried away toward headquarters. Shad watched him go, and turned toward Kedrick. "You know, we're sort of tied in with the company, an' I don't want to hang for 'em. Let's light a shuck out of here an' stick in the hills for a few days?"

"Can't. I've got to make that meeting with Burwick. But you might get out of town, anyway. Scout around and see what you can find of Goff and them . . . if they really left the country or not. Meet me at Chimney Rock about five tomorrow evening . . . make it later . . . about sundown."

Leaving Shad, Kedrick hurried to his room in the

St. James and bundled his gear together. He carried it down to the livery stable and saddled the Appaloosa. When that was done, he headed for headquarters, staying off the main street. Yet it was Connie Duane he wanted to see, and not Burwick or Keith.

There was no sign of any of them. Gunter was not around, and Burwick and Keith seemed to have vanished. Idling in the office, Tom heard a slight movement upstairs. He called out. Feet hurried along the floor above him, and then Connie was at the stair head. "Yes?" Recognizing him, she hurried down. "Is something wrong?"

Swiftly he explained, not holding anything back. "Nothing may come of it, although it wouldn't take much to start it, and they all know that the company gunmen are mostly out of town. Burwick, Keith, and your uncle must have lit out."

"Uncle John hasn't been around all day. I saw him at breakfast, and then he disappeared."

"I'll look around. Do you have a gun?" He shook his head then. "Don't much think you'll need it, most of them like you around here, and you've been pretty outspoken. But stay close to your room. The lid's going to blow off."

He turned away, but she called to him: "Tom?" He turned when he reached the door. He seemed to see pleading in her eyes. "Be careful, Tom."

Their eyes held for a long moment, and then he nodded. "I will if I . . . can."

He went out and paused on the steps. Burwick and

Keith might get out of the way, but whatever else Gunter might be, he was scarcely the man to leave his niece behind at a time of danger. Puzzled that he should be thus inconsistent, Kedrick paused and looked around him. The back street was bare and empty. The white, powdery dust lay thickly and had sifted into the foliage of the trees and shrubs.

Kedrick hitched his guns into place and walked slowly around the house. The stable lay behind it, but it was usually filled with horses. Now it seemed empty. He strode back, his spurs jingling a little and tiny puffs of dust rising from his boots as he walked. Once, nearly to the stable, he paused by a water trough and listened for noise from the town. It was quiet, altogether too quiet. He hesitated, worrying about Connie again, but then went on and into the wide door that gave entrance to the shadowed cool-ness of the stable.

The stalls were empty, all save one. He walked back, then paused. The chestnut was Gunter's horse, and his saddle lay nearby. Could he be somewhere around town? Kedrick considered that, then dismissed it. He removed his hat and wiped the band with his kerchief, then replaced it. His face was unusually thoughtful, and he walked to the far end of the stable, examining every stall as he walked back.

Nothing.

Puzzled, he stepped out into the bright glare of the sun, and heard no sound anywhere. He squinted his eyes around, then saw the ramshackle old building that had done duty for a stable before the present large one was built. He stared at it, and then turned in that direction. He had taken scarcely a step when he heard a rattle of hoofs, and swung swiftly around, half crouched, his hands wide.

Then he straightened. Sue Laine slid from her horse and ran to him. "Oh, I've found you, Tom!" she cried, catching him by the arms. "Tom, don't go to that meeting tomorrow. There's going to be trouble!"

"You mean, McLennon's framed something?"

"McLennon?" For an instant she was startled. "Oh, no! Not Mac!" Her expression changed. "Come home with me, Tom. Please do! Let them have this out and get it over with! Come home with me!"

"Why all this sudden worry about me?" He was sincerely puzzled. "We've met only once, and we seem to have different ideas about things."

"Don't stand there and argue! Tom, I mustn't be seen talking to you . . . not by either side. Come with me and get away from here until this is all over. I've seen Dornie, and he hates you, Tom. He hates you."

"He does, does he?" He patted her arm. "Run along home now. I've things to do here."

"Oh?" Her eyes hardened a little. "Is it that woman? That Duane girl? I've heard all about her, how beautiful she is, how . . . how she . . . what kind of girl is she?"

"She's a lovely person," he said gravely. "You'd like her, Sue."

Sue stiffened. "Would I? I wonder how much you

276

know about women, Tom? Or do you know anything about them? I could never like Connie Duane!" She shook his arm. "Come, if you're coming. I just heard this last night, and I can't . . . I won't see this happen."

"What? What's going to happen?"

She stamped her foot with impatience. "Oh, you fool, you! They plan to kill you, Tom! Now, come on!"

"Not now," he said quietly. "I've got to get this fight settled first, then maybe I'll ride your way. Now run along. I've got to look around."

Impatiently she turned and walked to her horse. In the saddle she glanced back at him. "If you change your mind. . . ."

"Not now," he repeated.

"Then be careful. Be careful, Tom."

He watched her go, then happened to glance toward the house. Connie Duane stood in the window, looking down at him, but as he looked up, she turned sharply away. He started for the house, then hesitated. There was nothing he could say now, nothing that would have any effect or do any good at all.

He started toward the front of the house again, then stopped. On an impulse he turned and walked swiftly back to the little old building and caught the latch. The door was weathered and gray. It creaked on rusty hinges and opened rheumatically. Inside, there was the musty odor of decay. Kedrick stood there for a minute watching the sunlight filter through the cob-webbed window and fall in a faint square upon the ancient straw that littered the earthen floor, and then he stepped forward, peering around the corner of the nearest stall.

John Gunter lay sprawled upon his face, his head pillowed upon one forearm, the back of his shirt covered with a dark, wide stain. Kedrick knelt beside him.

Connie's uncle had been stabbed in the back. Three powerful blows, from the look of the wounds, had been struck downward—evidently while he sat at a desk or table. He had been dead for several hours.

IX

Alton Burwick, for all his weight, sat his saddle easily and rode well. His horse was a blood bay, tall and long-limbed. He walked it alongside Tom Kedrick's Appaloosa, and from time to time he spurred it to a trot, then eased down. On this morning Burwick wore an ancient gray felt hat, torn at the flat crown, and a soiled handkerchief that concealed the greasy shirt collar. His shirt bulged over his belt, and he wore one gun, too high on his hip for easy use. His whiskers seemed neither to have grown nor been clipped. They were still a rough stubble of dirty, mixed gray. Yet he seemed unusually genial this morning.

"Great country, Kedrick! Country for a man to live

in! If this deal goes through, you should get yourself a ranch. I aim to."

"Not a bad idea." Kedrick rode with his right hand dangling. "I was talking about that yesterday, with Connie Duane."

The smile vanished from Burwick's face. "You talked to her yesterday? What time?"

"Afternoon." Kedrick let his voice become casual, yet he was alert to the change in Burwick's voice. Had Burwick murdered Gunter? Or had it been one of the squatters? With things as they were, it would be difficult or impossible to prove. "We had a long talk. She's a fine girl."

Burwick said nothing, but his lips tightened. The red cañon walls lifted high above them, for along here they were nearly five hundred feet above the bottom of Salt Creek. There was but little farther to go, he knew, and he was puzzled by Burwick's increased watchfulness. The man might suspect treachery, but he had said nothing to imply anything of the kind.

Tom's mind reverted to Sue's warning of the previous day—they intended to kill him—but who were "they"? She had not been specific in her warning except to say that he should not keep this rendezvous today. Kedrick turned the idea over in his mind, wondering if she were deliberately trying to prevent a settlement, or if she knew something and was genuinely worried.

Pit Laine, her gun-slinging brother, was one element in the situation he could not estimate. Laine had not been mentioned in any of the discussions and he seemed always just beyond reach, just out of sight, yet definitely in the background as was the mysterious rider of the mouse-colored horse. That whole story seemed fantastic, but Kedrick did not think Sue was inclined to fall for tall stories.

The cañon of Salt Creek widened out and several branch cañons opened into it. They left the creek bed and rode closer together to the towering cliffs, now all of seven hundred feet above the trail. They were heading south, and Burwick, mopping his sweating face from time to time with a dirty handkerchief, was no longer talking. Kedrick pushed back his hat and rolled a smoke. He had never seen Burwick so jittery before, and he was puzzled. Deliberately he had said nothing to any of the company about Gunter, although he had arranged with some of the townspeople to have the body moved. Tom was afraid it might precipitate the very trouble he was trying to end, and bring the fight into open battle. Moreover, he was not at all sure of why Gunter had been killed, or who had done it. That it could be retaliation for Singer's death was an answer to be considered, but it might have been done by either Keith or Burwick.

He drew up suddenly, for a horse had left recent tracks coming in alone from the northwest. Burwick followed his eyes, studying the tracks. "I've seen those tracks before," Tom Kedrick said. "Now whose horse is that?"

"We better step it up," Burwick said impatiently. "They'll be there before us."

They pushed on into the bright, still morning. The sky overhead was a vast blue dome scattered with fleecy puffballs of clouds, like bolts of cotton on the surface of a lake of pure blue. The red cliffs towered high on their left, and the valley on their right swept away in a vast, gently rolling panorama. Glancing off over this sagebrush-dotted valley, Tom knew that lost in the blue haze, some seven or eight miles away, was Malpais Arroyo and Sue Laine. Was she there this morning? Or was she riding somewhere? She was strangely attractive, that slim, dark-haired, dark-eyed girl with her lovely skin, soft despite the desert sun and desert wind. She had come to him, riding all that distance to bring him a warning of danger. Why? Was it simply that she feared for him? Was she in love with him? He dismissed that idea instantly, but continued to wonder. She was, despite her beauty, a hard, calculating girl, hating the country around, and wanting only to be free of it.

Heat waves danced out over the bottomland, and shadows gathered under the red wall. A dust devil lifted and danced weirdly across the desert, then lost itself among the thick antelope brush and the catclaw. Tom Kedrick mopped his brow and swung his horse farther east, the tall spire of Chimney Rock lifting in the distance, its heavier shouldered companion looming beside and beyond it.

"Look!" Burwick's voice held a note of triumph. "There they come!"

To the south, and still three or four miles off, they could see two riders heading toward Chimney Rock. At this distance they could not be distinguished, but their destination was obvious.

"Now that's fine!" Burwick beamed. "They'll be here right on time! Say . . ."—he glanced at his heavy gold watch—"tell you what. You'll be there a shade before them, so what say you wait for them while I have me a look at a ledge up in the cañon?"

In the shadow of the rock, Kedrick swung down. There was a small pool of water there. He let the Appaloosa drink and ground-hitched him deeper in the shade, near some grass. Then he walked back and, dropping to the ground, lit a smoke. He could see the two riders nearing now. One was on a fast-stepping chestnut, the other a dappled gray.

They rode up and swung down. The first man was Pete Slagle, the second a stranger who Kedrick had not seen before. "Where's McLennon?" he asked.

"He'll be along. He hadn't come in from the ranch, so I came on with Steelman here. He's a good man, an' anything he says goes with all of us. Bob'll be along later, though, if you have to have his word."

"Burwick came. He's over lookin' at a ledge he saw in the cañon over there."

The three men bunched and Steelman studied Kedrick. "Dai Reid tells me you're a good man, trust-worthy, he says."

"I aim to be." He drew a last drag on his cigarette and lifted his head to snap it out into the sand. For an instant, he stood poised, his face blank, then realization hit him. "Look out!" he yelled. "Hit the dirt!"

His voice was drowned in a roar of guns and something smashed him in the body even as he fell, then something else slugged him atop the head and a vast wave of blackness folded over him, pushing him down, down, down, deeper and deeper into a swirling darkness that closed in tightly around his body, around his throat. And then there was nothing, nothing at all.

Alton Burwick smiled and threw down his cigar. Calmly he swung into the saddle and rode toward the four men who were riding from behind a low parapet of rocks near Chimney Rock. As he rode up, they were standing, rifles in hand, staring toward the cluster of bloody figures sprawled on the ground in the shade. "Got 'em!" Shaw said. His eyes were hard. "That cleans it up, an' good!"

Fessenden, Clauson, and Poinsett stared at the bodies, saying nothing. Lee Goff walked toward them from his vantage point where he had awaited anyone who might have had a chance to escape. He stooped over the three.

Slagle was literally riddled with bullets, his body smashed and bloody. Off to one side lay Steelman, half the top of his head blown off. Captain Kedrick lay sprawled deeper in the shadow, his head bloody, and a dark stain on his body.

"Want I should finish 'em off for sure?" Poinsett asked.

"Finish what off?" Clauson sneered. "Look at 'em . . . shot to doll rags."

"What about Kedrick?" Fessenden asked. "He dead for sure?"

"Deader'n Columbus," Goff said.

"Hey!" Shaw interrupted. "This ain't McLennon! This here's that Joe Steelman!"

They gathered around. "Sure is!" Burwick swore viciously. "Now we're in trouble! If we don't get McLennon, we're. . . ." His voice trailed away as he looked up at Dornie Shaw. The soft brown eyes were bright and boyish.

"Why, boss," he said softly, dropping his cigarette and rubbing it out with his toe, "I reckon that's where I come in. Leave McLennon to me. I'll hunt him down before sun sets tomorrow."

"Want company?" Poinsett asked.

"Don't need it," Shaw said, "but come along. I hear this Bob McLennon used to be a frontier marshal. I never liked marshals no way."

They drifted to their horses, then moved slowly away. Dornie Shaw, Poinsett, and Goff toward the west and Bob McLennon. Alton Burwick, his eyes thoughtful, rode toward the east and Mustang and the others rode with him. Only Fessenden turned nervously and looked back. "We should have made sure they were dead."

"Ride back if you want," Clauson said. "They are dead all right. That Kedrick! I had no use for him. I aimed my shot right for his smart skull."

Afternoon drew on. The sun lowered, and after the sun came coolness. Somewhere a coyote lifted his howl of anguish to the wide, white moon and the desert lay still and quiet beneath the sky.

In the deeper shadow of towering Chimney Rock and its bulkier neighbor there was no movement. A coyote moved nearer, scented the blood, but with it there was the dreaded man smell. He whined anxiously and drew back, then trotted slowly off, turning only once to look back. The Appaloosa, still ground-hitched, walked along the grass toward the pool, then stopped, nostrils wide at the smell of blood.

Well down behind some rocks and brush, the shooting had only made it lift its head, then return to cropping the thick, green grass that grew in the tiny, sub-irrigated area around Chimney Rock. Nothing more moved. The coolness of the night stiffened the bodies of the men who lay sprawled there.

Ten miles north Laredo Shad, late for his meeting with Kedrick, limped along the trail, leading a badly lamed horse. Two hours before, the trail along an arroyo bank had given way, and the horse had fallen. The leg was not broken, but was badly injured. Shad swore bitterly and walked on, debating as he had for the past two hours on the advisability of camping for the night. But remembering that

Kedrick would be expecting him, he pushed on.

An hour later, still plodding and on blistered feet, he heard horse's hoofs and drew up, slipping his rifle into his hands. Then the rider materialized from the night, and he drew up, also. For a long minute no word was said, then Shad spoke. "Name yourself, pardner."

The other rider also held a gun. "Bob McLennon," he said. "Who are you?"

"Laredo Shad. My horse lamed himself. I'm headed for Chimney Rock. S'posed to meet Kedrick there." He stared at the rider. "Thought you was to be at the meetin'? What happened?"

"I didn't make it. Steelman an' Slagle went. I'm ridin' up here because they never come in."

"What?" Shad's exclamation was sharp. "McLennon, I was right afeared o' that. My bet is there's been dirty work. Nevah trusted that there Burwick, not no way."

McLennon studied the Texan, liking the man, but hesitant. "What's your brand read, Laredo? You a company man?"

Shad shook his head. "Well, now, it's like this. I come in here, drawin' warrior pay to do some gun slingin', but I'm a right uppity sort of a gent about some things. This here didn't size up right to me, nor to Kedrick, so we been figurin' on gettin' shut of the company. Kedrick only stayed on, hopin' he could make peace. I stayed along with him."

"Get up behind me," McLennon said. "My horse will carry double an' it ain't far."

X

His eyes were open a long time before realization came, and he was lying in a clean, orderly place with which he was totally unfamiliar. For a long time he lay there, searching his memory for clues to tie all this together. He was Captain Tom Kedrick—he had gone west from New Orleans—he had taken on a job—then he remembered. There had been a meeting at Chimney Rock and Steelman had come in place of McLennon, and then he had thrown his cigarette away and had seen those men behind the rocks, seen the sunlight flashing on their rifle barrels actually. He had yelled, and then dropped, but not fast enough. He had been hit in the head, and he had been hit in the body at least once.

How long ago was that? He turned his head and found himself in a square, stone room. One side of the room was native rock, and part of another side. The rest had been built up from loose stones gathered and shaped to fit. Besides the wide bed on which he lay, there was a table and a chair. He turned slightly, and the bed creaked. The door opened, and he looked up into the eyes of Connie Duane!

"Connie?" He was surprised. "Where is this place? What's happened?"

"You've been unconscious for days," she told him, coming to the bedside. "You have had a bad concussion and you lost a lot of blood before Laredo and Bob McLennon found you."

"What about the others?"

"Both of them are dead, and by all rights you should have been."

"But where are we? What is this place?"

"It's a cliff dwelling, a lonely one, and very ancient. It is high up in the side of the mountain called Thieving Rock. McLennon knew where it was, and he knew that, if word got out that you were alive, they would be out to complete the job at once, so they brought you here, McLennon did, with Shad."

"Are they still here?"

"Shad is. He hunts and goes to Yellow Butte for supplies, but he has to be very careful because it begins to look like they are beginning to get suspicious."

"McLennon?"

"He's dead, Tom. Dornie Shaw killed him. He went to Mustang to find a doctor for you, and encountered Dornie on the street. Bob was very fast, you know, but Dornie is incredible! He killed Bob before he could get a shot off."

"How did you get here?"

"Bob McLennon and Shad had talked about it, and also that Uncle John had been killed, so they came to me, and I came out here right away. I knew a little about nursing, but not much. Laredo has been wonderful, Tom, he's a true friend."

Kedrick nodded. "Who did the shooting? I thought it was Poinsett."

"He was one of them. I heard them talking about it but was not sure until later. Poinsett was there, Goff, Fessenden, Clauson, and Shaw."

"Anything else happened?"

"Too much. They burned Yellow Butte's saloon and livery stable, and they have driven almost half the people off the land. Their surveyors are on the land now, checking the survey they made previously. A handful of the squatters have drawn back into the mountains somewhere, under Pit Laine and that friend of yours, Dai Reid. They are trying to make a stand there."

"What about Sue?"

She looked at him quickly. "You liked her, didn't you? Well, Sue has taken up with Keith. They are together all the time. He's a big man now. They've brought in some more gunmen, and the Mixus boys are still here. Right now Alton Burwick and Loren Keith have this country right under their thumbs. In fact, they even called an election."

"An election?"

"Yes, and they counted the ballots themselves. Keith was elected mayor, and Fessenden is sheriff. Burwick stayed out of it, of course, and Dornie Shaw wouldn't take the sheriff's job."

"Looks like they've got everything their own way, doesn't it?" he mused. "So they don't know I'm alive."

"No. Shad went back there and dug three graves. He buried the other two, and then filled in the third grave and put a marker over it with your name on it."

"Good!" Kedrick was satisfied. He looked up at the girl. "And how do you get out here and back without them becoming curious?"

She flushed slightly. "I haven't been back, Tom. I stayed here with you. There was no chance of going back and forth. I just left everything and came away."

"How long before I can be up?"

"Not long, if you rest. And you've talked enough now."

Kedrick turned over the whole situation in his mind. There could be no more than a few days before the sale of the land would come off, and, if there was one thing that mattered, it was that the company not be permitted to profit from their crookedness. As he lay there resting, a plan began to form in his mind, and the details supplied themselves one by one as he considered it.

His guns hung on a nail driven into the wall close to his hand. His duffel, which he had brought away from the St. James, lay in the corner. It was almost dark before he completed his planning, and, when Laredo came in, he was ready for him.

"Cimarron?" Shad shook his head. "Bloomfield would be nearer. How's that?"

"Good!" Kedrick agreed. "Make it fast."

"That ain't worryin' me," Laredo said, rolling his

tobacco in his jaws. "They've been mighty suspicious lately. Suppose they trail this place down while I'm gone?"

"We'll have to chance that. Here's the message. Hurry it up!"

The sun was bright in the room when Connie came through the door with his breakfast. She turned, and her face went white. "Oh, you're up!"

He grinned shakily. "That's right. I've laid abed long enough. How long has it been?"

"Almost two weeks," she told him, "but you mustn't stand up. Sit down and rest."

There was a place by a window where he had a good view of the trail below. At his request Connie brought the Winchester to him, and her own rifle. He cleaned them both, oiled them carefully, and placed them beside his window. Then he checked his guns and returned them to their holsters, digging the two Welsh Navy pistols from his duffel and checking them, also.

Thoughtfully he considered. It was late to do anything now, but it was a wonder he had not thought of Ransome before. No more able legislator existed in Washington than Frederic Ransome, and the two had been brother officers in the War Between the States as well as friends in France during the Franco-Prussian War when Ransome had been there as an observer. If anybody could block the sale to the company, he could, even on such short notice. His telegram would be followed by a letter supplying all the details, and with that to go on Ransome might get something done. He was a popular and able young senator with good connections and an affable manner. Moreover, he was an excellent strategist. It would make all the difference in this situation.

The cliff-dwelling was built well back from the face of the cliff, and evidently constructed with an eye toward concealment as well as defense. They had called this, Connie told him, Thieving Rock long before the white man appeared, and the Indians who lived here had been notorious thieves. There was a spring, so water was not a worry, and there were supplies enough for immediate purposes.

Two days dragged slowly by, and on the morning of the third Kedrick was resuming his station by the window when he saw a rider coming into the narrow cañon below. The man was moving slowly and studying the ground as he came, although from time to time he paused and searched the area with careful eyes. Kedrick pushed himself up from his chair and, taking the Winchester, worked his way along the wall to the next room.

"Connie," he called softly. There was no reply, and after a minute he called a second time. Still no answer.

Worried now, he remembered she had said something about going down below to gather some squaw cabbage to add greens to their diet.

Back at the window, he studied the terrain care-

fully, and then his heart gave a leap, for Connie
Duane was gathering squaw cabbage from a niche in
the cañon wall, not fifty yards from the unknown
rider!

Lifting his rifle, Kedrick checked the range. It was
all of four hundred yards and a downhill shot. Carefully he sighted on the rider, then relaxed. He was
nearer the girl now, and a miss might ricochet and kill
Connie, for the cañon wall would throw any bullet he
fired back into the cañon itself and it might even ricochet several times in the close confines.

Yet, somehow, she had to be warned. If the rider
saw her tracks, he would find both the girl and the
hide-out. Suddenly the ears of his horse came up
sharply, and the rider stiffened warily and looked all
around. Carefully Kedrick drew a bead on the man
again. He hated to kill an unwarned man, but if necessary he would not hesitate.

Connie was standing straight now and appeared to
be listening. Tense in every fiber, Tom Kedrick
watched and waited. The two were now within fifty
feet of each other, although each was concealed by a
corner of rock and some desert growth including a
tall cottonwood and some cedars.

Still listening, both stood rigidly, and Kedrick
touched his lips with the tip of his tongue. His eyes
blurred with the strain, and he brushed his hand
across them.

The rider was swinging to the ground now, and he
had drawn a gun. Warily he stepped out from his

ground-hitched horse. Shifting his eyes to Connie, Tom saw the girl wave, and, lifting his hand, he waved back, then lifted the rifle. She waved a vigorous negation with her arm, and he relaxed, waiting.

Now the man was studying tracks in the sandy bottom of the wash, and, as he knelt, his eyes riveted upon the ground, a new element entered the picture. A flicker of movement caught the tail of Kedrick's eye, and, turning his head, he saw Laredo Shad riding into the scene. He glanced swiftly at the window and waved his hand. Then he moved forward and swung to the ground.

From his vantage point Kedrick could hear nothing, but he saw Laredo approach, making heavy going of it in the thick sand, and then, not a dozen yards from the man, he stopped. He must have spoken, for the strange rider stiffened as if shot, then slowly got to his feet. As he turned, Tom saw his face fully in the sunlight. It was Clauson!

What happened then was too fast for the eye to follow. Somebody must have spoken, but who did not matter. Clauson's gun was drawn, and he started to swing it up. Laredo Shad in a gunman's crouch flashed his right-hand gun. It sprang clear, froze for a long instant, and then just as Clauson fired, Shad fired—but a split second sooner!

Clauson staggered a step back, and Shad fired again. The outlaw went down slowly, and Laredo walked forward and stripped his gun belts from him, then from his horse he took his saddlebags, rifle, and ammunition. Gathering up the dead man, and, working with Connie's help, they tied him to the saddle, and then turned the horse loose with a slap on the hip.

Connie Duane's face was white when she came into the room. "You saw that?"

He nodded. "We didn't dare to let him go. If we had, we would all have been dead before noon tomorrow. Now"—he said with grim satisfaction—"they have something to think about!"

Shad grinned at him when he came in. "I didn't see that gun he had drawed," he said ruefully. "Had it layin' along his leg as he was crouched there. Might've got me."

He dropped the saddlebags. "Mite of grub," he said, "an' some shells. I reckon we can use 'em even though we have some. The message got off, an' so did the letter. Feller over to the telegraph office was askin' a powerful lot of questions. Seems like they've been hearin' about this scrap."

"Good! The more the better. We can stand it, but the company can't. Hear anything?"

"Uhn-huh. Somebody from outside the state is startin' a row about Gunter's death. I hear they have you marked for that. That is, the company is sayin' you did it."

Kedrick nodded. "They would try that. Well, in a couple of days I'll be out of here and then we'll see what can be done."

"You take some time," Shad said dubiously. "That passel o' thieves ain't goin' to find us. Although," he said suddenly, "I saw the tracks of that grulla day afore yestiddy, an' not far off."

The grulla again!

Two more days drifted by, and Tom Kedrick ventured down the trail and the ladders to the cañon below with Laredo and visited their horses concealed in a tiny glade not far away. The Appaloosa nickered and trotted toward him, and Kedrick grinned and scratched his chest. "How's it, boy? Ready to go places?"

"He's askin' for it," Shad said. He lighted a smoke and squinted his eyes at Kedrick. "What do you aim to do when you do move?"

"Ride around a little. I aim to see Pit Laine, an' then I'm goin' to start hunting up every mother's son that was in that dry-gulching. Especially," he added, "Dornie Shaw."

"He's bad," Laredo said quietly. "I nevah seen it, but you ask Connie. Shaw's chain lightnin'. She seen him kill Bob."

"So one of us dies," Kedrick said quietly. "I'd go willing enough to take him with me, an' a few others."

"That's it. He's a killer, but the old bull o' that woods is Alton Burwick, believe me, he is. Keith is just right-hand man for him, an' the fall guy if they need one. Burwick's the pizen-mean one."

With Connie they made their start three days later, and rode back trails beyond the rim to the hide-out Laine had established. It was Dai Reid himself who stopped them, and his eyes lighted up when he saw Kedrick.

"Ah, Tom!" His broad face beamed. "Like my own son, you are. We'd heard you were kilt dead."

Pit Laine was standing by the fire, and around him on the ground were a dozen men, most of whom Kedrick recognized. They sat up slowly as the three walked into the open space, and Pit turned. It was the first time Kedrick had seen him, and he was surprised. He was scarcely taller than his sister, but wide in the shoulders and slim in the hips. When he turned, he faced them squarely, and his eyes were sharp and bitter. This was a killing man, Kedrick decided, as dangerous in his own way as that pocket-size devil, Dornie Shaw.

"I'm Kedrick," he said, "and this is Connie Duane. I believe you know Shad."

"We know all of you." Laine watched them, his eyes alert and curious.

Quietly and concisely, Kedrick explained, and ended by saying: "So there it is. I've asked this friend of mine to start an investigation into the whole mess, and to block the sale until the truth is clear. Once the sale is blocked and that investigation started, they won't be with us long. They could get away with this only if they could keep it covered up, and they had a fair chance of doing that."

"So we wait and let them run off?" Laine demanded.

"No." Tom Kedrick shook his head decidedly. "We ride into Mustang . . . all of us. They have the mayor and the sheriff, but public opinion is largely on our side. Furthermore," he said quietly, "we ride in the minute they get the news the sale is blocked. Once that news is around town, they will have no friends. The band wagon riders will get off, and fast."

"There'll be shootin'," one old-timer opined.

"Some," Kedrick admitted, "but, if I have my way, there'll be more of hanging. There's killers in that town, the bunch that dry-gulched Steelman and Slagle. The man who killed Bob McLennon is the man I want."

Pit Laine turned. "I want him."

"Sorry, Laine. He killed Bob, an' Bob was only in town to get a doc for me. You may," he added, "get your chance, anyway."

"I'd like a shot at him my ownself," Laredo said quietly, "but somethin' else bothers me. Who's this grulla rider? Is he one of you?"

"Gets around plenty," the old-timer said, "but nobody ever sees him. I reckon he knows this here country better'n any of us. He must've been aroun' here for a long time."

"What's he want?" Shad wondered. "That don't figure."

Kedrick shrugged. "I'd like to know." He turned to Dai. "It's good to see you. I was afraid you'd had trouble."

"Trouble?" Dai smiled his wide smile. "It's trouble, you say? All my life there's been trouble, and where man is, there will be trouble to the end of time, if not of one kind, then another. But I take my trouble as it comes, bye." He drew deeply on his short-stemmed pipe and glanced at the scar around Kedrick's skull. "Looks like you'd a bit of it yourself. If you'd a less hard skull, you'd now be dead."

"I'd not have given a plugged *peso* for him when I saw him," Laredo said dryly. "The three of them lyin' there, bloody an' shot up. We thought for sure they was all dead. This one, he'd a hole through him, low down an' mean, an' that head of his looked like it had been smashed until we moved him. He was lucky as well as thick-skulled."

Morning found Laredo and Kedrick once more in the saddle. Connie Duane had stayed behind with some of the squatters' women. Together the two men were pushing on toward Mustang, but taking their time, for they had no desire to be seen or approached by any of the company riders.

"There's nothing much we can do," Kedrick agreed, "but I want to know the lay of the land in town. It's mighty important to be able to figure just what will happen when the news hits the place. Right now, everything is right for them. Alton Burwick and Loren Keith are better off than they ever were. Just size it up. They came in here with the land partly held by squatters, with a good claim on the land. That land they managed to get surveyed and they put in their claim to the best of it, posted the notices, and waited them out. If somebody hadn't seen one of those notices and read it, the whole sale might have gone through and nobody the wiser. Somebody did see it, and trouble started. They had two mighty able men to contend with, Slagle and McLennon. Well, both of them are dead now. And Steelman, another possible leader, is dead, too. So far as they are aware, nobody knows anything about the deaths of those men or who caused them. I was the one man they had learned they couldn't depend on, and they think I'm dead. John Gunter brought money into the deal, and he's dead and out of the picture completely. A few days more and the sale goes through, the land becomes theirs, and there isn't any organized opposition now. Pit Laine and his group will be named as outlaws, and hunted as such, and, believe me, once the land sale goes through, Keith will be hunting them with a posse of killers."

"Yeah," Laredo drawled, "they sure got it sewed up, looks like. But you're forgettin' one thing. You're forgettin' the girl, Connie Duane."

"What about her?"

"Look," Shad said, speaking around his cigarette, "she sloped out of town, right after McLennon was killed. They thought she had been talking to you before, and she told 'em off in the office, said she was gettin' her money out of it. All right, so suppose she asks for it, and they can't pay? Suppose," he added, "she begins to talk and tells what she knows, and they must figure it's plenty. She was Gunter's niece, and for all they knew he told her more than he did tell her."

"You mean they'll try to get hold of her?"

"What do you think? They'll try to get hold of her, or kill her."

Tom Kedrick's eyes narrowed. "She'll be safe with Laine," he said, but an element of doubt was in his voice. "That's a good crowd."

Shad shrugged. "Maybe. Don't forget that Singer was one of them, but he didn't hesitate to try to kill Sloan, or to point him out for Abe Mixus. He was bought off by the company, so maybe there are others."

At that very moment, in the office of the gray stone building, such a man sat opposite Alton Burwick, while Keith sat in a chair against the wall. The man's name was Hirst. His face was sallow, but determined. "I ain't lyin'!" he said flatly. "I rode all night to git here, slippin' out o' camp on the quiet. She rode in with that gunman, Laredo Shad, and this Kedrick *hombre*."

"Kedrick! Alive?" Keith sat forward, his face tense.

"Alive as you or me! Had him most of the hair clipped on one side of his head, an' a bad scar there. He sort of favored his side, too. Oh, he'd been shot all right, but he's ridin' now, believe me!"

The renegade had saved the worse until last. He smiled grimly at Burwick. "I can use some money, Mister Burwick," he said, "an' there's more I could tell you."

Burwick stared at him, his eyes glassy hard, then reached into a drawer and threw two gold eagles on the desk. "All right! What can you tell me?"

"Kedrick sent a message to some *hombre* in Washington name of Ransome. He's to block the sale of the land until there's a complete investigation."

"What?"

Keith came to his feet, his face ashen. This was beyond his calculations. When the idea had first been brought to his attention, it had seemed a very simple, easy way to turn a fast profit. He had excellent connections in Washington through his military career, and with Burwick managing things on the other end and Gunter with the money, it seemed impossible to beat it. He was sure to net a handsome profit, clear his business with Gunter and Burwick, then return East and live quietly on the profits. That it was a crooked deal did not disturb him, but that his friends in the East might learn of it!

"Ransome!" His voice was shocked. "Of all people!"

Frederic Ransome had served with him in the war, and their mutual relationship had been something less than friendly. There had been that episode by the bridge. He flushed at the thought of it, but Ransome knew, and Ransome would use it as a basis for judgment. Kedrick had no way of knowing just how fortunate his choice of Ransome had been.

"That does it!" He got to his feet. "Ransome will bust this wide open, and love it!"

He was frightened, and Burwick could see it. He sat there, his gross body filling the chair, wearing the same soiled shirt. His eyes followed Keith with irritation and contempt. Was Keith going bad on him now?

"Get back there," Burwick said to Hirst, "and keep me informed of the movements. Watch everything closely now, and don't miss a trick. You will be paid."

When Hirst had gone, Burwick turned to Keith and smiled with his fat lips. "So does it matter if they slow it up a little? Let them have their investigation. It will come too late."

"Too late?" Keith was incredulous. "With such witnesses against us as Kedrick, Shad, Connie, and the rest of them?"

"When the time comes," Burwick said quietly, "there will be no witnesses! Believe me, there won't be!"

XI

Keith turned on Burwick, puzzled by the sound of his voice. "What do you mean?" he asked.

Burwick chuckled and rolled his fat lips on his cigar. There was malice and some contempt in the look he gave Keith. How much better, he thought, had

303

Kedrick not been so namby-pamby. He was twice the man Keith was, for all the latter's commanding presence.

"Why," he said, "if there's no witnesses, there'll be no case. What can these people in town tell them? What they suspect? Suspicions won't stand in a court of law, nor with that committee. By the time they get here, this country will be peaceful and quiet, believe me."

"What do you want to do?" Keith demanded.

"Do? What is there to do? Get rid of Kedrick, Laredo Shad, and that girl. Then you'll take a posse and clean out that rat's nest back of the rim. Then who will they talk to? Gunter might have weakened, but he's dead. With the rest of them out of it. . . ."

"Not Connie?" Keith protested. "Not her! For heaven's sake, man!"

Burwick snorted and his lips twisted in an angry sneer as he heaved his bulk from the chair. "Yes, Connie!" he said. "Are you a complete fool, Keith? Or have you gone soft? That girl knows more than all of them. Suppose Gunter talked to her, and he most likely did? She'll know everything, everything, I tell you!"

He paced back across the room, measuring Keith. The fool! He was irritated and angry. The sort of men they made these days, a weak and sniveling crowd. Keith had played out his time. If he finished this job alive . . . well, Dornie didn't like Keith. Burwick chuckled suddenly. Dornie! Now there was a man! The way he had killed that Bob McLennon!

"Now get this. Get the boys together. Get Fessenden, Goff, Clauson, Poinsett, and the Mixus boys and send them out with Dornie. I want those three killed, you hear me? I want them dead before the week is out, and no bodies, understand?"

Keith touched his dry lips, his eyes haunted. He had bargained for nothing like this. It had all seemed such an easy profit, and only a few poverty-stricken squatters to prevent them from acquiring wealth in a matter of a few months. Everything had started off just as Burwick had suggested, everything had gone so well. Gunter had provided the money, and he had fronted for them in Washington. Uneasily now Keith realized that, if trouble was made over this, it would be he upon whom the blame would rest. Burwick somehow had been in the background in the East as much as he, Keith, had been kept in the background here. Yet it would be his guilt if anything went wrong. And with Ransome investigating everything had gone wrong.

He sighed deeply. Of course, Burwick was right. There was only one thing to do now. At least, Dornie and the others would not hesitate. Suddenly he remembered something.

"You mentioned Clauson. He's out of it, Burwick. Clauson came in last night tied to his horse. He had been dead for hours."

"What?" Burwick stopped his pacing and walked up to Keith. "You just remembered?" He held his face inches away from Keith's and glared. "Is anybody backtracking that horse? You blithering idiot! Clauson was dynamite with a gun, so if he's dead, shot, it has to be by one of three men, and you know it!"

Burwick's face was dark with passion and he wheeled and walked the length of the room, swearing in a low, violent voice that shocked Keith with its deep, underlying passion. When he turned again, Burwick's eyes were ugly with fury. "Can't you realize," he demanded hoarsely, "those men are dangerous? That every second they are alive we are in danger? You have seen Dornie in action. Well, believe me, I'd sooner have him after me than Kedrick. I know Kedrick! He's a former Army officer . . . that's what you're thinking all the time . . . an officer and a gentleman. But he's something more, do you hear? He's more. He's a gentleman . . . that's true enough, but the man's a fighter, he loves to fight! Under all the calmness and restraint there's a drive and power that Dornie Shaw could never equal. Dornie may be faster, and I think he is, but don't you forget for one instant that Kedrick won't be through until he's down, down and dead."

Loren Keith was shocked. In his year's association with Burwick he had never seen the man in a passion, and had never heard him speak with such obvious respect, and even—yes, even fear, of any man. What had Alton Burwick seen that he himself had not seen?

He stared at Burwick, puzzled and annoyed, but some of the man's feeling began to transmit itself to him, and he became distinctly uneasy. He bit his lips and watched Burwick pacing angrily.

"It's not only him, but it's Shad. That cool, thin-faced Texan. As for Laine . . ."—Burwick's eyes darkened—"he may be the worst of the lot. He thinks he has a personal stake in this."

"Personal?" Keith looked inquiringly at the older man. "What do you mean?"

Burwick dismissed the question with a gesture. "No matter. They must go, all of them, and right now." He turned and his eyes were cold. "Keith, you fronted us in Washington. If this thing goes wrong, you're the one who will pay. Now go out there and get busy. You've a little time, and you've the men. Get busy!"

When he had gone, Burwick dropped into his chair and stared blindly before him. It had gone too far to draw back even if he was so inclined, and he was not. The pity of it was that there had been no better men to be had than Keith and Gunter. Yet, everything could still go all right, for he would know how to meet any investigating committee, how to soft-pedal the trouble, turn it off into a mere cow-country quarrel of no moment and much exaggerated. The absence of any complaining witness would leave them helpless to proceed, and he could make it seem a mere teapot tempest. Keith was obviously afraid of Ransome. Well, he was not.

Burwick was still sitting there when the little caval-cade of horsemen streamed by, riding out of town on their blood trail. The number had been augmented, he noticed, by four new arrivals, all hard, desperate men. Even without Keith, they might do the job. He heaved himself to his feet and paced across the room, staring out the window. It went badly with him to see Connie Duane die, for he had plans for Connie—maybe. His eyes narrowed.

Out on the desert the wind stirred restlessly, and in the brassy sky above a lone buzzard circled as if aware of the creeping tension that was slowly gripping the country beneath it. Far to the north, toward Durango, a cattle buyer pulled his team to a halt and studied the sky. There was no hint of storm, yet he had felt uneasy ever since leaving town on his buying trip down to Yellow Butte and Mustang. There had been rumors of trouble down that way, but then there had been intermittent trouble there for some time, and he was not alarmed. Yet he was somehow uneasy, as though the very air carried a warning.

South of him, and below the rim, Laredo Shad and Kedrick turned aside from the Mustang trail and headed toward Yellow Butte. It was only a little way out of their line of travel, but both men wanted to see what had happened there. Yet, when they approached the town, aside from the blackened ruins of the destroyed buildings, everything seemed peaceful and still. Eight or ten families had moved back into the town and a few had never left. They looked up warily as the two riders drew near, then nodded a greeting.

They knew now that these two were siding with

them against the company, but hardship and struggle had wearied them, and they watched the two enter the settlement without excitement. The saloon had opened its doors in the large roomy office of the livery stable, and they went there now. A couple of men leaned on the bar, and both turned as they entered, greeted them, and returned to their conversation.

It was growing cool outside and the warmth of the room felt good. Both men stepped to the bar, and Kedrick ordered and paid. Shad toyed with his drink. He seemed uneasy, and finally he turned to Tom. "I don't like it," he said, low-voiced, "somehow or other Burwick is goin' to know about Ransome, an' he'll be in a sweat to get Connie out of the way, an' you an' me with her."

Kedrick agreed, for his own mind had been reading sign along the same trail. The only way out for the company now was to face the committee, if Ransome managed one, with a plausible tale and an accomplished fact, and then let them make the most of it.

"Burwick's a snake," Shad commented. "He'll never quit wigglin' until the sun goes down for the last time. Not that one. He's in this deep, an' he ain't the man to lose without a fight."

Horses' hoofs sounded on the road outside, and, when they turned, Pit Laine and Dai Reid were dismounting before the door. They walked in, and Laine looked at Kedrick, then moved on to the bar. Dai looked worried, but said nothing. After a minute,

Laine turned suddenly and went outside. "What's the matter?" Kedrick asked.

"It be worry, bye, and some of it shame, an' all for that sister o' his. Who would think it o' her? To go over to the other side? He's that shy about it, you would scarce believe. When a man looks at him, he thinks it's his sister they are thinkin' on, and how she sold out to that traitor to mankind, that rascal, Keith."

Kedrick shrugged. "Ambition and money do strange things. She has the makings of a woman, too."

Laine opened the door. "Better come out," he said, "we've got trouble."

They crowded outside. Men were hurrying toward the houses, their faces grave. "What is it?" Kedrick asked quickly.

"Burt Williams signaled from the top of the butte. There's riders coming from Mustang, a bunch of them."

As they looked, the small dark figure of a man appeared on the edge of the mesa once more. This time they saw his arm wave, once—two—three times, and continue until he had waved it six times. When he had completed, he gestured to the southeast. Then he signaled four more times from the southwest.

"Ten riders," Laine spat. "Well, we've got more than that here, but they aren't as salty as that crowd."

Burt Williams, favoring his broken arm, knelt behind a clump of brush on top of Yellow Butte and studied the approaching horsemen through the glass.

He knew all in this group by sight but not by favor. One by one he named them off to himself: "Keith, Dornie Shaw, Fessenden, an' Goff . . . Poinsett. No, that's not Poinsett. That's one of the Mixus boys. Yep, an' there's the other."

He swung his glass. The four riders, spaced well apart, were approaching at a steady pace. None of their faces was familiar. He stared at them a while, but finally placed only one of them, a badman from Durango who ran with Port Stockton and the Ketchum outfit. His name was Brokow.

Stirred, he searched the country all around the town for other movement, then turned back to the larger cavalcade of riders. Had he held on a certain high flat a minute longer he would have seen two unmounted men cross it at a stooping run and drop into the wide arroyo northeast of town. As it was, he had been studying the approaching group for several minutes before he realized that Poinsett was not among them. He was with neither group.

Worried, Williams squinted his eyes against the sun, wondering how he could apprise them of the danger down below, for the absence of Poinsett disturbed him. The man was without doubt one of the most vicious of the company killers, a bitter man, made malignant by some dark happening in his past, but filled now with a special sort of venom all his own. Williams would have worried even more had he seen Poinsett at that moment.

The attack had been planned carefully and with all

of Keith's skill. He surmised who they would be looking for, and hoped their watcher would overlook the absence of Poinsett, for it was he who Keith wanted in the right position for Poinsett was unquestionably the best of the lot with a rifle. At that moment, not two hundred yards from town, Poinsett and his companion, Alf Starrett, were hunkered down in a cluster of brush and boulders at one side of the arroyo. Poinsett had his Spencer .56 and was settling into position for his first shot. Starrett, with a fifteen-shot Henry .44, was a half dozen yards away.

Poinsett pulled out a huge silver watch and consulted it. "At half after two, he says. All right, that's when he'll get it." With utmost composure he began to roll a smoke, and Alf Starrett, a hard-faced and wizened little man, noticed that his fingers were steady as he sifted tobacco into the paper.

Bob McLennon had planned the defense of Yellow Butte, if such a defense became necessary, and, while Bob had been something of a hand with a gun, he definitely had not been a soldier or even an Indian fighter. Moreover, they had not expected an all-out battle for the town. Whatever the reason, he had committed a fatal error, for that pile of boulders and brush offered almost perfect concealment while affording complete coverage of the town, its one street, and the back as well as front of most of the buildings.

Keith had been quick to see this on his earlier visits to the town, and had planned to have Poinsett and Starrett approach the place some time before the main force moved in. In this, owing to their own experience, they had been successful.

Poinsett finished his cigarette and took up his rifle, then settled down to careful watching and checking of the time. He had his orders and they were explicit. He was to fire on the first target offered after half past two—and his first shot must kill.

Shad and Kedrick had returned to the saloon and Pit Laine was loitering in front. Dai had gone across the street. Laine was in a position out of sight of Poinsett, but the latter had glimpsed Dai. The Welshman, however, offered only a fleeting target and Poinsett did not consider firing. His chance came at once, however.

The door of one of the nearest shacks opened and a man came out. He wore a broad-brimmed gray hat, torn at the crown, and a large, checked shirt tucked into jeans supported by suspenders. He turned at the door and kissed his wife. Poinsett took careful aim with his .56, choosing as his target point the man's left suspender buckle. Taking a good, deep breath, he held it and squeezed off his shot.

The big bullet struck with a heavy thump. The man took a lurch sidewise, tried to straighten, then went down. His wife ran from the door, screaming. Up the street a door banged and two men ran into the street, staring. Starrett's first shot knocked the rifle from the hand of one, splintering the stock. Poinsett dropped his man, but the fellow began to drag himself, favoring one leg that even at this distance they

313

could see covered with a dark blotch at the knee.

Poinsett was a man without mercy. Coolly and carefully he squeezed off his second shot. The man stiffened, jerked spasmodically, and lay still.

"Missed my man," Alf said, apologetically, "but I ruint his shootin' iron."

Poinsett spat, his eyes cold. "Could happen to anybody," he said philosophically, "but I figured you burnt him anyways."

Within the saloon Kedrick had a glass half to his mouth when the shot boomed, followed almost at once by two more, their reports sounding almost as one.

"Blazes!" Shad whirled. "They ain't here yet?"

"They've been here," Kedrick said with quick realization. He swung to the door, glancing up the street. He saw the body of the last man to fall and, leaning out a bit, glimpsed the other. His lips tightened, for neither man was moving.

"Somebody is up the draw," he explained quickly. "He's got the street covered. Is there a back door?"

Kedrick dove for the door followed by the others as the bartender indicated the way, then caught up his shotgun. His pockets were already stuffed with shells. At the door Kedrick halted, then, flattened against the wall, stared up the draw. From here he could see the edge of the bunch of boulders and guessed the fire came from there. "Pinned down," he said. "They are up the draw."

Nobody moved. His memory for terrain served him

to good purpose now. Recalling the draw, he remembered that it was below the level of the town beyond that point, but right there the boulders offered a perfect firing point.

Scattered shots came from down the draw, and nobody spoke. All knew that the three men down there could not long withstand the attack and would fall back on the town to be taken in the rear.

XII

Kedrick made up his mind quickly. Defense of the town was now impossible and they would be wiped out or burned alive if they attempted to remain here. "Shad," he said quickly, "get across the street to Dai and Pit. Yell out to the others and get them to fall back, regardless of risk, to the cañon at the foot of Yellow Butte."

He took a step back and glanced at the trap door to the roof. The bartender saw the intent and shook his head. "You can't do it, boy. They'd git you from down the crick."

"I'm going to chance it. I think they are still too far off. If I can give you folks covering fire, you may make it."

"What about you?" Shad demanded.

"I'll make it. Get moving!"

Laredo wheeled and darted to the door, paused an instant, and lunged across the street. The bartender hesitated, swore softly, then followed. Kedrick picked up a bottle of the liquor and shoved it into his shirt, then jumped for the edge of the trap door, caught it, and pulled himself through into the small attic. Carefully he studied the situation.

Hot firing came from downstream, and evidently the killers were momentarily stopped there. He hoisted himself through, swung to the ridge of the roof, and carefully studied the boulders. Suddenly he caught a movement, and knew that what he had first believed to be a gray rock was actually a shirt. He took careful aim with his Winchester, then fired.

The gray shirt jumped, and a hand flew up, then fell loose. Instantly a Spencer boomed and a bullet tore a chunk from the ridgepole near his face and splattered him with splinters. Kedrick moved downroof a bit, then, catching the signal from the window across the street, he deliberately shoved his rifle and head up and fired four fast shots, then two more.

Ducking his head, he reloaded the Winchester. Another bullet smashed the ridgepole and then a searching fire began, the heavy slugs tearing through the roof about three to four inches below the top.

Kedrick slid down the roof, hesitated at the edge of the trap door, and, seeing a distant figure circling to get behind the men in the wash, he took careful aim and squeezed off his shot. It was all of five hundred yards, and he had only a small bit of darkness at which to aim.

The shot kicked up sand short of the mark by a foot or more as nearly as he could judge, and he knew he had missed, but the would-be sniper lost his taste for his circling movement and slid out of sight. Kedrick went down the trap door and dropped again into the livery stable office. Regretfully he glanced at the stock of whiskey, then picked up two more bottles and stuffed them into his pockets.

Hesitating only a second, he lunged across the way for the shelter of the livery stable. The Spencer boomed and he knew that the hidden marksmen had been awaiting this effort. He felt the shock of the bullet, staggered but kept going.

Reaching the livery stable, he felt the coldness of something on his stomach and glanced down. The bottle in his shirt had been broken by the bullet and he smelled to high heaven of good whiskey. Picking the glass out of his shirt, he located his horse's stall, led the Appaloosa out into the runway, and swung into the saddle.

The Spencer boomed again and again as he hit the road, riding hard, but he made it. The others cheered as he rode pell-mell through the cañon mouth and swung to the ground.

"This is no good," Laine said. "They can get behind us on the ridge."

Two men limped in from the draw, having withdrawn from boulder to boulder. Kedrick glanced around. There were fourteen men and women here who were on their feet. One man, he who had had the rifle knocked from his hand, had a shattered arm. The others were slightly wounded. Of them all, he had only seven men able to fight.

Quickly he gave directions for their retreat, then with Dai and Shad to hold the cañon mouth and cover them, they started back up the cañon.

Tom Kedrick measured his group thoughtfully. Of Laredo, Dai, and Laine, he had no doubts at all. Of these others, he could not be sure. Good men, some of them, and one or two were obviously frightened. Nobody complained, however, and one of the men whose face was pale took a wounded man's rifle and gave him a shoulder on which to lean. He led them to the crevasse, and down into it.

Amazed, they stared around. "What d'you know?" the bartender spat. "Been here nigh seven year an' never knowed o' this place!"

There were four horses with the group, and they brought them all into the cave. One of the men complained, but Kedrick turned on him. "There's water, but we may be glad to eat horse meat." The man swallowed and stared.

Laine pointed at Kedrick's shirt. "Man, you're bleedin'!"

Kedrick grinned. "That isn't blood, it's whiskey! They busted one of the bottles I brought away!"

Pit chuckled. "I'd 'most as soon it was blood," he said, "seems a waste of good likker."

The seven able men gathered near the escape end of the crevasse, and one of them grinned at Kedrick. "I wondered how you got away so slick. Is there another way out down here?"

He shook his head. "If there is, I don't know it. I

waited and got out through the cañon when it wasn't watched."

Laine's face was serious. "They could hold us here," he said anxiously. "We'd be stuck for sure."

Kedrick nodded. "I'm taking an extra canteen and some grub, then I'm going atop the butte to join Burt Williams. I'd like one man with me. From up there we can hold them off, I think."

"I'm your man," Laredo said quietly. "Wait'll I get my gear."

A rifle boomed, and then Dai Reid joined them. "They are comin' up," he said. He glanced at Kedrick. "One man dead in the boulders. I got the look of him by my glass. It was Alf Starrett. Poinsett was the other."

"Starrett was a skunk," Burnett, one of the settlers, said, "a low-down skunk. He kilt a man up Kansas way, an' a man disappeared from his outfit oncet that occasioned considerable doubt if he didn't git hisself another."

Kedrick turned to Pit Laine. "Looks like your show down here," he said. "Don't open fire until you have to, and don't fire even one shot unless it's needed. We'll be on top."

He led the way out of the crevasse and into the boulders and brush behind it. There was no sign of the attackers, and he surmised they were holed up, awaiting the arrival of some supporting fire from the rim back of the cañon.

Tom glanced up at the towering butte. It reared

itself all of a hundred and fifty feet above him and most of it totally without cover. As they waited, a rifle boomed high above them and there was a puff of dust in the cañon mouth. Burt Williams had opened up.

Yet their first move toward the butte drew fire, and Laredo drew back. "No chance. We'll have to wait until dark. You reckon they'll hit us before then?"

"If they do, they won't get far." Tom Kedrick hunkered well down among the slabs of rock at the foot of the Butte. "We've got us a good firing point right here." He rolled a smoke and lit up. "What are you planning when this is over, Shad? Do you plan to stay here?"

The tall Texan shrugged. "Ain't pondered it much. Reckon that will take care of itself. What you aimin' to do?"

"You know the Mogollons southwest of here? I figured I'd go down there and lay out a ranch for myself." He smoked thoughtfully. "Down in east Texas, before I came west, a fellow arrived there named Ikard. Had some white-faced cattle with him, and you should see 'em! Why, they have more beef on one sorry critter than three longhorns. I figured a man could get himself a few Hereford bulls and start a herd. Might even buy fifty or sixty head for a beginning, and let 'em mix with the longhorns if they like."

"I might go for somethin' like that," Laredo said quietly. "I always wanted to own a ranch. Fact is, I started one once, but had to git shut of it." He studied the end of his cigarette. "That was in the Texas Panhandle, a ways south of Tascosa. Quite a ways. It was rough country. I mean rough to live in, not rough like this is. Why, you could stand on your front step down thataway an' see straight ahead for three days! Coyotes? Why, you should see 'em! They'd whup a grizzly, or near it, an' make these coyotes around here look like jack rabbits." He stared down the cañon toward the mouth, his rifle across his knees. He did not look at Kedrick, but he commented casually: "We need luck, Cap'n, plenty of luck."

"Uhn-huh"—Kedrick's face was sober—"right now we're bottled up, and, believe me, Burwick will stop at nothing. I wonder who was on watch up the cañon? Or supposed to be?"

"Somebody said his name was Hirst. Sallow-faced *hombre*."

"We'll have to talk to him. Was he down below?"

"Come to think of it, he wasn't. He must have hid out back there."

"Or sold out. Remember Singer? He wouldn't have been the only one."

Laredo rubbed out the last of his cigarette. "They'll be makin' their play soon. You know, Kedrick, I'd as soon make a break for it, get a couple of horses, an' head for Mustang. When we go, we might as well take Keith an' that dirty Burwick with us."

Kedrick nodded in agreement, but he wasn't thinking of the men below. There were at least four good men aside from Shad, Laine, and Dai Reid. That left the numbers not too unevenly balanced. The fighting skill and numbers were slightly on the enemy's side, as they had at least twelve men when the battle opened, and they had lost Starrett. That made the odds eleven to eight unless they had moved up extra men, which was highly probable. Still, they were expecting defense, not an attack.

He studied the situation. Suddenly a dark figure loomed on the rim of the cañon some hundred and fifty yards off, and much higher. He lifted his rifle and fired even as both Shad and Kedrick threw down on him with rifles, firing instantly. The man vanished, but whether hit or not they could not tell.

Desultory firing began, and from time to time they caught glimpses of men advancing from the cañon mouth, but never in sight long enough to offer a target, and usually rising from the ground some distance from where they dropped. The afternoon was drawing on, however, and the sun was setting almost in the faces of the attackers, which made their aim uncertain and their movements hesitant. Several times Shad or Kedrick dusted the oncoming party, but got in no good shots. Twice a rifle boomed from the top of the butte, and once they heard a man cry out as though hit.

"You know, Laredo," Kedrick said suddenly, "it goes against the grain to back up for those coyotes. I'm taking this grub up to Burt, an', when I come back, we're going to move down that cañon and see how much stomach they've got for a good scrap."

Shad grinned, his eyes flickering with humor.

"That's ace high with me, podner," he said dryly. "I never was no hand for a hole, and the women are safe."

"All but one," Kedrick said, "that Missus Taggart who lives in that first house. Her husband got killed and she wouldn't leave."

"Yeah, heard one o' the womenfolks speak on it. That Taggart never had a chance. Good folks, those two."

Colonel Loren Keith stared gloomily at the towering mass of Yellow Butte. That man atop the butte had them pinned down. Now if they could just get up there. He thought of the men he had commanded in years past, and compared them with these outlaws. A pack of murderers. How had he got into this, anyway? Why couldn't a man know when he took a turning where it would lead him? It seemed so simple in the beginning to run off a bunch of one-gallused farmers and squatters.

Wealth—he had always wanted wealth, the money to pay his way in the circles where he wanted to travel, but somehow it had always eluded him, and this had seemed a wonderful chance. Bitterly he stared at the butte, and remembered the greasy edge of Burwick's shirt collar, and the malice in his eyes, Burwick who used men as he saw fit, and disposed of them when he was through.

In the beginning it hadn't seemed that way. His own commanding presence, his soldier's stride, his cold clarity of thought, all these left him despising Gunter as a mere businessman and Burwick as a conniving weakling. But then suddenly Burwick began to show his true self, and all ideas of controlling the whole show left Keith while he stared in shocked horror as the man unmasked. Alton Burwick was no dirty weakling, no mere ugly fat man, but a monster of evil, a man with a brain like a steel trap, stopping at nothing, and by his very depth of wickedness startling Keith into obedience.

Gunter had wanted to pull out. Only now would Keith admit even to himself the cause of Gunter's death, and he knew he would die as quickly. How many times had he not seen the malevolence in the eyes of Dornie Shaw, and well he knew how close Shaw stood to Burwick. In a sense, they were two of a kind.

His feeling of helplessness shocked and horrified Keith. He had always imagined himself a strong man, and had gone his way, domineering and supercilious. Now he saw himself as only a tool in the hands of a man he despised, yet unable to escape. Deep within him there was the hope that they still would pull their chestnuts out from the fire and take the enormous profit the deal promised.

One man stood large in his mind, one man drew all his anger, his hate and bitterness. That man was Tom Kedrick. From that first day Kedrick had made him seem a fool. Keith had endeavored to put Kedrick firmly in his place, speaking of his rank and his twelve years of service, and then Kedrick had calmly paraded such an array of military experience that few men could equal, and right before them all. He had not doubted Kedrick, for vaguely now he remembered some of the stories he had heard of the man. That the stories were true, and that Kedrick was a friend of Ransome's, infuriated him still more.

He stepped into the makeshift saloon and poured a drink, staring at it gloomily. Fessenden came in, Goff with him.

"We goin' to roust them out o' there, Colonel?" Goff asked. "It will be dark soon."

Keith tossed off his drink. "Yes, right away. Are the rest of them out there?"

"All but Poinsett. He'll be along."

Keith poured another stiff shot and tossed it off as quickly, then followed them into the street of Yellow Butte.

They were all gathered there but the Mixus boys who had followed along toward the cañon, and a couple of the newcomers who had circled to get on the cliff above and beyond the boulders and brush where the squatters had taken refuge. Poinsett was walking down the road in long strides. He was abreast of the first house when a woman stepped from the door. She was a square-built woman in a faded, blue cotton dress and man's shoes, run down at the heel. She held a double-barreled shotgun in her hands, and, as Poinsett drew abreast of her, she turned on him and fired both barrels, at point-blank range, and Poinsett took them right through the middle. Almost torn in two, he hit the ground, gasping once, his blood staining the gray gravel before their shocked eyes.

The woman turned on them, and they saw that she was no longer young. Her square face was red and a few strands of graying hair blew about her face. As she looked at them, her work-roughened hands still clutching the empty shotgun, she motioned at the fallen man in the faded, check shirt.

In that moment the fact that she was fat, growing old, and that her thick legs ended in the grotesque shoes seemed to vanish, and in the blue eyes were no tears, only her chin trembling a little as she said: "He was my man. Taggart never give me much, an' he never had it to give, but in his own way he loved me. You killed him . . . all of you. I wish I had more shells."

She turned her back on them and, without another glance, went into the house and closed the door behind her.

They stood in a grim half circle then, each man faced suddenly with the enormity of what they were doing and had done.

Lee Goff was the first to speak. He stood spraddle-legged, his thick, hard body bulging all his clothes, his blond hair bristling. "Anybody bothers that woman," he said, "I'll kill him."

XIII

Keith led his attack just before dusk and lost two men before they withdrew, but not before they learned of the hole. Dornie Shaw squatted behind the abutment formed by the end wall of the cañon where it opened on the plain near the arroyo. "That makes it easy," he said, "we still got dynamite."

Keith's head came up, and he saw Shaw staring at him, his eyes queerly alight.

"Or does that go against the grain, Colonel? About ten sticks of dynamite dropped into that crevasse an' Burwick will get what he wants . . . no bodies."

"If there's a cave back there," Keith objected, "they'd be buried alive!"

Nobody replied. Keith's eyes wandered around to the other men, but their eyes were on the ground; they were shunning responsibility for this, and only Shaw enjoyed it. Keith shuddered. What a fool he had been to get mixed up in this!

A horse's hoof struck stone, and as one man they looked up. Saddle leather creaked, although they could not see the horse. A spur jingled, and Alton Burwick stood among them.

Loren Keith straightened to his feet and briefly explained the situation. Burwick nodded from time to time, then added: "Use the dynamite. First thing in the morning. That should end it, once and for all." He drew a cigar from his pocket and bit off the end. "Had a wire. That committee is comin' out, all right. Take them a couple of weeks to get here, an' by that time folks should be over this an' talkin' about somethin' else. I'm figurin' a bonus for you all."

He turned back toward his horse, then stopped and, catching Dornie Shaw's eye, jerked his head.

Shaw got up from the fire and followed him, and Keith stared after them, his eyes bitter. Now what? Was he being left out of something else?

Beyond the edge of the firelight and beyond the reach of their ears, Burwick paused and let Shaw come up to him. "Nice work, Dornie," he said, "we make a pair, you an' me."

"Yeah." Dornie nodded. "An' sometimes I think a pair's enough."

"Well"—Burwick puffed on his cigar—"I need a good man to side me, an' Gunter's gone . . . at least."

"That company o' yours"—Dornie was almost whispering—"had too many partners, anyway."

"Uhn-huh," Burwick said quietly, "it still has."

"All right, then." Dornie hitched his guns into a firmer seating on his thighs. "I'll be in to see you in a couple of days at most."

Burwick turned and walked away, and Dornie saw him swing easily to the saddle, but it was all very indistinct in the darkness. He stayed where he was, watching the darkness and listening to the slow steps of the horse. They had a funny sound—a very funny sound. When he walked back to the campfire, he was whistling "Green Grow the Lilacs."

- - -

The attack came at daybreak and the company had mustered twenty men, of whom two carried packages of dynamite. This was to be the final blow, to wipe out the squatters, once and for all.

Shortly before the arrival of Burwick, Keith and Dornie Shaw with Fessenden accompanying them had made a careful reconnaissance of the cañon from the rim. What they found pleased them enormously. It was obvious, once the crevasse had been located, that not more than two men could fire from it at once, and there was plenty of cover from the scattered boulders. In fact, they could get within throwing distance without emerging in the open for more than a few seconds at a time. Much of the squatters' field of fire would be ruined by their proximity to the ground and the rising of the boulders before them.

The attack started well with all the men moving out, and they made twenty yards into the cañon, moving fast. Here, the great slabs fallen from the slope of Yellow Butte crowded them together. And there the attack stopped. It stopped abruptly, meeting a withering wall of rifle fire, at point-blank range!

Tom Kedrick knew a thing or two about fighting, and he knew full well that his hide-out would in the long run become a deathtrap. He put himself in Keith's place, and decided what that man would do. Then he had his eight men, carrying fourteen rifles, slip like Indians through the darkness to carefully selected firing positions far down the cañon from where Keith would be expecting them.

Five of the attackers died in that first burst of fire, and, as the gun hands broke for cover, two more went down, and one dragged himself to the camp of the previous night with a shattered kneecap. He found himself alone. The wife of Taggart had begun it—the mighty blast of rifle fire completed it. The company fighters got out of the cañon's mouth, and as one man they moved for their horses, Keith among them and glad to be going. Dornie Shaw watched him mount up, and swung up alongside him. Behind them, moving carefully as if they were perfectly disciplined troops, the defenders of the cañon moved down, firing as they came. A horse dropped, and a man crawled into the rocks, then jumped up and ran. Dai Reid swung wide of the group and started after him.

Another went down before they got away, and Kedrick turned to his group. "Get your horses, men. The women will be all right. This is a job that needs finishing now."

A quarter of a mile away, Brokow spotted a horse, standing alone, and started for it. As he arose from the rocks, a voice called out from behind: "A minute!"

Brokow turned. It was only one man approaching him, the Welshman, Dai Reid. He stared at the man's Spencer, remembering his own gun was empty. He backed up slowly, his eyes haunted. "My rifle's empty," he said, "an' I've lost my Colt."

"Drop the rifle, then," Dai said quietly. "This I've been wanting, for guns be not my way."

Brokow did not understand, but he dropped his rifle. He was a big man, hulking and considered powerful. He watched in amazement as Reid placed his Spencer carefully on the ground, and then his gun belt. With bowlegged strides, the shorter man started for Brokow.

The outlaw stared, then started forward to meet Dai. As they drew near, he swung. His rock-like fist smashed Dai Reid flush on the chin, and Reid blinked only, then lunged. Twice more Brokow swung, blows filled with smashing panic born of the lack of effect of that first punch. Dai seemed unable to avoid them, and both connected solidly, and then his huge, big-knuckled hand grasped Brokow's arm and jerked him near. The hand slipped to the back of his head and jerked Brokow's face down to meet the rising of the Welshman's head. Stars burst before Brokow's eyes, and he felt the bone go in his nose. He swung wildly, and then those big hands gripped his throat and squeezed till Brokow was dead. Then Dai Reid dropped the outlaw to the sand, and, turning, he walked away. He did not notice the horse that stood waiting. It was a grulla.

In the headlong flight that followed the débacle in the cañon's mouth, only Lee Goff had purpose. The hard-bitten Montana gunman had stared reality in the face when Taggart's wife turned on him. It was only coincidence that she so resembled his own mother, long since dead of overwork in rearing seven boys and five girls on a bleak Montana ranch. He headed directly for Yellow Butte and the Taggart home. He did not dismount, only he stopped by the door and knocked gently. It opened, and he faced Mrs. Taggart, her eyes red now, from weeping. "Ma'am," he said, "I guess I ain't much account, but this here's been too much. I'm driftin'. Will you take this here . . . as a favor to me?"

He shoved a thick roll of bills at her, his face flushing deep red. For an instant, she hesitated, and then she accepted the money with dignity. "Thanks, son. You're a good boy."

There's an old Mormon Trail across northern New Mexico into Colorado and Utah. Lee Goff's bald-faced sorrel stirred the dust on that road all the way across two states before its rider began to look the country over.

Behind him, had he known, Tom Kedrick was riding to Mustang. With him were Laredo Shad, Pit Laine, Dai Reid, Burt Williams, and the others. They made a tight, grim-faced little cavalcade, and they rode with their rifles across their saddle forks.

Due west of them, had they only known, another little drama was taking place, for the riders they followed were not all the riders who had abandoned the fight in the cañon. Two of them, Dornie Shaw and Colonel Loren Keith, had headed due west on their own. Both men had their own thoughts and their own ideas of what to do, and among other things Keith had decided that he had had enough. Whether the others knew it or not, they were through, and he was getting out of the country.

There was some money back there in Mustang, and, once he had that, he was going to mount up and head for California. Then let Ransome investigate. After a few years he would return to the East, and, if the subject ever came up, he would swear he had nothing to do with it, that he only represented them legally in the first steps of the venture.

What Dornie Shaw was thinking nobody ever guessed, and at this moment he had no thought at all in his mind. For his mind was not overly given to thought. He liked a few things, although he rarely drank, and seemed never to eat much. He liked a good horse and a woman with about the same degree of affection, and he had liked Sue Laine a good bit, but the woman who really fascinated him was Connie Duane, who never seemed aware that he was even alive. Most of all he liked a gun. When cornered or braced into a fight, he killed as naturally and simply as most men eat. He was a creature of destruction, pure and simple. Never in his life had he been faced with a man who made him doubt his skill, and never fought with anything but guns—and he vowed he never would.

The two rode rapidly and both were mounted well, so by the time Kedrick was leaving Yellow Butte and lining out for town, they reached the bank to Salt Creek Wash. Here Keith swung down to tighten his saddle cinch while his horse was drinking. After a moment, Dornie got down, too.

Absently Keith asked: "Well, Dornie, this breaks it, so where do you think you'll go now?"

"Why, Colonel," Shaw said softly, in his gentle boy's voice, "I don't know exactly where I'm goin', but this here's as far as you go."

It took a minute for the remark to sink in, and then Keith turned, his puzzled expression stiffening into blank horror, then fear. Dornie Shaw stood negligently watching him, his lips smiling a little, his eyes opaque and empty. The realization left Loren Keith icy cold. Dornie Shaw was going to kill him. He had been an utter fool ever to allow this to happen. Why had he left the others and come off with Shaw? Why hadn't he killed him long since, from behind if need be, for the man was like a mad dog. He was insane, completely insane.

"What's on your mind, Shaw?" Without realizing it, he spoke as he might to a subordinate. Shaw was not conscious of the tone. He was looking at Keith's belt line. The colonel, he reflected, had been taking on a little weight here lately. "Why, just what I say. You've come as far as your trail takes you, Colonel. I can't say I'm sorry."

"Burwick won't like this. We're two of the men on whom he relies."

"Uhn-huh, that's the way it was. It ain't now. Back yonder"—he jerked his head toward the butte—"he sort of implied he'd got hisself one too many partners." He shoved his hat back a little. "You want to try for your gun? It won't help you none, but you can try."

Keith was frightened. Every muscle within him seemed to have tightened until he could not move, yet he knew he was going to. But at the last, he had something to say, and it came from some deep inner conviction: "Kedrick will kill you, Dornie. He's going to win. He'll kill Burwick, too."

Suddenly he remembered something; it had been only a fleeting expression on Dornie Shaw's face, but, something. "Dornie?" he shot the word out with the force of desperation. "There behind you! The grulla!"

Shaw whirled, his face white, an almost animal-like fury on it. As he turned, Keith gasped hoarsely and triumphantly, and his gun swung up, but he had never coped with a fighter like Shaw. In the flashing instant that he whirled and found nothing behind him, Dornie hurled himself backward. The shot split wide the air where he had stood an instant before, and then Dornie himself fired from the ground. Fired once, then a second time.

Keith caught the bullet through the midsection, right where that extra weight had been gathering, and took the second one in the same place. He fell, half in the trickle of water that comprised Salt Creek. Feeding shells into his gun, Dornie Shaw stared down at the glazing eyes. "How did you know?" he asked sullenly. "How did you know?"

XIV

Fessenden rode well forward in the saddle, his great bulk carried easily with the movement of the horse. His wide face was somber with thought and distaste. Like the others, the wife of Taggart had affected him as nothing else could have. He was a hard man who had done more than his share of killing, but he had killed men ruthlessly, thoughtlessly, men in mortal combat where he himself might die as easily. Several times before he had hired his gun, but each time in cattle or sheep wars or struggles with equals, men as gun-wise as he himself. Never before had he actually joined in a move to rob men of their homes. Without conscience in the usual sense, he had it in this case, for the men who moved West, regardless of their brand, were largely men in search of homes. Before, he had thought little of their fight. Several times he had helped to drive nesters from cattle range, and to him that was just and logical, for cows needed grass and people lived on beef, and most of the range country wasn't suited to farming, anyway. But in this case there was a difference, he now realized, thinking of it for the first time. In this case men were not being driven off for cattle, but only for profit. To many, the line was a fine one to draw; to Fessenden and his like, once the matter was seen in its true light, that line became a gap, an enormous one.

Actually he rode in a state of shock. The victory

Keith had wanted seemed so near. The taking of the few left in the cañon had seemed simple. His qualms against the use of dynamite he had shrugged off, if uncomfortably. Yet he had gone into the cañon with the others to get the thing over with, to get his money, and get out. And then, long before they expected it, came that smashing, thunderous volley, made more crashing by the close cañon walls, more destructive by the way the attackers were channeled by the boulders.

Shock started the panic, and distaste for the whole affair kept some of them, at least, on the move. Yet it was hard to believe that Clauson and Poinsett were dead, that Brokow had vanished, that Lee Goff was gone. For alone of the group, Goff had told Fessenden he was leaving. He had not needed to tell him why.

Behind him rode the Mixus boys, somber with disappointment at the failure of the attack. They had no qualms about killing, and no lines to draw even at the killing of women. They were in no true sense fighting men; they were butchers. Yet even they realized the change that had come over the group. What had become of Brokow or Goff they did not know, only that disintegration had set in, and these men had turned into a snarling pack of wolves, venting their fury and their hatred on each other.

Mustang was quiet when they rode into town. It was the quiet before the storm, and the town, like that cattle buyer who had turned back to Durango, sensed the coming fury of battle. No women were on the street, and only a few hardy souls loitered at the bars or card tables. The chairs before the St. James were deserted, and Clay Allison had ridden back to his home ranch, drunk and ugly.

An almost Sunday peace lay over the town when Fessenden drew up before the Mustang Saloon and swung down from his weary horse. Slapping his hat against his leg to beat off the dust, Fessenden stood like a great, shaggy bull and surveyed the quiet of the street. He was too knowing a Western man not to recognize the symptoms of disaster. Clapping his hat all awry upon his shaggy head, he shoved his bulk through the doors and moved to the bar.

"Rye," he said, his voice booming in the cavernous interior. His eyes glinted around the room, then back to the bartender.

That worthy could no longer restrain his curiosity. "What's happened?" he asked, swallowing.

A glint of irony came into the hard eyes of the gunman. "Them squatters squatted there for keeps," he said wryly, "an' they showed us they aim to stay put." He tossed off his drink. "All hell busted loose." Briefly he explained. "You'd 'a' figured there was a thousand men in that neck of the rocks when they opened up. The thing that did it was the unexpectedness of it, like steppin' on a step in the dark when it ain't there." He poured another drink. "It was that Kedrick," he said grimly. "When I seen him shift to the other side, I should've lit a shuck."

"What about Keith?"

"He won't be back."

They turned at the new voice, and saw Dornie Shaw standing in the doorway, smiling. Still smiling, he walked in and leaned against the bar. "Keith won't be back," he said. "He went for his gun out on Salt Creek."

The news fell into a silent room. A man at a table shifted his feet and a chair creaked. Fessenden wet his lips and downed his second drink. He was getting out of town, but fast.

"Seen that girl come in, short time back," the bartender said suddenly, "that Duane girl. Thought she'd gone over to the other side."

Dornie's head lifted and his eyes brightened, then shadowed. He downed his own drink and walked jauntily to the door. "Stick around, Fess. I'll be back." He grinned. "I'll collect for both of us from the old man."

The bartender looked at Fessenden. "Reckon he'll bring it if he does?"

The big gunman nodded absently. "Sure! He's no thief! Why, that kid never stole a thing in his life. He doesn't believe in it. An' he won't lie or swear . . . but he'll shoot the heart out of you an' smile right in your face while he's doing it."

The show had folded. The roundup was over. There was nothing to do now but light out. Fessenden knew he should go, but a queer apathy had settled over him, and he ordered another drink, letting the bartender pour it. The liquor he drank seemed now to fall into a cavern without bottom, having no effect.

On the outskirts of town, Tom Kedrick reined in. "We'll keep together," he said quietly. "We want Keith, Shaw, Burwick, the Mixus boys, and Fessenden. There are about four others that you will know that I don't know by name. Let's work fast and make no mistakes. Pit, you take Dai and two men and go up the left side of the street, take no chances. Arrest them if you can, we'll try them, and"—his face was grim—"if we find them guilty, they'll have just two sentences . . . leave the country or hang. The Mixus boys and Shaw," he said, "will hang. They've done murder."

He turned in his saddle and glanced at the tall Texan. "Come on, Shad," he said, "we'll take two men and the right side of the street, which means the livery stable, the Saint James, and the Mustang." Kedrick glanced over at Laine. "Pit," he said, "if you run into Allison or Ketchum, better leave 'em alone. We don't want 'em."

Laine's face was grave. "I ain't huntin' 'em," he said grimly, "but if they want it, they can have it."

The parties rode into town and swung down on their respective sides of the street. Laredo grinned at Kedrick, but his eyes were sober. "Nobody wants to cross Laine today," he said quietly. "The man's in a killin' mood. It's his sister."

"Wonder what will happen when they meet?"

"I hope they don't," Shad said. "She's a right pretty sort of gal, only money crazy."

The two men with them stood hesitantly, waiting for orders. Both were farmers. One carried a Spencer .56, the other a shotgun. Shad glanced at them. "Let these *hombres* cover the street, Tom," he suggested. "You take the Saint James, an' I'll take the stable."

Kedrick hesitated. "All right," he agreed finally. "But take no chances, boy."

Laredo grinned and waved a negligent hand and walked through the wide door of the stable. Inside, he paused, cold and seemingly careless, actually as poised and deadly as a coiled rattler. He had already seen Abe Mixus's sorrel pony and guessed the two dry-gulchers were in town. He walked on a step and saw the barrel of a rifle push through the hay.

He lunged right and dove into a stall, drawing his gun as he went, and ran full tilt into the other Mixus! Their bodies smashed together, and Mixus, caught off balance, went down and rolled over. He came up, clawing for a gun. Laredo kicked the gun from under his hand and sent it spinning into the wide-open space between the rows of stalls.

With a kind of whining cry, Bean Mixus sprang after it, slid to his knees, and got up, turning. Laredo Shad stood, tall and dark, just within the stall, and, as Mixus turned like a rat cornered and swung his gun around, Laredo fired, his two shots slamming loudly in the stillness of the huge barn. Bean Mixus fell dead.

The rifle bellowed and a shot ripped the stall stanchion near Laredo's head. He lunged into the open, firing twice more at the stack of straw. The rifle jerked, then thundered again, but the shot went wild. Laredo dove under the loft where Abe Mixus was concealed, and fired two more shots through the roof over his head where he guessed the killer would be lying.

Switching his guns, he holstered the empty one and waited. The roof creaked some distance away, and he began to stalk the escaping Mixus, slipping from stall to stall. Suddenly a back door creaked and a broad path of light shot into the darkness of the stable. Laredo lunged to follow—too late.

The farmer outside with the shotgun was the man Sloan. As Abe Mixus lunged through the door to escape, they came face to face, at no more than twenty feet of distance. Abe had his rifle at his hip, and he fired. The shot ripped through the water trough beside Sloan, and the farmer squeezed off the left-hand barrel of his shotgun. The solid core of shot hit Mixus in the shoulder and neck, knocking him back against the side of the door, his neck and shoulder a mass of blood that seemed to well from a huge wound. He thought to get his gun up, but Sloan stepped around, remembering Bob McLennon's death and the deaths of Steelman and Slagle. The other barrel thundered and a sharp blast of flame stabbed at Abe Mixus. Smashed and dead, the killer sagged against the doorjamb, his old hat falling free, his face pillowed in the gray, blood-mixed dust.

Silence hung heavily in the wake of the shots. Into

that silence Laredo Shad spoke. "Hold it, Sloan!" He stepped through the door, taking no glance at the fallen man. "The other one won't hang, either," he said. "They were both inside."

The two men drew aside, Sloan's face gray and sick. He had never killed a man before, and wanted never to again. He tried to roll a smoke, but his fingers trembled. Shad took the paper and tobacco from him and rolled it. The farmer looked up shamefacedly. "Guess I'm yaller," he said. "That sort of got me."

The Texan looked at him gloomily. "Let's hope it always does," he said. He handed him the cigarette. "Try this," he told him. "It will make you feel better. Wonder how Kedrick's comin'?"

"Ain't heard nothin'!"

Pit Laine stood in a door across the street. "Everythin' all right?" he called.

"Yeah," the other farmer called back, "on'y you don't hafta look for the Mixus boys no more! They ain't gonna be around."

Captain Tom Kedrick had walked up the street and turned into the door of the St. James Hotel. The wide lobby was still, a hollow shell smelling faintly of old tobacco fumes and leather. The wrinkled clerk looked up and shook his head. "Quiet today," he said. "Nobody around. Ain't been no shootin' in days."

Guns thundered from down the street, then again and again, then silence, and the two solid blasts of the shotgun. Both men listened, and no further sound came. A moment later Pit Laine called out and the farmer answered. The clerk nodded. "Same town," he said. "Last couple of days I been wonderin' if I wasn't back in Ohio. Awful quiet lately," he said, "awful quiet."

Tom Kedrick walked down the hall and out the back door. He went down the weathered steps and stopped on the grass behind the building. There was an old, rusty pump there, and the sun was hot on the backs of the buildings. He walked over to the pump and worked the handle. It protested, whining and groaning at the unaccustomed work, and finally, despairing of rest, threw up a thick core of water that splashed in the wooden tub. When he had pumped for several minutes, Kedrick held the gourd dipper under the pump and let it fill. The water was clear and very cold. He drank greedily, rested, then drank again.

Far up the backs of the buildings at the opposite end of town, a man was swinging an axe. Kedrick could see the flash of light on the blade, and see the axe strike home, and a moment later the sound would come to him. He watched, then wiped the back of his hand across his mouth, and started along in back of the buildings toward the Mustang.

He moved with extreme care, going steadily, yet with every sense alert. He wore his .44 Russians and liked the feel of them, ready in his hands. The back door of the Mustang was long unpainted and blistered by many hot suns. He glanced at the hinges and saw they were rusty. The door would squeak. Then he saw the outside stair leading to the second floor, and, turning, he mounted the stairs on tiptoe, easing through that door, and walking down the hall.

In the saloon below, Fessenden had eliminated half a bottle of whiskey without destroying the deadening sense of futility that had come over him. He picked up a stack of cards and riffled them skillfully through his fingers, and there was no lack of deftness there. Whatever effect the whiskey had had, it was not on his hands. Irritated, he slammed the cards down and stared at the bartender. "Wish Dornie'd get back," he said for the tenth time. "I want to leave this town. She don't feel right today."

He had heard the shots down the street, but had not moved from the bar. "Some drunk cowhand," he said irritably.

"You better look," the bartender suggested, hoping for no fights in the saloon. "It might be some of your outfit."

"I got no outfit," Fess replied shortly. "I'm fed up. That stunt out there to Yeller Butte drove me off that range. I'll have no more of it."

He heard the footsteps coming down the hall from upstairs and listened to their even cadence. He glanced up, grinning. "Sounds like an Army man. Listen!"

Realization of what he had said came over him, and the grin left his face. He straightened, resting his palms on the bar. For a long moment, he stared into the bartender's eyes. "I knew it! I knew that *hombre* would. . . ." He tossed off his drink. "Aw, I didn't want to leave town, anyway!"

He turned, moving back from the bar. He stood, spraddle-legged, like a huge grizzly, his big hands swinging at his hips, his eyes glinting upward at the balcony and the hall that gave onto it. The steps ceased, and Tom Kedrick stood there, staring down at him.

Neither man spoke for a full minute, while suspense gripped the watchers, and then it was Fessenden who broke the silence. "You lookin' for me, Kedrick?"

"For any of your crowd. Where's Shaw? And Keith?"

"Keith's dead. Shaw killed him back up on the Salt after you whipped us in the cañon. I dunno where he is now."

Silence fell once more and the two men studied each other. "You were among them at Chimney Rock, Fessenden," Kedrick said. "That was an ambush . . . dry-gulcher's stunt, Fess." Kedrick took another step forward, then side-stepped down the first step of the stairs which ran along the back wall until about six steps from the bottom, then, after crossing the landing, came down facing the room.

Fessenden stood there, swaying slightly on his thick, muscular legs, his brutal jaw and head thrust forward. "Aw, hell!" he said, and grabbed iron.

His guns fairly leaped from their holsters, spouting flame. A bullet smashed the top of the newel post at

346

the head of the stairs, then ricocheted into the wall; another punctured a hole just behind Kedrick's shoulder. Tom Kedrick stepped down another step, then fired. His bullet turned Fessenden, and Kedrick ran lightly down four steps while Fessenden smashed two shots at him.

Kedrick dove headlong for the landing, brought up hard against the wall, and smashed another shot at the big man. It knocked a leg from under him, and he rolled over on his feet, colliding with the bar.

He had been hit twice, but he was cold sober and deadly. He braced himself and, with his left hand clinging to the bar, lifted his right and thumbed back the hammer. Kedrick fired two quick shots with his left gun. One ripped a furrow down the bar and hit Fessenden below the breast bone, a jagged, tearing piece of metal when it struck.

Fessenden fired again, but the bullet went wild, and his sixth shot was fired in desperation as he swung up his left hand gun, dropping the right into his holster. Taking his time, feeling his life's blood running out of him, he braced himself there and took the gun over into his right hand. He was deliberate and calm. "Pour me a drink," he said.

The bartender, lying flat on his face behind the bar, made no move. Tom Kedrick stood on the edge of the landing now, staring at Fessenden. The big gunman had been hit three times, through the shoulder, the leg, and the chest, and he still stood there, gun in hand, ponderous and invulnerable.

The gun came up and Fessenden seemed to lean forward with it. "I wish you was Dornie," he said.

Kedrick triggered. The shot nailed Fessenden through the chest again. The big man took a fast step back, then another. His gun slipped from his hand, and he grabbed a glass standing on the bar. "Gimme a drink!" he demanded. Blood bubbled at his lips.

Tom Kedrick came down the steps, his gun ready in his hand, and walked toward Fessenden. Holding his gun level and low down with his right hand, Kedrick picked up the bottle with his left and filled the empty glass. Then he pulled over another empty glass and poured one for himself.

Fessenden stared at him. "You're a good man, Kedrick," he said, shaping the words patiently. "I'm a good man, too . . . on the wrong side."

"I'll drink to that." Kedrick lifted his glass, they clicked them, and Fessenden grinned crookedly over his.

"You watch that Dornie," he advised, "he's a rattler . . . mean." The words stumbled from his mouth and he frowned, lifting the glass. He downed his drink, choked on it, and started to hold out a big hand to Kedrick, then fell flat on his face. Holstering his gun, Tom Kedrick leaned over and gripped the big right hand. Fessenden grinned and died.

XV

Connie Duane headed for Mustang only a short time after the survivors of the fight at Yellow Butte began to arrive. Restless, after leaving the men who were returning to the squatters' town, she had begun to think of what lay ahead, of Fred Ransome and the impending investigation, and of her uncle's part in it. All his papers as well as many of her own remained under lock in the gray stone house in Mustang, but if she was to get her own money back from Burwick, or was to clear any part of the blame from her uncle, she knew it must be done with those papers. She struck the old Mormon Trail and headed south. She was on that trail when the sun lifted, and she heard the distant sound of shots.

Turning from the trail, she reined her horse into the bed of Salt Creek and rode south, passing the point where only a short time later Loren Keith was to meet his death at the hands of Dornie Shaw. Once in Mustang she believed she would be safe, and she doubted if anyone would be in the stone house unless it was Burwick, and she knew that he rarely left his chair.

Arriving in Mustang, she rode quickly up the street, then cut over behind the stone house and dismounted. She went into the house through the back door and went very quietly. Actually she need not have bothered, for Alton Burwick was not there. Making her way up the old stairs, she unlocked the door to the apartment she had shared with her uncle, and closed the door behind her.

Nothing seemed to have been disturbed. The blinds were drawn as she had left them and the room was still. A little dust had collected, and the light filtering in around the blinds showed it to her. Going to her trunk, she opened it and got out the ironbound box in which she carried her own papers. It was intact, and showed no evidence of having been tampered with. From the bottom of the trunk she took an old purse in which there were two dozen gold eagles, and these she changed to the purse she was now carrying.

Among other things there was an old pistol there, a huge, cumbersome thing. This she got out and laid on the table beside her. Then she found a Derringer seven-shot .22 caliber pistol her father had given her several years before he died, and she put it in the pocket of her dress.

Hurrying across the room, she went into the next room and began to go through her uncle's desk, working swiftly and surely. Most of his papers were readily available, and apparently nobody had made any effort to go through them, probably believing they contained nothing of consequence or that there would be plenty of time later. She was busy at this when she heard a horse walk by the house and stop near the back steps.

Instantly she stopped what she was doing and stood erect. The window here was partly open and she could hear the saddle creak very gently as whoever it was swung down. Then a spur jingled, and there was a step below, then silence.

"So? It's you."

Startled by the voice, Connie turned. Sue Laine stood behind her, staring with wide eyes. "Yes," Connie replied, "I came for some things of mine. You're Sue, aren't you?"

Without replying to the question, the girl nodded her head toward the window. "Who was that? Did you see?"

"No. It was a man."

"Maybe Loren has come back." Sue studied her, unsmiling. "How are they out there? Are they all right? I mean . . . did you see Pit?"

"Yes. He's unhappy about you."

Sue Laine flushed, but her chin lifted proudly. "I suppose he is, but what did he expect? That I was going to live all my life out there in that awful desert? I'm sick of it! Sick of it, I tell you!"

Connie smiled. "That's strange. I love it. I love it, and every minute I'm there, I love it more. I'd like to spend my life here, and I believe I will."

"With Tom Kedrick?"

Sue's jealousy flashed in her eyes, yet there was curiosity, too. Connie noticed how the other girl studied her clothes, her face.

"Why . . . I . . . where did you ever get that idea?"

"From looking at him. What girl wouldn't want him? Anyway, he's the best of the lot."

"I thought you liked Colonel Keith?"

Sue's face flushed again. "I . . . I . . . thought I did, too. Only part of it was because Tom Kedrick wouldn't notice me . . . and because I wanted to get away from here, from the desert. But since then . . . I guess Pit hates me."

"No brother really hates his sister, I think. He'd be glad to see you back with him."

"You don't know him. If it had been anybody but someone associated with Alton Burwick, why. . . ."

"You mean, you knew Burwick before?"

"Knew him?" Sue stared at her. "Didn't you know? Didn't he tell you? He was our stepfather."

"Alton Burwick?" Connie stared in amazement.

"Yes, and we always suspected that he had killed our father. We never knew, but my mother suspected later, too, for she took us and ran away from him. He came after us. We never knew what happened to mother. She went off one night for something and never came back, and we were reared by a family who just took us in."

A board creaked in the hall, and both girls were suddenly still, listening.

Guns thundered from the street of the town, and both girls stared at each other, holding their breath. There was a brief silence, then a further spattering of shots. Then the door opened very gently and Dornie Shaw stood there, facing the two girls.

He seemed startled at finding the girls together, and looked from one to the other, his brown eyes bright, but now confused. Then he centered his eyes on Sue

Laine. "You better get out," he said. "Keith's dead."

"Dead?" Sue gasped. "They . . . they killed him?"

"No, I did. Up on the Salt. He drew on me."

"Keith . . . dead." Sue was shocked.

"What about the others? Where are they?" Connie asked quickly.

Dornie turned his head sharply around and looked hard at her, a curious, prying gaze as if he did not quite know what to make of her. "Some of 'em are dead," he said matter-of-factly. "They whupped us. It was that Kedrick"—he spoke without emotion or shadow of prejudice as though completely indifferent—"he had 'em set for us an' they mowed us down." He jerked his head toward the street. "I guess they are finishin' up now. The Mixus boys an' Fessenden are down there."

"They'll be coming here," Connie said with conviction. "This is the next place."

"I reckon." He seemed indifferent to that, too. "Kedrick'll be the first one. Maybe"—he smiled—"the last one." He dug out the makings, glancing around the room, then back at Sue. "You git out. I want to talk to Connie."

Sue did not move. "You can talk to us both. I like it here."

As he touched his tongue to the paper, his eyes lifted and met hers. They were flat, expressionless. "You heard me," he said. "I'd hate to treat you rough."

"You haven't the nerve!" Sue flashed back. "You

know what would happen to you if you laid hands on a woman in this country! You can get away with killing me, but this country won't stand for having their women bothered, even by a ratty little killer like you!"

Connie Duane was remembering the Derringer in her pocket and lowered her hand to her hip within easy grasp of the gun.

A sudden cannonade sounded, then a scattering of more shots. At that moment Kedrick was finally shooting it out with Fessenden. Dornie Shaw cocked an inquisitive ear toward the sound. "Gettin' closer," he said. "I ain't really in no hurry until Kedrick gets here."

"You'd better be gone before he does come." Connie was surprised at the confidence in her voice. "He's too much for you, and he's not half frightened like these others are. He'll kill you, Dornie."

He stared at her, then chuckled without humor. "Him? Bah! The man doesn't live who can outdraw Dornie Shaw! I've tried 'em all! Fess? He's supposed to be good, but he don't fool with Dornie! I'd shoot his ears off."

Calmly Connie dropped her right hand into her pocket and clutched the Derringer. The feel of it gave her confidence. "You had better go," she said quietly. "You were not invited here and we don't want you."

He did not move. "Still playin' it high an' mighty, are you? You've got to get over that. Come on, you're coming with me."

"Are you leaving?" Connie's eyes flashed. "I'll not ask you again!"

Shaw started to speak, but whatever it was he planned to say never formed into words, for Connie had her hand on the Derringer, and she fired from her pocket. Ordinarily she was a good shot, but had never fired the gun from that position. The first bullet burned a furrow along Dornie Shaw's ear, notching it at the top, the second shot stung him along the ribs, and the third plowed into the table beside him.

With a growl of surprise, he dove through the door into the hall. Sue was staring at Connie. "Well, I never!" Her eyes dropped to the tiny gun that Connie had now drawn from her pocket. "Dornie Shaw! And with that! Oh, just wait until this gets around!" Her laughter rang out merrily, and despite herself Connie was laughing, too.

Downstairs, near the door, Dornie Shaw clutched his bloody ear and panted as though he had been running, his face twisting as he stared at his blood. Amazed, he scarcely noticed when Kedrick came up the steps, but, as the door pushed open, he saw him. For a fatal instant, he froze, then he grabbed for his gun, but he had lost his chance. In that split second of hesitation, Kedrick jumped. His right hand grasped Dornie's gun wrist, and Kedrick swung the gunman bodily around, hurling him into the wall. Shaw's body hit with a crash and he rebounded into a wicked right to the wind.

Shaw was no fighter with his hands, and the power

of that blow would have wrecked many a bigger man. As it was, it knocked every bit of wind from the gunman's body, and then Kedrick shoved him back against the wall. "You asked me what I'd do, once, with a faster man. Watch this, Dornie!"

Kedrick lifted his right hand, and slapped the gunman across the mouth. Crying with fury, Shaw fought against the bigger man's grip while Kedrick held him flat against the wall, gripping him by the shirt collar, and slapped him, over and back. "Just a cheap killer," Kedrick said calmly. "Somebody has already bled you a little. I'll do it for good."

He dropped a hand to Dornie's shirt and ripped it wide. "I'm going to ruin you in this country, Dornie. I'm going to show them what you are . . . a cheap, yellow-bellied killer who terrorizes men better than himself." He slapped Dornie again, then shoved him into the wall once more, and stepped back.

"All right, Shaw! You got your guns! Reach!"

Almost crying with fury, Dornie Shaw grabbed for his guns, but as he whipped them free, all his timing wrecked by the events of the past few minutes, Kedrick's gun crashed and Shaw's right-hand gun was smashed from his hand. Shaw fired the left-hand gun, but the shot went wild, and Kedrick lunged, chopping down with his pistol barrel. The blow smashed Dornie Shaw's wrist and he dropped the gun with a yelp.

He fell back against the wall, trembling, and staring at his hands. His left wrist was broken, his right thumb gone, and, where it had been, blood was welling.

Roughly Kedrick grabbed him and shoved him out the door. Shaw stumbled and fell, but Kedrick jerked him to his feet, unmindful of the gasps of the onlookers, attracted by the sounds of fighting. In the forefront of the crowd were Pit Laine, Dai Reid, and Laredo Shad, blinking with astonishment at the sight of the most feared gunman in the country treated like a whipped child.

Shaw's horse stood nearby, and Kedrick motioned to him. "Get on him . . . backwards!"

Shaw started to turn and Kedrick lifted his hand and the gunman ducked instinctively. "Get up there! Dai, when he's up, tie his ankles together."

Dornie Shaw, befuddled by the whipping he had taken, scarcely aware of what was happening, lifted his eyes. He saw the grulla tied near the stone house. It was the last straw; his demoralization was complete.

Feared because of his deadly skill with guns and his love of killing for the sake of killing, he had walked a path alone, avoided by all, or catered to by them. Never in his life had he been manhandled as he had been by Tom Kedrick. His ego was shattered.

"Take him through the town." Kedrick's voice was harsh. "Show them what a killer looks like. Then fix up that thumb and wrist and turn him loose."

"Turn him loose?" Shad demanded. "Are you crazy?"

"No, turn him loose. He'll leave this country so far behind nobody will ever see him again. This is worse than death for him, believe me." He shrugged. "I've seen them before. All they need, that kind, is somebody to face them once who isn't afraid. He was fast and accurate with his guns, so he developed the idea he was tough. Other folks thought the same thing. He wasn't tough. A tough man has to win and lose, he has to come up after being knocked down, he has to have taken a few beatings, and know what it means to win the hard way. Anybody can knock a man down. When you've been knocked down at least three times yourself, and then get up and floor the other man, then you can figure you're a tough *hombre.* Those smoke poles of Shaw's greased his path for him. Now he knows what he's worth."

The crowd drifted away and Connie Duane was standing in the doorway. Tom Kedrick looked up at her, and suddenly he smiled. To see her now, standing like this in the doorway, was like life-giving rain upon the desert, coming in the wake of many heat-filled days.

She came down the steps to him, then looked past him at Pit. "Your sister's upstairs, Pit. You'd better talk to her."

Laine hesitated, then he said stiffly: "I don't reckon I want to."

Laredo Shad drew deeply on his cigarette and squinted through the smoke at Laine. "Mind if I do?" he asked. "I like her."

Pit Laine was astonished. "After this?"

Shad looked at the fire end of his cigarette. "Well," he said, speaking seriously, "the best cuttin' horse I ever rode was the hardest to break. Them with lot of git up an' go to 'em often make the best stock."

"Then go ahead." Pit stared after him. Then he said: "Tell her I'll be along later."

XVI

For three weeks there was no sign of Alton Burwick. He seemed to have vanished into the earth, and riders around the country reported no sign of him. At the end of that time three men got down from the afternoon stage and were shown to rooms in the St. James. An hour later, while they were at dinner, Captain Tom Kedrick pushed open the door and walked into the dining door. Instantly one of the men, a tall, immaculate man whose hair was turning gray at the temples, arose to meet him, hand outstretched. "Tom! Say, this is wonderful! Gentlemen, this is Tom Kedrick, the man I was telling you about. We served together in the War Between the States! Tom . . . Mister Edgerton and Mister Cummings."

The two men, one pudgy with a round, cheerful face, the other as tall as Frederic Ransome with gray mutton-chop whiskers acknowledged the introduction. When Kedrick had seated himself, they began demanding details. Quietly, and as concisely as possible, he told them his own story from his joining the company in New Orleans.

"And Burwick's gone?" Edgerton asked. He was the older man with the mutton-chop whiskers. "Was he killed?"

"I doubt it, sir," Kedrick replied. "He simply vanished. The man had a faculty for being out of the way when trouble came. Since he left, with the aid of Miss Duane and her uncle's papers, we managed to put together most of the facts. However, Burwick's papers have disappeared, or most of them."

"Disappeared?" Edgerton asked. "How did that happen?"

"Miss Duane tells me that when she entered the house before the final trouble with Shaw, she passed the office door and the place was undisturbed and the desk all in order. After the crowd had gone and when we returned, somebody had been rifling the desk and the safe."

"You imply that Burwick returned. That he was there then?"

"He must have been. Connie . . . Miss Duane . . . tells me that only he had the combination and that he kept all the loose ends of the business in his hands."

Cummings stared hard at Kedrick. "You say this Shaw fellow killed Keith? How do we know that you didn't? You admit to killing Fessenden."

"I did kill Fessenden. In a fair fight, before witnesses. I never even saw Keith's body after he was killed."

"Who do you think killed John Gunter?" Cummings demanded.

"My guess would be Burwick."

"I'm glad you're not accusing Keith of that," Cummings replied dryly.

"Keith wouldn't have used a knife," Kedrick replied quietly, "nor would he have attacked him from behind as was obviously the case."

"This land deal, Kedrick," Ransome asked, "where do you stand in it?"

"I? I don't stand at all. I'm simply not in it."

Cummings looked up sharply. "You don't stand to profit from it at all? Not in any way?"

"How could I? I own nothing. I have no holdings or claim to any."

"You said Burwick promised you fifteen percent?"

"That's right. But I know now that it was merely to appease me long enough to get me on the spot at Chimney Butte where I was to be killed along with the others. Burwick got me there, then rode off on the pretext that he wanted to look at a mineral ledge."

"How about this girl? The Duane girl?" Cummings asked sharply. "Does she stand to profit?"

"She will be fortunate to get back the money that her uncle invested."

"See, Cummings?" Ransome asked. "I told you Kedrick was honest. I know the man."

"I'll give my opinion on that later, after this investigation is completed. Not now. I want to go over the ground and look into this matter thoroughly. I want to investigate this matter of the disappearance of Alton Burwick, too. I'm not at all satisfied with this situation." He glanced down at the notes in his hand, then looked up. "As to that, Kedrick, wasn't Fessenden a duly elected officer of the law when you shot him? Wasn't he the sheriff?"

"Elected by a kangaroo election," Kedrick replied, "where the votes were counted by two officials who won. If that is a legal election, then he was sheriff."

"I see. But you do not deny that he had authority?"

"I do deny it."

Connie Duane was awaiting him when he walked back to his table. She smiled as he sat down, and listened to his explanation. She frowned thoughtfully. "Cummings? I think there is something in Uncle John's papers about him. I believe he was acting for them in Washington."

"That explains a lot." Kedrick picked up his coffee cup, then put it down abruptly, for Laredo Shad had come into the room, his face sharp and serious. He glanced around and, sighting Kedrick, hurried toward him, spurs jingling. Kedrick got to his feet. "What's wrong? What's happened?"

"Plenty! Sloan was wounded last night and Yellow Butte burned!"

"What?" Kedrick stared.

Shad nodded grimly. "You shouldn't have turned that rat loose. That Dornie Shaw."

Kedrick shook his head irritably. "I don't believe it. He was thoroughly whipped when he left here. I think he ran like a scared rabbit when he left, and, if he did want revenge, it would be after a few months, not so soon. No, this is somebody else."

"Who could it be?"

Tom's eyes met Connie's and she nodded, her eyes frightened. "You know who it could be. It could be Burwick."

Burwick had bothered him, getting away scotfree, dropping off the end of the world into oblivion as he had. Remembering the malignant look in the man's eyes, Kedrick became even more positive. Burwick had counted on this land deal, he had worked on it longer than any one of them, and it meant more to him.

"Shad," he said suddenly, "where does that grulla tie in? It keeps turning up, again and again. There's something more about all this than we've ever known, something that goes a lot deeper. Who rides the grulla? Why is it he has never been seen? Why was Dornie so afraid of it?"

"Was he afraid of the grulla?" Shad asked, frowning. "That doesn't figure."

"Why doesn't it? That's the question now. You know, that last day when I had Shaw thoroughly whipped, he looked up and saw something that scared him, yet something that I think he more than half expected. After he was gone down the street, I looked around, and there was nothing there. Later, I stumbled across the tracks of the grulla mustang. That horse was in front of the house during all the excitement!"

Frederic Ransome walked over to their table. "Cum-

363

mings is going to stir up trouble," he said, dropping into a chair. "He's out to get you, Kedrick, and, if he can, to pin the killing of Keith on you, or that of Burwick. He claims your story is an elaborate build-up to cover the murder of all three of the company partners. He can make so much trouble that none of the squatters will get anything out of the land, and nothing for all their work. We've got to find Burwick."

Laredo lit a cigarette. "That's a tough one," he said, "but maybe I've got a hunch."

"What?" Kedrick looked up.

"Ever hear Burwick talk about the grulla?"

"No, I can't say that I did. It was mentioned before him once that I recall, and he didn't seem interested."

"Maybe he wasn't interested because he knowed all about it," Shad suggested. "That Burwick has me puzzled."

Connie looked up at him. "You may be right, Laredo, but Pit and Sue Laine were Burwick's stepchildren and they knew nothing about the horse. The only one who seemed to know anything was Dornie Shaw."

Tom Kedrick got up. "Well, there's one thing we can do," he said. "Laredo, we can scout out the tracks of that horse and trail it down. Pick up an old trail, anything. Then just see where it takes us."

On the third day it began to rain. All week the wind had been chill and cold and the clouds had hung low and flat across the sky from horizon to horizon.

Hunched in his slicker, Laredo slapped his gloved hands together and swore. "This finishes it!" he said with disgust. "It will wipe out all the trails for us."

"All the old ones anyway," Kedrick agreed. "We've followed a dozen here lately, and none of them took us anywhere. All disappeared on rock, or were swept away by wind."

"Escavada's cabin isn't far up this cañon," Shad suggested. "Let's hit him up for chow. It will be a chance to get warm, anyway."

"Know him?"

"Stopped in there once. He's half Spanish, half Ute. Tough old blister, an' been in this country since before the grass came. He might be able to tell us something."

The trail into the cañon was slippery and the dull red of the rocks had been turned black under the rain. It slanted across the sky in a drenching downpour, and, when they reached the stone cabin in the corner of the hills, both men and horses were cold, wet, and hungry.

Escavada opened the door for them and waved them in. He grinned at them. "Glad to have company," he said. "Ain't seen a man for three weeks."

When they had stripped off their slickers and peeled down to shirts, pants, and boots, he put coffee before them and laced it with a strong shot of whiskey. "Warm you up," he said. "Trust you ain't goin' out again soon. Whiskey's mighty fine when a body comes in from the cold, but not if he's goin' out again.

It flushes the skin up, fetches all the heat to the surface, then gives it off into the air. Man freezes mighty quick, drinkin' whiskey."

"You ever see a grulla mustang around, Escavada?" Laredo asked suddenly, looking up at the old man.

He turned on them, his eyes bright with malicious humor. "You ain't some of them superstitious kind, be you? Skeered o' the dark like? An' ghosts?"

"No," Kedrick said, "but what's the tie-up?"

"That grulla. Old story in this here county. Dates back thirty, forty years. Maybe further'n that. Sign of death or misfortune, folks say."

Laredo looked inquiringly at Kedrick, and Kedrick asked: "You know anything about it? That horse is real enough. We've both seen the grulla."

"So've I," the old man said. He dropped into a chair and grinned at them. His gray hair was sparse, but his eyes were alive and young. "I seen it many times, an' no misfortune come my way. Not unless you call losin' my shovel a misfortune."

He hitched his chair nearer the woodpile and tossed a couple of sticks on the fire. "First I heerd of it was long ago. Old folks used to tell of a Spanish man in armor, ridin' a mouse-colored horse. He used to come an' go about the hills, but the story back of it seems to be that a long time back some such feller was mighty cruel to the Injuns. That story sort of hung around an' a body heered it ever' now and again until about fifteen, sixteen years back. Since then she's been mighty lively."

"You mean, you heard the story more since then?" Kedrick asked.

"Uhn-huh. Started with a wagon train wiped out by Injuns up on the Salt. Ever' man jack o' them kilt dead . . . womenfolks, too, the story was. There was a youngster come off scotfree, boy about five or six years old. He crawled off into the brush, an', after, he swore them Injuns was led by a white man on a grulla horse, a white man in armor!"

"Wild yarn," Shad said, "but you can't blame the kid, imaginin' things after what he must've seen."

"He said that *hombre* in the armor went around with a long knife, an' he skewered ever' one of the bodies to make sure they was real dead. He said once that *hombre* looked right square at him, layin' in the brush, an' he was skeered like all git out, but must've been he wasn't seen, 'cause he wasn't bothered."

"An' this grulla has been seen since?" Shad asked. "Reg'lar?"

"Uhn-huh, but never no rider clost enough to say who or what. Sometimes off at a distance, sometimes just the horse, standin'. Most folks git clear off when they see that horse."

He got up and brought back the coffee pot. "Right odd you should ast me about him now," he commented. "Right odd."

Both men looked at him, and, sensing their acute interest, he continued. "Been huntin' here lately. Ketched me a few bees off the cactus an' mesquite, figurin' to start a beeline. Well, I got her started, all right, an' I trailed them bees to a place far south o' here. South an' west, actually. Most o' this country hereabouts is worked out of bees. I been at it so long I was workin' a good ways off. Well, my beeline took me over toward the Hogback. You know that place? She's a high-curvin' ridge maybe five or six hundred feet at the crest, but she rises mighty close to straight up for four hundred feet. Crawlin' up there to locate the cave them bees was workin' out of, I come on a cave like a cliff dwellin', on'y it wasn't. She was man-made, an' most likely in the past twenty years or so. What started me really lookin' was my shovel . . . the one I lost. She was right there on that ledge, so I knowed it hadn't been lost, but stole off me, so I began huntin' around. I found back inside this place it was all fixed up for livin'. Some grub there, blankets, a couple of guns, an' under some duffel in the corner an old-time breastplate an' helmet."

"You're serious?" Kedrick demanded incredulously.

"Sure as I'm alive! But"—Escavada chuckled—"that ain't the best of it. Lyin' there on the floor, deader'n last year's hopes, was a young fellow. He had a knife, an old-time Spanish knife that a feller in armor might have carried, an' it was skewered right th'ough him!"

"A young man . . . dead?" Kedrick suddenly leaned forward. "Anything odd about him? I mean . . . was he missing a thumb?"

Escavada stared. "Well, now, if that don't beat all!

He was missin' a thumb, an' he was crippled up mighty bad in the other arm. Carried her in a sling."

"Dornie Shaw!" Laredo leaped to his feet. "Dornie Shaw, by all that's holy!"

"Shaw?" Escavada puckered his brows, his old eyes gleaming. "Now that's most odd, most odd! Shaw was the name o' that boy, the one who didn't git killed with the wagon train!"

Kedrick's face was a study. Dornie Shaw—dead! But if Dornie had been the boy from the wagon train, that would account for his superstitious fear of the grulla mustang. But to suppose that after all these years Dornie had been killed by the same man, or ghost if you believed in ghosts, that killed the rest of them so many years before was too ridiculous. It was, he thought suddenly, unless you looked at it just one way.

"Man can't escape his fate," Escavada said gloomily. "That boy hid out from that knife, but in the end it got him."

Kedrick got up. "Could you take us to that place, Escavada? Down there on the Hogback."

"I reckon." He glanced outside. "But not in this rain. Rheumatiz gits me."

"Then tell me where it is," Kedrick said, "because I'm going now!"

They were crossing the head of Coal Mine Creek when Laredo saw the tracks. He drew up suddenly, pointing. The tracks of a horse, well shod. "The grulla," Kedrick said grimly. "I'd know those tracks anywhere."

They pushed on. It was late and the pelting rain still poured down upon their heads and shoulders. The trails were slippery, and dusk was near. "We'd better find us a hole to crawl into," Shad suggested. "We'll never find that horse in this weather."

"By morning the tracks will be gone, and I've a hunch we'll find our man right on that cliff dwelling where Escavada saw Dornie's body."

"Wonder how Dornie found the place?"

"If what I think is right," Kedrick replied, wiping the rain from his face, "he must have run into an old friend and been taken there to hide out. That old friend was the same rider of the grulla that killed his family and friends with the wagon train, and, when he saw that armor, he knew it."

"But what's it all about?" Shad grumbled. "It don't make sense! An' no horse lives that long."

"Sure not. There may have been half a dozen grullas in that length of time. This man probably tried to capitalize on the fears of the Indians and Mexicans who live up that way to keep them off his trail. We'll probably find the answer when we reach the end of our ride."

The Hogback loomed, black and ominous, before them. The trail, partly switchback and partly sheer climb, led over the sharp, knife-like ridge. They mounted, their horses laboring heavily at the steep and slippery climb. Twice Tom Kedrick saw the tracks of the grulla on the trail, and in neither case could those tracks have been more than an hour old.

Kedrick glanced down when they saw the opposite side, then dismounted. "This one is tricky," he said grimly. "We'd better walk it."

Halfway down, lightning flashed, and in the momentary brightness Laredo called out: "Watch it, Tom! High, right!"

Kedrick's head jerked around just as the rifle boomed. The bullet smacked viciously against the rock beside him, spattering his face with splinters. He grabbed for his gun, but it was under his slicker. The gun boomed again, five fast shots, as fast as the marksman could work the lever of his rifle.

Behind Tom Kedrick the anguished scream of a wounded horse cut the night and Shad's warning yell was drowned in the boom of the gun again, and then he flattened against the rock barely in time to avoid the plunging, screaming horse! His own Appaloosa, frightened, darted down the trail with the agility of a mountain goat. The rifle boomed again, and he dropped flat.

"Shad? You all right?"

There was a moment before the reply, then it was hoarse, but calm. "Winged me, but not bad."

"I'm going after him. You all right?"

"Yeah. You might help me wrap this leg up."

Sheltered by the glistening rain-wet rock, with gray mist swirling past them on the high ridge of the

Hogback, Kedrick knelt in the rain, and, shielding the bandage from the rain with a slicker, he bound the leg. The bullet had torn through the flesh, but the bone was not broken.

XVII

When the wound was bandaged, Kedrick drew back into the shelter of the slight overhang and stared about. Ahead and below them was a sea of inky blackness. Somewhere down that mountain would be their horses, one probably dead or dying, the other possibly crippled. Around them all was night and the high, windy, rain-wet rocks. And out there in the darkness a killer stalked them, a killer who could at all of three hundred yards spot his shots so well as to score two hits on a target seen only by a brief flash of lightning. Next time those shots could kill. And there was no doubt about it. Now the situation was clear. It was kill or be killed.

"Sure," Laredo said dryly, "you got to get him, man. But you watch it. He's no slouch with that Spencer!"

"You've got to get off this ridge," Kedrick insisted. "The cold and rain up here will kill you."

"You leave that to me," Shad replied shortly. "I'll drag myself down the trail an' find a hole to crawl into down on the flat below this Hogback. Might even find your palouse down there. You got grub an' coffee in those saddlebags?"

"Yeah, but you'd better not try a fire until I come back."

Shad chuckled. "Make sure you come back. I never did like to eat alone."

Slipping his hands under his slicker through the pockets, Tom gripped his guns. His rifle, of course, was in his saddle scabbard. He was going to have to stalk a skilled killer, a fine marksman, on his own ground in absolute darkness with a handgun. The killer had a Spencer .56.

Lightning flashed, but there was no more shooting. Somewhere out there the killer was stalking them. He would not give up now, or retreat. This, for him, was a last stand unless he killed them both. His hide-out now was known, and, if they escaped, he would no longer be safe. That he did not intend to be driven from the country was already obvious by the fact that he had stayed this long.

Kedrick crawled out, using a bush to cover his movement, and then worked along the windy top of the ridge toward a nest of boulders he had seen ahead of him by the lightning flash. The wind whipped at his hat, and flapped the skirt of his slicker. His right-hand gun was drawn, but under the slicker.

He crawled on. Lightning flashed and he flattened out on the rocks, but the Spencer bellowed, the bullet smashing his eyes and mouth full of gravel. Rolling over, he held his fire, spitting and pawing desperately at his blinded eyes.

There was no sound but the wind and rain. Then in

the distance, thunder roared and rumbled off among the peaks, and, when the lightning flashed again, he looked out along the high ridge of the Hogback. Lashed by the driving rain, its rocks glistened like steel under clouds that seemed a scarce arm's length above Kedrick's head. Mist drifted by him, touching his wet face with a ghostly hand, and the little white skeletons of long-dead pines pointed their sharp and bony fingers toward the sky.

Rain pelted against his face, and he cowered, fearing the strike of a bullet at each flash of lightning, smelling the brimstone as the lightning scarred the high ridge with darting flame. He touched his lips with his tongue and stared until his eyes ached with strain. His mouth was dry and his stomach empty, and something mounted within him. Fear? Panic? He could stay still no longer. With infinite patience, he edged forward, working his way a little over the edge of the ridge toward the hulking black clumps of some juniper, ragged trees, whipped to agonized shapes by generations of wind.

There was no sound but the storm, no sight of anything. He moved on, trying to estimate how far away the cliff house would be, to guess if he could reach it first or get between it and the killer out there. Flame stabbed the night and something burned sharply along his shoulders. He let go everything and rolled, went crashing down a dozen feet before he brought up in a tangle of dead limbs.

But the killer was not waiting. He loomed suddenly

dark on the crest, and, crouching like a hunted animal, every instinct alert, Kedrick fired! The dark figure jerked hard, and then the Spencer bellowed. The bullet plastered a branch near him, and Kedrick knew that only his own shot had saved his life. He fired again, and then deliberately hurled himself backward into the night, falling, landing, crawling. He got to his feet and plunged into the absolute darkness, risking a broken limb or a bad fall, anything to get the distance he needed. Then lightning flashed, and, as if by magic, the Spencer boomed. How the man had followed his plunging career he could not know, but he felt the stab and slam of the bullets as they smashed about him. This man was shooting too close. He couldn't miss long.

His shoulders burned, but whether that shot had been a real wound or a mere graze he did not know. Something fluid trickled down his spine, but whether it was rain water through the slit coat or his own blood, he could not guess.

He moved back, circling. Another shot, but this slightly to his left. Quickly he moved left and a shot smacked right near where he had been standing. The killer was using searching fire now, and he was getting closer.

Kedrick moved back, tripped and fell, and bullets laced the air over him. Evidently the man had a belt full of ammunition, or his pockets stuffed. Kedrick started to rise, but his fingers had found a hard smoothness, not of rock, but of earth and gravel!

Carefully he felt about in the darkness. The path! He was on a path, and no doubt the path to the cliff house.

He began to move along it, feeling his way carefully. Once, off to his left, he heard a rock roll. He took a chance and fired blind, then rolled over three times and felt the air split apart as the shots slammed the ground where he had been. He fired again, then again, always moving.

Lightning flashed, and he saw a hulking thing back on the trail the way he had come, a huge, glistening thing, black and shining. Flame sprang from it, and he felt the shock of the bullet, then steadied himself and fired again.

Deliberately then, he turned and worked his way down the path. Suddenly he felt space before him, and found the path here took a sharp turn. Another step and he might have plunged off! How near was his escape he knew in another instant when lightning flashed and he saw far below him the gray white figure of the Appaloosa standing in the rain.

He worked his way down the cliff, then found a ledge, and in a moment his hands found the crude stone bricks of the cliff house. Feeling his way along it, he felt for the door, and then, pushing it open, he crawled into the inner darkness and pushed the door shut behind him.

After the lashing of wind and rain the peace seemed a miracle. Jerking off his soaking hat, he tossed it aside, and threw off the slicker. There was a chance the killer would not guess that he knew of this place, and undoubtedly, had he not known, he would have passed it in the darkness and storm. Working his way along the floor, he found a curtain dividing this from an inner room. He stepped through it and sat down hard on the bunk. Feeling for his left-hand gun, he found the holster empty, and he had fired five shots with his right gun. Suddenly the curtain stirred and there was a breath of wind, then it vanished. The killer was in the other room! He had come in!

Kedrick dared not rise for fear the bed would creak, but he heard a match strike, and then a candle was lighted. Feet shuffled in the other room. Then a voice. "I know you're in there, Kedrick. There's water on the floor in here. I'm behind a piece of old stone wall that I use for a sort of table. I'm safe from your fire. I know there's no protection where you are. Throw your guns out and come with your hands up! If you don't, I'm going to open fire an' search every inch of that room!"

Over the top of the blanket curtain, which was suspended from a pole across the door, Tom Kedrick could see the roof in the other room. The cave house was actually much higher than need be; evidently the killer had walled up an overhang or cave. Kedrick could see several heavy cedar beams that had served to support a ceiling, now mostly gone. If that was true in the other room, it might be true in his, also.

He straightened to his feet, heard a sudden move, then fired! From the other room came a chuckle.

"Figured that would draw fire! Well, one gun's empty. Now toss out the other an' come out. You haven't a chance!"

Kedrick did not reply. He was reaching up into the darkness over his head, feeling for the beams. He touched one, barely touched it, then reached up with both hands, judging the distance he had to jump by the width of the beams in the other room. What if it were old and would not support his weight? He had to chance that.

He jumped, his fingers hooked well over the edge, and soundlessly he drew himself up. Now Kedrick could see into the lighted room, but he could not locate the killer. The voice spoke again. "I'm giving you no more time, Kedrick. Come out or I start to shoot! Toss that other gun first!"

Silence lay in the room, a silence broken by the sudden bellow of a gun! The killer fired, emptied a six-gun, then emptied another. Tom Kedrick waited, having no idea how many guns the man had, or what he might have planned for. Then six more carefully spaced shots were fired, one of them ricocheting dangerously close to Kedrick's head.

A long pause, and then a sound of movement. "All right, if you're alive in there now, you got a shot comin', but if you want to give up, you can. I sort of want you alive." Suddenly the blanket was jerked from its moorings, and Alton Burwick stood in the opening, a gun gripped in his fist, ready to fire. Kedrick made no sound, and the man stared, then rushed into the room. Almost whining with fury, he jerked Kedrick's hat from the bed, then the slicker, and, as the latter fell to the floor, with it fell Kedrick's other pistol, which falling from the holster had hooked into some tear in the slicker. He stared at it furiously, and then jerked the bed aside. Almost insane with fury, he searched, unbelieving and whining like an angry hound on a trail.

He stopped, his pent-up fury worn away, and stood there, his chest heaving with his exertions, his fist still gripping the pistol. "Gone! Gone!" he cried, as if bereft. "When I had him right here!"

Kedrick's fingers had found a tiny sliver of wood, and deliberately he snapped it against Burwick's cheek. The fat man jerked as if stung, then looked up. Their eyes met, and slowly he backed away, but now he was smiling. "Oh, you're a smart one, Kedrick! Very smart! Too bad it couldn't have been you with me instead of that weakling Keith! All front and show, but no bottom to him, no staying quality! But"—he sighed—"I've got you anyway, and you'll suffer for what you've done." He scooped Kedrick's other pistol from the floor and backed away. "All right, get down!"

Kedrick dropped to the floor, and the fat man waved irritably at the gun he clutched. "No use to bluff. That's empty. Throw it down!"

"What's it all about, Burwick?" Tom asked suddenly. "Why this place? The armor? What about Dornie Shaw?"

"Ah? How did you know about that? But no matter, no matter." He backed to the wall, watching Kedrick and holding the gun. "Why, it was gold, boy! Gold, and lots of it! It was I stirred those Indians up to attacking that caravan. I wanted the gold they carried, and most of it belonging to Dornie's pa. I knew about it. Followed them from Dodge. Knew when they drew it from the bank there, and how much. They fooled me, though. When the Indians hit, they'd buried it somewhere. It could have been a lot of places, that was the trouble.

"They might have buried it sooner, somewhere else along the trail. I've dug and I've hunted, but I've never found it. Maybe I will someday, but nobody else is going to! Wondered why I wanted the land? Profit, sure. But I wanted this place, a couple of sections in here, all for myself. Figured on that, working it out somehow. The gold's somewhere between here and Thieving Rock. Has to be."

Kedrick nodded. "That clears up a lot of things. Now you drop that gun, Burwick, and come as my prisoner."

Burwick chuckled fatly. "Try to bluff me? I'd've expected that from you. Nervy one, huh? Bet you got that Connie Duane, too. By the Lord Harry, there's a woman! No scare to her. Not one bit. Drop your gun, boy, or I'll put my first bullet through your kneecap."

He was going to shoot, and Tom Kedrick knew it. Coolly he squeezed off his own shot, an instant faster. He shot for the gun hand, but the bullet only skinned the thumb knuckle and hit Burwick in the side. The fat man jerked and his face twisted, and he stared at the gun, lifting his own. Coolly Kedrick fired again, then again. The bullets struck with an ugly smack, and Burwick wilted, the gun going from his limp fingers to the floor. Kedrick stepped in and caught him, easing him down. The flabby cheeks were suddenly sagging and old.

Bitterly the man stared upward at him. "What happened? That . . . that . . . ?"

"The gun was a Walch twelve-shot pistol," Tom explained. "I started carrying them a few days ago, replacing the Forty-Four Russians."

Burwick stared at him, no hatred in his eyes. "Smart," he said. "Smart! Always one trick better than me, or anybody. You'll . . . do, boy."

XVIII

On the streets of Mustang the sun was warm after the rain. Tom Kedrick, wounded again but walking, stood beside Connie Duane. Shad was grinning at them. "Look mighty fine in that tailored suit, Tom. You goin' to be gone long?"

"Not us. We'll be married in Santa Fé, and then we're headin' for the Mogollons and that ranch."

"Seems a shame not to hunt for that gold," Laredo complained. "But, anyway, the real treasure was that box full of Burwick's papers. Sure made Cummings hunt his hole. But I do regret that gold."

"I don't," Connie replied. "It's caused too much trouble. Alton Burwick spent his life and a good many other lives after it. Let it stay where it is. Maybe a better man will find it, who needs it more than we do!"

"Gosh," Laredo said suddenly, "I got to light a shuck. I'm late to meet Sue. So long, then!" They watched him go, waiting for the stage.

Everything was quiet in Mustang—three whole days without a killing.

Additional Copyright Information

Center Point Publishing
600 Brooks Road ● PO Box 1
Thorndike ME 04986-0001 USA

(207) 568-3717

US & Canada:
1 800 929-9108
www.centerpointlargeprint.com